This Might
Sting a Bit

This Might Sting a Bit

A charmingly dysfunctional family.
A closet full of skeletons.

CLAIRE ADLAM

Quickfox

Published by Quickfox Publishing,
PO Box 50660 West Beach 7449
Cape Town, South Africa
www.quickfox.co.za | info@quickfox.co.za

This Might Sting a Bit
ISBN 978 0 620 94715 2

First edition

Editor: Alexia Lawson
Cover design: Claire Adlam
Cover image: Ambra
Typesetting and production: Quickfox Publishing
Printed by Kasey Print

DISCLAIMER
This is a work of fiction. Any resemblance of characters to actual persons,
living or dead, or actual events is purely coincidental.
Furthermore, the fictional storyline and its point of view are not intended as
a substitute for professional medical advice, diagnosis or treatment. Should
you or a loved one find yourself struggling with substance abuse, please seek
advice from a qualified healthcare professional who will assist with finding
appropriate treatment.

For Mom,
thank you.

He is no hero who never met the dragon, or who, if he once
saw it, declared afterwards that he saw nothing.
Equally, only once one who has risked the fight with the
dragon and is not overcome by it wins the hoard, the
'treasure hard to attain'. He alone has a genuine claim to
self-confidence, for he has faced the dark ground of his self
and thereby has gained … an inner certainty which makes
him capable of self-reliance.

CARL GUSTAV JUNG

Prologue

The worksheet said:

Life-story guidelines:
- *Part A: describe your childhood*
- *Part B: describe your adulthood*
- *Part C: describe the last six months, i.e. your life and events preceding your arrival here.*

In all sections, focus on the unmanageability of your life and factors leading you into active addiction.

Well, this is going to be one exercise I won't forget in a hurry, I thought, chewing the end of my pen. I opened my blank notebook and began to write.

Part A: Childhood

1

As a child, I'd often heard adults discussing Suicide Month. October in Zimbabwe, our hottest, driest month. A month when the searing African heat could tip the scales and make you top yourself. Apparently. But surely one had to be depressed in the first place? Surely summer heat couldn't take all the blame?

Either way, for years I'd had a mental image of a bunch of miserable folk getting together, watching the mercury rise, and one day late in October saying, 'Bugger it, let's see if the weather upstairs is more bearable.' Then, in my mind, they'd either cuddle a loaded shotgun or find a piece of hosepipe and a car that idled well. I'd never known anyone who'd ended their woes in October, so I'd not lost a whole lot of sleep over it. For us kids it was simple, if you're hot, get in the pool. Why did adults always have to over complicate things? It's just weather.

We were a few days off Suicide Month and it was, indeed, sticky as we headed through the farm workshops, weaving between the old tractors and a graveyard of tyres, pointing our horses in the direction of our dam.

'Kat, can we go back past the house?' shouted Rolo from behind me. 'I've left my cellphone.'

'You're kidding?' I laughed. 'You want to text while riding? There isn't even a signal out there.' That was Rolo. Ditzy at times.

'But what if he calls?'

Rolo had a new admirer, Jason. A secret crush that was, in fact, no secret at all because when a girl fancies the living daylights out of a boy she can't keep quiet about it. She gave me the 'pleeeeeez' look.

'Sorry Jobb, we'll be quick-quick,' I said, swivelling in my saddle to face my caretaker of sorts. I was forbidden to ride alone on the farm as local drifters – odd bods, my mother called them – often strayed onto our land, sometimes with criminal intent. As long as I was with Jobb, I could ride wherever and whenever. Jobb, our proud self-titled Horse Manager, didn't have much call for gadgets so he didn't get the whole cellphone thing, although they were new for us too. He just grinned about Rolo, his stark white teeth a bright flash against his hot, shiny aubergine skin.

Rolo had spent the last week with us. Her aunt in South Africa had popped her clogs, as Rolo so eloquently put it, and she'd declined the funeral trip to Johannesburg with her parents. We were the closest friends, a relationship filled with all the stuff of normal fifteen-year-old girls. Her parents also farmed in Raffingora, and we'd both attended the local junior school. Now, being at different senior schools, we saw each other only in the holidays and on the occasional weekend pass when we stayed in Harare with her brother Jack instead of trekking home to the farm.

Rolo, once called Caroline – but her nickname had stuck much to her father's dismay – was one of the few people who got me. She had a refined sense of humour, a huge heart and she could be as intelligent and nerdy as she could be a big flaky bimbo. Tall, slim and blonde, the boys went nuts for her but Rolo was blissfully unaware of it.

Trotting my horse Savannah up our driveway, I saw a few dusty trucks parked under the jacaranda trees, all belonging to friends from the district. Damn, I thought, remembering Mom had told us to make ourselves scarce that afternoon as she had friends coming. I'd seen these gatherings at our house before, on neighbouring farms too. Sometimes they met at the Country Club. I'd once asked what they were about but Mom had shrugged it off with a vague answer, only making their gatherings even more mysterious.

'We chat about life and stuff. You know, Adult Issues,' she'd said. But these gatherings never looked like her regular tea parties or coffee mornings. They were different, more serious. Boring. There wasn't much laughing.

Rolo's horse caught sight of our bantam cockerel squawking and running for its life, my two boxers in hot pursuit. Boxers versus bantams was an old dispute that played out daily. Sometimes the boxers won and feathers flew, sometimes the bantams won and there'd be embarrassed boxers with bloodied snouts. Today Gertie, my bitch, held back, but my male puppy Titus, better known as TightArse or Tighty, wasn't having any of it. The cockerel whipped under Rolo's horse before the fight was taken to the kitchen door where, judging from a loud shriek, Cookie had stepped in as referee. In many ways, Cookie held far more authority in our home than my mother did. We had wanted to use his real name, but Cookie was a title to aspire to. Nobody messed with their Cookie if they knew what was good for them and ours ran a tight ship.

'Kat, can you go grab my phone?' Rolo was struggling to control her horse, thanks to the dogs.

I ran inside, trying to avoid being seen knowing I'd get a royal bollocking if caught anywhere near Mom's gathering. They were all sitting in the front lounge. Sure enough, another heavy atmosphere and no light-hearted banter. Grabbing Rolo's phone, I tore back down the stairs, then I paused in the hall, unseen.

'My name is Maddie and I am at it,' I heard.

'Hi Maddie,' the others replied in a sing-song voice.

Okay, so Maddie was there and Maddie was 'at it'. But at what? Maddie and her husband had been farming in Raffingora for years and were no strangers to the community. Her son Pete was one of our closest friends. So why on earth was Maddie telling them her name like a first-time introduction? And what's with the sing-song reply like kids at crèche? Weird. I was dying to eavesdrop some more, fascinated by the curious séance. Tearing myself away, I ran out and handed Rolo her phone.

'Right, let's get down to the dam before it gets too late,' I said, back in my saddle.

'Kat, he's asked me to his school dance!' Rolo's eyes were glued to her phone.

'Who? Fiddlypoop?' I smiled, happy for her.

'Yes, Jason Fiddlypoop!'

The afternoon heat was relentless, the dust making my eyes gritty, catching in the back of my throat, and sticking to my bare arms where it mingled with sweat. Yesterday's wildfire in the foothills on our boundary had left long, thin flecks of ash dancing in the air. They dissolved the second they touched skin, leaving only black smudges and a fleeting bitter smell. The msasa trees looked like flames themselves. Leaves of reds and oranges that would turn a vivid lime when the rains eventually came. I breathed in the heat and rich scents, imagining shapes in the distant watery mirage being thrown up by the rising heat. Sunrise and sunset were the most humane times to ride during Suicide Month, but our horses were already glistening with sweat.

Jobb rode silently behind us. My farm bodyguard, a silent force always there. He was a Shona, the people of the Mashonaland province. I had once asked the origin of his name and he'd shared the wonderful story of how his grandfather believed if you always had a job, then life would be good. Jobb, a skilled rider himself, had a gift with horses and had taught me well. There was no ducking and diving either. Jobb made me do all the grunt work – grooming, feeding and mucking out, even spending nights in the stable with a sick horse a few times.

We heard a truck coming up behind us. It was my father doing his late-afternoon crop checks. Slowing down, he stuck his head out the window. 'Kat, keep your knees in! There's enough space between them and your horse to park a bloody bus. You have no idea how sloppy you look from behind.' I had to laugh. I was hardly in a show ring.

It occurred to me that Dad didn't partake in Mom's 'gatherings', yet one or two other men did so it wasn't women only. I definitely needed to find out more.

Before Dad went on his way, he stretched his arm out to give Rolo a white rose, making her giggle. He'd obviously been at the new flower sheds. Our farm, Raffingora's biggest, had been in his family for over sixty years. We grew tobacco and maize in summer, wheat in winter, Mom had a few dairy cows, and Dad had ventured into export roses more recently.

We spotted the quad bike parked at the end of the track by the dam and then saw Chris. At seventeen, my brother was already earmarked to be the family rebel, which I thought was a pretty accurate bit of family forecasting.

We had our moments as siblings with the usual bickering matches but, overall, we got on. With his blue eyes and Mediterranean complexion, girls fell for Chris and went a bit stupid around him, Rolo included. He just lapped it up.

Maddie's son Pete came stumbling through the long grass. He and Chris were inseparable during school holidays. Rolo waved, but they were engrossed in their pellet-gun game – tossing rusty cans in the air and trying to blast them to smithereens. Clearly drunk or stoned – more likely both – they couldn't have hit a stationary train from two metres. Weaving around, Pete tripped on a stone, landing face first in the mud with a delicious squelch, and accidentally firing the pellet gun as he fell. Chris turned as white as a sheet, his eyes the size of dinner plates when the lead nugget whistled past his ear.

Rolo and I joined them while Jobb let the horses drink. Abandoning their tin-can game, Chris sat down to roll a fat joint in soggy newspaper, giggling away with Pete. I'd seen them smoking weed before so it was no great revelation but, if Dad found out, Chris's life would be over. Pete offered me a drag which I declined, having been violently ill the only time I'd ever tried it. Rolo, however, wanted to impress Chris and graciously accepted a drag of the soggy mess. Unable to inhale, she had a monumental coughing fit. Jobb was sitting on a rock watching, but he'd never rat on us. Marijuana was common in their compound, a part of farm life, and, if no real harm came of it and nobody went batshit crazy, nobody seemed to care.

The sun sets fast in our part of Africa, and with only half an hour before dark, Jobb insisted we go home. Leaving the boys to their own antics, we headed straight down the farm's long dirt airstrip, giving our horses their heads. They picked up speed quickly, knowing there'd be bran at the other end. Halfway down the strip, we heard the quad bike coming up behind us. We reined in the horses and moved to the edges of the strip. The boys quickly overtook us, whooping like lunatics, still stoned.

I saw it coming. The quad hit a slight bump and took off, flipping before landing on its side. Chris and Pete flew straight through the air and landed free of the quad, luckily. In the clouds of dust Jobb dismounted tossing me his reins as he ran to help them. They were lying on top of each other, unhurt and still giggling, but the quad wasn't going anywhere.

'Oh shit. Shit. Shit,' said Chris, standing up, dusting himself off, and then pulling Pete up. 'How are we gonna get this one past Dad?'

'Maniacs! Bloody hell!' I shouted, also checking that Rolo was okay on her horse.

'*Eish, Bwana* Chris,' said Jobb, shaking his head at the boys. 'You're riding back with us now. It's getting too dark to walk.'

Chris had the decency to look shamefaced and got up behind Jobb on his horse. Pete rode home with me as Rolo was having enough trouble calming her horse after all the drama.

'I will come sort the quad bike later tonight,' said Jobb. 'But, *eish*, Chris, don't smoke *mbanje* and ride the quad again. Please, you are too stupid by far.'

'Sorry Jobb. And thank you. *Tatenda shamwari.*'

It was a slow walk home on three very uptight horses. On the way, I asked Pete why his mom was at our house. I felt him answer behind me with only a shrug. The boys definitely knew a lot more about those gatherings than I did and curiosity was eating at me.

'But Pete, I heard your mom say hello and then say her name like she didn't know the people there, and then she said she was "at it".' I felt him shrug again. I decided to drop the subject, for now.

At the stables we quickly rubbed down the horses before making our way back to the house. The air had finally begun to cool. Dust particles were shimmering in the air, iridescent in the fading daylight. We saw one of the tractors heading towards the compound, pulling a trailer filled with sweaty, tired but cheerful workers. They would pass the house so we hitched a ride. Rolo was engrossed in her cellphone again, fascinating the workers with her 'portable talk box' as they called it. Chris was very subdued and Pete looked shattered too. My mind was still on Maddie and what I'd overheard – all of us lost in thought. The tractor stopped at the gate and the four of us ran up the driveway and into the kitchen.

'Cottage pie, twenty minutes,' said Cookie when he saw us. Then, noticing the state of Chris and Pete and their glassy eyes, he shouted to one of his kitchen helpers, '*Eish!* Put the second cottage pie in, the little boys have been smoking the *mbanje* again. Munchy munchy tonight!' Even our kitchen staff knew the signs.

There was no sign of Maddie or anyone else from the gathering, just Mom and Dad on the patio catching up on the day, enjoying the peace and sounds of the African evening as crickets and frogs warmed up for the night. Two hot but happy boxers were sprawled out on the patio couches.

'Pete,' Mom called out, seeing us come in through the French windows, 'Maddie couldn't wait for you so you're staying the night. She'll fetch you tomorrow.'

'Thanks Mrs Hay,' said Pete. I was the only one close enough to hear him add under his breath, 'That's if she remembers.'

I shot him an odd look. Then I saw Dad notice the state of Chris. I held my breath, wondering what was coming.

'Boys, let's take the Cessna up in the morning,' he said. 'After the fire yesterday, I need to recheck our fire breaks. Chris, if you're not still bleeding from the eyeballs and can see straight, I'll let you log an hour.'

Dad knew they were stoned! Luckily for Chris, it seemed he wasn't going to make a big deal of it. Hell, he was even offering Chris a flying lesson and an hour towards his private pilot's licence which he'd started last year, Dad being his flying instructor and an occasional pilot himself.

Later that evening when I was brushing my teeth, Pete came into the bathroom. 'You misheard my mom, Kat.'

'Mmhuh?' I grunted, my gob full of Colgate.

'She didn't say "at it", she said "addict".' And with that, Pete scuttled out.

Bugger Pete, shooting off like a long dog before I could ask him anything. But Maddie is a wife and mother, I thought. She's a normal, sane lady, not a scumbag. How on earth could she be an addict? Gatherings, drug addicts – there was definitely something odd going on. Slapping some body cream on my tanned summer skin and tying up my hair for the relief of cool air on my neck, I headed for bed, confused.

Rolo fell asleep quickly, escaping into fantasies of school dances and sexy dresses, but I lay awake for ages. The nightjar's call was close, breaking through the night-time chatter of crickets and frogs, while the sprinklers tick-ticked across the garden, splashing the windows on each cycle. It was still terribly hot and having Tighty sprawled out across my bed didn't help.

He may have been a puppy but he left little space for me. A while later, I felt him lift his head about three seconds before I heard the faint 'phut-phut' of the quad bike. Jobb had gone back – probably with one of the mechanics – and when Dad passed through the garages in the morning, he'd see the quad parked as and where it should be and he'd be none the wiser about the accident.

It had been a normal day really. Buggering around on the farm. Chris doing things that invariably had to be hidden from Dad. Rolo all worked up about boys. Thinking about Maddie, I replayed her words in my mind, now that I knew them.

'My name is Maddie and I am an addict.'

2

A few days later, I was kicking around with nothing to do and very bored. Chris and Dad had taken the plane on a short hop up to Kariba for the Air Rally. They weren't competing, but had gone for the festivities and would return with the biggest hangovers of the year. Rolo's parents were back from the funeral so she'd gone home, reporting back within an hour on her takings. There was little more exciting for a Zimbabwean teen than a parent's South African-stocked suitcase full of treats. So bored, I even attempted to finish a school project on the Zambezi god, Nyaminyami, but that quickly became tedious. It was far too hot to march my brain through lists of African gods. I ambled into the kitchen for a snack and found Cookie taking out a batch of peanut butter biscuits.

'Ah KitKat,' Mom said, busy sealing jars of hot marmalade. 'If you've got nothing better to do, won't you take some jam and biscuits up to the Jacksons?'

'Mmm hmm,' I grunted with a mouth full of warm buttery biscuits.

The air was oppressive and very still. Ruby-red and cerise bougain-villaeas against the wild dark skies made a dramatic picture, but the heavy clouds that rolled in each afternoon just wouldn't break. I saw a flash of lightning over the far-off hills and, ever the farmer's daughter, counted the seconds between it and the thunder to calculate the storm's distance from us. The thunder was barely audible. Today was not the day I'd get to stand in a torrential downpour, thick red mud oozing through my toes, each step making a satisfying schlurp. At least I had jacaranda music, gentle popping sounds, as I walked up the driveway over the silky purple carpet of fallen flowers.

Tim Jackson, Dad's farm manager, lived with his wife Linda and daughter Ela, a year younger than me, in the manager's house not too far from ours. Genuine, down-to-earth and hard-working, Tim was also a close friend to Dad. After a few beers, Dad would say, 'Tim, if you were better looking, I'd marry you!' Then there'd be some buff macho talk with Tim saying, 'Listen, *boet*, don't come here with your bloody moffie talk, my Linda will string you up by your bollocks.' He and Linda had come to the farm six months after my grandfather suddenly died and Dad had just been thrown in the deep end.

With them came Ela, who, unknown to us, would change our lives. Ela, with her glorious auburn hair, porcelain skin, a voice like Swiss chocolate, and startling tanzanite eyes, was as blind as a bat. She'd been born with an eye condition, and from about the age of eight her sight had begun to deteriorate. At first it was slow and she'd managed with glasses but, by thirteen, Ela needed a white stick, and then came her guide dog, Mojo, the most beautiful golden retriever. Together, the redhead and the blondie were quite a sight. Ela's eyes had not changed or clouded over, as was often the case with the blind. They'd remained an almost violet blue, misleading and disarming at first. So pretty, yet so cruel. Her crystal-clear eyes were an imprisoning wall of blue, standing between the world and her mind, allowing nothing in. Yet Ela was the most serene person I knew. She'd handled the transition into her dark world with such maturity, and I was endlessly filled with admiration for how she'd gone from a regular child to a blind teenager.

Ela had had time to prepare. Knowing her world would one day become utterly dark, she'd sapped up every sight and colour she could lay her eyes on, hungry for the visual side of life. Her signature phrase became, 'Let me see, before the lights go out.' Tim and Linda took her travelling when she was nine, just old enough to start grasping world history and foreign cultures. They took her to see Buckingham Palace, the Eiffel Tower, the Mona Lisa, the Statue of Liberty. The pyramids. Bedouins in the Sahara. Tigers in India. Kangaroos and koalas. Snow on the Alps. She swam with dolphins off the Mozambique coast and, of course, saw many summer sunsets over Lake Kariba and Mana Pools. Tim and Linda spent every cent they'd ever saved educating Ela who had locked within the most vivid mental photo album. Even now, she often shared her overseas sights with Chris and me as we'd not travelled nearly so far. Ela would hand us her holiday photos and ask us to describe every picture in minute detail, reliving her travels using our eyes and her memory.

I headed to the garages to get the quad bike, too hot to walk all the way. Jobb sure had done a fine job of covering up Chris's little accident and there wasn't a mark on it. Tighty hopped up behind me, his front paws on the back of my shoulders. His velvety black jowls soon started flapping in the wind as we picked up speed, me giggling as the wet slaps right in my ear grew louder. The workers always howled with laughter when they saw us and had recently presented me with a fabulous charcoal sketch of Tighty and me on the quad.

We turned into the Jackson's gates, the phut-phut of the quad and Tighty's yaps announcing our arrival. Ela was lying under a msasa tree paging through a Braille textbook. She lifted her head in our direction and smiled. Linda waved hello from inside. She was at her computer, probably preparing schoolwork for Ela. She'd been able to attend the first few years of junior school with us but, after her travels and her sight failing fast, Linda, a special needs teacher before marrying Tim, decided to home school her. Ela would still write O and A Levels like us, and was already ahead in her curriculum.

'I've been sent with PB biscuits,' I shouted to Linda, getting a thumbs up in reply.

Ela and I sat on the lawn, chatting for ages. Hearing how Chris and Pete had got stoned and pranged the quad, Ela eagerly asked where Chris was. She adored him and it wasn't a one-way street. He'd do anything for her and we all wondered if one day it would become something more than friendship. Chris often took Ela up in Dad's funny old microlight, doing a few circuits over the farm. She would weave exotic stories about what was below them, telling Chris that they were flying next to the Eiffel Tower, or hovering over the pyramids – so close she could touch them. The rich fantasies lit her dark world and became a way for her to escape her reality. In the air, she felt free. After seeing Ela, Chris was always a dreamy fool.

She somehow calmed the hooligan in him, albeit temporarily. I could only hope he would never break her heart.

'El,' we heard Linda calling a while later. 'Mrs Clapham is here for your lesson.'

'Agh. The Clap,' grumbled Ela.

Ela's piano teacher, Mrs Clapham – The Clap, as we called her – was an austere, and somewhat uptight, elderly lady, complete with blue rinse. She was a gifted pianist with a few Albert Hall concerts under her garter belt, and had also been the bookkeeper and music teacher at our old district school. After a decade of home piano lessons, The Clap and Ela had developed a very special bond, which I didn't get, but didn't question either. It was rare to see The Clap smile. She had a tight little mouth, lips permanently pursed and puckered into a remarkable resemblance of a cat's bum. We always grumbled about old Cat's Bum Clap being super strict but deep down she was a dear old duck.

I decided to stay for Ela's lesson. Inside, Ela sat at her piano, playing a funky little tune while munching on a biscuit.

'Ela! Christ Almighty! Can you get rid of that biscuit? Crumbs on the ivory – tsk!' said The Clap in a clipped voice, pulling a particularly serious cat's bum, her tightly curled hair jiggling.

They soon settled into the lesson and I sprawled out on a couch with Mojo and Tighty. A while later I heard Tim coming home. He found Linda in her study and, despite their hushed voices, I worked out there'd been a drama of sorts.

'Maddie is becoming a serious liability. Can't you and Gill do something more for her?' Tim was clearly upset and frustrated.

Catching words here and there, I gathered that Maddie, while driving through town, had knocked a man off his bike. He was only grazed but his bicycle was buggered. Maddie, high as a kite, had gone absolutely berserk at the poor man for scratching her truck, despite it being entirely her fault. Tim happened to be passing and had had to stop Maddie belting the innocent man she'd nearly killed with her reckless driving.

'Nine in the morning, Linds, nine o'clock in the bloody morning and she was completely roasted. Finished. Rat faced. Next time she'll kill someone,' Tim said.

Ela had heard Tim too. Still playing, she turned to me, knowing I was listening. 'Maddie again,' she said, mid-Mozart.

The Clap made a disapproving face complete with wide eyes and lips in an even tighter cat's bum. It twitched as if wondering whether to trust a fart to be just a fart.

'Mom, what's up with Maddie. Is she sick?' I asked a few days later as we drove into town with a cream delivery for the local supermarket.

'She's not sick per se, not sick like needing a doctor or hospital, but she's having some emotional problems,' said Mom.

'Is she having a nervous breakdown? Is she headed for the loony bin?'

'Kat! That's a little unkind. Maddie is a good person and a dear friend. She just needs support right now.'

'What happened with her and the guy she knocked off his bike?'

'Where on earth did you hear about that?' Mom looked at me sideways.

'Tim was telling Linda about it the other day. We overheard.'

'Ah. Well, Maddie is on some heavy medication and she made the mistake of having a glass of wine. She shouldn't have mixed the two and she shouldn't have been driving.'

'Oh,' I said, wondering what kind of a special occasion it had been that had had Maddie knocking wine back with her morning cornflakes. 'Didn't you do something similar once, Mom?'

I regretted the words as soon as I said them. Maddie's incident had sparked a hazy memory of Mom having a prang when I was about five. I braced myself.

'You remember that?' Mom's tone was slow and considered.

'I remember more the fight you and Dad had afterwards. Went on for days.'

'That's all behind me now.'

'So how can we help Maddie?' I asked, relieved Mom wasn't going to nail me for my cheeky comment. Much as I was dying to know more about the addict label Maddie seemed to have earned, I'd realised it wasn't the right time to fish in that pond.

'We're helping Maddie as best we can. Pete just needs you lot, his mates, around for support.'

'I like Pete. A bit shy at times but he's a sweetie.'

I didn't want to say anything about Pete getting wasted with Chris at every chance they got. This time I managed to hold my tongue.

3

Our family had a slightly different living arrangement to most when it came to my grandparents. Dad's mother and Mom's father – a widow and a widower – shared a house on the farm.

Mom was an only child. Her parents Dan and Polly, British by birth, had been in tea in India before the war. In the late 1940s, once Hitler had had his arse kicked, they'd moved to Africa where, in Nyasaland before it became Malawi, my grandfather had owned a large tea estate. On retiring in the late 1950s, they'd moved to what was then Salisbury.

The claustrophobia of city living after the wide-open spaces of India and Malawi had led to a rethink and, within a year, they'd accepted a post managing a smallholding in the Mazoe Valley, an hour outside Salisbury. Compared to tea, it was a much smaller enterprise, producing fruit and veg. Granny Polly lost a cancer battle when I was two so I had no real memories of her. Grandpa, bereft without his soul mate, took her death hard. Worried that he'd become a hermit, Mom had moved Grandpa to our farm shortly afterwards.

Dad's side of the family had roots in South Africa's Cape Winelands. A branch of the family had explored work opportunities further afield, and his great-grandparents had been among the first white farmers in Rhodesia. As a youngster, Dad's father Arthur had fallen in love with Jillian, the daughter of a wealthy English Lord who'd been widowed young and had chosen to raise his only child in colonial Africa. Arthur married Jillian and two years later along came Dad, followed by twin girls five years later. My aunts had shipped out of Rhodesia in the 1970s once it was clear that Ian Smith's days were numbered and political change loomed. Both went back to their Cape roots where both had married wealthy wine farmers.

Arthur, a passionate polo player, died in a freak riding accident the year after Mom and Dad married. During a match at the Country Club, a flock of birds had spooked his horse. Arthur was thrown, snapped his neck on landing and died instantly, bang in the middle of the polo field – dead as a doornail.

Jillian, or GranJilly as we called her, had always been a touch psychic and able to tell fortunes when she put her mind to it. She'd had a shiver down her spine over breakfast and had begged Arthur not to play polo that day, but Arthur, with no time for 'mumbo bloody jumbo spooks and sorcery shit', ignored her. He'd polished off his bacon and eggs, looked in on his tobacco in the curing sheds, gone to polo, and was stone dead two hours later. GranJilly had never quite recovered from the shock. Her hair turned snow-white practically overnight.

Liked and well respected, Arthur's sudden death had rocked the community. The funeral had turned into a drunken affair with umpteen toasts and lots of 'Best way to go, that's our Arthur, no indignity, jammy bloody bastard.' Unfortunately, our grief-stricken GranJilly kept on toasting Arthur well after his death and became firm friends with the gin bottle. She turned into a raging alcoholic very quickly and was never too far from a bottle. Gin-soaked and torn apart by grief, she was useless without the love of her life by her side. There was no consoling her and it was around about then that people started calling her Jill-bey, after her preferred gin brand, Gilbey's.

While Dad had been groomed to take over the farm, he was shell-shocked when called to duty early. Not only that, he also had to contend with a gin-marinated mother who'd be plastered by ten in the morning. On top of which, three months after Arthur's death, Dad and Mom put their first bun in the matrimonial oven – Chris.

Dad just rolled up his sleeves and got stuck into his new roles. He didn't have a whole lot of choice. Unable to cope with GranJilly, Dad admitted defeat and summoned his sisters to straighten out their drunkard of a mother. There'd been heavy resistance from Jill-bey but my aunts cracked it and, nobody knows how, they got her off the gin. There was even talk among the workers that an African witch doctor had been summoned. The name Jill-bey was dropped, GranJilly got her shit together, broke up with the gin bottle and didn't touch booze again.

And so Mom and Dad found themselves each with an ageing, widowed parent they needed to keep an eye on. It was decided that Grandpa and GranJilly would become housemates, living in the third house on the farm – a cottage down by the dam. Initially Grandpa kicked up a stink as he'd never cared for GranJilly but, being a true gentleman, he didn't let on to his true opinion of her. Except for a few arguments and bickering matches still today, a happy medium was found. In fact, Grandpa and GranJilly were rather like an old married couple themselves, just without geriatric sex. Chris had always speculated about their sexual arrangements, once asking me over Sunday lunch in a not-so-soft whisper if I thought they ever shagged. Grandpa later took Chris and me aside to set the record straight, saying he'd sooner shag Attila the Hun.

GranJilly could be an exceptionally bad-tempered, crotchety old bat with a seemingly never-ending list of things to bitch about. Poor Grandpa suffered the brunt of it, but had perfected the art of zoning her out. Brave soul, my Grandpa was, and ever the family clown. I utterly adored him and we had a special relationship that is difficult to describe.

With only two days left before we'd head back to school in Harare, I decided to find Jobb, saddle up and ride down to visit Grandpa and GranJilly. As Jobb and I slowly made our way along the dusty farm roads, he told me all about his daughter, who was getting married soon, and the *lobola* he'd received from the man. It was to be quite the district wedding and I loved seeing Jobb so excited and proud.

Grandpa and GranJilly's cottage was surrounded by old gum trees that threw off a scent of eucalyptus, freshening the still, unbearably hot air. Their lush garden, drenched by the sprinklers each night, was an almost cruel contrast to the parched farmland, so desperate for the rains to come.

As we neared the cottage, we heard the popping of a pellet gun.

'Goddamn bastard crows! I've had a gutful of being woken by their bloody shrieking,' fumed Grandpa, appearing with GranJilly's two Jack Russells yapping at his heels.

Crows were his pet hate. I had to agree that their squawking at dawn was enough to put you in the foulest of moods. They'd sit, their claws scratching the tin roof like nails on a blackboard, teasing the dogs that would yap wildly in return. It really was the most abrasive way in which to be woken. In African legend, it is said that to eradicate crows you simply kill one and spread its carcass on the roof. The other crows see their mate is toast, and gather around the carcass for a Crow Funeral. Then they get the message and bugger off, never to return. The snag was that a Crow Funeral could last for days and the noise escalate to maddening levels, so it had to get worse before it got better. Dad had done it at our house with success, but Grandpa remained plagued by the glossy menaces and seemed to have a dead crow permanently pegged on the roof, a Crow Funeral in full swing. Personally, I thought the Jack Russells were more the problem, given their innate ability to wind the crows up.

'KitKat! We've hardly seen you lately. Aren't you due back at school this week?' said Grandpa, smiling broadly, forgetting his crows for a second.

'Yup, we head back Monday night,' I said, dismounting.

Jobb stretched over to take my reins and headed to the back garden where we kept a barrel of water for the horses. He'd find GranJilly's Cookie and probably join him in the sun on the back step with a huge mug of sweet milky tea and doorstopper Sun Jam sandwiches.

'Come inside Kat. Perfect timing – your GranJilly is fighting with the computer again. Please save her before the gin bottle starts winking at her,' said Grandpa, wicked as always.

Inside we found GranJilly bollocking on her computer. 'Windows? Why do I need windows on a computer, you stupid bloody machine! And if I see your paper clip smiley face offering help one more time I'm going to throw this godforsaken machine in the dam,' she grumbled on, and then saw me. 'Oh KitKat, angel, you're just in time. Please help.'

I took a deep breath and sat next to her. We'd done this before. I must have given her fifty hours of computer lessons already.

'Go. Away,' she said to the paper clip man in a slow hostile voice. Then she clicked her mouse another twenty times in rapid succession and the computer let out an angry beep.

'SHIT!' GranJilly scraped her chair back and stood up in a huff, her nostrils flaring, practically scoring the ground with her foot like an angry bull.

'Jillian! I'll wash your mouth out with soap,' chuckled Grandpa, winking at me. 'Your Gran sure turns into a guttermouth when she's on that thing.'

'Lemonade? Made a fresh jug this morning,' GranJilly offered, ignoring Grandpa.

'Mmm, thanks,' I replied, sitting down to assess the myriad of error messages. She had eight text documents open, three spreadsheets running, the spell check active, the music player on mute, she had number-locked the keyboard, and had six print jobs queued when she didn't even have a printer. No wonder it was paralysed.

Mom had recently given her our very old computer and the only reason she persevered was that The Clap, her best friend, was computer literate and the two old farts could get horribly competitive. GranJilly refused to look incompetent and Mom had tasked her with the farm's dairy bookkeeping to keep her mind active. She made more and more mistakes every month and Mom actually re-did the books herself, unbeknown to GranJilly. It was a total farce, but Mom wanted her to have a reason to get out of bed every morning.

'I can't see the fascination with these computers,' said Grandpa. 'Nothing wrong with a ledger and a typewriter. We ran an entire tea estate that way.'

'Oh shut up will you, Dan. If Betty Clapham can master technology, then so can I,' said GranJilly, grizzling at Grandpa through the kitchen hatch as she clinked ice cubes into glasses of lemonade.

Grandpa and I snorted in amusement. He found The Clap about as tiresome as GranJilly and he'd been thrilled to hear our likening of her mouth to a cat's arse.

'Kat, tell us your news. Is your brother still being a hooligan? Is he still wooing Ela?' asked GranJilly, handing me a glass of her too tangy, strip-the-enamel-off-your-teeth lemonade.

Computer fixed, I rattled off the family news. I told them about my project on Nyaminyami and Grandpa was immediately in his element, the perfect person to ask about Zambezi Valley history. He went straight to his dusty bookcase to pull out his photo albums. He had incredible photos of

Kariba's Operation Noah which he'd seen in the late 1950s when the Valley was flooded to build the power station at Kariba, requiring the massive wildlife relocation exercise.

I was soon engrossed in the faded photographs and Grandpa's tales. I never tired of his beloved albums. We paged through his Malawi chapter too, the black-and-white photos turning into faded colour around the 1970s. We laughed at pictures of Mom as a little girl paddling in Lake Malawi, and at pictures of her showjumping days sporting elaborate rosettes for her horsey achievements. Then the photos of Mom and Dad as newlyweds, back in the days when Dad had a little more hair.

I noticed that in nearly every early photo of Mom, she had a glass of wine in her hand and was in party mode. Then it struck me – something I'd not seen before. From when I was about five, the standard-issue glass of wine was missing from her hand. Cigarettes and still smiling, yes, but the booze was missing. Something else made me stop and stare – a picture I'd seen before but never really examined in detail.

It was Mom as a teenager in Malawi. She was looking rather tubby, not her usual slender self. I looked more closely, observing her dark and haunted look – a sharp contrast to other photos where she appeared bright and bubbly. There was definitely something strange about the photo, I couldn't quite put my finger on it.

'Mom looks a bit bleak there, Grandpa?' I said, fishing.

'Mmm. I think she'd had a bad bout of malaria,' he said, and quickly turned the page.

A fresh round of crow squawks brought us all back to the present. Hearing the enemy, Grandpa sat back in the couch, hands behind his head as he closed his eyes and gently took a long, slow, very deep breath.

'Here we go again!' said GranJilly, rolling her eyes and tilting her head mockingly at Grandpa. 'The crows are to him what the paper clip man is to me. More lemonade, Kat?'

'No, thanks.' My teeth were still recovering from the first glass. 'I better make tracks. Jobb will want to settle the horses before dark.'

'Come on then, Kat, let's get you home,' said Grandpa.

We found Jobb outside, sitting in the shade with Cookie who was peeling carrots for supper. Between him snacking as he peeled and Jobb feeding them to the horses, there'd be one carrot each for supper.

'Jobb, old chap, how's Kat's riding?' asked Grandpa. 'Any chance of her showjumping like her mother?'

'*Eish Baas*, I've tried to make her jump but, *aikona*, she's not interested,' said Jobb.

It was true. Jumping terrified me. I was yet to attempt a jump that didn't end with me lying face down in the dust and my horse belting off into the sunset.

'Next holidays we'll build some new obstacles and try her on them. Come on Kat, off you go,' said Grandpa, giving me a leg-up. As I slipped my feet into the stirrups, he smacked my horse's flank, making her bolt off down the driveway, with me only just clinging on.

I heard Grandpa roar with laughter behind me. 'Keep your bloody knees in Kat, could park a bus between them and the horse!'

I threw my arm up in a wave as Jobb and I gave the horses their heads. We were back at the stables in no time at all.

The clouds were rolling in again. Fat, heavy and black with more promise of rain. Thunder rumbled, teasing the thirsty crops. As I headed home from the stables, a few drops of rain fell, great big splodges that left little craters in the dust, rolling around in a shimmery dance. The scent was delicious and I turned my face to the sky, loving the drops on my skin, mingling with the sweat and dust that coated me. I opened my mouth to catch the sweet, salty African rain. Tighty and Gertie, who'd been waiting for me at the stables, also jumped and twisted with their heads to the sky in a weird boxer rain dance, catching drops on their floppy pink tongues. Then it stopped. Just a brief taunt from above.

The evening felt heavy and still. The clouds hadn't blown over and the air remained pregnant with a storm. After supper, with nothing decent on TV and the air marginally cooler outdoors, I joined Mom and Dad on the patio. Despite our ankles and arms embalmed with repellent and a huge citronella candle doing its best, the mosquitoes were relentless and I couldn't bear it for long.

I went in to find Chris. He was recording a talking book for Ela, sitting on his bed reading Roald Dahl's *James and The Giant Peach* to an old tape recorder. Last week he'd done *Animal Farm* and *The Secret Diary of Adrian Mole*. Hours of reading done completely of his own accord. His ritual was to give Ela a set of new talking books whenever we went back to school. Chris had an amazing voice and was brilliant at accents, though there'd been much embarrassment when his voice had broken about a year ago. For Ela, he'd persisted through the sudden squeaks and odd rasping sounds, before finding his adult voice which Ela described as all manly and 'like he gargles warm honey', which had only made me cringe.

He stopped the tape when I plonked myself on his bed. Tighty leapt up too. As we sprawled out, drained by the incessant heat, I looked at Chris's bookcase – a jumble of novels, flying magazines and pop culture collected over the years. A framed photo of our family reminded me of my armchair travels with Grandpa.

'I was looking at Grandpa's albums today,' I said.

'Mmm,' said Chris.

'Mom used to drink, hey? I mean drink booze.'

'Umm, yup.' He glanced at me sideways.

'And now she doesn't?' I both stated and asked.

'Nope, she's not touched a drop in about eight years, not since her trip to that "health farm".' His fingers wiggled in an air quote. The term 'health farm' was obviously a load of bollocks.

'Health farm?' I said, suddenly starting to remember. Bits and pieces of memories were coming back to me but the details were fragmented, like a jigsaw puzzle yet to be done.

'What's brought this on? Did Grandpa say something?' asked Chris.

'No. I think it's all the drama with Maddie that's making me curious. Tell me more, Chris? I know there's a story!'

And so Chris, the only person in the world to share my genes, began to unpack and make sense of my jumble of memories and dozens of questions.

4

'Okay, so you already know the story about GranJilly and her nickname Jill-bey,' said Chris. 'Well, Mom and GranJilly were actually quite similar. Dad told me once that when he met Mom she was the life and soul of every party. Okay, so drinking is practically the national sport in Zim but, in her twenties, Mom's drinking got a bit hectic and she became something called a binge drinker.'

'Binge drinker?'

'Yup. Do you know what an alcoholic is?'

'Yes, it's some smelly, dirty dude who gets hammered all day, staggers around and lives in a ditch or on a park bench. A bum. A loser,' I said, pleased with my answer.

'Not really! An alcoholic can also be the most lah-di-dah upper-class and successful person. They're not always hobos or scumbags.'

'Oh?'

'Yes. And there are different varieties of alcoholics. Some, like GranJilly, wake up and drink before their feet even hit the floor in the morning. They lurch around in a stupor from dawn till dusk. They're the everyday drinkers. Then others, the binge drinkers, who don't necessarily drink every day but, when they do, they give it horns. They drink and drink until they're snot-flying drunk and can't remember their own names. They might only do it a few times a year, but they're still alcoholics.'

'Lovely,' I said.

'Basically, whatever type of drinker they are, once they get going it all turns into a bit of a dog show. Most people know when they've had enough, when to stop drinking. Alcoholics don't.'

'And?'

'Mom was an alcoholic of the binge variety. About once a month, she'd get totally hammered, disgrace herself and embarrass the crap out of Dad. They'd have the most awful fights over her outrageously bad behaviour. Dad even chucked her out once. Sent her to stay with Grandpa. You were just a toddler.'

'But Dad drinks. I've seen him drunk too.'

'Dad knows when to stop. And he doesn't go berserk if he can't have a drink or the booze cabinet runs dry.'

'Oh.' I was a bit confused. The story was getting more interesting by the minute. I knew there was some dirt in our family.

'Mom didn't drink when she was pregnant with us. Dad said they all hoped she'd change her ways when she became a mother. She didn't put her drinking boots away for good, and drank from time to time after I was born but, on the whole, she was more controlled. Then she got preggers with you, Kat, and stayed sober until you were about three. Suddenly she went full throttle and, two years later, her binge drinking hit an all-time high. Dad said she'd find every reason under the sun, however obscure, to drink. When the rains came, when the tobacco fetched a high price at the auctions, when it fetched a low price, when there was a birth on the farm, a death, when shit happened, when shit didn't happen – anything was a reason to drink. You're lucky you don't remember the fighting. It was horrid to hear them always laying into each other.'

'I remember a few fights, and that Mom never wanted to play with me.'

'Yup, me neither. Anyway, then Mom's hooching shifted from the binge pattern to every day. She started to get sneaky, hiding it from Dad, denying being drunk yet reeking of booze and slurring. Dad then brought in a "no booze" rule in the house. Cookie and co all knew Mom had a problem anyway. Shit, I used to cringe when I saw Cookie cleaning up her vomit. Poor Jobb took some flack too. Remember when Mom broke her arm?'

'Yes. She said someone spooked her horse and she tumbled?'

'She did tumble, only the horse was standing dead still in the yard. So pissed, she passed clean out and toppled off. She came round face first in the dust with her arm bent at a funny angle. Jobb saw it all from across the yard. Despite Mom's insistence that she'd been thrown, Dad believed Jobb.'

'No ways!' I was actually quite shocked.

'Yup. Once Mom knew everyone was watching her like a hawk, she got crafty. Alcoholics are great at hiding their habit. I was always finding half-jacks in the linen cupboard and other weird places. I remember swigging from her glass of orange juice at breakfast and getting a nice little hit. Barely any orange in it, just vodka.'

'Wow, so Mom was quite the nutter?'

'Oh yeah! Then, because Dad's sisters had managed to kill GranJilly's romance with the gin bottle, he flew them here to do the same for Mom. But she refused point-blank to listen to anyone. GranJilly even tried but there was no reasoning with her. Remember how she used to fly into rages?'

'I do, actually. But she doesn't really freak out like that anymore.'

'It was the hooch that made her screech like a deranged fishwife. Things got worse and worse. I remember Doctor Roberts often being called out when Mom would puke and puke, basically vomiting herself into such extreme dehydration that she needed a drip. We often spent weekends with Tim and Linda. Dad did everything he could to shield us from the drama.'

'So what happened? How and when did she change?'

'Dad had pretty much given up on ever seeing her sober again and started talking about divorce. Then, on a trip to see his cousins in Cape Town, a family friend who counselled recovering addicts sat him down and gave him some guidelines on approaching Mom about getting sober. He came home full of hope and followed the suggestions, but failed. I think the counsellor lady had banked on it not going well so had created a Plan B for Dad. Plan B was more hardcore. Plan C was divorce.'

'Hardcore? Plan B?'

'Plan B was flying in someone trained in treating alcoholism to talk to Mom. Mom never knew a thing about this person coming to the farm and, well, she got ambushed. It was an Intervention.'

'What's an Invention?'

'No man, an In-*ter*-vention. It's when a neutral third party oversees a drama and mediates, I think. An umpire. I don't know what they said to Mom, but several people were there – Dad, GranJilly and Grandpa, Tim and Linda, Maddie's husband Kevin was there, Doc Roberts, and a few others. I saw everyone leave after an hour, all looking distraught and like they needed a stiff drink themselves. Mom and the lady from Cape Town talked alone for another two hours. From that day on, there was no more shouting. That night, the air and vibe in the house lifted slightly, like clouds clearing after a big storm.' Chris paused for a while, remembering, suddenly rather sad.

I was lost for words.

'Mom packed a suitcase and the next day she flew back with the lady to Cape Town. Dad told us she was going to see his cousins and then go to a health farm to get some rest, and that she'd be home and healthy soon.'

'Wait! I remember that,' I said. 'I remember sitting on their bed while she was packing and she kept hugging me, crying, and saying she loved us all.'

'Yeah. Well, health farm my arse. Mom went to rehab.'

'REHAB? Like for drug add—' I stopped, hearing footsteps coming down the passage. A second later Mom stuck her head round the door.

'What are you two yakking about, huh? Chris, honey, do some school packing please,' said Mom.

She hadn't overheard us, thank God!

'Night Ma,' said Chris and I together, waiting to hear her bedroom door close before continuing.

'That was close,' said Chris.

'But this is not a big secret is it, Mom's drinking?'

'Nah, not really, it's kinda in the past but I know Mom still feels shit and guilty. Maybe she thinks you're still too young to know all the gory details.'

'Well, the other day I asked her about the time she knocked that guy off his bike and she didn't freak out like I thought she would. She was pretty calm about it.'

'Hmm, interesting. She has mellowed a lot – it was so long ago.'

'Okay, finish the story,' I said. 'So she went to rehab, not a hospital?'

'Yup. Rehabs are different to normal hospitals. I think you do get doctors and nurses in them, mainly psychologists and psychiatrists – don't ask me the difference. They're both head doctors, though. Mom was there for three months.'

'And she's not had a drink since?'

'Not a drop.'

'Now what I want to know is why? Why did she drink?'

'Kat, that I can't answer. Your guess is as good as mine.'

'Can't we just ask her?'

'I think you'll get a short answer. I have a feeling something hectic happened in Malawi when she was a teenager. I'd steer clear though. Curiosity killed the Kat!'

'Well, thanks for the, err, bedtime story! I can't quite get my head around it all, but anyway.'

'One day it will all come out. Bugger off now. I need to finish Ela's tape.'

I lay in bed listening to the high-pitched drone of mosquitoes scouting for a juicy piece of exposed flesh. Curiosity killed the Kat indeed, I thought, wondering if I could ever look at my mother the same way again.

So, my mother is an alcoholic. And she was tossed into rehab.

Super. Lovely. Good to know.

Two days later, our black tin trunks packed, our squash rackets, cricket bats and hockey sticks flying everywhere, Chris, Pete, Rolo and I converged in the driveway dressed in our uniforms and ready for school. It was Mom's turn to do the school run into Harare.

Linda had brought Ela down to say goodbye. She had blinked back tears after Chris presented her with a new set of talking books. It was tough for her during school terms but she was getting better at the goodbyes. There were, after all, at least three of these driveway scenes every year.

Mom and Linda stood chatting quietly to one side.

'I'll spend a night or two in Harare once I've dropped the kids off. I want to get to a meeting and chat to them about Maddie too,' Mom said, making sure Pete was out of earshot.

'Great. Let me know what they say,' said Linda.

'Will do. Right, you lot,' said Mom, turning back to us. 'Let's move!'

'Mom, who are you meeting in town?' I blurted out as Linda and Ela drove off.

Pete and Rolo were engrossed in something on her cellphone, but Chris was standing slightly behind Mom, and made a face behind her back to say 'Eeeek, you're toast', his eyes wide. I held my breath, knowing I shouldn't have asked.

'Kat, I told you the other day, we're helping Maddie get through a rough patch. I'm meeting with some people in Harare who've been in the same boat as us and can give me some advice. It's called AA,' said Mom, her voice low and one eye on Pete.

Chris's eyes grew even wider, shocked to hear Mom's calm answer.

'But I thought AA sold road maps and fixed broken cars,' I said. 'Has Maddie got car troubles as well as emotional ones?'

Chris spluttered, doing a poor job of hiding his laugh. Mom half turned to look at him and she, in turn, raised one eyebrow.

'This is another AA,' said Mom, clearly unimpressed.

I decided to quit while I was ahead. It hadn't escaped me that Mom had said 'the same boat as *us*', lumping herself in the same category as Maddie. It certainly tied in with what Chris had told me.

'Well, aren't you being the ballsy one today,' Chris said to me as Mom walked off to find her keys.

We reluctantly piled into our own school bus, an old VW kombi that belonged to Rolo's mom. It should have been retired years ago, but it was the only vehicle big enough for the four of us and all our school gear. Last year, Rolo and I had been allowed to paint daisies all over it, much to the boys' embarrassment.

Mom would deliver Rolo to Baxter High, Chris and Pete to their all-boys Catholic school, St Edwards and I'd get dumped at the all-nuns Dominican Convent.

At the back of the hot kombi, Rolo filled me in on the boy news. Jason was still chasing her and she was dying to see him again. He was a day scholar, not a boarder like us, also at St Edwards. Hearing Jason's name, Chris and Pete couldn't wait to tell tales.

'Hey Pete,' said Chris, 'remember last term, when Jason got cuts and his arse was so knackered he had to stand in class for two days?'

Cuts were any form of punishment issued via any stick-like, welt-inducing object, something Chris was familiar with. In fact, Chris had a long association with his housemaster's cane and currently held the 'Edwards Record' for Most Cuts In One Term, something his peers considered a top-notch achievement and worthy of idol status.

'Why did Jason get cuts?' asked Rolo.

Pete started sniggering and moved closer to prevent Mom overhearing. 'He got caught smoking some Mary Jane in the loos,' said Pete.

'Don't believe you!' said Rolo. 'He's not like you two – he wouldn't smoke weed.'

'Wanna bet?' asked Chris.

I saw Mom watching us in the rear-view mirror, but the boys had their backs to her so she couldn't hear much.

'He got lucky,' said Chris. 'He flushed the evidence before the master saw it and got punished just for regular smoking.'

'Well, it's not like you two have ever turned down the Mary Jane,' I said.

'Okay, okay. Shush now,' said Chris, glancing over his shoulder at Mom. 'Seriously though Rolo, Jason is a good dude. I like him. He does seem to have girly groupies always chasing him, but Pete and I will sort him out if he messes you around, okay? You just give the word.'

Chris was as protective of Rolo as he was of me. He really would sort Jason out and defend Rolo's honour, no matter the consequences.

'Who are you taking to the school dance?' Rolo asked the boys.

'Umm, don't know yet,' said Pete.

'And you, Chris?' asked Rolo.

'There's a chick called Samantha at Baxter,' said Chris. 'I met her at cricket last term. She's super cute, hey Pete?'

'Oh yeah, a serious hottie,' said Pete.

'Ooooh! We've not heard about a Samantha before. This is news,' I said.

'I know how silly you girls get whenever I like someone. Don't even start on me now,' said Chris.

'No man, I want to know more,' I said. 'She's at Baxter? Rolo, do you know her?'

'Think I know who you mean, Chris. But nah, can't say I know her well,' said Rolo.

'What does she look like?' I asked.

'She's a stunner,' said Chris. 'Long, dark, curly hair, cute freckles and legs a mile long.'

'Oi, you guys, when is the dance?' shouted Mom from upfront. The woman had the hearing of a bat.

'End of November,' replied Pete.

'Where?' asked Mom.

'Rugby field. No hotel will have us again,' said Chris.

Last year at the dance, someone had thrown a waiter into the hotel pool and puked all over the lobby.

'They're putting up a marquee and getting caterers in. So we'll just puke on the rugby field this year,' added Pete.

'Rolo, what are you wearing?' Mom asked.

'Mom is going to Jo'burg on another shopping trip so I've placed an order for a little black dress and strappy heels,' said Rolo.

'Pete,' I said, an idea forming, 'I'm just thinking about a date for you. There's this girl at Convent who—'

Pete interrupted me mid-sentence. 'Kat, please would you be my date?'

'Oh,' I said, surprised. 'Well, sure. Okay then. That'll be a blast, thanks Pete.'

'Oooh Pete!' said Chris, thumping him on the arm. 'You dirty dog – my little sister?'

Pete started blushing, Chris started laughing, and Rolo elbowed me in my ribs.

'Mom!' I bellowed to the front of the bus. 'I need a dance dress too.'

Mom winked and smiled at me in the mirror. She'd already guessed that secretly I was thrilled, having felt left out of all the dance talk. The only dance I'd ever been to had been at the district junior school and the hall had had the ambience of a jail cell with every last fluorescent light blazing.

'Cool! We're all going then,' Rolo said.

'Yup, more importantly, I can check out this Samantha then too,' I said, laughing as Chris sighed and rolled his eyes.

It was all rather mundane in the first half of term until one day, Lucy, one of my dorm mates and the biggest nerd ever, suddenly decided she wanted to start squash. I was on the school team and she coerced me into giving her lessons during our free time on Sundays. I always enjoyed the slightly quirky Lucy and loved anything that got me out on a Sunday, the worst day in boarding school. Harare Sports Club was a ten-minute walk from school, and didn't require a nun escort as long as we weren't tempted by evil and came straight home.

There was a great vibe at the courts and we became friends with some of the boys who played league each week. Lucy soon had a clear admirer who'd taken it upon himself to help with her coaching. She was secretly delighted and I'd even caught her doodling hearts in class – the universal symbol of a massive schoolgirl crush.

And I'd met Anthony, another St Edwards boy, just a few months older than me. Drop-dead gorgeous, tall, lean yet muscular, fascinating green eyes that transfixed me, and a floppy blond hairstyle. Ignoring all the other girls in too-short, too-tarty squash skirts always trailing after him, he seemed to seek me out, always with compliments, be they about my hair, my tan or my serve. After a long debate about Shakespeare one day, I realised he was quite smart too. Life suddenly became one big Anthony-flavoured daydream. And so I officially joined the ranks of Lucy and Rolo, with a crush on a guy who set off butterflies in me and made me, too, doodle hearts in geography.

I wrote to Ela about it, always wanting her to feel she was still a part of our lives during school terms. I knew telling her about Anthony meant Linda would learn about him and probably Mom too, but I was okay with that. I had letters back from Ela, two in Linda's handwriting and one in Grandpa's, which was a first. He must have popped in and got coerced into taking a dictation. I couldn't stop laughing at the slightly deranged-looking cat Grandpa had drawn at the end of the letter.

My weekend bag packed, I waited at the school gates for Mom to collect me for the four-day half-term break. Grandpa needed to see the optician and was coming in too, and we'd sleep at the flat Grandpa kept in Harare. It was small, but fine for a few nights when the three-hour drive back to the farm wasn't worth the trek. Mom had to get home by Sunday night so Chris and I would spend the last night with Rolo at her brother Jack's house. At thirty-two, Jack was already a highly regarded lawyer and was soon to marry Anna, a kindergarten teacher whom we all adored.

Hearing a familiar dog bark, I swung round to see Mom in her dusty truck with both Grandpa and Mojo hanging out the window. It meant one thing – Ela was here too.

'Ela?' I said, excitedly, at the car window.

'Surprise!' said Mom and Ela at the same time.

'Ah, this is so cool,' I said, jumping in. 'This is a first. You coming for half-term?'

'Nothing else to do on the farm so I coerced your mother,' said Ela. 'Might be a bit squashed with Mojo but I wanted to see you guys.'

'How're you KitKat?' asked Grandpa. 'Been terrorising the nuns, I hope.'

'I have made a concerted effort, yes,' I said, leaning forward to kiss him.

'That's my girl,' he chuckled.

At St Edwards, Chris and his mates were tossing a rugby ball around. Again, Mojo's barking announced our arrival and Chris ran to the car, grinning.

'Ela! How awesome,' he said, squeezing into the back with us. 'Mom, Grandpa, KitKat, howzit, howzit, howzit!'

'Before we go, Chris, please take Mojo for a quick walk. I'm sure she needs to pee,' said Ela.

While Chris and Mojo were doing a lap around the rugby field, I was happily checking out the other boys when I spotted Anthony at the far end of the car park.

'Oh my God!' I said to Ela. 'He's over there.'

'Who? Yummy squash boy?' asked Ela.

'Yes. Yummy Anthony.'

Mom turned around, smiling at me. 'Yummy Anthony? Is he someone I should know about?'

'Look Ma, that one there, floppy blond hair, tall, divine. He plays squash at the club and he's to die for, don't you think?'

'Mmm, he is rather cute,' said Mom.

'He's a little young for you, Gill,' joked Grandpa, who then blatantly craned his neck out of the window and let out a loud, shrill whistle that echoed around the courtyard and made all the boys turn.

'GRANDPAAAA!' I hissed, thumping him on the arm.

Of course Anthony turned and saw us all ogling. He waved, and next thing I knew, he was sauntering over. I could have died.

'Agh, shit,' I muttered.

Mom and Grandpa started laughing at me as I rolled my window down and Anthony stuck his head in.

'Hey Kat,' he said.

Oh, those eyes! I promptly turned into a moron and couldn't speak.

'Hi there,' he said to Ela, Mom and Grandpa. 'I'm Anthony.'

'Lovely to meet you, Anthony. I believe you're a brilliant squash player,' said Mom.

Ela, meanwhile, was jabbing me in the ribs, making me squirm. Looking like the village idiot, I grinned at Anthony.

'Umm, I don't know about brilliant, Mrs Hay. Kat's pretty good herself,' said Anthony.

'Anthony, this is Ela, and that's the mother and the grandfather,' I said, suddenly finding my voice, then letting out a stupid girly giggle. This boy stuff was hellish.

'Nice to meet you all. Have a great weekend Kat, see you at squash next week, I hope,' said Anthony, winking at me.

With that, he ambled off, saying hi to Chris and patting Mojo as they walked past him to the truck. Thank God I was sitting. My knees would never have kept me upright.

'So, he's cute,' said Mom, starting the car. 'How exciting! Kat's got a boy in her life.'

'What?' said Chris, having missed the whole discussion. 'Kat, you're into Anthony?'

I sighed. 'Yes, alright, so I like him. Let's not make a big deal of it. We just play squash together.'

'Well, well, well,' said Chris, sounding like an old man. 'He's a nice guy, but he's always got a heap of girls after him. At cricket, most of the girls are there only to perve over him.'

I shrugged. I wasn't surprised, I'd seen it at squash. Mom winked at me in the rear-view mirror. The subject was dropped, thankfully.

After a long lunch at Wimpy, Grandpa took himself to the optician and Mom suggested she and I shop for my dance dress, leaving Chris and Ela yakking.

The boutique's shop assistant was the type to insist you look stunning in a bin bag, just to make a sale. Her leopard print jeans and ghastly blue eyeshadow made me take her gushing with a pinch of salt. The first eight dresses off the rail were hit-and-miss but number nine was a winner.

'Mom, I love it!' I said, doing a twirl in the dress – burgundy velvet, thin spaghetti straps crisscrossing the very low-cut back, and the neckline sprinkled with tiny, tasteful specks of diamante.

'Oh, now that is gorgeous! Might need to address the footwear though,' she said, looking at my school shoes.

'You don't think these shoes work? Jolly comfy though,' I laughed.

'Well, that was easy,' said Mom as we went back to find the others. 'Do you know how hard it is to find the perfect dress, never mind in the first shop you try?'

While describing it to Ela and letting her run her hands over the plush velvet, I couldn't help wishing it was Anthony who'd be seeing it on the night.

Grandpa soon strutted back, sporting a new pair of glasses. Smoothing his hair and posing in the middle of Wimpy like it was a catwalk, he asked us how hot he looked.

'As cool as ever, Grandpa,' said Chris. 'All the grandmas will be beating down your door.'

'Ah, so many blue rinses, so little time,' sighed Grandpa, winking at an old lady in the corner. She spluttered, sending her grandchildren into fits of giggles.

The weekend flew by, one big laugh with Grandpa putting his own spin on everything. Too quickly we were saying good byes again as Mom left us with Rolo, Jack and Anna on Sunday afternoon.

Never in a million years did I imagine my life was about to change course quite dramatically.

'Right, now show me this amazing dance dress?' said Rolo within five minutes of us arriving.

'That is incredible Kat. Wow, you look about twenty-five,' said Anna, who'd come to inspect it too. 'Have you got shoes yet? I have the perfect pair you can borrow.'

'I've got flat silver sandals,' I replied.

'Nope. You need heels with that dress,' said Anna, dashing off to fetch a very sexy pair of strappy stiletto sandals.

'Are you sure you don't mind lending them to me?' I asked. They were perfect.

'Absolutely. They look stunning on you. Just practise walking in them so you don't fall and make a tit of yourself on the big night. And here, paint your toenails – you have such pretty feet,' she said, tossing me a bottle of cherry-red nail varnish.

'Anna …' Jack stuck his head round the door, stopping to give a wolf whistle when he saw me all dressed up. 'Wow Kat, that's quite a dress! Anna, the boys are coming to watch the rugby and have a braai later. Do you want to ask your brother? Might be nice company for Chris.'

'Ah. Good idea,' said Anna.

'I'll pick him up when I go get some beers,' said Jack, marching off in 'guy braai' mode.

Anna went to make salads, leaving Rolo and me to paint our toenails. I changed out of my dress but kept the heels on to practise my balancing act, suddenly feeling super elegant. Jeans and stilettos weren't exactly my usual farm look.

An hour later, Jack and three mates lugged in a cooler box packed with beer and meat. Cracking open a beer each, they were perfectly synchronised as they set about the holy rugby braai ritual. Anna, Rolo and I were in the open-plan kitchen making garlic bread when I turned around to get the fright of my life. There was Anthony, standing on the other side of the lounge. Rolo noticed me gawking, my mouth open, and followed my eyes. She looked at me, her expression asking 'what's wrong?'

I quickly dropped a spoon, giving me a reason to sink behind the counter and out of Anthony's sight. Rolo, catching on to my diversion tactic, dropped another spoon far too obviously and joined me on the floor. Anna peered down at us and just started laughing.

'Rolo, who the hell is that?' I whispered, indicating that I meant Anthony. A stupid question really as I knew full well who it was.

'Oh, that's just Ant, Anna's brother. Ant Lawson. Great guy.' She paused. 'Why? Your face is a picture.' Her eyes widened as the penny dropped. 'Oh my God, Kat! Wait, is that your Yummy Anthony from squash?'

'Yup.'

'Oh shit, how funny!'

'Pfft! Glad *you* think so.'

'Small world,' Rolo chuckled softly. 'I never even made the connection. I only know him as Ant and you call him Anthony.'

I could have happily hidden all night, but Anna prodded me with her foot, her flapping hand a signal that we might want to get off the floor. Slowly we stood up, with me trying to find some composure, jabbing Rolo in the ribs with the spoon to stop her giggles. Ant, Anthony, yummy guy from squash – whoever he was – had come over to the kitchen, smiling broadly.

'Howzit Rolo, how you doing?' he said. 'And Kat? Hey! What are you doing here?'

Two seconds and bam, those green eyes had me in a trance.

'Umm … w-well …' I stuttered and held my breath. 'So, you see, Rolo lives on the farm next door to me and we're really good friends and we're staying with Jack tonight 'cos my mom had to get home. Then, umm, Jack is taking us back to school tomorrow and well, umm, that's why I am here. Hello Anthony.'

What a blithering idiot. I'm such a moron, I thought. I was never such an airhead when I saw him at squash, but chance encounters were evidently a problem – something I needed to work on, fast.

Realising I hadn't drawn breath since, well, he'd arrived, I then gave my idiot act a grand finale by taking a gulp of air in the most unladylike manner imaginable. All I could do then was smile gormlessly, not trusting myself to speak again. Ant laughed, a slow deep laugh that was as sexy as hell, but he was laughing with me about the bizarre situation, not at me.

'Well, it's awesome to see you, an awesome surprise.'

His knee-weakening smile nearly had me on the floor again.

'Great shoes. Love the red toes too,' he added.

Shit. I'd forgotten I was still wearing Anna's heels. A whole new avenue for embarrassing myself had just opened up. With Ant there, it was pretty much a done deal that I'd fall on my face before the night was out. Oh well, sink or swim, do or die, I thought. Taking them off would just seem lame.

Jack, looking all focused, strode into the kitchen to marinate the meat and said, 'Oh Ant, meet Kat, old family friend from Raffingora.'

'Actually, I know Kat,' Ant said, winking at me.

'Cool. Well, you guys do your own thing. Have a beer, Ant, but don't go overboard or your mom will shoot me,' said Jack, walking off to check on his fire.

Ant, as I now knew him, opened a beer, still watching me with a sparkle in his eyes. Could these waters be any more unchartered?

Chris ambled in. Seeing Rolo barely keeping a straight face, Chris quickly worked out what had happened and, when Ant moved off, he too laughed at my profound discomfort.

'I take it you didn't realise your squash boyfriend was Ant Lawson? I thought you knew he was Anna's brother,' he said.

'No! And thanks for telling me. Knob!' I hissed, cracking him on the head with a roll of tin foil.

A while later, all the boys, including Ant and Chris, were nicely sloshed, yelling at the ref on TV and making casual bets. Rolo and I were looking for some juice in the kitchen, and saw an open bottle of white wine on the counter. Both thought the same thing.

'Probably not a good idea,' I said.

'Ah come on, let's have a swig. They're getting pissed, why can't we?' Rolo stroked the bottle, an evil glint her eye.

Actually, I thought, when else would I get to hang out with Ant like this? Perhaps I could redeem my earlier bout of moronic behaviour. Looking at it that way, I agreed that a slurp of wine seemed like an incredibly bright idea. Unseen, we each took a swig. Then another. And a few more. Next, Rolo grabbed a beer and yanked me out the back door.

'Come on, no one will notice,' said Rolo. The beer opened with a satisfying pop and we had half each.

I'd had wine and beer before but it hadn't blown my hair back. It tasted pretty foul actually. But tonight, it set off a warm, fuzzy glow and, with Ant in the next room, I quickly felt more confident. Surprisingly, I was suddenly steadier on the stilettos too.

Feeling braver, we rejoined the party and I boldly perched on the arm of the couch next to Ant. He smiled at me and, in one smooth move, hooked his thumb into my belt. The rugby soon ended, though I couldn't say who'd been playing, let alone who won.

When everyone moved outside to eat, Rolo and I held back to whip another beer before joining them. It turned into an amazing evening and suddenly I was filled with wit and interesting things to say. Ant and I sat on the lawn and chatted for ages – so much better than the stilted small talk at squash where we were always interrupted. I lay back on the cooling grass and floated, looking at the evening stars and rising moon. Chris sprawled out too, giving Rolo a drunken guide to the galaxy.

Needing to pee, I managed to amble across the lawn relatively gracefully. The high heels sank into the soft lawn and made walking even trickier. I knew Ant was watching and was definitely not admitting stiletto defeat.

In the loo, I heard Rolo giggling outside the bathroom window. Then I heard Chris and then Ant too, all three now skulking around the back of the house. After a quick fluff of my hair and a swipe of lip gloss, I peered out the back door, finding them lurking outside the laundry. A slightly sweet smell hit me.

'Really? Weed again?' I said to Chris. 'What if Jack smells that?'

'Nah, he won't. It's nearly finished. Have the last drag KitKat,' said Rolo, in between giggling at some clothes pegs.

Ant was dead quiet, looking at me terribly seductively, his green eyes staring out from under his fringe. My head was spinning as it was but I buckled under peer pressure, not wanting to seem a prude. I took a small drag, managing not to disgrace myself again. Chris stomped the end of the joint into the flower bed and we weaved our way back to the party.

With his arm around my waist, Ant pulled me close. 'You always smell so good …' It felt like a promise. A blockbuster movie trailer. A film I knew I had to see.

Jack's mates were playing touch rugby, pumped up by the match. Everyone was pretty well plastered, except Anna who was sitting to one side with a girlfriend having what seemed to be a serious heart-to-heart. Jack hauled Chris and Ant into the rugby game.

'Come Kat. You're with me, gorgeous,' said Ant, grabbing my hand.

We positioned ourselves by the pool and I tried to look upbeat despite a series of bright dots dancing in my vision and making me horribly confused. I took a deep breath, hoping the cool, sharp evening air would resolve the difference between reality and wherever Kat was. The ball was being tossed higher and harder by the minute and soon enough it came flying at me. Still in the heels, I jumped, arms stretched and ready for an impressive catch. It was a bad idea and I knew it.

The second my feet left the ground, I knew it.

Jack's swimming pool was artistically set into the side of a small hill, with a three-metre drop from the top of the hill into the deep end. A fountain spout protruded from the retaining concrete façade and, directly below it, a shallow sitting step in the pool. The rugby ball was actually well out of my reach and I didn't realise how close I had drifted to the edge of the pool until I went one backward step too far. I teetered wildly as a stiletto caught the edge of the paving and I went flying, aware only of Ant lunging for me, screaming 'Kaaaat!'

As my world went black, all I thought was, 'This isn't going to end well. Bad idea stilettos, weed and wine. Told you.'

5

It was only by piecing together other people's versions of my spectacular fall that I knew what had happened. Between playing rugby and coming round in hospital, my mind could tell me nothing about the accident. One big blank.

Apparently, when my heel caught the edge of the paving, I'd fallen sideways, knocking my head on the concrete. The momentum saw me roll over the edge and down the three-metre drop into the pool, hitting the fountain spout before landing hard on my shoulder on the shallow sitting step. Then I'd rolled off the step and sunk like lead, straight to the bottom of the pool's deep end. The doctors said I was probably already unconscious at that stage.

They all watched it happening in slow motion, Rolo said. Knowing I was a strong swimmer, they had waited, expecting me to come up and laugh at my own stupid klutzy behaviour. When I didn't surface, Jack, Ant and Chris dived in. They had struggled with my dead weight in the dark watery depths of the pool, but eventually managed to drag me out.

I was out cold and not breathing at all when they laid me on the grass. Anna, a teacher, knew CPR and immediately started resuscitation, pounding on my chest. Still I wasn't breathing. Minutes passed and, despite thinking I was already gone, Anna kept at the CPR, desperate for signs of life.

Jack called an ambulance and the sirens were heard within seconds, the hospital just a few blocks away. As the medics bolted across the garden,

Anna finally got me to splutter. With water gushing from my lungs, out of my mouth and through my nose, I finally came round. Anna collapsed beside me, exhausted and sobbing. Everyone else just stood around, paralysed by shock.

The medics quickly placed a manual ventilator over my mouth, soothing me as I continued to retch violently. A cut above my eye was pouring blood, with the badly torn skin exposing stark white brow bone. By then, I was looking waxy and grey, every inch of me telling a tale of oxygen starvation. Still at the poolside, the medics worked hard to stabilise me, I was shaking uncontrollably. They unbuckled the stilettos and started cutting off my jeans, looking for other injuries, hacking through the wet denim that stuck to me like beauty-parlour leg wax. Ant stood by with blankets and a dry T-shirt. When they moved me, I screamed hysterically in pain – that part I remembered. I vomited all over the medics before losing consciousness again. At that point, no one knew if the lack of oxygen during the near drowning had caused any brain damage.

I remembered drifting in and out of consciousness in the ambulance, aware that Chris and Anna were with me, but disoriented, not knowing why I was in so much pain. Anna clutched Chris's hand. Her maternal instincts had kicked in as she tried to get us both through the awful accident that had just happened in her home.

In Casualty, a team of doctors were primed and waiting. Once the layers of vomit and blood had been sponged off, they stitched the gash on my head. The pain! I didn't think it humanly possible to feel such extreme agony. Both my head and shoulder were on fire. My ribcage throbbed. My throat felt like I'd swallowed a thousand razor blades and thrown them back up again. My lungs burnt with every breath, as if I had inhaled a thousand angry hornets. And, unable to get the air I needed, I then had a full-scale panic attack on top of everything else. That's when the doctors knocked me clean out with heavy painkillers and sedatives. Relief at last. I drifted off, never wanting to wake again if it meant feeling even a fraction of that white-hot pain.

I drifted while arrangements were made to admit me to ICU. Chris, head bowed, was bargaining with God for my recovery and insisting it had all been his fault. It was such a strange sight that I wanted to giggle but I didn't know how to. My body could barely cope with essential functions, never mind laughter.

Jack had followed the ambulance and brought Rolo and Ant with him to the hospital. Only once the doctors had finished the preliminary tests and were reasonably confident that I was not brain-damaged did Jack call his parents. It was Anna's suggestion that they call his mom first. Rolo later told me it was the first time she'd ever seen Jack, as an adult, crying. Their mom quickly offered to call mine, realising Jack was a gibbering wreck himself.

Sometime after midnight, I went into ICU. Jack, Ant and Rolo went home but Chris and Anna sat outside throughout the night in hard, cold, sanitised plastic chairs. Funny, I thought, how those desperately needing comfort are given added discomfort in which to wait it out.

An hour later, my vital signs nosedived. My lung functions hit the skids and I crashed. It was terrifying. I felt like I was suffocating, wrapped in cling film. Suddenly my limbs went rigid and my jaw locked, my face contorted into an unbecoming 'O'. Someone hit a button and nurses came running from various corridors, rushing into position like a well-trained army, almost stealth-like, looking to their leader for a command. I noticed they were strangely quiet. I did hear one nurse say 'seizure' and 'near drowning' in a low voice. The formation of nurses seemed to know exactly what to do after those three words and one plunged a needle into my butt cheek, another jammed a mask on my face. Sedatives and oxygen had been brought into the battle.

The end result of my botched rugby catch was eight stitches above my eyebrow, an angry graze down my face and ear, extensive cranial bruising, a dislocated shoulder which would be manipulated under anaesthetic the next day, severe concussion and three broken ribs. The ribs were Anna's handiwork. Desperate to revive me and not be haunted by my death for all her days, her pounding on my chest had been a little over-zealous. In short, I was a mess. All from trying to impress Yummy Anthony from squash.

'Mom, Dad, thank God you're here,' said Chris.

It was dawn when I heard Chris's voice in the ICU waiting room, sounding all wobbly. Mom and Dad had left the farm as soon as they'd had the call from Jack's mother and had driven like the clappers to Harare.

Anna, looking beyond shattered, was still at the hospital too.

'Hi Mom, Dad,' I said, groggy.

'Oh my God, KitKat,' said Dad. 'Shit, you gave us such a fright, sweetheart. How're you feel—' And then he dissolved, unable to speak as he gulped back his tears, chin trembling. Meanwhile Mom was openly bawling her eyes out and looked even more buggered than me. She seemed to have several tissues on the go.

'It's sore, so sore,' I said, struggling to talk with all the drugs sloshing around in me.

'Sore where, sweetie? Your arm or head?' asked Mom, sniffing.

'Both. Everything. Everywhere. Sore. It hurts all over. So fucking sore.'

Dad forgot his tears and let out a big laugh at my foul language which, in the norm, would have earned me a mammoth lecture. 'That's my girl! Feisty,' he told a nurse checking my drip.

'Jack has explained everything,' said Mom. 'And Anna, sweetheart, you saved her life. I can't begin to thank you.' And Mom was gone again, launching into a fresh round of sobs.

'She gave us quite a fright, Mrs Hay,' said Anna. 'One minute everyone was laughing and tossing the rugby ball around, next minute Kat, wearing stilettos, was lifeless on the bottom of the pool.'

'Stilettos?' asked Mom, one eyebrow raised.

'Long story, Mom, long story,' I said with a weak smile.

'And Chris, are you okay?' asked Dad. 'You look completely stuffed too.'

'I thought she was a goner. She was just lying there, on the bottom in the dark water.' Chris's voice was shaky, he was clearly exhausted.

I suddenly realised that I was actually very lucky to be alive – not in a coma, not brain-dead from the few minutes without oxygen, not in the morgue. Seeing the worry and relief around me put it all into perspective.

More nurses shuffled in, scribbling on the all-important clipboard at the end of my bed before asking everyone to give them some space.

'Right Chris and Anna, let's get you two home,' said Dad, relieved to be in his usual place of authority and able to take charge now that he'd actually seen me alive with his own eyes. 'Anna, you've been incredible, I am lost for words. Chris, come, we'll go to the flat and try catch a nap.'

'Mom, stay with me for a while,' I asked.

'Of course. I need to see your doctor anyway.' All choked up, Mom turned to Anna. 'Anna, thank you again, my God, thank you.'

'I'm so sorry that this happened while the kids were with us. We feel totally responsible,' said Anna, the only composed one around my bed.

'Oh Anna, it's not your fault at all. You saved her life,' said Mom, hugging her tightly.

'Oi, you lot,' I slurred. 'Enough with the tears, my funeral ain't gonna be for years yet.'

Anna, picked up her handbag and kissed me on the forehead. 'Bye Kat,' she said. 'I'll pop back after work this afternoon. Oh, and sorry I knackered your ribs.'

'Sorry I knackered your shoes, Anna!'

I started to stabilise over the following week in hospital. My shoulder was manipulated back into place once my lungs could withstand the general anaesthetic. Physiotherapy helped the swelling from the dislocation but my shoulder and collarbone were black with bruising. Time would heal my ribs and I'd have a nice scar above my eyebrow for life. An MRI scan revealed significant bruising of my brain, serious enough to keep me in a few extra days. The neurosurgeon casually told me that if the swelling persisted, to save me from being a cabbage for life, he'd drill into my skull to release the pressure. The heavy anti-inflammatories and steroids worked and forty-eight hours later my brain was much improved, thank goodness. I hadn't liked the sound of someone taking a Black+Decker to my pip. I had probably gone at least two minutes without oxygen but Anna's CPR had made the difference between brain damage and the full recovery I would now make.

Chris was definitely a touch traumatised too. He visited every afternoon and, when Mom and Dad were out of earshot, he told me that the casualty doctor had asked Anna if I'd been drinking, to which she'd said no. Chris had obviously kept quiet about the joint but, to me, he insisted it was all his fault, that if it weren't for his weed I'd have been more compos mentis playing rugby and none of it would have happened. Poor Chris didn't realise that Rolo and I had swiped a few drinks. I had to put an end to his guilt.

'Chris, relax, I was actually more pissed than stoned,' I assured him. 'That drag of weed actually did nothing for me. I was the fool for playing touch rugby in stilettos and trying to be cool in front of Ant.' I could see the weight lifting off his shoulders.

If there was an upside to my exploring the bottom of a swimming pool, it was Ant's visits. The minute I was allowed non-family visitors, he appeared with a massive bunch of exquisite white roses. I met his lovely mother and Ant got to meet Dad. Not the usual setting for boyfriend–girlfriend parental introductions, around a hospital bed, but at least it was done and out the way.

Each afternoon, our parents would go downstairs for a coffee to leave Ant and me alone. On his first visit, to my relief, I no longer blurted out stupid things, loving the happy drugs for fixing that for me. Happy, too, that he hadn't run a mile after seeing me at my worst – covered in puke and blood, blue in the face, shirtless and without jeans – I only hoped I'd at least been wearing a decent bra and knickers that night. Despite all that, he was at my bedside every day, so I tentatively assumed the attraction was mutual.

'Okay, so at least you nearly drowned for a gorgeous guy,' said Mom one day after Ant left, 'and not for a weedy, spotty, run-of-the-mill chap.'

Dad humpfed, and then made jokes about using his 'bloody shotgun' on Ant, rattling off the usual paternal warnings which always went along the lines of if-he-lays-a-finger-on-my-little-girl-I'll-have-his-guts-for-garters. With the best-kept shotgun in the district, Dad had long been dreading this phase of my life.

Jack, the poor man, would probably never have us to stay again. He spent days apologising to my parents. Meanwhile, I had smoker's remorse, swearing I'd never touch a joint again, or drink as a means to fine-tune my flirting skills. There'd certainly been nothing appealing about me lying practically naked and out cold in front of the very boy I'd wanted to impress.

Dozens of visitors came. Grandpa, holding the fort with Tim at home, rang several times a day, making me giggle with his farm stories. Ela and Linda made a special trip to town to see me. Rolo managed to wangle a school pass and coerced Dad into collecting her for a visit. GranJilly, Maddie, and even Jobb and Cookie, phoned. Mother Superior visited, bringing a card signed by my classmates. She insisted on praying for me, which made Mom and Dad a little uncomfortable. Ha ha, I thought, welcome to my world, folks!

After ten days in hospital, my neurological team prescribed another two weeks at home, so it was back to the farm with Mom and Dad. Battered, bruised and somewhat embarrassed by the fuss I'd caused.

Around about then my recurring nightmares about water started. The onset of panic attacks, that just arrived with no warning, weren't much fun either. I knew if I was to prevent a full-blown phobia, I needed to get back on the proverbial horse and make swimming part of my overall recovery.

The first few days at home, I slept. Until then, I could count on one hand the number of headaches I'd had in my life. Now, they were relentless. The persistent pain drove me to distraction and all I could do was turn to the prescription painkillers I'd been sent home with, brutes that rendered me useless. The neurosurgeon had said to expect some headaches, but I never dreamt they'd be so bad.

The rains had finally come and Dad was flat out on the farm, but he'd pop home to have lunch with me. If I wasn't out for the count in the evenings, he'd help me with the schoolwork that Mom had rather ambitiously collected for me. Most days I'd just blob on my bed or sit with Tighty under the trees outside, reading or cloud watching, sometimes being the ref in the boxers versus bantams wars.

Grandpa visited every day, one day deciding I needed some catapult lessons which, unfortunately, ended in me killing a bantam stone dead by mistake. We managed to clear the crime scene before Mom saw it and I think Cookie took it home for supper. Grandpa then wrote a letter to the pharmaceutical company that I was currently keeping in business, asking them to add catapults to the list of machinery one should not operate when high as a kite on their product.

Ela also helped the days pass. I'd told her about the drinking and weed, knowing she never judged. For a girl who lived practically in isolation from the world, she was incredibly open-minded. She had tried drinking alcohol herself a few times, as curious as any other teenager. She'd crack terrible jokes about being blind drunk and having double vision. That was Ela – always owning her disability, never a victim.

One day Mom asked me if I had, in fact, been drinking that night. I was surprised she knew there'd been a possibility of it. I wasn't a good liar so I confessed, though I kept quiet about Chris's joint.

'Your doctor suspected you'd been drinking but you kids all denied it. It just worsened your already complicated ordeal,' said Mom.

'Oh,' I said, sheepishly. 'But don't be cross with Jack. He never knew we'd been drinking.'

'I'm not cross with Jack at all. I'd have been coffin shopping last week if he and Anna hadn't jumped around. And I'm not angry with you either. A little upset, but not angry. Surprised too. It's not like you to go wild.'

The word 'coffin' hit me between the eyes.

'You're not even sixteen. Don't grow up so fast, Kat. If you try all the adult stuff now, what's left to look forward to later? And don't think I don't know what Chris gets up to, but he is that much older and seems able to handle it, not that I approve though.'

Was she referring to his drinking or smoking weed, I wondered. Best keep quiet either way.

'I don't even like booze. I just wanted to seem cool in front of Ant. I was totally thrown when I saw him at Jack's house.'

'He obviously really likes you so—'

'You think?' I interrupted.

'Pfft! Definitely! I was watching him with you at the hospital. There's certainly a feeling or two there. And hasn't he phoned you every day?'

'Yes, he has called a lot, hey? I guess he does like me.'

'Of course he likes you. But you don't need to get blotto just to make yourself more appealing. You're beautiful and funny, and you have a heart the size of Africa. Booze doesn't add anything, in fact it takes away from your beauty. A drunk woman is not attractive to men. They like nothing less than crass, unladylike behaviour, take it from me.'

'But didn't you try these things when you were young? Didn't you get all stupid and boy-shy too?'

'Oh, I was the worst! The biggest wallflower, all awkward and geeky. Of course I tried these things, which is why I understand. I also made some awful mistakes. However, this isn't a pious or self-righteous sermon. I talk from first-hand experience. Trust me, Kat, leave all that stuff for when you're older. I include sex too, by the way.'

'Mom! Urgh! Sex? Do you really have to talk about that?' I got horribly embarrassed whenever she mentioned the dreaded birds and bees.

'Of course! It might be the furthest thing from your mind, but now you have Ant. I've heard of girls at it like rabbits from the age of twelve and there's always huge peer pressure.'

'Eeew! I'm not having sex with Ant. Well, probably not.' Despite my embarrassment, I'd begun to wonder how the whole shagging thing worked, but like hell I'd admit that to Mom any time soon.

'I'm not saying you will. Anyway, today is not the day for the sex, teenage pregnancy and STD sermon either. I've got to nip into town to fetch the post now.'

Phew. Awkward talk was over.

'You've got dark rings under your eyes. Is your head sore again?' asked Mom, gently moving a strand of hair that had caught on my stitches.

'Yup, it's killing me. I'm going to lie down. Laters, Mom.'

While we'd been talking about drinking, at the back of my mind were thoughts of Mom's drinking, of Maddie and the AA gatherings. I wanted to ask her more about it all, but couldn't muster the energy today. There'd be another time for that talk too.

On my eighth day home, I thought I was going to die – drop-kicked into the corner by my worst migraine yet. When I started vomiting uncontrollably, Mom called Doc Roberts who dashed over. Within the hour, I'd had a super-sized shot of painkiller mixed with anti-nausea medicine. I felt the unmistakable kick of the drugs as they hit my bloodstream, a tangible jolt, head to toe, that was oh-so soothing.

In that instant, when the narcotics kicked in, I noticed how I'd shift into an altered reality – part dream, part hallucination with its own storyline. And I didn't just notice it – in an odd way that I didn't quite understand, I started to welcome it. It was always cosy, like stepping out of a chilly pool and being wrapped in a huge, warm, fluffy towel. A soft cloak. Soothing and safe. Today I felt like an explorer from a bygone era, setting out on an epic adventure into the unknown, about to face great thrills and untold dangers. A sweet, sexy narcotic kick. The best part was that my painkiller meanders never involved water or panic attacks, as if the drugs cured that fear too. It had only been two weeks since our introduction in hospital, but one could say a decent impression had been made and the friendship was developing.

The drugs worked fast and I realised I would live.

Mom spoke to the neurosurgeon the next day. Concerned there was perhaps some residual swelling in my brain, he phoned through a script for a more specific neurological anti-inflammatory and painkiller. I was also signed off school for another week, and booked in for more neck and spine X-rays and another MRI brain scan in Harare. There was concern that a vertebra had taken a beating, causing the continued spasm in the surrounding tissue.

After a day or two on the new meds, my headaches became more manageable. However, I was pretty much plastered all day and every day.

I was pleased to be home for Jobb's daughter's wedding. The traditional Shona ceremony was always quite an affair. Mom, Dad, Grandpa and I went along as the guests of honour. It was a loud and colourful day, but my head ached in the hot sun and we headed home early. They'd all 'shake shake' and party through the night, getting hammered on *Chibuku*, a lumpy opaque African beer with an alcohol content that could make a horse's eyes water.

As we left, Dad discretely handed Jobb an envelope, a wedding gift of cash. Jobb could feel it was a sizeable wad and was truly appreciative.

'Thank you, Boss, *mazvita*! Eish, God bless you Big Boss and Big Bwana Grandpa Boss, and you Mrs Madam Boss, also you Miss Madam KatKat. God bless you all,' Jobb said, our family rankings all sounding like a rap song, making me giggle. He had never quite got my name right.

Dad was good to his workers and they respected him. Many old-school farmers in Zimbabwe were utterly racist – practically slavers – treating their workers appallingly and giving them the most basic housing. On those farms, disaster often struck. Dad was always saying to Chris and me, 'what goes around comes around' and, 'do unto others as you'd have done to you.' Mom added, 'whatever we put out there, into the Universe, comes back to us tenfold, good or bad.' It was true, and Dad had a happy and loyal workforce. He paid well, ensuring they had decent homes, food, and that no one on our farm was ever cold in winter.

A different storm was brewing though, and it had farmers worried. Our esteemed President had made an announcement regarding nationwide land redistribution or 'Land Grabs', depending on which side of the fence you sat. Commercial farmlands were to be freely taken and handed to the 'War Veterans' and the white farmer wouldn't have a leg to stand on. Mugabe openly admitted he wanted the country rid of the 'British'.

'I'm not bloody British. I am a Zimbabwean, born and bred. And I have personally worked my arse off, cultivating land to feed this very nation.' Dad would rant. He and his farming muckers would get terribly upset when discussing the topic. Every last white farmer in Zimbabwe was quietly shitting himself after the announcement threatening his livelihood, and every conversation tended to include the phrase 'we're screwed' or variations thereof. Nobody really knew when it would all kick off. Many were in complete denial, insisting it was too ludicrous to happen. They were the ones who didn't work on a Plan B and would be the ones who, one day, would lose everything they'd ever worked for.

Nobody knew then that violence, arson, intimidation and even murder would go hand-in-hand with the scheme. Not even Dad, and he knew a thing or two, but he had started his Plan B.

6

At the end of my second week home, I packed again and tried to ready myself mentally for school. First, I'd have the tests in Harare, after which I'd hopefully get the all-clear from the neurosurgeon and head back to the nun house. The school dance was only three weeks off and I really didn't want to leave Pete dateless.

I'd managed a smidgen of schoolwork at home, but the minute my head and neck pain kicked off I'd be back on my bed travelling to galaxies far, far away. I'd had a bad spate of nightmares about water, often waking in the night to find myself thrashing around, tangled in my sheets and drenched in sweat. I made a point of swimming every day, quite happy in the pool, but apparently my subconscious was lagging behind, still ironing out a few issues around drowning in general.

We hit the road early on Monday morning. Mom and I drove in comfortable silence, not needing chatter to fill the space. Waking with a throbbing head again that morning, I'd scoffed some painkillers and was definitely dopey as I watched the world whizz by. We drove through some heavy rain not far from home.

'I really hope that storm makes it to the farm,' said Mom, as we came out the other side of it. 'The dam is dropping fast. Next thing your father will be using the D word.'

D was for drought, a big hairy, scary word for farmers. The scariest thing after Land Grab.

A while later, Mom caught me completely off guard. In fact, I'd have been less surprised if we'd been overtaken by Eskimos on a sled drawn by huskies.

'Kat, I've been thinking long and hard. I think it's time I told you the whole story. My story,' Mom said, pausing, watching my expression.

'Your story?'

'My old drinking habits, AA, meetings, Maddie – that story.'

'Oh. Okay,' I said, gobsmacked. 'Chris told me parts. He seems to know your, err, story.'

'Yes, most of it. I didn't think you were old enough to grasp it all, until now. I don't want you thinking it's all a big shameful secret shrouded in mystery, because it's not.'

'How did it start?' I asked, suddenly a bit more alert and keen to, at last, get the facts.

'It started when I was a teenager in Malawi. I was about seventeen when I discovered booze, much like you and Rolo. It was at the Country Club. Grandpa was playing cricket and us kids were left to our own devices. One of the boys got his hands on a half-jack of gin and we passed it around down on the empty golf course. The booze made me all warm and fuzzy. Brave and confident—'

'Yes! I know that feeling,' I interrupted.

'Well, soon enough it became quite the norm for me to swipe booze here and there. I had no close friends in Malawi and got quite lonely and bored.'

Mom had said before that being an only child made for a lonely childhood, especially on a tea estate in Malawi.

'Did Grandpa ever catch you?'

'No, but my mother did, once. She went berserk but didn't tell Grandpa. I got the whole sermon about it not being ladylike, etcetera. She caught me smoking too.'

'Ouch!'

'At eighteen, I'd been drunk more times than I could count. If there was alcohol anywhere, I couldn't resist it. It made me feel so much better about life, like I was a different person. I'd even be shit-faced at my showjumping events, which was both stupid and dangerous. The horsey parties afterwards would also get out of hand. I could have gone so much further with my showjumping if I'd been less focused on being a drunkard and a rebel.'

'So what happened when you met Dad?'

'By then I was of legal age and drinking was a common part of life. I'd started my secretarial and accounting job in Salisbury. We worked hard and played hard. We led a fairly normal social life, lots of braais, evenings in nightclubs like Sandros, pubs like Red Fox, and regular Kariba houseboat trips. It was good fun. You've seen the photos.'

'Mmmm.' Indeed, I had seen the photos of Mom always attached to a wine glass.

'After we got married, my drinking got excessive and Dad started to get on my case about it. I would totally embarrass him when I gave it stick. He used to beg me not to drink, but I couldn't help myself. Though I knew how much it upset him, it was as if something was sitting on my shoulder, a little devil, always egging me on, telling me the world was a better place when pissed.'

'Chris said you were a binge drinker.'

'Yes. I wouldn't drink every day but, when I did, I didn't stop until I fell over.'

'And then you stopped drinking when you got pregnant?'

'Yes. And round about then Grandpa Arthur died and GranJilly was drinking heavily too. Dad was under a huge amount of pressure and I just added to it. But I was so happy to be starting our family that I swore I'd never touch a drop again.'

'So, what happened?'

'After Chris was born, I went a full eighteen months sober, not a drop. I'd been coping fine, but then, I don't know why, I just felt like having a toot one day. It was at a party at Tim and Linda's house, everyone drinking, having a ball, smoking joints too. I felt left out so I had a vodka.'

'Did you get hammered?'

'That's such an awful word – hammered,' Mom laughed. 'But no, I didn't. However, I had a few drinks, greatly enjoying that old feeling of being part of the fun and like another person. My passion for booze was instantly reawakened and, soon enough, I was binge drinking again. Your father went apeshit. He pleaded with me, but the devil on my shoulder was more convincing than ever before.'

'So then?'

'Then I got preggers with you and remained sober for about two years.'

'What made you go back to the bottle?'

'Dunno really. Life. Boredom. Haunted by old emotional issues. It was always there, an urge to get numb. Poor Dad, I became the most horrendous person to live with and was such a bitch to him.'

'Chris said Dad was going to divorce you.'

Mom took a deep breath and exhaled heavily. 'Dad did threaten divorce and he was going to fight for custody of you two, my precious babies, unless I came right. I don't blame him. Grandpa was at his wits' end too. There was no reasoning with me.'

'Chris said you went from bingeing to getting drunk all day and every day.'

'Yes. As soon as I started to sober up, I would top up again. It was a vicious bloody cycle and I drove everyone away – refusing to admit I had a drinking problem, insisting I could stop anytime I wanted to. I couldn't. That's the sticky part they call denial.'

'I don't understand how you can know something is bad, know how it upsets people, feel so guilty, and yet keep at it.'

'Well, darling, that's the disease of alcoholism and addiction. It was not in my nature to practise moderation. Don't get me wrong, I hated myself for what I was doing to Dad and you two.'

'Chris said you'd often stay in bed for days.'

'That was the alcohol poisoning, and dehydration from the vomiting. God, it turns my stomach to remember those hangovers. I also became very depressed. I didn't want anyone near me, preferring to be left alone in my own haze and misery. I stopped taking an interest in the farm. I ignored my share of the work, like doing the accounts. I stopped seeing my friends too and was always arguing with someone, or finding fault to deflect my own faults. No one really wanted to spend time with me. I was very bitter and twisted, a right miserable cow! Then I knocked that guy off his bike, just like Maddie did, and Dad took my car keys away and cleared the house of all alcohol, leaving me housebound and the house dry. Dad also told Cookie and the maids that they'd be fired if I they brought me alcohol.'

'Did they?'

'To their credit, no, despite some hefty bribes I offered. However, we had a new gardener who was not above making an easy buck and was very happy to bring me gin and vodka on the sly. We had a cunning arrangement. I'd leave cash under a certain shrub in the garden and he would replace it with a bottle. Suddenly I was a terribly keen gardener, but was only concerned about one shrub.'

'That's actually quite funny.'

'Needless to say, Dad found out – actually it was Cookie who grassed me up – and that gardener promptly got his arse kicked and then fired by Dad. I remember hearing Cookie and the gardener having awful fights about him being my gin mule. One day they got into a tussle over it and the buggers completely destroyed my one special shrub. Anyway, when I got booze, I stashed it in weird places. I once hid a bottle in the chimney, wedged on a little ledge inside the rough brickwork. It didn't occur to me that it was winter and, when Dad lit the fire, there was an awful sound of glass breaking and a rush of flames as the alcohol caught fire.'

I snorted, both amused and shocked.

'I think that was the final straw for Dad. He went absolutely nuts. He took you and Chris to stay with Grandpa. Then he went to see his cousins in Cape Town a few days later, saying he'd start a custody battle on his return.'

'So, you did come close to divorce?'

'Very close. I begged and pleaded and made great promises to change, but he was very, very angry. He told me to get my act together, once and for all, while he was away, outlining just how much I stood to lose.'

'So, he just left you? Went to the Cape?'

'He was right in what he did. I really put him through hell. He was working so hard to provide for us, meanwhile I'd long stopped being a wife and mother. I'd become a third child, who needed more care than you and Chris. Dad had also had to deal with Arthur's sudden death and GranJilly's drinking.'

'Chris said that Dad met with drinking experts in Cape Town.'

'Drinking experts? That's funny! They were more help-people-*stop*-drinking experts. Anyway, Dad sat me down to talk the night he got back. Needless to say, I'd been drunk the entire time he'd been away, even though

I knew where it would all lead. Dad's words fell on deaf and drunk ears and I flew off the handle. That was the night I hit him.'

'You hit Dad? Jeeez Ma!'

'I know. I lashed out. Ironically, when I clobbered him, my wedding ring caught his brow and cut him. When I saw the blood, I knew I'd gone too far.'

Mom paused again, her face sad and heavy as she hauled out the difficult memories.

'So then?' I asked.

'Dad went to stay at the cottage with you two and Grandpa. I was left to stew on my own. Two days later I was called into a meeting at the house.'

'That's when the drinking expert rehab lady came to get you.'

'Yup, I didn't know anything about it in advance. I called it my ambush! Anyway, next thing I knew, I was sitting in the lounge facing the firing squad.'

'Who was in the firing squad?'

'Dad, GranJilly, Grandpa, Tim, Linda, Doc Roberts and Mrs Clapham.'

'Cat's Bum Clap? Why was the old prune there? You aren't that friendly, are you?'

'No, it wasn't about being friends. Mrs Clapham's husband died a roaring drunk. She'd been through much the same as Dad and gave him a lot of support, surprisingly enough.'

'What did they all say?'

'They'd each prepared a few lines to say to me. It was awful, very emotional and everyone in tears. Linda broke down completely and was actually ill for a few days afterwards, it was that difficult for her. Basically, they begged me to stop drinking. If I didn't want to stop and do it for myself, as opposed to just paying lip service with more empty promises, Dad would walk away from our marriage that very day, and keep you and Chris on the grounds that I was an unfit mother. I'd be asked to leave the farm immediately. Grandpa said there'd be no running to him either, that he wouldn't save my arse. He also asked me to think about how my mother would feel if she could see me, if she'd be proud of how I was traumatising my children.'

'Did the talk help?'

'I hit my rock bottom that day, Kat. It was the talk of losing you kids and what Grandpa said about my mother. I realised I was done with drinking. Seeing the pain I was inflicting, knowing I was about to lose everything and everyone I loved just for booze – which made me sick as a dog anyway – it was madness and I finally saw it. I was ready to accept the help being offered.'

'What's rock bottom?'

'It's when you can't sink any lower and life simply can't get any worse. Addicts and alcoholics get to a point when they have hurt themselves enough to want to stop. It's the deepest, darkest pit of despair imaginable, when you're finally buggered enough to end the self-destruction.'

'That was the day I sat on your bed watching you pack a suitcase?'

'Yup. The conditions laid out in that intervention were that I fly to Cape Town the next day and do a month in rehab.'

'But you were gone longer than a month.'

'Most people only need a month in treatment but the more difficult nuts to crack need a longer stint. At thirty days, the counsellors and psychiatrists thought I was undercooked and, if I left then, there was a high likelihood of relapse.'

'So, you were a tough nut?'

'One of the toughest! After thirty days, I was moved into what's called secondary care, slightly less hectic than primary care, and I stayed another fifty days.'

'What happens in rehab? Were you with grungy drug addicts, criminals and drunken hobos and stuff?'

'No, though rehab is not particularly glamorous. You first go through detox, when all the booze or drugs leave your system. It's all hard and detox is bloody awful. Physical pain I didn't think possible. My entire body ached, but there's no lying in bed feeling sorry for yourself in rehab. We had to be up and dressed by eight and listen to many talks about alcohol and drugs and their physiological effects.'

'What happened in the secondary rehab?'

'It was more like living in digs – about fifteen inmates in a big house, where we had to cook, clean and start edging ourselves back into normal life. It was still strict and we always had a counsellor around, but we were allowed out more and attended lots of external AA meetings.'

'Do you miss the hooch at all?'

'I did at first, but it destroyed my life. In rehab I found myself, and started to face a lot of old emotional issues. I clawed my way out, no longer needing to forget.'

'And what's the connection with Maddie? Is she an alcoholic? And what is AA?'

'Alcoholics Anonymous is a fellowship of similar people who help each other overcome their drinking problems. We just share our hard-won lessons and offer support to those still struggling. There's also a set of Steps that we try to live by. As for Maddie, she abuses tranquillisers on top of her drinking, and is an addict. She's basically at her rock bottom now and we're trying to get her into a rehab too, but they don't have the money for it. It's jolly expensive and there are no specialised rehabs here in Zim.'

'I have another question.'

'Fire away.'

'Why did you drink? Why did you want to be someone else all the time? What did you want to forget? Who hurt you?'

Mom took a very deep breath. 'When I was seventeen, I was raped. I wanted to forget the rape.'

My mouth fell open, dumbstruck. The air in the car suddenly became heavy, almost cloying. Those three words – *I was raped* – had sucked the oxygen out.

'Let's finish this another day, I can see your brain is on overload now. You've got black rings under your eyes again,' said Mom.

'Well yes, you could say I have brain overload! Does Chris know about the rape?'

'No. I didn't get to that part with him, not yet.'

'Grandpa?'

'Yes.'

'Dad?'

'Of course, we don't have secrets.'

'Holy crap, Mom.' It was all I could say.

I stared out the car window, silently processing everything. I was pleased to know the truth at last, though it was a lot to take in and my headache was back, pounding away merrily. The wispy blond grasslands were mesmerising, like driving past a sheet of shimmering gold paper. Plump local women, their babies strapped to their backs with cheerful bath towels, were selling huge baskets of equally plump mangoes in laybys on the road. I saw men on bicycles, pedalling along sedately. Overcrowded buses crawled along, belching out black smoke, crates of live chickens strapped to the roofs and even goats hanging out the bus windows amidst the sea of shiny faces.

Normal life continued around me, yet a layer, a membrane, had just been placed over it and my view of it had all suddenly changed. Like I had put on too-strong reading glasses. I wanted to take the glasses off and rewind, but couldn't. I could never unhear The Story.

Mom squeezed my hand, leaving it there for now.

Two hours and more painkillers later, we were done with my X-rays and MRI scan. We headed to the flat and I had a much-needed nap.

'Your eyes look a bit clearer,' said Mom when I woke. 'Fancy an early supper at Coimbra?'

The scruffy little Portuguese restaurant was a Harare ritual for many. Basic furniture, dusty plastic ferns and other deadbeat décor, but they made the best peri-peri chicken – garlicky and swimming in oil – one's arteries got nervous just hearing the word Coimbra.

'Sounds good,' I said, realising I was starving.

'Shall we see if Ant can join us? And his parents. Maybe Jack and Anna too?'

Ant! The mere mention launched a butterfly attack. We'd been speaking every day since my accident. If there was one benefit to going back to school, it was being in the same town as him again.

Ant gave me a long, tight hug when we arrived. Anna just winked at me from behind him, setting off a major blush. All evening, I failed to contribute anything interesting or remotely intellectual to the conversation, distracted by Ant's thigh pressed against mine, loving every minute. For the first time in weeks, I wasn't thinking about pain and when it'd strike next. Seeing Jack and Anna again made me realise we all had a weird bond, forever linked by the rugby catch gone wrong. Needless to say, I got some more light abuse from Jack about my stupid move that night, but my ribs, still tender, suddenly reminded me that any laughing was to be approached with caution.

Stuffed and full of garlic as we walked to the cars much later, Ant and I lagged behind. He pulled me close, his embrace warm and safe.

'You're looking so much better,' he said. 'I just hope your doctors can get a handle on the headaches now.'

'I'm sure they'll go away in time,' I said, trying to sound breezy and like it wasn't all dragging me down. 'It's been a pretty crazy few weeks. A bit hazy in parts!'

'I broke my arm a few years back. I know what those painkillers do to you. Kinda fun at first but I was very happy to come off them.'

I was about to say I was in the 'kinda fun' stage of my relationship with painkillers, but Ant might have run a mile and I held my tongue.

'Jeez, when I saw you go flying into that pool then disappearing into the dark water, I shat myself ...' I could have sworn I detected a lump in Ant's throat but he quickly shook off the wobble. 'Can I call you after you've seen the neuro guy and had your results tomorrow?'

'Of course! Can't say I feel like going back to school on Wednesday. This term has been one big disjointed mess.'

'All I want is to see my Kat back at squash, healed and happy.'

'I'll probably suck, Ant. I'll be right back to square one, old Captain Codeine here!'

My MRI results showed that the brain swelling had nearly gone, but my X-ray revealed a neck far straighter than it should be, the muscle all in a spasm and knocking out the natural curve. And they confirmed a faint fracture in one vertebra. There was little to be done for it though. Things would knit back in time, much like my broken ribs.

The neurosurgeon asked some detailed questions about my headaches and migraines before thoroughly examining my neck and back. I'd whacked my neck so out of alignment it wasn't funny and the dislocated shoulder had impacted my spine too.

'So, where to now?' Mom asked the doctor. 'How do we get her neck back into alignment and will her headaches then stop?'

'Kat, I'm pretty sure your headaches stem from the head and neck trauma, especially if you were never prone before,' he said. 'Intensive physiotherapy will help. There's a great physio opposite your school so you can walk over. Continue with the anti-inflammatories for another two weeks and I'll also repeat your painkiller script.'

'Can I get back on the squash court, Doc?' I asked.

'Not yet young lady. Squash will trigger a flare up. Besides, you'll be in a neck brace.'

'God no!' I blurted out, horrified. 'Those look so ugly.'

'I agree, they're hardly a fashion statement but will help. You want to be free of headaches, don't you?'

'They just look so uncomfortable,' I said, despairing at the thought.

'Right then,' said the doctor. 'You can go back to school, and I'd like you to keep a headache diary to help identify the triggers. See me again at the end of term before you go home.'

All the way to the medical supplier, I bitched and moaned about the brace. Eventually Mom got fed up and told me to wind my neck in. I started giggling at her unintended pun, only for my ribs to stop me. Fortunately, new stock had come in and I could get a brace in pink.

We had a quiet night at the flat. While Mom organised all my medication, ready to give to my dorm matron, I had a long yak to Ant on the phone, me moaning about my pink foam-rubber necklace.

Later, Mom and I, sharing the main bedroom, lay chatting about Ant.

'He's a great kid, I approve,' said Mom. 'Enjoy this part. Oh, what I'd give to feel that first rush of love and crushes again.'

'It's nerve-wracking Mom.'

'Oh yes, but totally worth it.'

I managed a smile. It'd been a long two days of doctors and tests and everything was sore, the pain wearing me down more than usual. As loaded on painkillers and exhausted as I was, I wanted to know more about Mom's story.

'Who did it, Mom?' I asked.

'Did what?'

'Raped you?'

'Oh,' Mom said. She was silent next to me, then we both sat up in bed.

'How did it happen?' I asked.

'It was our manager in Malawi. Grandpa's right-hand man,' she said, pausing before she said his name slowly. 'Patrick Houghton-Brown.'

The name hung heavy in the air.

She said it again, slower, 'Patrick … Houghton … Brown … the fucking bastard.' She took a deep breath before continuing …

'Patrick had a wife, Molly, and two small kids. Molly was lovely but there was something odd about Patrick. My mother didn't like him, said he was shifty and had sly eyes, but Grandpa never saw it. He thought Patrick was just a normal family man, and an excellent and capable manager. They'd have the odd social together – the usual farm stuff. Molly was a bit of a mouse, painfully shy and skittish. One day Mom popped in to see her and found her sporting a black eye.'

'Did Patrick beat her?'

'She insisted she'd only tripped on a step, although it was pretty obvious that Patrick slapped her around. He was a piss artist too. Anyway, that day I was out riding on the estate, on my own. Mom had gone into town and Grandpa was mediating a labour dispute. I'd had a tummy bug for days and was desperate for the loo, about to be caught short. Their house was closest so I rode there. Only Patrick was home. Molly was out for the day and there were no staff around.'

My stomach was already starting to churn.

'After I used the loo, Patrick offered me some juice which I accepted, not wanting to seem rude. He'd been drinking, totally pissed at midday so I was very uncomfortable. I took one look at him, saw his eyes and knew something horrendous was about to happen. Next thing, he cornered me, forced my jeans down and tore my shirt open. He was a huge man. The more I struggled, the more excited he got, heaving over me, panting, his booze breath sour and sweat dripping from his forehead onto me. I was pinned down and couldn't get away, but I did manage to bite him on his forearm. I sank my teeth in as deeply as possible. He didn't seem to notice I'd drawn blood, he was in such a frenzy. With his huge hands clasped tightly round my neck, barely allowing me air, he raped me on his kitchen floor – no one around to hear my screams throughout the brutal attack.'

Saliva flooded my mouth as I fought a wave of nausea.

Mom went on. 'He really bruised and tore me, so badly I had to walk my horse home. I blanked out a lot of the detail, but remember walking for what seemed like hours though it was only ten or fifteen minutes. Grandpa happened to drive by with his workshop manager and stopped when he saw me walking my horse. Then he saw my torn shirt, my jeans still gaping open and the zip broken, and me looking like a zombie, unable to talk by then. He flew out of the truck, knowing something was very, very wrong. He asked his workshop chap to ride my horse back to the stables and then he helped me into the truck. I started sobbing, my whole body shaking violently. Grandpa kept asking me over and over, "Who did this? Who Gill, who?" And he swore he'd kill the bastard.'

'So, he knew you'd just been raped?'

'Oh yes, he knew immediately. He drove hell for leather to our house and, thankfully, my mother was back from town. Grandpa explained how he'd found me. Mom just held me while I cried and retched. When I'd calmed down a bit, to confirm their suspicions she asked, very tenderly, if I'd been raped. I nodded, saying only one word – Patrick. Grandpa turned on his heel and left the room, shielding me from the rage that had overcome him. Mom helped me into a bath. I was bleeding a lot, and my wrists and throat were badly bruised. I then started to describe it all, including how I had bitten him. Grandpa called our local police station. In those days, the police actually did see that laws were kept in the district. An hour later, I was being interviewed at home. The police asked if anyone had witnessed the attack or seen me at his house. Again, I described biting his arm.'

'Did they arrest him right away?' I was clutching a pillow against my chest.

'No. Apparently, that afternoon the police went to his house. No one was home. They then found him in the estate offices, doing paperwork, and he insisted he'd been there all day. He categorically denied the accusation even though no one could verify his story. Then the sergeant saw the angry bite on his arm and asked how he'd been hurt. Patrick just brushed it off and said his new puppy had nipped him.'

'The bastard,' I whispered.

'Patrick knew there were no witnesses and he thought he was home free. Little did he know that, before the policemen entered his office, they had lingered unseen in the corridor, overhearing him on the telephone. He must have been talking to one of his revolting beer-guzzling mates and the sergeant heard him say, "Yeah, told you I'd have her, pop her cherry. The little whore was begging for it, came looking for me on the pretence of needing the loo. She was nice and feisty too, put up a very enjoyable little struggle".'

'So why didn't they take him into custody?'

'Well, there were no witnesses and, despite the bite and overhearing his phone call, the sergeant chose not to lock him up. They had a far better plan,' said Mom. 'Grandpa fired Patrick that night and gave him twenty-four hours to get himself and his family off the estate. However, early the following morning, Molly went to Grandpa in a state – Patrick was missing, he hadn't come home the night before. Molly knew nothing of the police being there or the rape charges as she'd got home late the previous night. Patrick hadn't been around and she'd assumed he was working late or out drinking. Come morning, she got worried so Grandpa filled her in. Apparently, the look on Molly's face simply confirmed that her husband was a violent monster and entirely capable of rape. Grandpa then sent out a search party and they soon found Patrick, floating face down, stone dead, in the dam.'

'Drowned? Or murdered?'

'That same police sergeant, who'd interviewed me the day before, came out to investigate and proclaimed Patrick's cause of death to be "accidental drowning due to drug and alcohol intoxication". There was no further investigation into his death. I just heard he was dead. Years later, Grandpa told me that it had definitely not been accidental, rather our workers had taken justice into their own hands.'

'Huh?'

'The story goes that the workshop manager, who'd been with Grandpa when he found me walking home, had later gone back to the workers' compound and told all the men there what had happened to me, their boss's daughter. With just one look at me, he too recognised that a rape had just happened. The workers didn't like Patrick. He was a racist shit to them, but was sneaky and only ever laid into them behind Grandpa's back.

Apparently that police sergeant left Patrick's office – having overheard the bragging phone call and seen the bite on his arm – and gave a symbolic nod to the large group of workers who'd gathered outside waiting for news of the investigation. The nod was a subtle signal, a code if you like, that the matter was out of police hands and was now in theirs, the workers' hands. Basically he gave Grandpa's workers carte blanche to do as they wished. They were beyond angry, disgusted at what Patrick had done to me. He never stood a chance and, that night, the workers went after him. They tied him to the back of his own truck with ropes and chains. They dragged him, face down, for a few kilometres along the gravel road, to our dam. He'd still been alive when they bound his hands and feet with rope, attached a few bricks, crammed plastic bags into his mouth and threw him in.'

'Did the workers ever admit to doing it?' I asked, fighting the bile sitting in the back of my throat.

'No, but everyone knew how Patrick met his maker. The case was closed. And everyone knew he had raped me, my statement was never doubted. The sergeant's nod to the workers had been the go-ahead for an act of informal farm justice, for things to be set right in whatever way the workers saw fit. It's something called Bush Court, and our Bush Court saw fit to kill him. The police coroner simply ignored the severe grazing all over Patrick's body, as well as the ropes and the plastic bags jammed in his mouth. The way in which it was handled had a lot to do with Grandpa's status in the district. By default, I held the same status. Such was the power and loyalty of our workforce and their utter disgust at Patrick. The police took his body away in a flimsy pine coffin. That night, the workers gathered at the dam to perform a cleansing ritual where the local witch doctor purged the water of Patrick's evil spirit. And that was the end of that. And that, Kat, is why I drank and what I wanted to forget.'

We were both silent for a few minutes as I absorbed the horror.

'This Bush Court thing is fascinating. I've never heard of it,' I said, starting to pick over the details.

'It's very powerful. Effective too, but ask any African about Bush Court and they will categorically deny its existence. It's a "don't ask, don't tell" thing, obviously totally illegal, but an age-old justice system that's still used today. I've never seen it on our farm, but am willing to bet we have one too. Touch wood, we've just never had a real crime or violent incident that required it to kick in.'

'And Patrick's family?'

'My mother bumped into Molly a few years later. Said she was a new woman, remarried to a lovely man and glowing with happiness. Patrick's death had been a blessing for her.'

'So what did you do after it happened?'

'I had to move forward, but my life changed forever that day. If I hadn't needed the loo, my life would have been very different …' Mom suddenly paused, as if she needed to say more, but she swallowed her thought, whatever it was.

'We must sleep now Kat. You've got school in the morning.'

'Mom, I don't even know what to say,' I said, so very sad for her.

'There's nothing to say, it's all in the distant past. It's just part of my story and there's nothing you have to say, think, or do, sweetheart. I just wanted you to know the root of my alcoholism, why I wanted to get numb.'

'Well, now I understand why I always have to ride with Jobb,' I said.

Mom smiled and nodded. I turned off the light and fell asleep holding her hand.

7

Early the next day, Mom had a long handover with my dorm matron Sister Norah, explaining my medications, which were promptly locked up in her medicine cupboard. On hearing I was to go to physio, ever the suspicious nun, she said she'd escort me there and back, like I was going to score crack or get pregnant between the school gate and the physio, whose door I could see from my dorm window.

Physio was outrageously sore and I was given specific exercises as homework. My headaches improved slightly, though several times a week I had to ask Sister Norah to unlock her magic cupboard and let loose some of my painkillers. Relentless pain gnawed at me. I'd try to get by without the pills, but some days it was unbearable and I couldn't, despite the fuzz they caused, and despite being so loaded that one day I spent an entire lesson working from a geography text book in a French class, wondering why I was lost. The brace felt horribly tight in the mid-summer heat too. Sod's Law it hadn't happened in winter.

Finally, the weekend of the St Edwards dance arrived and my room-mates all shared in the fun of getting ready. With my thick hair held up by pretty diamante clips, wearing subtle make-up, new high heels and the rich velvet dress, I was finally all set. I even managed to paint my toenails without being seen. Nail varnish, especially whorish siren-red tones, was banned at the Convent.

Sister Norah looked in on me. 'Kat, I don't suppose I can convince you to wear your neck brace tonight. Correct?'

'Err, correct indeed, Sister. Pink and burgundy would constitute an outright fashion crime,' I said, smiling. Not in a month of Sundays would I wear it to a dance and Sister knew it wasn't a battle worth getting into.

'You look very nice, Kat. That's a rather lovely dress.' She glanced at my feet and, bless her, ignored my red toenails.

While waiting for the St Edwards bus that was collecting the girls who were going to the dance, Sister Norah reminded me of my 11.30 p.m. curfew. It was as if Dad had donned a habit and was standing there with his shotgun.

The marquee on the St Edwards rugby field was magnificent. Decorated like a Bedouin tent, it had drapes of jewel-coloured silk everywhere. Swathes of fabric created a low ceiling and dim lighting finished off the rich and exotic Arabian Nights theme.

Pete made me laugh with his awkward compliment when I arrived. 'Wow, Kat! You look amazing. Your brother is going to be busy tonight – all the boys are already perving over you and you've not been here two minutes.'

Rolo looked like a model in her new slinky black dress and I finally got to meet the famous Jason, who really was ridiculously good-looking – Rolo had not been exaggerating. Dark, almost black, hair, incredible dark-blue eyes, and a long scar on his jaw line from flying through a glass door as a kid that made him even more interesting. I was delighted for Rolo, who was smiling with her eyes, not just her mouth.

And then we met Samantha, Chris's date. The Samantha. She was very pretty, just as Chris had said. She had long, deep-red curly hair, freckles, a cute smile and a great figure, all toned and athletic. However, she had nothing in the boob department, her chest as flat as a breadboard. She towered over Chris in insanely high stilettos – more like showgirl shoes, borderline fancy dress. But there was something odd about her and, even before we were introduced, my first impression wasn't great. She had some hefty airs and graces, was totally up her own bum and it showed. As we watched Sam and Chris approach, Rolo and I were on the same page straight away.

'Sam, this is my sister Kat. Rolo, you know Sam, don't you?' said Chris.

'Kind of, I've seen you at school,' said Rolo. 'Love your dress, Sam.'

Sam was in a peacock-blue taffeta dress that was too fluffy, too frilly, and too shiny. I knew damn well that Rolo was being sarcastic.

'Nice to meet you, Sam,' I said, and smiled warmly at her. 'Been hearing all about you from the boys.'

'All good, I hope. If not, then don't believe a word,' she said, rather predictably.

And then she laughed. Oh my God, that laugh! It was more of a donkey's bray. It really was the oddest sound that came barrelling out of her mouth. How could Chris put up with that? I caught Rolo's eye, both of us thinking the same thing, and I had to look away before we got the giggles.

Chris, realising that Rolo and I were amused at something, glanced nervously at me with a look, to say 'Please go easy on her'. I composed myself, but Sam had caught wind of my inner snigger and, within a minute of our meeting, it was as if war had been declared. Sensing the tension, Chris quickly suggested he and Sam get drinks. Rolo and I were only too pleased for our group to disperse and went to find our table.

I was in deep conversation with Pete when I heard Sam give a hee-haw and realised she'd joined us.

There was an awkward silence at the table and it struck me how intimidating it must be for her. We probably seemed to be a very closed circle. That said, Jason wasn't bothered, was doing a splendid job of fitting in, but Sam was struggling. I decided, for Chris's sake if not hers, to be more welcoming. My good intentions were short-lived. Uncomfortable at how all chatter had stopped when she'd sat down, Sam threw senseless chit-chat in my direction.

'So then, isn't this such fun?' she said, smiling too brightly. 'Now, Kat, I heard *all* about your little rugby accident. Chris told me everything, didn't you, Poppet?' She leant into Chris and pinched his cheek sharply, leaving a red mark.

I couldn't quite believe what I was hearing but figured the fun was just kicking off. Poppet? God give me strength!

'The thing is Kat,' Sam continued, 'it takes, like, forever, to get used to wearing proper high heels. It comes with practice. You'll get there. I remember when, many, many years ago, Mommy bought me my first pair. Murder at first, though I can't say I tried out for rugby in them. Ballet was more my thing, far more elegant and ladylike. Anyway Kat, I digress. One day you'll ask yourself how you ever lived without heels.'

Sam sat back in her chair, looking pleased with herself. Then she tweaked the end of Chris's nose and gave another hee-haw.

I didn't dare look at Rolo. My face must have been a picture as I began to boil. Bloody patronising little bitch! Stuck-up cow! Shit, screw being nice, you can sod off, I thought. And who under the age of sixty uses the word 'digress'? How the hell did Chris find all that even remotely attractive or endearing, on top of her donkey laugh? I picked up my drink and took a slow sip, considering my reply. Sam was smirking, watching me intently. You could have cut the air with a knife while everyone waited for my response.

I smiled sweetly. 'You know, Sam, you're absolutely right and I'm *so* glad to hear I will get used to wearing heels in time. Gosh, that's such a relief,' I said, still with a saccharine smile. 'You'll find the same when you eventually start wearing a bra. It's murder at first but soon feels quite natural—' I casually dropped my eyes to her chest before continuing, 'but judging from things in that department, you've still got a couple of years before you and Mommy go bra shopping.'

Pete spluttered, spraying a mouthful of drink and splattering Sam's stupid peacock dress and then he kicked me under the table. Rolo had her hand over her mouth, her shoulders shaking from stifled laughter. Jason didn't even bother hiding it and was laughing openly at Sam's expense. Chris was mortified.

The precious Sam stood up and announced in a terse, pissy tone that she needed to 'powder her nose'. She motioned for Chris to stand up too. 'Will you come with me please, Poppet, and wait by the door?' It was an order, not a request.

Like a docile puppy, Chris followed as Sam flounced off. He glared back at us and mouthed, 'Thanks a fucking lot!'

We collapsed in hysterics. Tears were soon streaming down Rolo's face, she didn't care that she was buggering up her mascara. She put her forehead on the table, making the tableware rattle as she giggled. Jason pretended to powder his nose on a napkin, making loud, rasping donkey sounds. Pete called me Poppet and pulled my nose, and then Rolo made a great show of fiddling with her bra straps and thrusting out her fair-sized boobs and cleavage, which Jason greatly enjoyed.

'What a little bitch,' I said, laughing myself. 'I was honestly going to be nice to her and then the little tart starts with that condescending bullshit.'

'I love it!' said Pete. 'Your reply was classic.'

'Don't you agree that was a bit offside of her? The cheek of it! What have I ever done to her?' I said.

'Oh, she was totally offside,' said Jason. 'Totally, dude.'

'Pete, what on *earth* does he see in her?' asked Rolo, sniffing loudly as her tears of laughter subsided.

'Agh, general opinion is that Sam is easy. Some of the guys have come very close to, you know, getting a leg over,' said Pete.

'Slapper,' said Rolo. 'And that dress is SO hideous.'

'Ignore her, Kat, she's nothing special,' said Jason. 'Chris will just get mad if you snipe at her all evening. He obviously digs her, though why is anyone's guess.'

'I'm actually surprised at Chris, I must say,' I said. 'I thought he'd choose someone deeper than the average bath, not just a fluffy nothing.'

'Thing is she actually seems pretty serious about Chris,' said Pete. 'Even the guys in our class who've taken her behind the proverbial bike shed say it's unusual for her to date, or even like, a guy for more than a fortnight. But she's been at every sporting fixture this term, always to see Chris.'

'Oh shit. I wish he'd just stick with Ela. She's much better girlfriend material,' I replied.

'Ah, but Chris doesn't think Ela likes him in that way,' said Pete.

'Rubbish! Of course she does, she adores him,' Rolo said.

Sam and Chris eventually returned to the table, but I chose to ignore Sam. Her ego bruised, she then threw barbed comments into the conversation in an attempt to make me rise to the bait. However, I'd had the last word and let her silly behaviour wash over me. She looked particularly pissed off when Jason got up to go to the loo, telling Rolo his nose needed powdering.

'Don't be long, my Poppet. Shall I wait at the door?' replied Rolo. Chris and Sam threw looks to kill.

Giggling, I turned to Pete. I was far more interested in catching up with him than indulging some jumped-up little princess. 'How's your mom doing Pete? My mom said she's going through some heavy stuff at the moment.'

'Yup. I swear she has turned into a nutter recently. Did your mom tell you about her drinking problem?' he asked.

'Actually she did, and that your mom mixes booze with pills, or something.'

'Shit, I don't know what she does anymore. My dad is at his wit's end and, much as I hate boarding school, I'm dreading school holidays and Christmas. KitKat, she's a frigging nightmare once she gets going. At least Karen is coming out for Christmas.' Karen was Pete's much older sister who'd lived in America for yonks.

'Well, if it's any consolation, my mom told me that she used to be the same, also a nutjob,' I said.

'I know, Chris told me. I just get angry. Why can't she sort her shit out? I mean, your mom came right.' Pete's voice was heavy and sad.

'But Pete, my mom only came right after going to some fancy clinic down south, not on her own.'

'Yeah, I know. It's just that Mom acts like a spoilt, overindulged toddler. It's tiresome. Dad and I find every excuse to get out of the house, just for some normality and sanity. Rehab is definitely what she needs, but Dad's finances aren't great so she'll have to kick the pills and booze on her own. But hey, at least your mom is around for her, which is more help than you know. Your mom is my hero. I can't imagine her ever being as much of a nutter as mine currently is.'

I had a heavy heart talking to Pete, but was pleased he'd opened up a bit. He obviously trusted Chris and me with his family shame and drew strength from the fact that our mother had come right, eventually.

After dinner, the headmaster gave a short speech that absolutely nobody listened to. Sam was still glowering, though I couldn't care less. If she wanted to hang around Chris and be a part of our circle, then she was going to have to change her sulky, bratty ways. Finally, the disco kicked off, the lights dimmed, and people started to party.

Later, Chris, Pete and Jason disappeared around the back of the cricket pavilion. Sam, thankfully, went to talk to some other girls while Rolo and I caught up.

When we went to the loo, we caught sight of the boys hidden in the shadows, drinking from someone's hip flask. There didn't seem to be any evidence of joint for a change. Seeing Rolo and me, they called us over and offered us a swig of vodka. Rolo happily took a slug but I passed, having munched some painkillers earlier. Pharmaceuticals, vodka, and Sister Norah waiting up for me, would not have a happy ending. Then Sam, also on her way to the loo, spotted us in the shadows and came flouncing over. I groaned softly and Chris quietly told me to 'fucking cork it'.

'Incoming, six o'clock,' said Jason, watching Sam approach. 'It's the S.A.M.'

'S.A.M?' Rolo asked Jason.

'Smart Arsed Madam!' sniggered Jason, setting off more giggles in Rolo and me.

'Self Absorbed Muppet, more like,' Rolo muttered.

'There you are Chris Poppet, you naughty boy,' gushed Sam. 'I've been looking for you everywhere.'

I sighed. I mean, what was Chris – five years old? He offered Sam some vodka that she, of course, drank. She then got brave and looked pointedly at my shoes.

'No voddies for you in those shoes, KitKat,' she said, closing with a hee-haw.

I seethed. I'd had enough. 'Samantha,' I said, 'firstly, it's Kat to you. Calling me KitKat is a rite of passage, which you are yet to enjoy, if ever. Secondly, I don't know what your fucking problem is or who pissed on your batteries. Up until two hours ago, I'd never clapped eyes on you let alone done you wrong, so I don't know where you get off being so bitchy and sarky, but you and your sour diva attitude are not going to ruin my evening. May I suggest you either wind your precious little neck in or piss off and give me a wide berth from here on out.'

Silence. Well, apart from a gasp from Rolo, and Jason openly laughing at Sam again. I walked off. Jason, Pete and Rolo followed me back into the tent, none of them said anything. They didn't need to. It was official. Nobody liked Sam and she'd made an utter balls-up of first impressions. What a bizarre girl. The sad part was that she obviously thought smart talk and cutting insults were the way to impress a guy. Usually, I was friendly and approachable but she had brought my claws out.

Back at our table, Sam approached me. I gave her a sideways look, warning her with my eyes, practically curling my lip.

'My apologies, Kat. I'm sorry,' said Sam. 'You're right, my comments were out of line. I guess it's just 'cos I really like your brother and wanted to be funny to impress him. I got it all wrong. So, I'm sorry. Can we wipe the slate clean? Friends?'

I looked at her, thinking carefully before I spoke. 'Sam, I have a very low tolerance for unfounded bitchiness and bullshit. I speak my mind and make no apologies for doing so. If you can handle that, and not be a horrible bitch, then sure, we can be friends. But know one thing, if you insult me, you insult my brother. You've mucked things up with Chris tonight, he's just too polite to say anything.'

It was just gone 11 p.m. by then and a teacher told us the bus was waiting to take us girls home – if the Convent could be called home. It hadn't been a great evening. Sam had done a good job of ruining it and my first dance had felt like a bit of an anticlimax. I couldn't wait to get into bed, my head was rowdy with yet another throbbing headache.

Back at the nun house, Sister Norah was waiting up, doing her embroidery and reading her Bible at the same time. Fascinating multi-tasking skills these nuns have, I thought.

'Hello Kat. Was it fun?' she asked.

'Yes, thanks Sister.' There was no need to tell her about my brother's fascination with the snobby town bike.

'You look tired. How are you feeling?' she asked, gently linking her arm into mine as we walked to my dorm.

I smiled tiredly. Her concern was strangely comforting. We stopped off at her magic cupboard where she handed me two painkillers and then she went to make me some warm milk. Relieved to finally flop into bed, I found myself wondering about Maddie. Having now heard Mom's reasons behind her own drinking, I wondered if something similarly horrendous had happened to Maddie. Poor woman. Poor Pete, too.

8

Five glorious weeks of Christmas holidays stretched out in front of us and Rolo, Chris, Pete and I couldn't wait to get home. My birthday was in two weeks' time, Pete's was a day before mine, and then we'd all be at Jack and Anna's wedding, Ant included.

I loved this time of year on the farm. The rains had arrived, cooling everything down, winter's dust long since washed away. The oranges and browns of the dry season were giving way to the colours of a wet, tropical summer, and bright, crisp, emerald-greens and limes were everywhere.

It was litchi season too, and that meant our annual Long-Spit-Litchi-Pip tournament. Many years ago, Chris, Ela and I had sat gorging under the litchi trees and had had a pip-spitting contest, the furthest spit winning. It had grown into a summer tradition. Grandpa, who'd coached us all in the art of a perfect pip spit and what factors affected pip trajectory, was always the referee and sponsor of the prize, which was double pocket money for the month. It always got extremely competitive but Long-Spit-Litchi-Pip wasn't about winning, it was about not losing. Rules stated that the loser had to cut Grandpa's toenails, which he grew specially for months in advance. And one thing you didn't invite was a session with an old man's toenails. Ela had never actually lost in the history of the game, luckily for Grandpa because who really wants a blind chick wielding sharp objects around your toes? As we got older, Grandpa had introduced another prize. The winner could now opt to have a beer with him afterwards.

I was nine when I won Long-Spit-Litchi-Pip and, as the rules stated, I was duly offered the beer. Feeling terribly important, I got horribly drunk and promptly vomited up half a tree of litchis. Last year, GranJilly and The Clap had formed their own Over 60s league, only to laugh it all off when The Clap spat not just a pip impressively far but her dentures too. Unfortunately, Tighty had been first on the scene when the teeth landed on the far side of the lawn and had already given them a good slobbery lick by the time The Clap got to them. As she lunged to grab his collar, Tighty got a wild look in his eyes and bolted off into the bushes. Eventually Dad found him hiding under a shrub, gently gnawing on the teeth. The Clap refused to put them back in her mouth without full sterilisation. Grandpa had suggested a quick whizz in a boiling kettle but she'd sped off home in embarrassment. All gums, she'd pulled the cat's bum to end all cat's bums. Laughing so hard, I had come close to another major litchi vomit.

A few days after getting home, Ant rang to say he was coming out early with Anna to help with wedding preps and would be around for a good ten days, including my birthday. I knew it was due to Anna, creating ways for us to hang out together. I promptly adopted my stupid grin again until Grandpa said that my gormless look was scaring the dogs, and asked me to stop it.

Knowing Pete was having a tough time at home – Maddie still being a bit of a wild card – I proposed he and I have a joint birthday party. He seemed genuinely touched by the idea and we decided on a farm-style 'free for all' at the dam.

When Mom and I did the party shopping, she allowed me to get some beer for shandies, in honour of my sweet sixteenth. Despite its measly alcohol content, I still got the obligatory lecture.

'Remember what I said – don't go overboard, have fun and be a lady. I think it's safe to say that Ant likes you just the way you are. And do NOT drink on top of your painkillers,' said Mom.

'Got it!' I replied, wondering if such a window of opportunity would ever present itself. I didn't go a day without taking painkillers. Just two days ago, I'd had another horrendous migraine and was still coming right.

The morning of my birthday started with the tradition of a family breakfast and gift-giving after which Cookie and I prepared enough party food for an army. Dad and the boys headed to the dam to set up while Mom and

I waited for everyone at the house. Linda and Ela soon arrived with Jack, Anna, Rolo and Ant right behind them.

Rolo thrust a present in my hands and gave me a huge hug. 'Sweet sixteen, and for sure you're gonna be kissed today,' she teased.

After everyone had birthday-hugged me, Ant finally got his chance. He'd stood back, greeting Mom first and getting serious Brownie points for spotless manners.

'Happy birthday, my gorgeous,' he said. 'You are truly the sweetest sixteen ever.' He rather embarrassingly planted a big kiss on my lips, bold as brass in front of Mom.

I raced upstairs to put my presents in my room and, as I thundered back down, I ran into Ant in the hall, everyone else waiting outside. Ever the opportunist and flashing me his famous smile, he quickly took me in his arms, pulling my body into his before kissing me. Heaven. I'd died and gone to heaven. With a stopover in Paradise. Outside, Mom blasted her hooter which got Tighty howling, swiftly bringing us back to the present.

'Happy birthday,' said Ant, holding my hand as we walked out. 'So glad I can be here. I don't think I have ever seen you look so hot.'

I was tanned enough to carry off a white-and-red polka-dot bikini top and little denim shorts. Such a simple outfit, one I had spent days planning and I was giving myself a day off from wearing my neck brace too.

'I'm also having a hard time keeping my thoughts pure and my hands off you, but *hokoyo* – beware my father. I swear I saw him with his shotgun just now,' I said laughing and blushing at the same time.

At the dam, Dad was rigging up the foofie slide and Tim had found some old tyre tubes to float around on. Grandpa was at the braai with Jobb, lording it up over proceedings, beer in hand, no shirt, belly hanging out, and wearing funky black sunglasses à la Tom Cruise. God knows where he'd got them but he looked a right clown. As the beers went down, so Grandpa slipped further into his natural colonial persona and posh English accent, well on his way to getting pissed and becoming sillier by the minute. GranJilly was there with The Clap, who I didn't realise had been invited – the two old ducks already yakking away under an umbrella.

Ant and I went over to Grandpa. I just knew he was going to go all colonial on Ant.

'Ant, old chap, splendid to see you, young man, splendid,' started Grandpa. 'I believe you witnessed young KitKat's appalling rugby skills. Teach her how to tackle, won't you? More of a cricket man myself but anyway—' He then suddenly bellowed over Ant's shoulder. 'Jobb! That fire is way too bloody hot. Get those steaks off for now! Oh, sorry, Ant old cock, what were you saying?' said Grandpa, having now deafened Ant. All we could do was laugh.

Maddie was looking fresh and pretty in a sundress and big straw hat. There'd been some doubt that she'd show up but today her eyes were clear and bright, not glazed over, and she seemed happy. I was pleased to see her making an effort for Pete. Pete's sister Karen from the States came over to say hi. She was gorgeous – tall, very short bleached blonde hair, a nose stud – and looked a bit like a supermodel. Rolo and I, after intense discussion, decided she'd definitely had a boob job. Barely covered by her tiny bikini top, her very firm, perfectly round knockers, were too high to be anything but a surgeon's handiwork. All the boys were transfixed. Chris couldn't take his eyes off her and I even caught Ant gawking when he thought I wasn't watching. Jack, also feasting his eyes on Karen's cleavage, promptly received a whack across the back of his head from his soon-to-be-wife. Grandpa, cottoning on to what they were all staring at, caught sight of Karen, or rather her boobs, and sauntered over for a closer inspection.

'Grandpa, meet Pete's sister Karen,' I said.

Grandpa shook her hand far too vigorously, making her boobs jiggle. 'It's my pleasure indeed. You're a splendid looking girl Karen, I must say—' Grandpa suddenly paused, peering intently into Karen's face, his nose almost touching hers. 'Good God child, you've got a piece of shrapnel lodged in your left nostril. Do you want me to get it out?'

'No Grandpa, it's a nose stud, leave it alone!' I said, smacking his hand as it hovered over Karen's nostril.

Karen just laughed. 'I paid good money for that shrapnel actually. Bled like a stuck pig too.'

'You mean you actually pierced your snout and that bit of old tin is lodged in there intentionally? Doesn't it get rusty, old girl?' asked Grandpa, fascinated. He'd only ever seen piercings in ears before. 'How do you manage to pick your nose without snagging your finger?'

Karen grinned at Grandpa who then ambled off to find Chris.

'Chris, old boy,' said Grandpa, lowering his voice slightly, 'how about some of that wacky 'backy of yours? Come on, let's go have a puff on the other side of the dam.'

Oh. My. God! Grandpa was asking Chris for joint! Incredible, I thought, absolutely incredible how adults always knew our secrets. Chris's face was a picture, Pete's too. Ant couldn't stop chuckling, delighted by my mad grandfather, saying it was the best laugh he'd had in ages. With over thirty people at the dam party, it sure was a baptism of fire for poor Ant, finally seeing the slightly weird rural world I lived in, and experiencing my slightly crazy family and friends all at once. He was very relaxed though, taking it all in his stride.

Grandpa had found the old rowing boat in the workshops and he and Jobb had taken it down to the dam where, so far, it was afloat. After lunch, he convinced GranJilly and The Clap to get into it and gave the rickety boat a huge shove out into the deeper water. There was a wicked belly laugh from Grandpa who had intentionally forgotten to hand them the second oar so they were gaily going round in circles. Everyone stopped to watch and sent up a loud cheer from the banks for GranJilly and The Clap, who were starting to look a bit distressed.

Soon there were loud shrieks and cries from their direction and a frantic waving of arms. The little boat was taking in water. Within minutes, it disappeared completely and GranJilly and The Clap were both splashing around, their cotton sundresses bobbing around their shoulders much to everyone's amusement, Grandpa's mainly. Sure as nuts, he'd known that boat would sink with the weight of two people. He'd planned the whole thing and was roaring with laughter, slapping his knees as they thrashed about in the water with indignant squeaks that only a geriatric can make. Dad and Tim swam out to rescue them, the old dears clinging to tyre tubes as they were dragged back to shore. They came up the bank, their grey permed curls hanging in limp ringlets, The Clap with the tightest cat's bum lips ever when she realised her wet dress was completely see-through. We waited for the tirade and for Grandpa to get severely bollocked on, but then GranJilly and The Clap took one look at the state of the other and dissolved into laughter.

'Oi, Dad, I hope you're not going to let that boat rot away in my bloody dam?' said Dad to Grandpa.

'Don't stress James, I'll ring the army divers tomorrow,' joked Grandpa, turning to Jobb. 'How's your scuba diving, Jobb old chap? Got a wet suit and goggles?'

Later, Ant and I managed to clamber onto one of the big tyres. Grabbing an oar, I rowed us round to a quieter, more secluded corner of the dam, hidden from view by reeds and trees that arched low and dipped into the water's edge. The afternoon sun beating down on us was heavenly. Ant had a complexion that went brown in five minutes and, looking at him in board shorts, taking in his muscular body and six-pack, I was hard pushed to find anything wrong.

'Kat, I love this laid-back farm life of yours. You're lucky.'

'Nah. It can get pretty boring stuck out here during the holidays.' I smiled as Ant ran his hand suggestively down my shin, playing with my cherry-red painted toenails. Super ticklish, I jerked sharply and we both toppled into the water. It was just shallow enough for me to stand, the water lapping at my shoulders. Ant quickly came to me. His kiss felt different this time, more intense. Even in the slightly chilly water, he radiated heat as he moulded his body into mine. I hooked a leg firmly around his hip. I was surprised at myself, being so brazen. The few shandies I'd had were definitely helping and they had been mixed with some painkillers after all. I wasn't letting a headache ruin my day.

Ant ran his fingers down my back, pulling my leg even tighter around his hip. He teasingly played with the bow on my bikini top. 'Now what would happen if I pulled this?'

'Only one way to find out ...'

My bikini top floated in the water next to us ... the feeling of skin on skin was sublime and exciting. I'd never known a feeling like it. We just stood there, stuck in the moment.

Knowing we were taking a risk with my father not that far away, Ant was the one to pull away a while later. 'Let's go back. The last thing I need is for you to get grounded so I can't see you again this week.'

I groaned. 'You may well have a point,' I said, grabbing my bikini top and turning to let Ant re-tie the back.

We rejoined the party. Ant gave me a peck on the cheek, winked and then buggered off with Chris and the other boys. They quickly disappeared into the longer grass where I knew bloody well there would be joint or two smoked.

'Ooh, and who just had a hot 'n steamy make-out?' said Rolo as I sat next to her and Ela. 'I'll have you know your mother was on the prowl but I distracted her for you.'

'Oh God! Thanks. I owe you,' I said, grinning.

'Just taking one for the team,' chuckled Rolo.

Grandpa was stretched out flat on his back on the bank next to us, enjoying a siesta after his steak and a dozen beers, also working on his best dose of sunstroke ever. He was snoring like a steam train with his mouth wide open. Jack deftly lobbed bits of ice at him as he slept. One chunk landed perfectly in his open mouth and, nothing to Grandpa, he just snorted like a bull, swallowed it and licked his lips without stirring from his sleep.

Much later, with the sun sinking fast, it was time to call it a day. We loaded up the trucks again and hauled our sunburnt bodies home. I sat on Ant's lap as we trundled along, thinking it'd been my best birthday ever, but the main thing was Pete had loved his party. He'd come out of his Maddie-induced funk for the day. He, Chris and Ant all wore the signs of having smoked some weed, not that I was bothered. Then I realised my head was pounding again.

I climbed into bed later, tired and with a crazy headache and more painkillers in me, but incredibly happy and all floaty about Ant.

9

The next morning, before I even woke fully, I knew I was about to be knocked sideways by the migraine to end all migraines. Mom came to find me just as I was aiming my head over the loo. A while later, I crawled back to my bed, the room as dark as I could make it. Little white spots danced in front of me and the pain reached into every cell. It was a new pain. Normally, the attacks tore only my head apart. Two bites of dry toast was all I could manage as a lining for the double dose of painkillers I threw back. Within minutes, both toast and pills were on their return trip as the vomiting continued. The acidic bile tore at my throat and the migraine was galloping faster than ever before.

Doc Roberts, summoned by Mom despite it being a Sunday, came striding into my room an hour later, finding me beyond buggered, my neck so stiff I could barely turn. Seeing my very limited range of movement, he did some gentle neck massage and manipulation, followed by acupuncture which was a first for me. The needles, dotted around, began to release some of the spasm, but only after a double shot of pethidine and meds to kill the nausea did things start to ease. It was the same process and one I was becoming too familiar with. Frustration, agony and a tornado in my head, then the sharp prick of the needle that promised to release me.

I taxied down the runway yet again, knowing I would come through the storm and land safely the other side.

I woke up groggy and disoriented, registering that it was nearly dark. Apparently I'd slept the entire day. It was hot and muggy. I could smell and hear gentle rain with thunder rumbling a way off. The fading storm had cast a surreal, dark twilight as the sun set behind the heavy cloud.

I ambled downstairs to find everybody. There was a power cut, judging from the candles and paraffin lamps dotted around the house, and wonderfully quiet. We had a generator because power cuts were increasingly common, but tonight Dad had chosen to enjoy the rain and peace of a Sunday evening without the TV blaring or Chris pumping his techno music through the house. It was so tranquil I could hear the faint sound of an African woodpecker busily tapping his way into a tree and guinea fowl in the distance. I found Mom and Dad reading their books by lantern light on the patio, enjoying the relief of the cooling air.

'KitKat,' said Dad, seeing me. 'You're awake. How's your head?'

'Mmm. Feel like Tyson gave me a going over again,' I said.

'Sweetheart, even Doc Roberts said that was your worst one yet,' said Mom.

'Mmm,' I grunted again, still fuzzy and drugged. 'Felt pretty bad to me too.'

'Think you can handle some macaroni cheese?' asked Mom.

'Urgh,' I said, pulling a face.

'You must eat something, sweetheart.'

'Urgh.'

I so hated these migraines. Even once the pain lifted, my entire body felt the effects for a good twenty-four hours afterwards, like a migraine hangover. Aftershocks.

With every attack, I became less trustful of my body and, as Jack and Anna's wedding approached, found myself pleading with it to give me a couple of clear days. I'd promised to help Rolo with her bridesmaid duties, but I also wanted to spend every minute possible with Ant, who had just glided into our farm circle as if he'd been hanging out with us for years. It was easy, comfortable. And the more I got to know Ant, the more I wanted more. The chemistry between us was sizzling.

The next morning, I could barely contain my excitement about spending the day with Ant, now we were officially a couple. I slipped on a strapless white linen sundress with a fitted bodice, grading into a floaty skirt dotted with flowers and a hot pink sash cinching in my waist. I spent an hour straightening my normally wild, curly hair, topped off with a big straw hat that I'd decorated with fresh roses. Feeling guilty for not wearing my neck brace as often as I should have, I put it on. Within ten seconds it was tossed back into the corner and the idea laughed off. Throwing some lip gloss and a few painkillers in a little bag, I found myself ready two hours early, twiddling my thumbs.

Ant was waiting outside Rolo's house for me, looking like he'd walked out of a magazine advert, in chinos and all country-wedding-groomsman. Taking me in from head to toe, his hug was intense. 'Can we not just run away now?' he whispered, taking a deep breath.

I suddenly felt coy and in danger of saying silly girly things. Thankfully Rolo came bouncing over, showing off in her glorious bridesmaid dress. She did an over-the-top spin. Swirls of delicate silk and chiffon – red, orange and flashes of hot pink flew up around her, her knickers on full display.

'Check you, KitKat, all scrubbed up. You two make a revoltingly good-looking couple,' she said. 'Anna looks magnificent too. Her dress is insane! We've been drinking champagne in my bedroom for hours so I am a touch plastered, for the record.'

'Yes, and with the level of giggling I heard, I'm surprised any of you are standing,' said Ant.

The ceremony was beautiful, held under a massive msasa tree, its low branches hung with crystals on orange silk ribbons that danced in the breeze, and red flame lilies everywhere. I noticed Jack wipe an eye ever so quickly as Anna walked the aisle in the garden. Once the formalities were over, Ant barely left my side. We danced and laughed all evening. I flattened two large glasses of champagne, which brought on a lovely glow. Mom saw it but didn't make a big fuss, just delivered a condensed version of her now standard 'be a lady Kat, don't go berserk' lecture. She was keeping her beady eye on Chris more than on me so it was easy to fly under the radar. He and Pete kept ducking off, I suspected for a puff of joint, in between their drinking. Sure enough, Chris was soon lurching around like Uncle Fester and by midnight he was well and truly wasted. Sneaking some more champagne with Rolo, I also began to spin.

The music got louder as the party kicked up a notch and we were all on the dance floor when we suddenly heard a shriek. Chris had stumbled and gone flying into the fish pond which had been incorporated as a centrepiece among all the tables, the marquee was so big. Chris just sat there in the pond, drenched and laughing while Pete fell on the floor in hysterics.

'Oh God, look at him. What a tit,' I said to Ant, also pissing himself laughing.

'Ah, your brother. He's a special one,' said Ant.

Chris made no move to get out of the pond, making some prized koi very nervous. There was even one floating on the surface, dead as a doornail.

'Sushi, anyone?' shouted Chris, holding up the dead fish. I saw Mom hissing something at Dad who promptly hauled Chris out of the pond. Jack clearly thought it was jolly amusing and went to fetch dry clothes for Chris. Mom decided to call it a night with a wet, drunk and stoned Chris in tow.

'Kat, we're off, before your brother humiliates me again,' said Mom, finding Ant and me on the dance floor. 'Do you want to stay with Rolo tonight? I'll fetch you in the morning.'

'Ah cool, yes!' I was nowhere near ready to end my evening with Ant.

Slowly, people drifted home or to their guest beds on farms all around the district and, by two in the morning, only a handful of us were left in the marquee. My feet ached and I slipped off my sandals to feel the relief of cool grass underfoot. When Rolo announced she was going in to change, Ant suggested we take a stroll. He pulled me close to warm me in the nippy night air as we sat on an old bench in the rose garden. There was no need to fill the space with chatter, now so comfortable around each other. However, my butterflies weren't any less energetic. I leant back onto Ant, swung my legs over the end of the bench and we listened to the night's sounds.

'I was watching you from the top table during the speeches. Couldn't take my eyes off you. Neither could any of the other guys here, I might add,' said Ant a while later, playing with a strand of my hair.

Sitting there, warmed by his arms, I thought of the revoltingly cheesy expression 'all of me feels alive' and found, irritatingly, that it made perfect sense. The buzz I got from Ant was better than any high I'd ever had from alcohol or joint or even the painkillers.

Rolo suddenly started bellowing from the house. 'KAAAT!' Her voice echoed around the garden, shattering the moment. Even the tree frogs swallowed their thoughts and a massive owl in a tree above us thumped its wings as it took off in fright.

'God that girl's timing is awful,' I said.

Ant chuckled. We both took a deep breath, a synchronised acknowledgment of the building sexual tension between us. We wanted more than a few minutes alone snatched here and there. It clearly wasn't going to happen tonight.

'What, Rolo?' I yelled back through the shadows, making the frogs pause again.

'Mom says you gotta come inside now. Ant, she says you're to go to bed too. On your own! The only shagging allowed tonight is between Jack and Anna,' she yelled, forgetting there were about twenty guests in the house, all listening.

I groaned softly. 'Oh shit.'

'Okay, we're coming now-now,' Ant shouted.

'Chop-chop lollipops!' Rolo yelled back, loud enough to wake the dead.

We just sat there, snatching more time, reluctant to move. Wanting to be as close as possible, I sat squarely on Ant's lap, the two of us eye to eye. His hands quickly slid under my dress, firm and warm on my thighs. There was enough moonlight to see his face and, even in the dim light, his eyes transfixed me.

'I hope you realise, Anthony Lawson, just how much of my head you occupy on a daily basis,' I said. 'If someone had told me three months ago that I would be sitting on my best friend's farm with the hottest guy from squash, one all the chicks are mad about, I'd have accused them of smoking crack.'

'Puleez – I never even dared hope you'd go out with me. I thought you were way out of my league. Do you know how thrown I was when I found you making garlic bread in Anna's kitchen that awful night? I was terrified you'd think I was some lame-arse kid outside squash.'

'Me out of your league? Pfft! And you didn't look thrown at all that night.'

'Big time! I'd been fascinated by you for ages, just didn't know how to take it to the next level. And suddenly the moment presented itself. It was a bit rude of you to invite the paramedics, but I'd had an awesome evening up till that part.'

'Those buggers ruined a perfectly good pair of jeans, hacking them off like that. Not the standard way to show a guy your knickers, but hey, at least it hasn't been boring babe.'

'I don't think you have an ounce of boring in you. Come, let's go in. You're just distracting me now, talking about your knickers. And I don't want you getting into shit with Rolo's mom.'

Carrying my shoes and wearing my straw hat, Ant walked me up to the house. I raced up to Rolo's bedroom, dying to rehash every detail of the day with her but she was already half asleep.

'Mmm, g'night Kat, sorry your fun with Fiddlypoop got cut short. What a stunning day huh?' Before I could reply, she nodded off.

10

Christmas was only two weeks away and Christmas lunch would be at our house, with Tim, Linda and Ela, Pete, his folks and Karen. The Clap was coming too, with her English niece, out for the holidays.

Christmas always started with morning service at the district church. It was more a social event than honouring 'J', as Chris referred to the chap who'd supposedly been born that day. Everyone from the district would catch up on news and wish each other well. It was a day the community came together and usually counted its blessings. This year though, the mood wasn't terribly cheerful. I stood outside with Dad while he and some fellow farmers chatted about the land-reform policy.

'I think they may actually get away with it, taking land with no compensation. There's already been trouble down in Matabeleland,' a neighbouring farmer said.

Matabeleland, the province stretching across the bottom of Zimbabwe, was home to Bulawayo, the largest city after Harare, and the Ndebele tribe who were old foes of our Shona people.

On the topic of land redistribution, as we were supposed to refer to the latest brainwave of a policy, Dad – and pretty much every white farmer in Zimbabwe – was worried, and rightly so. The mere mention made them twitch. Already the economy was deteriorating at alarming speeds with vital elements of its infrastructure failing too. Electricity was down more often than not and the water reserves and municipal supply systems were struggling.

It also marked the start of an era of fuel shortages and rationing. Queues at petrol stations could be up to a hundred cars long and one could sit for twelve hours, even overnight, just for a quarter of a tank. I'd queued with Mom and had been amazed at the sense of community that prevailed amidst the ridiculousness and inconvenience. People would bring drinks and snacks, share magazines, play loud music and get a party going, or just pass the time chatting with complete strangers, united by the madness we were expected to live with.

Bladder and bowel control also had to be considered when joining a particularly long queue, but the worst part was being two cars from the fuel pump when the supply ran dry. We'd heard of an eighty-year-old lady who, pipped at the post after a thirteen-hour wait, laid into the pump attendant and had to be restrained. The fuel shortages had also given rise to a new community cause – Tanker Spotting. It only took a sighting of a fuel tanker somewhere for phones everywhere to start ringing as people spread the word of a possible fuel delivery, some even taking a gamble and following the tanker to the next town, hoping like hell it actually was on a delivery and not empty and on its way back. Anyone accurately breaking news of a fuel delivery would enjoy elite status in the community for a few hours. Fuel queues and shortages had even become a perfectly acceptable excuse for being late for work or not showing up at all.

It wasn't a cheerful topic, the state of our nation, particularly on Christmas morning. One of our neighbours read my mind.

'It's Christmas day. Let's be grateful for what we *do* have and let's hope that this time next year we are all still here and our farms and families are safe. Let's drink to that today,' he said.

There was a low rumble of gruff 'hear hears' but the flat tones and heavy expressions told another story, one of dread and impending doom. Little did they realise just how bad things were about to get.

Back home, everyone gathered around the Christmas tree. Dad and Grandpa, both in Santa hats with flashing lights, cracked open their first beer and served presents. For the next hour, all worries were set aside as we gave, received, unwrapped, thanked, ooh'd and aaah'd with splatterings of ooh-how-lovely-I-always-wanted-one, and don't-eat-it-all-at-once. Chris and I then kept to our own tradition of spending time with our house and garden staff and their families, and dishing out gifts to all. I loved seeing the sheer delight on the kids' faces. After a quick game of soccer with them, we went in to help with lunch.

Cookie had done most of the preparations while we were at church. He loved helping us prepare the feast and, no matter how much Mom insisted he take the day off, he would insist on working. Their Christmas morning battle was as traditional as mince pies and it'd become quite theatrical over the last twenty years, performing their own kitchen pantomime. Cookie would eventually concede to just an hour off for lunch and we'd be allowed to step into his kitchen. I was tasked with making gravy and stuffing the pudding with silver coins. Dad strolled in to empty his pockets of change, saying next year we might well be shoving foreign currency into the pudding.

Tim, Linda, Ela and Mojo arrived with yet more gifts. Maddie, Kevin, Pete and Karen strolled in too, Karen's enormous boobs again on display in an almost indecently low-cut dress. Today her piercings included a line of studs running up the side of one ear and a tiny diamond in her nose. Maddie appeared to be sober, but was definitely looking a little strung out with a slightly wild glint in her eyes. Now there's a loose cannon, I thought, wondering how the day would pan out. A while later The Clap arrived with her niece Sarah. I put her in her early twenties, pretty in a plain Jane way, yet fashionable too. I rather fancied her white linen pants and red leather belt with a chunky silver buckle. That said, she was wearing a rather odd and ugly pair of sandals that looked like they belonged on a German backpacker bus. I noticed she wore a wedding ring too. None of us knew anything about Sarah. Her Aunty Clap had never even mentioned her until now.

The house quickly became loud as everyone got to grips with pre-lunch cocktails – Mom, Maddie and GranJilly on the non-alcoholic version. Chris and Pete were climbing into the beer again and I was allowed a shandy, diligently mixed by Grandpa. The first was just amber lemonade so I lodged a formal complaint. Grandpa then went to the other extreme and the rest were basically neat beer, and most enjoyable too. An extreme buzz hit me and I remembered only later that I'd had painkillers on toast for breakfast. Grandpa himself was working hard on a bottle of gin and he and Pete spent half an hour discussing the cricket score, neither of them realising there wasn't even any cricket on.

Ela sat at the kitchen table, yakking away while I made gravy, Mom darted in and out to check on the turkey of ostrich proportions. Chris and Pete were lingering in the kitchen too, looking evil. I could see they were up to something. Sure enough, when Mom left the kitchen to join her guests, Chris and Pete struck.

'Okay ... now Pete!' said Chris in a loud whisper. 'Quick!'

I was digging in the fridge. When I turned, I caught Pete dumping a pile of what looked like dried herbs in my gravy pan. Except it wasn't herbs, it was marijuana.

'You little fuckers!' I shrieked. All I got was an evil grin from the boys who'd obviously smoked, eaten or somehow ingested some weed already.

I peered into my gravy, assessing the situation. There was no way I could fish it out. Ground so fine, it had quickly dissolved into the simmering gravy. The heat and fat would have already activated its mind-altering effects and there was no time to start a fresh batch. Besides, Mom would only question why I poured a perfectly good pot of gravy down the drain.

'Shit man, you two. What the hell are you playing at?' I hissed.

'Agh, it's really mild stuff,' said Chris. 'One of the workers swindled us and it's shit quality. Wouldn't hurt a fly. Don't stress Kat, just leave it.'

'Now what's he done?' asked Ela, knowing Chris was up to no good.

'He's only gone and dumped a whack of dope in my gravy, Ela.'

Pete and Chris were now in full giggle mode. 'Come on Kat, lighten up. It's J's birthday today and we should celebrate. Pretty sure J used to do some weed himself. You don't get to walk on water without some help,' said Pete.

'Arseholes!' I hissed again and kicked Chris in the shin, making him yelp.

I had little choice but to roll with the punches and serve what had been delicious gravy, now just a thick, brown hallucinogenic sauce that would knock the socks off everyone. I, the sane one of the family, was about to get everyone stoned.

'Rats ... bastards ...' I mumbled. I was about to call them fuckwits but swallowed the compliment when Mom came striding into the kitchen.

'Right, let's eat,' said Mom. 'Mmm, gravy looks good Kat.' She dipped her finger in it and licked it. 'Great flavour!'

Yeah Mom, and it ain't just your bog-standard Bisto in there, I thought. Chris and Pete shot out the back door. They couldn't have looked more suspicious if someone had written 'guilty' across their foreheads in red permanent marker.

'Oi, you two,' Mom shouted after them. 'Come and help us serve.'

Oh well, I thought, bugger all I can do now so I may as well enjoy the fun, starting to see the humour in it. Once seated, the cracker pulling started and everyone began to squabble over the made-in-China-by-illegal-child-labour toys that flew around the room.

Dad topped up everyone's glasses and made his annual toast. 'To our family and friends – present, absent, dead and departed. To good rains. To peace and health.'

'And bollocks to Land Grabs,' added Grandpa.

Dad carved and the gravy boat started its trip round the table. Pete, Chris, and I literally didn't take our eyes off it as it passed each person.

'And what are you two finding so amusing?' GranJilly asked Pete and Chris, sensing some mischief. Mom looked sideways at them, her antenna twitching too.

No one knew they were pouring lashings of narcotics over their turkey.

Sarah was seated next to Grandpa who was now half a bottle of gin worse for wear. 'So, young lady, what do you do to earn a crust?' Grandpa asked her.

'I'm a pharmacist,' replied Sarah.

'Aah, nothing like a few recreational narcotics to liven up a party,' replied Grandpa approvingly.

I sniggered. Little do you know Grandpa, I thought. More and more I suspected Mom got her infamous nutter genes from him.

Grandpa turned to Karen who was opposite him. Still deeply fascinated by her, he began to count aloud the number of studs in her ear. 'You really are a fan of shrapnel-like adornments, aren't you?' he asked. 'Has good old-fashioned classic jewellery, like rings, necklaces and bangles, gone out of fashion, or am I just an old-fashioned fool?'

'Oi, which bit of the turkey do you want?' Dad said to Grandpa, interrupting him and brandishing his carving knife.

Grandpa, without taking his eyes off Karen's cleavage, didn't miss a beat. 'Oh, today I'm a breast man, thanks old chap.'

Tim and Kevin started laughing, Dad just shook his head. Then Grandpa proudly and very loudly recited his favourite poem, one we'd always hear at Christmas lunch where he was the turkey talking to the pig: *Lucky little sucking pig, lucky little swine. Sage and onions up your arse, sausages up mine!*

The Clap and GranJilly were served first at the other end of the table, and after the 'don't-wait-it-will-get-cold' signal from Mom, they tucked in. Sure enough, about ten minutes later I saw the first signs of the gravy kicking in. Ever so slowly, it all started to get rowdy.

Ela, sitting beside me, said softly, 'Oh boy Kat, I can sense the silliness coming.'

It came past Ela and me. 'Gravy?' Mom offered.

'Umm, okay.' I took a tiny amount. Normally I drowned my food in gravy so Mom, now certain something was going on with us, looked at me sideways again but made no comment.

'Want some Ela?' I asked.

'Duh! Of course,' she whispered. 'Sorry, I gotta experience this one.' I slopped a generous amount of gravy on her plate.

'Kat, this is splendid gravy,' said Kevin, helping himself to more.

I didn't dare look at Chris. At the other end of the table, The Clap was giggling at the streamers, pointing at the motionless paper ribbons lying on the table and insisting they were dancing. Then GranJilly started, insisting her carrots and peas were smiling at her. Dancing streamers and happy carrots, I thought, here we go! Maddie had also perked up considerably and started chatting to Sarah.

'Are you married or engaged Sarah,' Maddie asked her, pointing at her ring finger.

'What? This child married?' said Grandpa, butting in. 'Never! She's barely eighteen, surely?' He took a huge gravy-soaked mouthful of turkey.

Sarah started grinning. She'd almost cleared her plate and had distinctly flushed cheeks. 'I'm twenty-three actually,' she said. 'And no, I'm not married per se, but am in a committed relationship.' Sarah paused. 'With my life partner,' another pause, 'Amanda.'

Well, he may have been gin-soaked as well as stoned, but Grandpa absorbed that last bit of information in milliseconds. He nearly choked, a mouthful of peas flying straight out of his mouth, a few landing in Karen's cleavage opposite him. Chris threw his head back and howled with laughter, literally.

'Hang on, hang on, old girl,' said Grandpa, picking a few half-chewed peas off the tablecloth. 'Let's back up a bit. You're a … you know … LESBIAN?'

'Yup,' said Sarah, laughing. 'I like girls. Big fan of girls. Lovely creatures, girls.'

'Well, I have to agree with you there, but you don't like willy? Not at all? Not even from time to time or on special occasions? Birthdays, no?' asked Grandpa, captivated. I don't think he'd ever met a real live lesbian.

'Dad! Cut it out. Now!' ordered Mom from the head of the table, horrified to hear him being so graphic. By then Chris had his forehead on the table, his entire torso was shaking with laughter, making the glasses rattle. Mom tried to kick him under the table and kicked Ela instead, who yowled with indignation. Pete had his hand clasped over his mouth and was red in the face, doing an awful job of hiding his amusement. The Clap was pulling, without doubt, her best and tightest cat's bum ever after Sarah's sexual confession.

'So, you definitely like girls, Sarah.' Grandpa persisted. 'Only girls?'

'Yup. I did date a few men. Nice enough to wine and dine with, but, my God, they bored me in bed,' said Sarah, the mousey girl who had been so quiet until now. The entire table was all ears, muffled fart-like squeaks escaping from behind Pete's hand.

'Well, old girl, that's 'cos you didn't date me,' replied Grandpa.

'Carpet muncher!' I heard Chris mumbling to Pete. 'We have a carpet muncher in our midst.'

Dad's face was a picture, not knowing who was more of a pig – his father-in-law or his son.

Grandpa suddenly sat back in his chair, looking thoughtful. We held our breath, no one knowing what outlandish thing he'd say next. He then leant sideways to look at something under the table, flicking up the tablecloth to get a better view.

'Dad, I'm warning you ...' Mom growled at him.

'Aha!' he said to Sarah, reappearing from under the table. 'I knew there was something off with your sensible shoes. Lesbian Adventure Sandals. Makes perfect sense now!'

With that, Pete was finished. I thought he'd actually wet his pants he left the table with such haste, his face beetroot red. As he reached the doorway, we all heard him completely dissolve into hysterics, letting out a massive fart. In the hallway, his back against the wall and still laughing, he slowly slid down into a squat, then collapsed completely onto the floor. I even saw Cookie, back from his break, stick his head around the corner to see if Pete was having some kind of seizure.

I could barely breathe for giggling and thought I was about to wet my pants myself. Dad, Kevin and Tim couldn't keep a straight face either, in fact Dad had tears rolling down his cheeks, even with Mom glaring at him to shut up and not egg Grandpa on.

Meanwhile Grandpa blazed forth. 'Oi, Betty, old girl,' he said to The Clap, 'you never told us about your naughtylicious niece. Kept that one very quiet, didn't you? You dirty mare.'

'Dad! Will you bloody cork it,' hissed Mom again, but I could see she was about to crack up any second herself. There wasn't a single person not loving the lunchtime conversation, except maybe The Clap.

Suddenly we heard Karen join in. 'Hats off to you Sarah,' she said, raising her glass and casually fishing Grandpa's peas out of her cleavage before lobbing them straight back at him. 'It takes a lot to come out of the closet. I know. You go girl.'

'Jesus Christ! Are you a fanny fanatic too?' Grandpa asked Karen, his bushy grey eyebrows now level with his receded hairline and his eyes showing way too much white.

'I've dabbled. I'm more bi though,' said Karen, laughing.

'Bi-curious or bi-sexual?' asked Sarah, suddenly looking at Karen in a whole new light.

'No, not bi-curious as I've done my field research and cured the curiosity. Bi-sexual, yes. I enjoy men and I enjoy women too,' Karen said. 'Sometimes both at once, on special occasions,' she added, winking at Grandpa.

'Oh, I'll bet you do,' Grandpa came right back, grinning at Karen with a wonderfully naughty face. He raised his glass. 'Well, here's a toast to two very charming and utterly enthralling young women. And I commiserate with all the hot-blooded men who must surely mourn your crossing over to the other team, Sarah. At least young Karen has not defected entirely. We can give thanks for small mercies, well, double D mercies actually.' Grandpa's eyes were firmly back on Karen's cleavage. I could have sworn I saw Sarah taking an appreciative look in the same direction.

Unfortunately, round about then, it became clear that Maddie was off her face. I didn't believe it was only the gravy, she must have surreptitiously popped a tranquilliser or something because suddenly she was slurring. She raised her glass of water and, with her words tumbling into each other, she made a toast too. 'Yes, here's to the lezos. Always wanted to try it myself actually. I'm bi-curious too.'

It was Dad's turn to splutter and spit food. Mom and Linda were eyeing each other, obviously concerned about Maddie blurting out her lesbian fantasies. After all, it was a fairly outrageous thing to announce in front of your husband and kids over Christmas lunch.

I sat back and, as the meal continued, looked at our crazy lunch table. Three generations, pretty much all stoned, getting a crash course in lesbianism. Even my head was buzzing differently after my tiny helping of gravy. Dad was grinning away like a fool, Tim and Linda were totally chilled and looking like a pair of hippies, Kevin too. Mom, not a big fan of gravy, was the only lucid person there. Ela was having the time of her life, listening to all the voices and different conversations going on at once. Having gone from shy girl to bright, gregarious and outspoken lesbian in a matter of minutes, Sarah was discussing the merits of sexual freedom with Grandpa. Maddie had her eyes closed and, every so often, her head would jerk as she napped upright in her chair. As for the Stoned Rangers, Chris and Pete, well, they were the most wasted except for maybe Grandpa. An hour later there was plenty of food left over, but not a drop of gravy.

After about two hours of craziness and more bizarre conversations we all shuffled out to lounge on the patio. It was raining again, it always did on Christmas afternoon, and the storm had cooled the air beautifully. Gertie, Tighty and Mojo were firmly ensconced on the couches and refused to move so we all plonked down around them while Cookie served pudding out there. Like fat, bloated ticks we sat in peace and contentment until Grandpa began to fart wildly, much to Mom's disgust.

'Bloody hell, Dad, you're worse than my children. Stop being so revolting,' she said. 'Look, the pong has made Tighty move away.'

'No worse than his own farts. Can't take me anywhere, I know,' he chirped back at Mom, not really giving a rat's arse.

Most of us started to nod off. Maddie was already in a deep slumber on the couch and unattractively snoring like a steam train. It would be a Christmas long remembered for the laughter but, other than Ela, Pete, Chris and me, nobody knew just why they had laughed so much that day.

11

After all the excitement of my birthday, the wedding, Ant, and Christmas, life suddenly felt dull on the farm. I was dying to ride, but Mom had put the kibosh on that, saying even wearing my brace I was asking for trouble getting on a horse with a still temperamental neck. I took a few spins on the quad bike, taking Ela with me and describing to her the beauty of an African farm in mid-summer. The rains had been good this year and the earth was soft, muddy and restored from dust. The msasa trees, having shed their winter colours were now bright green and brimming with birdlife. We saw large flocks of guinea fowl everywhere, with chicks in tow. The mahobohobo trees, wild loquats, were dropping their fleshy fruit – huge carpets of juicy orangey-honey balls.

I'd lie in bed listening to the rain at night or watching forks of lightning strike the granite kopjes in the distant hills. There wasn't much that could beat a bone-shaking thunderstorm. However, this summer, it was bittersweet because I had noticed a clear link between the thunderstorms and my headaches. As the atmospheric pressure built, so would my headaches, often subsiding only when the clouds started to dump their load of rain. One way or another, between the persistent niggling headaches, the severe migraine attacks and my spasm-prone neck, I'd not felt a hundred per cent since my accident. It was as if I had been hung upside down, shaken long and hard, and my brain hadn't found its way back since. I also had bouts of light-headedness and double vision, and some days I'd be as dizzy as a flea on a dog's bollocks after a dip. It was extremely disconcerting when my eyes suddenly played broken telephones with my brain and told me there was two of everything. While I was still munching the strong painkillers, I noticed I was building a definite tolerance to them. Occasionally it took three or four, not the prescribed two, to make the pain clear off.

Mom had voiced her concerns. 'See if you can go without Kat. They're loaded with codeine and a tranquilliser to boot, so they are highly addictive.'

Given my alleged genetic predisposition to addict-style nutter behaviour, I was conscious of how many I was munching, but headaches seemed to have become part of life. I always had one niggling and just resigned myself, remembering that I had a knackered vertebra which would take time to heal. And when it did, the pill munching would stop.

Now sixteen, I was legal to drive and had started lessons with Grandpa. Mom had appointed him as family driving instructor when Chris came of age, saying we would drive her back to drink. Grandpa jumped at any reason to get out of the house away from GranJilly, and he took on the role happily. Apparently, he and Chris had had some awful rows but they'd pushed through the pain and Chris could actually drive quite well. It was ironic that he'd been flying planes and microlights far longer than he'd been driving cars.

Years ago, Dad had been at the auctions in Harare and won a bid for a buggered shell of an old beach buggy, which he and Grandpa restored. Now bright red, complete with a Ferrari horse on the bonnet, it was our learning-to-drive car. Grandpa built a special seat in the back for Tighty, who loved the buggy as much as he loved the quad bike. Its open engine mounted at the back sounded like a dozen angry Harley Davidsons, drowning out conversation. The suspension was awful – you'd feel a jolt driving over an ant. It had no roof or canopy, making wet weather driving out unless someone fancied holding up an umbrella. The speedometer didn't work, instead speed was gauged by how high-pitched a scream the engine made. Despite all the defects, the buggy was great and we couldn't exactly break it.

Bored to sobs, I phoned Grandpa to ask if he'd come up and give me a lesson. He claimed he was sick with a 'potentially fatal dose of flu', but he'd rise from his death bed just for me. Then he mumbled something about GranJilly's nursing and revolting chicken soup being more lethal than his flu or my driving. After all the huffing and schnuffling he said, 'See you in nine minutes.'

Sure enough, within minutes Grandpa, looking hale and hearty, came roaring up the driveway on his dirt bike. He strode in but, suddenly remembering he was supposed to be dying, made a big production of blowing his nose loudly and saying stronger men had been hospitalised for lesser ailments. Grandpa had a Man Cold, end of story. When he saw Mom, he insisted she feel his forehead for signs of a fever.

'Yes, Dad, you'll be dead by supper,' said Mom, her hand on his brow. 'Is your Will in order or shall we knock up a new one quickly?'

'Now, is that nice? Your poor old long-suffering Pa is dying and you're talking wills,' said Grandpa.

'Oh, go on you two, get out from under my feet,' said Mom. 'Kat, your neck brace.'

'Urgh,' I said, putting it on begrudgingly. I'd hoped Mom wouldn't notice my bare neck.

Grandpa, Tighty and I jumped in the buggy, Tighty assumed his position in the back barking like a nutjob. I started the buggy and promptly stalled it. After a few more attempts and several bunny hops in reverse, I managed to get it facing forward.

'Kat, release the clutch slowly, child!' shouted Grandpa above the engine's roar. 'Be gentle on the pedals, don't be so bloody cack-handed. Oh Lord, I think I may die today after all.'

I got into first gear and managed a fairly smooth nine metres forward. Just as I prepared to change into second, Grandpa pre-empted me and starting yelling.

'Don't-look-down-at-the-gear-stick-keep-your-eyes-on-the-bloody-road. Eyes-ON-the-fucking-road.'

His cacophony of orders threw me and I promptly stalled, again. Tighty was having a blast, barking madly over my shoulder and I was already half deaf, what with both his and Grandpa's barking.

'Right, jump out young lady, let me refresh your memory. You've obviously forgotten every bloody thing I taught you last time. At least you already have your neck in a brace so whiplash ain't a problem for you, but it is for me.'

He took the wheel, telling me to watch his feet. He then demonstrated the art of gently releasing the clutch. He did it several times, smooth stops and starts and not a single hop worthy of bunnies or kangaroos. When he changed gear, he craned forward, chin on the steering wheel staring straight ahead like a loon to make an over-exaggerated point. Then he refreshed me on 'the art of gentle braking'. Only after fifteen minutes of all that was I allowed back behind the wheel.

I got going and, as we trundled along the dirt road next to the maize field, I even managed to get into fourth gear. The noise of the buggy and barking flushed out every bird in a five-kilometre radius. The workers waved wildly, cheering when they saw us with Tighty in the back, phut-phutting along.

Our farm was crisscrossed by small streams that flowed into the dam and we soon came to a little concrete slab that served as a crossing but could hardly be called a bridge. Barely three metres wide, it had no wall or parapets. We went down the slight decline and I was doing fine with my approach until Grandpa started shouting and there wasn't even an error to shout about.

'Don't put us in the bloody stream, Kat. Watch the road, watch the road, watch … the … bloody … road … oh Christ here we go again!'

Totally flustered, I lost focus and looked at the gear stick as I lined the buggy up to cross. I swerved, lost traction and all control, veering left, down the small incline and into the marshy banks of the stream. We didn't actually land in the drink per se, but we were well and truly stuck in the mud. Tighty leapt out and began cavorting around in the thick bog. I sat dead still, staring ahead, clutching the steering wheel with white knuckles, and cowering. I waited for the bollocking of a lifetime, sure Grandpa was going to go batshit.

'Humpf,' said Grandpa after a few moments, still sitting in the passenger seat and finishing his cigarette. 'Well then …' he paused. 'Shit. Shit. Fuck and bugger.'

He then reached into his pocket and hauled out a bottle of cough syrup, glugging half the bottle in one sip. I watched in amazement, realising he'd had a good helping of it before our lesson.

'What?' he said, looking at me. 'Don't give me that look. Closest thing I have to a stiff drink right now.'

Still I waited for the tirade, but it never came. Grandpa was pretty chilled and I could only think the cough syrup's alcohol content was my saving grace.

'Right then, come on young lady, don't just sit there. Let's see how we're gonna get ourselves out of this bloody mess.'

We both climbed out and immediately sank up to our calves in mud. We walked around the buggy, more squelching than walking, examining it from all sides.

The back wheels weren't in the deeper mud, just balancing on some rocks. Grandpa went to the front to see if he could somehow raise that section. He then instructed me to start the engine, put it in reverse and put foot. He would grip the underside of the front fender and give it an upwards and backwards heave while I accelerated, hoping the rocks would give the back wheels enough traction to reverse out. We didn't move at all. If anything, we ended up deeper in the mud and Grandpa got a face full of sprayed muck and leaves. He was soon panting and red in the face.

'Gonna blow my sodding haemorrhoids at this rate, Kat. Fine bloody mess you've got us into,' he said, catching his breath. Meanwhile, Tighty stood there watching Grandpa. If dogs could laugh, Tighty would have been slapping his knees in hysterics. He was giving Grandpa such a quizzical look, his little ears pricked up and giving a typical boxer wrinkled frown, that I got the giggles. A look of warning from Grandpa, as he leant on the bonnet still trying to breathe, quickly wiped the smile off my face. I got out again and joined him at the front to assess the situation. It wasn't looking hopeful.

There was an old rope in the buggy so Grandpa's next bright idea was to tie it under the back fender and hook it around a tree slightly higher up the bank. Then, using the tree and rope to create a pulley, he'd draw the rope tighter and tighter while I revved the buggy in reverse again. I was dubious, but Grandpa told me to shimmy under the buggy and attach the rope.

'My fingers are buggered with arthritis so I can't tie a decent knot,' he said.

I got down and, lying on my back in the mud, I fiddled around trying to attach the rope. Unable to see what I was doing, I went by touch. My neck brace made it harder to move around under the buggy.

'How're you doing under there, Kat?' Grandpa had lit another cigarette and was casually polishing off the last of his cough syrup like it was cocktail hour.

'I can't tie the rope properly. Can't see what I am doing,' I muttered.

Next thing, I felt the buggy start to shift. The back wheels were moving on the stones, now very precariously balanced.

'GrandPAAA!' I yelled. 'Don't lean on it. It's gonna fall on my fucking head!'

'Language, young lady! That's filthy language,' he muttered. 'And I'm not fucking leaning on it.'

And then it shifted again. I scrambled, terrified of being squashed alive, crushed into the mud. As I struggled to move out of the way in time, Grandpa leapt into action. He took hold and lifted up the back end of the buggy, taking its full weight in his hands so I could scramble out from under it. I shimmied backwards as fast as I could but, just as I thought I was clear, Grandpa lost his grip, the rocks rolled and the edge of the back fender came down, whacking me on the side of my head. My world went black, the colour of unconscious.

I came around at home on the patio, laid out on the big sofa and caked in mud. Dad was sitting with me. I caught the sharp odour of Dettol as he gently wiped mud off my face and arms. Actually, I saw two Dads, everything in double vision. I also saw two Grandpas sitting there. Both Grandpas, white as a sheet, were holding their heads in their hands. Two of Chris, too. Well now, I thought, would ya' look at that, I got me some twin brothers!

Mom was on the phone inside, talking in a slightly hysterical tone that made me wonder why she was so upset. 'Please hurry. I suspect another head injury.' Her voice was shrill and she hung up abruptly.

I realised that I was the one causing the drama. I opened my eyes a bit wider as Mom came galloping out to the patio.

'Doc Roberts is on his way, luckily he's not far, fifteen minutes max,' she announced. Then she noticed I'd opened my eyes. 'Oh thank God, Kat, you're awake. Don't move, love, lie still.' She took over Dettol duty from Dad.

'I'll get her a Coke,' said Dad.

Then I felt it. The pain. Oh my God, the obscene pain. Again. I tried to sit up but Mom said not to. I put my hand up to my head, registering that I had my brace on, but utterly confused as to what had happened. I could have sworn I'd been having a driving lesson down by the river so how had I landed up here?

'Honey, I need you to lie as still as possible until Doc Roberts arrives and checks your neck,' Mom said softly.

'What happened this time?' I asked, fragmented memories started to come. 'We weren't playing rugby, were we? The last thing I remember was cough syrup, Grandpa.'

'Cough syrup?' Mom asked Grandpa, who flapped his hand dismissively and deftly ignored Mom's question.

'And stones and mud. Lots of mud,' I added.

Grandpa, now perched next to me, looked vastly relieved that I was awake and talking at last. I noticed his hands were shaking.

'Driving lesson,' he said. 'We landed in the stream, remember? You were trying to tie the rope when the buggy came down on the side of your head. Luckily it didn't pin you down.'

'How did we get home?' I slurred.

'I happened to drive by,' said Dad, handing me a Coke with a straw so I didn't have to sit up. 'I found Grandpa, plastered in mud, leaping around on the bridge and we managed to haul you out. You've got a nasty cut on your arm from a sharp rock and an ostrich-sized egg on your head.'

'Thank God you were wearing your neck brace,' said Mom. 'I think it protected you from a far worse injury. God, I can't believe this. Another head injury and you've barely recovered from the last one.'

And then I went from double vision to triple vision. The four people sitting around me morphed into a crowd of twelve. I closed my eyes and drifted, unable to deal with the pain and a family three times its normal size.

A while later I opened my eyes to find Doc Roberts gently examining me. He helped me into a sitting position and unfastened my brace, which had a lovely mud veneer even on the inside.

'You poor child. How many?' said Doc Roberts, holding up two fingers.

'Two and a half,' I replied. 'Maybe three and a quarter. Dunno.' Everything was blurry.

'Yup, she's severely concussed. Her neck seems okay but it's going to go into spasm again,' he said. 'She's going to need more X-rays to check that already fractured vertebra. Thank goodness you were wearing the brace, Kat.'

'Shit! My head. Sore.' It was all I could say. I had flashbacks to being in the ambulance with half a swimming pool in my lungs.

Doc Roberts then asked Mom to put me in a bath and get the mud washed off so he could see exactly what other injuries I had sustained. Dad carried me through to the bathroom and left Mom to help me. I just lay there, watching the water turn a pretty orangey-red colour from the mixture of blood and mud, thinking how pretty my hallucinations made everything seem. In clean clothes, I climbed onto my bed and Doc Roberts was able to finish checking me over.

'Right, that's a nasty gash on your forearm. I need to disinfect it,' he said, preparing a wad of cotton wool doused in peroxide. 'This might sting a bit,' he warned.

Might sting a bit, my fucking arse! I nearly went clean through the thatched roof. He may as well have doused my arm in paraffin and flicked a match onto it. I howled with pain, which made my sore head pound even harder. Even Tighty came running, leaping onto my bed, getting as close to me as he could, and giving Doc Roberts a look as if to say 'hurt her again and you and I will have a problem'.

Once the fire settled, Doc Roberts assessed the range of movement in my neck. Every move sent me into new heights of agony.

'I can't examine her when she's in this much pain. It's too much for her to bear, Gill. I'm going to load her up with pethidine,' he told Mom.

Ooh yes, now that sounds far more agreeable, I thought.

'Do what you need to do, just give her some relief,' said Mom, now looking green herself.

The drugs hit my bloodstream fast and I was taxiing down the runway again, headed back to that delicious destination where pain did not exist. My landing gear up and gaining altitude, I got the giggles about Tighty, peering intently into my face. If he'd been human, he'd have been holding my hand saying 'There, there, have a nice trip'.

I woke up five hours later, stiff, and bruised all over. Grandpa was sitting in the corner, reading my book. Tighty had moulded himself along the length of my body. He and Grandpa sitting vigil. Grandpa saw me stir and came over, gently taking my hand. Tighty sat up too, two worried and wrinkled faces staring at me.

'KitKat, I'm so sorry. It was entirely my fault. I don't know what on earth possessed me to send you under the buggy.'

'Mmm, it's okay Grandpa,' I slurred. 'May I have some water please?'

'Of course, I'll get Mom too.'

I lay staring at the ceiling, listening to Grandpa thundering down the stairs shouting for Mom.

'How're you feeling?' she asked, coming in and sitting next to me.

'Knackered. Fuzzy. Fu'knackered. Sore, basically,' I replied. 'What was Doc Roberts's verdict?'

'Relieved you were wearing your brace but says your neck will probably get quite inflamed. He's put you back on the anti-inflammatories. The cut on your arm should heal fine, may leave a bit of a scar though.'

Chris was hovering at the door. 'And you *okes* think I'm the hooligan. At least I never planted the buggy in the river.'

'I'll head home now,' said Grandpa, kissing me on my forehead. 'I'm so sorry KitKat.'

As Mom walked Grandpa out, I heard him say, 'Was stupid of me Gill, so stupid. Sorry.'

'Well, yes,' replied Mom. 'I can't say sending her under the buggy was your brightest idea yet, but she'll be fine Dad. Just a freak accident, don't beat yourself up.'

The next few days were a bit hazy. My concussion subsided, but I lived from dose to dose of painkillers and anti-inflammatories, both of which were starting to hurt my stomach. Nevertheless, they kept the pain at bay and I mostly stayed in bed. Mom arranged a new neck brace too, purple this time. Cookie had tried to scrub my old one, but it was stained with mud and smelt like old-man socks.

After hearing of my latest wheels up, Ant commented that his girlfriend did seem to be quite the klutz and prone to freak accidents. He was sweet about it and I loved hearing him use the word 'girlfriend'. I longed to spend time with him again.

Ela visited a few times. Lying side by side on my bed we'd play her talking books, although I kept nodding off. Pete popped by too with a bunch of flowers and chocolates from Maddie and I'd often wake from an afternoon nap to find Grandpa sitting in my bedroom, just passing the time and reading my trashy magazines.

A week later, Dad went to the tobacco auctions in Harare. Arriving home the next morning, he marched in to say hello and that he had a special Get Well treat from Harare. I looked up from my book to see Ant standing in my bedroom. I was convinced the hallucinations had started again.

'Hi gorgeous,' he said, coming to hug me. I leapt off my bed in such a hurry that I stumbled.

'Woah, careful. Don't let me be the cause of another accident,' he said, breaking my fall.

'What the ... but how ...' I babbled, doing my best goldfish imitation and suddenly wishing I'd washed my hair that morning.

Ant told me he'd been scheming, looking for a way to visit me. After I'd mentioned Dad going to Harare, Ant phoned him directly, first to ask permission to visit me and then for a lift to the farm. He was staying three nights, going back with Tim who had to collect a cousin from the airport. And everyone in the house, including Ela, had been in on the surprise. I really did have quite a cool family.

Leaving Ant and me alone, Dad walked out, throwing a quick warning over his shoulder. 'Ant, you're sleeping in the guest room downstairs. And Kat, this bedroom door stays open at all times.'

Ant later told me that Dad had casually left a full pack of bullets for his shotgun on the seat in the car. I did love Dad's dry sense of humour.

All pain, headaches and lacerated arms were forgotten and I spent an idyllic few days with Ant, not doing anything terribly energetic but doing it together. I was deeply impressed by the lengths he'd gone just to see me – the balls it must have taken to set it up with my father. Ant had banked enough Brownie points to last him a very long time and I think even Dad was secretly impressed by his initiative.

A week later, with only five days until school started, Mom decided we'd head into Harare a few days early so that I could have some much-needed physio, get the X-rays, and see the neurosurgeon. The radiologists couldn't believe I'd whacked my head again. The X-rays showed that the fracture in my vertebra had extended slightly so I'd definitely taken several steps backwards. Yet more physio, anti-inflammatories, painkillers, neck brace, and no sport for another month. Basically, a re-run of the first sentence when I hadn't even finished serving it.

And so the school year started, and I went back feeling anything but refreshed and focused. I had to pull it together though, as I was now in my O Level year and knew it would be my toughest one yet. I was writing nine subjects and my results would directly influence whether or not I would write A Levels, without which there was zero chance of getting into any South African university, not that I had decided on university but I wanted to have the option. What a bizarre few months, I thought, while unpacking in my dorm. I realised that, aged sixteen, I had been both drunk and stoned, and that I might just have fallen in love. My new head and neck problems had seen me start using painkillers consistently and I'd not gone a day without drugs for months. Even I had noticed my increasing fondness for the package deal of warm, pleasant fuzz and pain relief.

Part B: Adulthood

12

I was hot, bothered, and sitting in the traffic on one of Harare's highways. The term 'highway' was ambitious though, because Borrowdale Road was merely a dual carriageway with marginally fewer potholes than the roads in suburbia. A police roadblock up ahead appeared to be causing the traffic backlog and the policemen manning it looked as hot and irritable as I was. The air conditioning in my little Toyota, my nineteenth birthday gift from Mom and Dad, was on the blink.

I had a headache too. Nothing unusual there, but today I had a hangover on top of it. Hangovers were also common, if I were honest with myself. The headaches and migraines stemmed from my injuries when I was sixteen and still no doctor or specialist had been able to rid me of them. Many, many doctors and so-called specialists had poked, prodded and tested me, but with no success. Headaches were just a way of life for me. And so, as a result, were painkillers.

The last meeting at work had been difficult and now I was late for visiting hours at the hospital. I was going to visit Sam, Chris's Samantha, the same Sam I'd butted heads with all those years ago at the St Edwards school dance. I resigned myself to being late and picked up my cellphone to let Chris know.

It was a stupid move and one of the policemen caught me red-handed. I saw him smirk, pleased to have an excuse to give some grief. Sadly, tensions with any authorities ran deep these days, the stress and strife of the failing economy and the land-reform scheme trickling into everyday life. The cop sauntered arrogantly up to my car, leaning his shiny face a little too far into my open window. I was hit by an acrid smell of sweat and stale halitosis. Pissed off, I lit a cigarette and deftly puffed smoke his way, a clear suggestion that he should step back and take his face out of my personal space. He couldn't exactly fine me for smoking in my own car.

He scowled at me, demanded my driving licence and continued his arrogant saunter around my car. As luck would have it, my indicator light had blown and I'd forgotten to get it fixed. He proudly wrote two tickets: *Inappropriate use of cellular technology while in command of a moving vehicle* and *Defective rear indicator.* I was dying to flick my own indicator, the one involving my middle finger.

I could be grateful that he wasn't going to breathalyse me. Last night's bender had been notable, and I probably still had a large quantity of alcohol partying its way out of my system. Two tickets later, I was finally on my way to the hospital. The flowers I'd got for Sam were all but dead from an hour in a hot car, and even the helium 'Congratulations' balloon was deflating before my eyes as it bobbed around, tied to the back door handle.

Sam and Chris had started dating seriously when they were eighteen. It hadn't fizzled out as Rolo, Pete and I had hoped, though I had grown to accept Sam, despite our prickly start. However, to this day, I could not see what Chris saw in her. Her donkey laugh had become worse, a far deeper – almost masculine – hee-haw that always made people stare. Sam was still a little too fond of herself, still said 'Mummy' and 'Daddy', all sickly sweet. Still a princess.

Throughout school, Chris had remained a hooligan with his drinking and weed habit. The archetypal wild child. Pete remained close to us all and even he – Rolo too – had repeatedly questioned Chris's fascination with Sam. Chris always defended her though, and asked us just to be happy for him. Mom and Dad seemed to think she was good for Chris, calmed him down a bit. Little did they know that she had a wild streak herself and was a Weed and Wine club member. Unable to get past the spoilt brat, I just didn't trust Sam, bottom line.

The worst part had been what their romance did to Ela. She still adored Chris, as he did her. They probably even loved each other. I knew they had kissed once or twice, but Chris had never taken things to a more serious level which saddened me terribly. There would always be strong feelings between them. Ela was like a sister to me, and I wanted her to enjoy the same things we all did, including passion, romance and true love. For a long time, I'd had a sense that Chris did not actually know *how* to love Ela. For anyone, teen or adult, living with a disabled person was complex.

I remembered that Christmas in clear detail, the December when the bomb dropped. Chris and Sam had just written their A Levels, had left school, and were embarking on adult life. Following his pilot dream, Chris was about to start his commercial licence at a flying school in South Africa. Sam was off to study law at Rhodes University. They'd continue their relationship long distance, though it wasn't exactly long as Rhodes was only an hour's drive from the flying school. Then, three days before Christmas, Chris announced that Sam was pregnant.

Mom had looked like she was about to keel over from shock.

'How far along?' Dad asked.

Eight or so weeks, Chris had told us. Sam had mentioned the possibility a few days prior, piddled on a stick, saw one too many blue lines, and then Chris got the phone call that would forever change his life.

Chris and Sam decided to face it head on and be nineteen-year-old parents. Sam would postpone her law degree and do it via correspondence, one day. Chris could have condensed his flying and qualified inside seven months, but the absentee lifestyle of a pilot was notorious for wreaking havoc on marriages so, instead, he chose to pursue his creative skills, studying advertising, graphic design and production, also via correspondence. He made the ultimate sacrifice and his lifelong passion would only ever be a hobby, not a career.

Sam's father had hauled out the proverbial shotgun and used it as motivational tool to see Chris trot down the aisle, highlighting that any other decision would land Chris's bollocks in grave danger. And so Sam had waddled down the aisle with her five-month bump. The wedding was a bittersweet affair.

Chris had looked absolutely terrified. It was all I could do not to run up and tell him he was making the mistake of his life. Pete had been best man and, along with Rolo, Ela and me, wore a plastic smile, each of us finding it hard to disguise our sentiments. We felt we were mourning rather than celebrating. In a way we were. We were saying farewell to the happy, carefree days when the five of us roamed around having good, clean fun and always had one another's back. We were mourning our childhood that was coming to an abrupt end, ironically due to a child.

The farce of a wedding catapulted us all into a new, more adult, phase that frankly none of us was ready for, Chris included. Our little circle had been fractured and it quickly started to disintegrate. Sam would never quite 'get' us or belong. Chris was leaving the circle rather than bringing Sam into it and it left a big hole in our lives. It was hardest for Ela, still doing her studies from home and living quite an isolated life. The rest of us had, at least, new paths opening up – Ela's world remained dark and often lonely, not that she ever said as much. How I'd longed to be able to go back and recapture the good old days but it was all gone. We couldn't press pause on our childhood and we'd all been deeply affected by Chris and Sam's shotgun wedding. It certainly taught us a bloody good lesson in contraception.

They'd had a girl, Katie Ela Hay. We were all surprised about the choice of middle name, and I realised then that Sam was oblivious to the strong feelings between Chris and Ela. She was so self-involved, she'd never considered someone with a disability could be more appealing than her, or a threat. Rolo called it vanity, plain and simple.

Chris and Sam had set up a home in Harare. Sam's father, a filthy rich businessman, was a true entrepreneur with fingers in many pies – you didn't ask what he actually did for work. His wedding gift had been a small house in Borrowdale, their starter home. I had to admit, Sam was a brilliant mother and created a beautiful home. She and Chris seemed happy enough on the surface, but I sensed Chris's wanderlust. There was a yearning in him to explore the world, to fly planes to exotic places, to sit in the bush and paint. He needed to be more than just a young father and husband. He had landed a great job in Harare's biggest advertising agency and whenever he could, in his spare time, he'd fly. Sam meanwhile had it quite good and was perfectly happy with her lot in life.

Benjamin Daniel Hay, Chris and Sam's second child, had been born last night. It had been a difficult pregnancy and, three weeks early, Ben had decided he was cooked and wanted out.

In the hospital car park, I swallowed a few painkillers before making my way to Sam's private room that 'Mommy and Daddy' got for her. As I waited for the lift – the back of my cotton top damp from sitting in a hot car – I remembered being in that same hospital after I'd nearly drowned in Jack's pool. It seemed like a lifetime ago and brought back so many memories.

I could hardly move for flowers and people in Sam's suite. Ben, the cutest little baby ever, lay fast asleep in my arms, his little hands clenched in tight fists tucked under his chin. Chris was beaming, pure joy in his eyes in sharp contrast to Katie's arrival. Chris and Sam had been so shell-shocked, so terrified of their little bundle, so worried they'd break her.

In her latest princess outfit, little Katie was there too, cute as a button in pink frills from head to toe. She was clinging to Chris, fascinated, yet a little suspicious of the blob that was her new brother.

'Daddy, can Ben play fairy games with me when he comes home?' she asked, making us all laugh.

'No, my sweet. You'll have to wait a year or two before he can be a fairy,' said Chris, smiling at the look on his father-in-law's face

I had to laugh. Chris was still terrified of Peter, though they'd come a long way. He and his wife Jean were wonderful grandparents and, as they left, Peter gave Chris a bear hug.

'Thanks, my boy, for giving me the two most precious grandchildren. I'm proud of you, both of you, and now I'm glad I didn't actually shoot or castrate you for getting my daughter up the duff.'

'Daddy,' Katie said to Chris, 'what's the duff?'

'Ask Grandpa when you're twenty-one. He'll tell you what happens to boys who do that,' said Chris, winking at Katie.

As Sam's parents left, ours arrived. Mom and Dad had left the farm as soon as they heard Sam had gone into labour, and had sat with Chris at the hospital all night. Mom started telling Katie stories about when Chris and I were babies. Katie's eyes were wide with surprise to hear that we'd once been the size of Ben, thinking that adults were born big.

There was genuine love around Sam's bedside that afternoon, and she and Chris were the happiest I'd seen them. Leaving them to it, I made moves to leave.

'Will you be home tonight?' asked Mom.

'Yup. I'm meeting the girls for a quick drink and then I'll be home,' I replied.

Home for me these days was a little cottage in Umwinsidale, one of the last residential suburbs on the outskirts of Harare – bordering on farmlands, yet only a fifteen-minute drive into town. It was all part of our family's Plan B, Dad's survival plan as a result of the land-reform policy. The repossession of white-owned farms was still being orchestrated countrywide.

The white farmers' fear and dread about the policy had turned out to be well-founded. Mugabe and his cohorts had indeed started helping themselves to agricultural land and hundreds of farmers across the country had already been displaced, most left high and dry. There had been outbreaks of violence and vandalism, targeted at those who'd resisted their takeover, with several murders in the white farming community as well. The promise that the farmers would receive fair compensation for their land and equipment had never materialised. Farming families were literally told to clear off, and anyone who begged to differ paid a serious price – sometimes it cost them their life. We'd heard reports of diehard farmers who thought that they'd beat the system by lining the pockets of their local dignitaries. And some farmers just stayed in situ, believing that it could never happen to them, and didn't plan ahead. It did happen.

Quite understandably, there'd been a sharp rise in people heading to South Africa, UK and as far as Australia and New Zealand. Families were being shattered and scattered all over the world. Not even the international news coverage deterred our leader, hell-bent on ridding the country of its old colonial ways. He said that, come what may, equality would be restored to those who'd fought in the liberation struggle, the so-called War Veterans – except those pitching up to take the farms were about twenty years too young to have fought in the freedom struggle.

About nine months ago, Mom and Dad, being realistic about the storm brewing over land, had started working on their Plan B, which was to buy a property in Harare. They still actually farmed in Raffingora, but knew it was just a matter of time until they were forced to leave. The house in Harare was the family bolthole. Farmers who'd already been served their

Section Eights – the title of the forced eviction notices – but who had made no alternative plans, had lost everything. Dad wasn't going to be one of them. At that point, residential properties or smallholdings that fell within Harare's bounds were safe, so he bought such a smallholding, ten hectares, in Umwinsidale on which he was setting up a horticultural venture. The company that dominated the local fruit and vegetable supply chain into supermarkets had given Dad a supply contract for green beans and peppers. While Dad continued on the old farm, he had also started preparing the land and infrastructure for his new veggie venture in town.

The Umwinsidale property was breathtaking. It had beautiful fertile soil, stables, a pool, a prolific water supply from two boreholes and a small reservoir. The main house was huge, and Mom had already furnished it with many items from the farm mixed up with new furniture. It was starting to resemble a home, so when the folks came to Harare they stayed in it.

I had been given a self-contained cottage on the property. I loved my little home with its rustic charm, its thatch and low ceilings. I had a monstrous main bedroom with French windows opening onto the lush garden. In the small study, I'd set up my desk, my computer and my library of books. An open-plan kitchen, lounge, and dining area all opened out onto a wide, covered patio that I'd furnished with large sofas, Indian day beds, and opium couches with huge cushions. Every morning I'd sit there and take in the stunning view, down and across the valley and onto farmlands. I had planted up some flowerbeds in my patch and massive lavender and rose bushes permanently scented the air, while magnificent msasa trees housed much birdlife. It was idyllic. Rolo, green with envy, would often escape her crazy housemates and spend weekends with me. We'd hosted a few notable parties and many a hangover was slept off on my patio.

Worried about security, as the property was so isolated, Dad had offered Jobb the role of town bodyguard. Knowing what side his bread was buttered on, Jobb was delighted to have a secure job unthreatened by the land reform. We had moved three horses to Umwinsidale where Jobb continued his Horse Manager role, and he was also in charge of the workers who were jacking up Mom's new garden and clearing Dad's land for the veggies. Jobb was ever so proud to be in charge of the workforce in town. He took his bodyguard role seriously too and no matter what, come nightfall, Jobb was always on the property.

Dad wanted my caretaker to be able to drive and had recently told Jobb that if he got his driver's licence, he'd get a handsome reward for his decades of loyalty to our family – one of the farm's old bakkies which was already in Umwinsidale. Jobb was beside himself with excitement and immediately set about passing his learner's licence. Grandpa, still the family driving instructor, gave him the odd lesson and, on weekends, I'd see Jobb practising in the old truck, zooting around the property and reversing around drums, always with local pop star, Oliver Mtukudzi, blaring from the tiny radio. On Sundays, Jobb would spend hours lovingly polishing what would soon be his very own car.

If I felt brave, I'd let him practise on real roads by driving me to the local café for the newspaper and cigarettes. Secretly, I loved watching Jobb show off to his new muckers who gathered at the café on Sunday afternoons, all dead impressed that Jobb got to drive his madam around AND had an Oliver Mtukudzi tape. I don't know who'd taught him about car etiquette, probably Grandpa, but he always made a great show of parking and leaping out to rush round and open my door for me, making his friends cheer and laugh every time.

Dad came to town about once a month. In the interim, Jobb ran a tight ship. The veggie venture would only start in earnest once Dad got his Section Eight and left the farm for good. Nobody knew when that would be.

After the hospital visit, I went to the Keg, a bar in Borrowdale that was our generation's local watering hole. We were familiar faces there – familiar drinkers, rather – and, on a Wednesday or Friday night, we were guaranteed to know most of the crowd. It all got a bit incestuous and claustrophobic at times, but such was Harare's nightlife.

Rolo was already at the Keg with Vicky, an old school friend. English, the daughter of expats from Harare's British High Commission, Vicky was supermodel-stunning with her super-short hairstyle and classic 'peaches and cream' complexion. She could be high maintenance, but I was used to her quirky ways. It wasn't uncommon to get a call from her at two in the morning, embroiled in some nightclub brawl, and have to rescue her – she'd done the same for me a few times. Vicky was hard not to like, and most men in Harare felt the same. She went through boyfriends at an alarming rate and, at nineteen, she already had a higher than average shag count.

'Possibly twenty … but there was vodka,' she'd once told us. Vicky didn't care in the slightest about being called a slapper, saying life was too short to not live big. When we'd get all tarted up for a big night out, she'd put on her purple Wonderbra, manoeuvre her sizeable tits as high and her cleavage as deep as possible, and chant 'Carpe Diem, the devil rides tonight!'

Once a round of vodkas was on its way, I told the girls about baby Ben. Rolo and I chuckled to remember the St Edwards dance where I first crossed swords with Sam, describing the infamous bra-and-high-heels quips to Vicky.

'I'd have kicked her straight in the fanny if she'd said that to me. One time, boom, in the squirrel, with boots on,' said Vicky, shooting from the hip as always.

'Ah guys, look, I have to put up with her. She's not that bad. The donkey laugh still needs work, granted,' I said. 'She's marginally less of a princess now she's a mother and wiping shitty arses all day.'

'I can't believe they've had another kid,' said Rolo. 'I gave them two years tops before they got divorced.'

'I'd have your brother any day, Kat. He can fertilise my eggs, sunny side up, with pleasure,' said Vicky. She'd always had the hots for Chris.

'Oh, how's Ela, by the way?' asked Rolo.

'She's good. I spoke to her this morning,' I said. 'She's about to write her finals. I still can't believe she's a shrink.'

Ela, or Doctor Ela Jackson, the most intellectual and highbrow of all of us, had just completed her psychiatry degree and held a diploma in speech therapy. She was about to start work in Harare at a child welfare centre for orphaned and abused handicapped children. Our Ela was finally leaving the farm and joining us in town where she'd live at the welfare centre.

'Our very own Mother Theresa,' said Rolo. 'I'm so proud of her. Wish I had half her brains and dedication.'

'Daaaahlings!' A voice bounced around the pub. It could only be Andrew.

'Daahlings daahlings daahlings. My three poppets,' he said, strutting in.

I had first met Andrew when I'd ordered event décor for a work function from his floral shop, and we'd become close friends. Back then, he'd been agonising on how to 'come out' to his family. It had been rocky for a while, but he was so much happier living loud and proud. He'd been successful in business too, running a landscaping venture on the side, usually redoing some rich, bored housewife's garden. Always up for a party, Andrew was the best person to take on a big night out. Gorgeous too. He regularly made both sexes drool.

After some dramatic 'mwah mwah' air kisses for effect, Andrew flopped into a chair.

'Right girls, tequila. My back is killing me, I've been bending over all day.'

'Who's the lucky guy?' asked Vicky.

'No man,' he tsk'ed. 'I've been bending over Mrs Goldstein's sodding roses, pruning all day. Oh, and look,' he held up a plastered thumb in a flourishing diva gesture, 'Goldstink's little rat of a poodle bit me. Revolting thing. If I ever get it on its own, its fluffy little Jewish dog bollocks are gonna disappear right up its own arse, I'll hoof it so hard. Anyway. Where's your hot hunk, KitKat?'

'Ant's on the river again,' I said, pulling a sad face.

'Oooh, those lucky hippos,' Andrew said with an evil grin, handing me a tequila and flapping his hand to say I should knock it back without delay.

'Fiddlypoop has gone again?' Rolo asked. 'When does he get home?'

'Probably only in about three weeks,' I said. 'Depends on what bookings they get, but even so it will only be for a weekend.'

Ant. My gorgeous Ant was still the love of my life. We'd been proverbial childhood sweethearts ever since my sixteenth birthday. Finally, what all the great poets and authors had been banging on about for centuries – love – made sense.

Ant had done two years of dentistry at university in Cape Town but had never been happy with his degree choice. At the end of his second year, he'd gone on a Zambezi canoe safari and had been fascinated by the whole safari and river-guiding scene. He'd horrified his folks when he'd announced he was chucking in dentistry to work on the Zambezi River. Ant had really come into his own up in the Valley, truly happy for the first time ever. These days he was based in Victoria Falls, mostly doing white-water rafting, convinced he had the best office location in the world and making good money out of tourists too.

My tall hunk with his chiselled abs, long scraggy and streaky hair, and permanent tan, still made my knees a little wobbly. He made other girls' knees wobbly too and I was forever catching girls drooling over my boyfriend. It certainly hadn't been plain sailing all the way and I'd struggled when he went to university. Long-distance love had sucked. I'd been the one left behind, while he had a whole other life I couldn't be a part of. Then, in the first year, we broke up for three months after he started messing around with another girl at varsity.

I was devastated, ripped in two, when he came clean. Plus, we broke up on the phone so I couldn't even go round and kick him in the shins. Ant insisted it had been a once-off drunken blunder, that he'd been so wasted he hadn't actually managed to shag the girl – like that was meant to make me feel any better. With a very bruised ego, I then went on a series of benders myself. I turned into a version of Vicky for a while, pointed out to me by Vicky herself. A lot of meaningless sex was my way of proving that I could still pull, despite the empty 'I'm a big slag' feeling it left the morning after. I don't know who took the break-up harder, but Ant and I were miserable without each other. After dozens of remorseful letters, I finally agreed to try again. I then had a trust issue to deal with, on top of the long distance. Many nights I'd lie awake imagining all the things he could be up to, asking myself if all the angst was worth it. I couldn't escape the fact, I truly loved him.

Things had improved when he came home. I was settled in my own job, always busy and more grounded, and far more chilled about our relationship. Once Ant had followed his dream and found the life he wanted, he became more grounded too. It was still a long-distance relationship but somehow the Harare–Vic Falls distance was more manageable. If Ant had a long stint away in peak season, I would often hop on a flight and spend a weekend with him in either Vic Falls or Kariba.

Now everyone was waiting for wedding bells, except me. The last thing on my mind was settling down. I was having way too much fun, working hard and partying harder. I thought my social life was entirely normal for a girl my age. Ant thought otherwise, and frequently rode my case about my wild partying, sparking massive fights. It wasn't like he himself ever said no to a good piss-up, yet I was the excessive one and I thought it was a load of bollocks. Ever since Mom had dropped the 'I'm an alcoholic' bombshell, I'd been acutely aware of where it could all land me, and I swore I'd never let myself get to that point. So, the second Ant started moaning, I'd flare up and lash out, denying outright that I was anything but normal. It was a recurring argument that bored me – a murky area in our relationship.

'Earth to Kat,' Andrew was waving his hand in front of my face, snapping his fingers. I was miles away, lost in thought.

'Sorry, was thinking about Ant,' I said, downing the rest of my vodka and then another tequila before realising how late it was. 'Shit! I said I'd spend some time with Mom and Dad tonight. I'd better make a move.'

'I'm gonna head too,' said Rolo. 'I've got an early meeting tomorrow.' Rolo was the personal assistant to the chief executive of one of Harare's big IT firms, a very cushy and well-paid job.

'What's everyone doing on Friday night?' asked Vicky. 'Shall we go to that Summer Rave?'

'I'm in,' said Andrew without even thinking, just hearing the word 'rave'. We were all into the trance culture and we'd stay on the dance floor for hours, losing ourselves, soaking in the music, the vibe, the heaving mass of people who danced more with their arms than their feet. And soaking in the drugs, of course. A rave always meant a high of some flavour or another, and we were no strangers to that either.

Driving home, I thought again about Ela now becoming a doctor. I felt positively dim next to her with her fancy degree, and no tertiary education to my name. My last years at school had been notable only for the ongoing feud I had with Mother Superior, Sister Maria. It had kicked up a notch when my O Level results came out. Religious Studies had been a compulsory subject for all Convent girls but I'd announced to Mom and Dad, well in advance, that I would not waste one minute studying religion and would allocate the time to other subjects more relevant for real life.

Yet, no one believed me when I told them to expect a U for Religion. I passed all my other subjects well, but, when results came out, Sister Maria hauled me over the coals.

'Katherine Hay, never in the hundred-year history of this Convent has a pupil got a U for Religion. It's a despicable mark for a Convent girl. You're an utter disgrace. How can this be?'

I told her my 'U' was hardly surprising given that I had written merely two words on my paper – my name – and then pointed out that at least I'd made history. Mother Superior had growled like an irritable old dog. Then she changed her tune and invited me back to complete high school and write A Levels at the Convent, saying I was still the most honest girl there, even if I didn't give a toss about God or about going to hell. We didn't quite 'high five' on it, but I accepted. I passed my A Levels and had briefly considered university too. Not being the most disciplined character, I decided that another three years of studying wasn't for me, despite the student life of wild parties I'd heard so much about.

While I pondered life after school and what to do, Alice Moyo, my old dorm mate, had introduced me to her cousin Stephen Mlambo who was in public relations and I liked what I heard. He had recently returned from the UK where he had spent five years building a small but exclusive PR agency in London and was ready to open an African branch. He offered me the job as a junior account manager, and I took to PR like a duck to water. He had also worked as a journalist and taught me how to write for mainstream media and big business. Despite the political turmoil, corporates were booming and any company worth its salt retained a PR agency. The industry had come a long way and PR was no longer just about pretty bimbos organising gin-and-tonic golf days and company Christmas parties. After six months on the job, Stephen put me onto one of his conference-organising committees and soon I was handling all the admin. The events were hard work and the long hours of being fabulous and charming to hundreds of people did get tiring, but it was never dull and I loved my job.

I found Mom and Dad just sitting down to supper when I got home. Grabbing a plate and a glass of wine, I joined them at the table.

'So, what's happening at work these days? Anything exciting?' asked Dad.

'Mmm,' I said, dribbling spaghetti down my chin, 'we're organising the big hospitality and tourism convention next month so we're all balls-to-the-wall.'

'Where are you holding it this year?' asked Mom.

'We've just accepted quotes from a lodge in Victoria Falls.'

'Well that's cool. You'll get to see Ant?' asked Dad.

'Not sure he'll be there. He's waiting for a group to confirm a booking, but I should get to see him for one night at least.'

I finished my wine and sat back, tired after a long day, a bit tipsy and still with an awful headache that I tried to ignore. Dad and I lit cigarettes, making Mom scowl. She'd quit six months ago, something I needed to consider too. I was stupid to have started in the first place but I'd been eighteen, drunk and curious.

After clearing the table, we moved outside for some cool night air. A big storm was building, and the wind picked up and forks of lighting bounced off the granite boulders way off in the distance.

'So, tell me the family news. What's happening at the farm? How's GranJilly?' I asked, kicking off my high heels and putting my feet on the table.

'Shame, she's getting increasingly frail,' said Dad.

GranJilly had fallen and broken her hip a few months back. She'd had complications with the surgery, as well as pneumonia, and the ordeal had knocked her.

'We think she'll need a full-time nurse soon,' said Mom.

'Is she still staying at the house with you?' I asked.

'Yup. I can't expect Grandpa to nurse or bath her,' said Mom. 'He's at the house with her now, while we're here. But shit, she can be a cantankerous old bat – drives us all round the bend most days.'

As we moved on to happier family news – Dad beaming at the mention of little Ben – Mom's cellphone rang and she dashed inside.

'Oh my God! When?' we heard Mom say. 'I can't believe this. How awful.'

Dad and I looked at each other, both raising our eyebrows. 'Sounds like bad news,' I said.

'The most awful thing,' said Mom, coming back out a while later and wiping away tears. 'Poor old Betty Clapham is dead.'

'What?' I replied. 'How?'

'That was Grandpa on the phone. It happened today. When she didn't surface after her normal afternoon nap, her Cookie went to her room and found her dead. Doc Roberts says she must have just died in her sleep. She was eighty-two after all.'

'Agh shame,' I said. 'Ela will be very upset.'

'What a way to go, though – no illness, no fuss or big drama – perfect, like when my father died,' said Dad, raising his glass in a toast to dear old Cat's Bum Clap.

Needing my bed, I said goodbye to Mom and Dad who were leaving at dawn the next day. I was now quite used to their coming and going between town and the farm at least once a month. I climbed into bed and, via text message, told Ant I loved and missed him. Reading his sweet reply from a tented camp somewhere on the banks of the Zambezi, I'd have given anything to be in his sleeping bag that night.

I lay awake for a while, my mind chasing its tail despite being so tired. The sprinklers were tick-ticking their way in circles around the lawn, reminding me of the farm life I missed so much. Oh, to be a kid again, running around barefoot with no bigger worry than where to ride my horse or who'd lose the Long-Spit-Litchi-Pip contest and have to cut Grandpa's toenails. What a weird day it had been, a day that had brought both death and birth. The headache I'd woken up with was still there when I fell asleep.

13

The next morning my alarm clock grated through me as I woke, still with a foul headache. I smacked the clock into silence and lay there, fighting waves of nausea.

I'd get two distinct varieties of headaches, either alcohol related, a term I found infinitely more acceptable than 'hangover', or neck related. Today was the latter and pain ripped up my neck and into the left side of my head, radiating into my eye. I rummaged in my handbag for my painkillers and took three, the nearly empty bottle reminding me to get to the chemist later. I had a busy day ahead at work and couldn't afford to fall by the wayside. The painkillers would just have to get me through. Thinking for a second, I then took a fourth.

I was hugely frustrated that no doctor had been able to rid me of the incessant and often debilitating pain I lived with. Mom had even taken me to a Headache Clinic in South Africa where they had done test after test. We all knew it was from the neck injuries. Unfortunately, identifying the source hadn't made them stop. Neck aside, I'd been told I was prone to migraines anyway. Doctors labelled me a 'migraineur', my neck injuries had only compounded the situation. It wore me down and I rarely had a totally pain-free day.

The painkillers helped, but several years down the line I'd developed a high tolerance, needing higher and higher doses just to keep on top of the pain. Up to a year ago, I had been able to manage with the more benign over-the-counter painkillers, now I guzzled the far stronger prescription varieties. The doctors, short on answers, just kept prescribing more, and stronger, painkillers. I was now just one level down from the strongest drugs available. One of the many doctors I'd seen reckoned I was getting rebound headaches, the extended use of painkillers to treat headaches was manifesting into more headaches. A vicious bloody cycle!

Mom was extremely worried that I was becoming dependant on the drugs and was on a slippery slope. I just wanted to get ahead in life, lock down my career and live like a normal twenty-something woman. Yet most days I walked around in a haze of codeine, functioning at less than my best. Sometimes I saw my consistent pain as a disability, like Ela's blindness. However, there was possibly light at the end of the tunnel. The neurosurgeon had proposed a more aggressive treatment and, in two weeks, I would start nerve-blocking injections directly into my neck and eye, to turn off some nerve endings. I was absolutely dreading it.

Wearily, I got dressed for work and then got back on my bed for ten minutes to let the drugs kick in – I would have given anything to just lie there all day. I hauled myself up. After some gut-lining Pronutro, I half-heartedly dragged my arse to work.

'You look a bit rough, Kat. Feeling okay?' said Stephen when I got to the office.

'I have a moody head again,' I replied. Stephen knew how I suffered and was compassionate, but I always downplayed things with him. Our clients had to come first.

By two o'clock my head was worse and I was heading for a complete 'man-down-fall-in-a-heap' session. I had struggled through a meeting, so nauseous I feared I might redecorate the client's boardroom with my breakfast. On the way back to the office, Stephen commented on my greenish tinge and told me to knock off early. It was a long weekend anyway.

I went straight home and tossed back several more painkillers. It was about the seventh lot of the day and I was beyond blasted. I put my cellphone on silent and dozed restlessly, waking up a while later to the sound of gentle knocking on my bedroom window. I lurched outside. It was Jobb, wanting to tell me we needed horse bran.

'*Eish*, sorry Miss KatKat, you are sick,' said Jobb, instantly noticing the black shadows around my eyes. Even Jobb knew about my torturous head.

'Yes, sorry Jobb. Let's talk about the horses tomorrow,' I mumbled.

'Yes, Miss KatKat. You want me to phone Boss Chris, tell him you sick?' he offered.

'It's okay, Jobb, I'll be fine. Thank you,' I replied, thinking how fortunate I was to have him around. Not your normal family nurse but his presence was comforting.

'Okay. You need me to come, then you call. I can come sleep here outside, Miss KatKat,' he said matter-of-factly. He'd slept on my verandah before when I'd been ill.

I smiled in thanks and promised I'd call him if it got worse, letting him get on with his evening lock-ups. As I walked back to my bed, my world started spinning. White spots danced before me and I just made it to the bathroom. Vomiting over and over, for the next hour I was unable to move off the bathroom floor. I felt like a red-hot poker had been plunged into my left eye and I knew it was now a full-blown migraine. I tried to sip some water, knowing from experience that I'd quickly dehydrate.

An hour later, I had to call for help. Chris was just leaving the hospital after a late visit to see Sam and Ben.

'You sound like shit,' Chris said.

'Chris, it's a bad one,' I said shakily.

'Migraine?'

'Yup.'

'Casualty?'

'Please,' I replied. There was no need to elaborate. Chris had been through this with me many times, knowing the only way to kill it was to bring out the big guns and get me into Casualty for a painkiller shot.

I splashed some cold water on my face and, while I waited, I stepped outside needing fresh air. Jobb was sitting on my patio reading a tiny Bible in the dim light. He'd probably been there all evening, a silent comfort, keeping an eye on me and ready to take action if needed. Holding onto the door, I smiled at him.

'Now shall I call Boss Chris?'

'I beat you to it. He's on his way, thank you, Jobb.' I had to run inside to vomit again. The pain was vicious, like sharp metal teeth sinking into my skull, raking and clawing down my throat too.

Moments later Chris arrived, with Katie.

'Owee?' said Katie, reaching up to place her little hand on my head. Katie had also seen me like this before.

'It's very very owee, sweetheart. Thanks for coming Chris,' I said, my voice all raspy.

'Right, let's get you there,' said Chris. Familiar with the drill, he grabbed my handbag, a dampened hand towel and a kitchen bowl.

'Don't want you puking all over my car again,' he said. He'd learnt the hard way and had battled to clean his car after his maiden voyage with me in migraine mode.

The same doctor who'd treated me the last time was on duty and he knew immediately why I was there. After a drip was up, he loaded me with the good stuff, the shot that would bring me back from the edge – a cocktail of pethidine, an anti-inflammatory, an anti-emetic to stop the vomiting, topped off with a mild tranquilliser. Seconds after the prick, relief washed over me as the pain subsided. For the first time that day, I thought I might live. The drugs were heavenly and I became a feather, gently floating back to sanity.

The drip ran quickly and the doctor came back to chat to me.

'Right, Miss Hay, that was a baddie and the second in six weeks. I had to give you a slightly higher dose today.' Helping me into a sitting position, he examined my neck. 'Your neck is as hard as cement. Are you getting anywhere with your specialists?'

'They're starting me on those nerve-blocker shots in about two weeks.'

'Ouch! That's a pretty heavy-handed approach. I hope he told you what to expect.'

'A black eye. And the nerve endings in my eye and neck will go numb,' I replied.

'You will definitely get a shiner but it should help things.'

'Doc, I can't live like this, always munching pills. I'll do anything to lessen this awful pain I live with, even if it involves black eyes.' I suddenly came over all tearful, feeling exhausted and overwhelmed.

'I hear you, poor thing. I once wrote a paper on chronic pain patients and that's how I classify you. Go home now, get some rest. Your neurosurgeon is one of the best in Africa, I'm sure he will get to the bottom of this.'

He signed my release form and I was good to go.

'Damn, you're properly blasted,' said Chris, noticing my glazed eyes as we went to the car.

'Yup, was a big sucker tonight,' I slurred.

At home, Chris ran me a bath then went to watch TV. Katie sat in the bathroom with me, telling me all the fairy games she had planned for Ben.

After Chris made me a cup of sweet tea, I insisted he take Katie home, now dead on her feet. It was 11 p.m. and the night had vanished.

'You'll be okay on your own?' asked Chris.

'Of course. Thanks so much for taking me in.'

When I locked up, Jobb was still sitting on my patio. Even if I insisted I was now okay, I knew he wouldn't go to his own bed and would sit there through the night. The wind had picked up, bringing in a chill. I went inside to fetch him a blanket, found a packet of biscuits and made him a big mug of sweet milky tea. Taking them from me, he smiled. I bowed my head and tapped my cupped hands together to thank him for being there. He gave a small nod of respectful acknowledgment.

I fell asleep detesting my body for failing me, again.

I woke up feeling like a new person. I put a pot of coffee on, made some toast, picked up the newspaper and went to sit in the morning sun. The paper was full of reports of violence and vandalism surrounding the land-reform scheme. There didn't seem to be any sequential plan or timeline to the exercise, but it was gaining ground nationwide. Families were still being run off their land, homes burnt to the ground, and anyone resisting was likely to get seven shades of shit beaten out of them. The latest wave of unrest had been in a district not too far from ours.

I heard a car coming up the driveway. It was Rolo. She came in swinging a bag of fresh croissants, with Sally, her huge bull mastiff, in tow. Mom's town bantams squawked loudly at Sally as she lumbered around after them, jowls flapping, slobber flying and flab wobbling, trying to get up enough speed to catch herself some breakfast.

Rolo was looking fresh and summery in a pretty white dress, a chunky turquoise-and-silver necklace and a mass of bangles jingling on one arm. She was always so poised, always elegant and immaculately groomed with a fantastic sense of style. No wonder all the boys adored her.

'I've brought breakfast,' Rolo said, hugging me.

'You fine woman,' I said. Noticing a long strand of dog slobber in her messy blonde hair, all swept up in a topknot, I wiped it off with a tissue. 'I'm assuming this is Sally's?'

'Well, I certainly didn't get lucky last night so it must be,' chuckled Rolo. 'But you're not looking too sharp yourself. Troublesome head?'

'Yup. Same old story.' I told her about last night's cocktail hour in Casualty.

We pulled up some sun loungers and sat chilling, catching up.

'Hey, so did you hear about Ela and The Clap?' Rolo asked.

'I know she died.'

'Apparently, they have already had the reading of her Will. Bizarrely, she propped it against her bedside lamp the day she died – must have known her time was up. It seems she was quite a wealthy old duck. Without a husband or any kids to leave it to, Ela is the main beneficiary.'

'You're kidding!'

'Serious, and we're talking quite a hefty sum. She left a letter for Ela too, saying that the money is to help Ela set herself up in life, that maybe one day she'll find a worthy cause or set up her own practice or a counselling centre.'

'Well, I'll be buggered!'

'Yup, now I wish I'd taken piano lessons too,' laughed Rolo.

'Who'd have thought, huh? Old Betty Cat's Bum Clap. I must give Ela a call later actually. She's arriving in town this weekend and I promised I'd give Tim and Linda a hand with getting her organised in her house at the welfare centre. Her first day at work is Tuesday.'

'Aren't you just thrilled for her, Kat? God, imagine being blind and then leaving home, leaving everything you know, to embark on a new life.'

'Well, at least the welfare centre has other blind counsellors and therapists. Plus we're all around, so she won't get lonely.'

Ela had been able to set her own pace with her home schooling and was one of a handful of people internationally who had written A Levels aged fifteen, three years before the norm. She'd graduated at twenty, most of her degree done via correspondence with the last six months on campus at

Wits University in Johannesburg. She'd placed second in her year, not bad for a blind girl four years younger than her peers.

As Rolo and I got stuck into other gossip, Ant phoned. I'd picked up dozens of missed calls last night, only managing to get a sms through to him that morning.

'Hi babe!' I answered with a spark in my voice.

'Sweetness, you okay? I was worried when you didn't answer last night. How's the pip?'

'Much better,' I said. 'All praise the God of Pethidine!'

Ant couldn't chat long. His next tour group was arriving and he still had to check the weapons and pack up all the trucks to head back into the Valley.

'I'll try call later. Love you, KitKat, wish I was there with you girls. Love to Rolo.'

'Bye, love you too. And I miss you like hell,' I replied. Ant still made me flutter inside.

'Bye, love you, Ant! Miss you!' yelled Rolo into my phone. All I heard was Ant laughing as he hung up.

Rolo sat there grinning at me.

'Yes? And what's that look for?' I asked.

'For you. For you and Ant. I know you two have had your share of shit and have got one dating divorce under your belts, but can you see yourself with him for life? Perhaps the pitter-patter of baby River Rats and little KittyKats?'

'Hell no! Well, not now, I mean. I love him to bits and just wish we were together more. Kinda gets lonely. I mean, I'm in a serious relationship but my day-to-day life is that of a single girl. Where are the perks?' I said, asking myself the question more than asking Rolo. 'It's the weekends that get to me. It's hard to go out and see couples together and be the one feeling like a fart lost in a suppository factory.'

'I guess. Can't be fun.'

Rolo had had her fair share of heartache too. She'd gone through a few relationships since school but was currently single. Her last break-up had been brutal. She'd taken a hard knock when her boyfriend of two years realised he was gay. Andrew's gaydar had gone off a long time before, and he'd alerted her, but Rolo had been adamant that her boyfriend was definitely straight given his superior bedroom skills. We'd never doubted the accuracy of Andrew's gaydar since. Rolo currently had her eye on a man she worked for, or, to be more accurate, her boss, the financial director. Not only was he much older, he was married with small kids. I'd completely freaked when she first mentioned him in the 'I'd-quite-like-to-shag-him' context. I totally disapproved of affairs and was a staunch traditionalist, believing that infidelity in any relationship was just not cricket.

'Talking of men,' I said, 'I hope you've declared your financial director out of bounds. Please tell me you've dropped the idea?'

'Nothing has happened, I promise. He's definitely coming onto me – I'm doing my best to sit on my hands, as it were. He's delicious though, you have to agree. He can audit my books any day.'

He was delicious, I couldn't argue that. We'd bumped into him out one night. With slightly shaggy black hair and intense eyes the colour of sapphires, he looked a lot younger than he was. Still, for all his hotness, I couldn't approve. Rolo and I had been friends long enough to call each other out when a line was being crossed and I wasn't hiding my disdain.

'Just leave him alone and steer clear. You could lose your job and your father will shoot you.'

'Okay, okay! So he's out of bounds. Find me another unmarried distraction then. Doesn't Ant have any decent River Rat friends who can take me for a canoe? Never mind golf widows, you and I could be river widows together.'

'I wouldn't wish this river widow life on anyone.'

The late morning sun was starting to roast our shoulders despite heavy black clouds rolling in, threatening a storm. I thought how good for the land the rain would be. We dragged our sun loungers into the shade of a msasa tree next to Sally, now a hot slobbery mound after her bantam games.

Next we had a call from Jack and Anna, inviting us to a celebration braai that night.

'What are we celebrating?' Rolo asked, switching to speaker phone.

'Well,' said Anna, 'eight months from now there'll be an Aunt Rolo and Uncle Ant—'

'Oh my God!' shrieked Rolo, scaring Sally. 'You're preggers?'

'Yup. We're pregnant,' said Anna.

'Wow! Congrats!' I said, shouting into the phone too. 'When did you find out?'

'A few days ago. After piddling on the stick, I was waiting for a blood test to confirm it.'

'Anna, I just spoke to Ant actually. I take it he doesn't know yet?' I asked.

'Nope, tried to call him earlier but his phone was off,' said Anna.

'He leaving now for a trip but try him again tonight,' I suggested.

'Will do, and I'll see you girls later,' she said and hung up. Rolo and I grinned stupidly at each other. They'd been trying for a baby for a while so it was happy news.

'Talking of babies, affairs and lovers, Kat, there's been something bugging me lately, but I've not known how to broach it with you,' said Rolo. 'I'll just say it straight.'

'Oh shit, this sounds ominous,' I said, fearing it may be about Ant.

'I think Sam is having an affair. There, I said it.' Rolo had a weird look of relief on her face.

'Huh? Sam? Sam Sam? My sister-in-law, Sam?'

'Yes.'

'Umm, wanna elaborate?'

'I saw her at lunch, four or five days before Ben was born. The restaurant was packed so she didn't see me. Thing is, she was having lunch with some man and there was very definitely something between them, a vibe. I really do think she is messing around behind Chris's back. Sure of it, actually. It all looked very inappropriate.'

'Whaaaat? You serious? Heavily pregnant and with another man?' I was gobsmacked.

'Seems so. She was looking huge, I must say. I hadn't seen her in ages.'

'She was huge last week. Did you get a good look at him? Anyone we may know?'

'Nope, I couldn't see much of his face without gawking and drawing attention. He looked a bit older, fat, dark hair. I saw him brush his hand over Sam's.'

'Holy shit! What do we do now?' Not for a minute did I doubt what Rolo had seen and now believed.

'Dunno Kat. Do *you* think she could be screwing around?'

'I've always thought that if anyone was going to stray it would be Chris, not her. So, you say there was some kind of chemistry between them. It couldn't have been one of her cousins?'

'Nah, this dude was a little more than a friend or relative,' she said. 'As I say, I've been wondering how to tell you.'

'Glad you did. I reckon we keep this to ourselves for now. If the chance to mention it to Chris comes up, then I will. God, imagine if she is having an affair, Rolo. Worse – while pregnant.'

'Dirty whore. The mind boggles. Pregnant sex – eeeew, that's just wrong.'

Suddenly feeling drained, I realised I needed a nap if I was going to make Anna's celebration later. Rolo, yawning too, gathered up Sally and headed home, promising to fetch me later for the braai.

I made myself a sandwich and climbed onto my bed with my book. I couldn't concentrate though, my mind going in circles about Sam. I eventually slept, out for the count for two hours solid.

It was a special night, with Jack and Anna both glowing. I had a glass of champagne with everyone else and, before I knew it, I'd made short work of a bottle of wine and felt incredibly mellow. It wasn't a late evening and by eleven o'clock I climbed into my bed which was, very inconsiderately, spinning. I decided to see if I could get hold of Ant, longing to be with him again. He answered right away.

'Sweetheart,' I said, 'did Anna get hold of you yet?'

'Nope, I've only just turned my phone on and the signal out here is horrid. Why?'

'I know I should let them tell you, but I can't keep it in any longer. Anna is pregnant. She was trying to call you today.'

'Serious? Wow, that's amazing news! And just as they were starting to consider fertility treatment.'

'Yup, you gonna be Uncle Ant,' I started giggling at how funny it sounded. There was a long pause on Ant's side. 'You still there? Ant?'

'Urr, Kat, where've you been tonight?'

'Tonight? I told you, Jack and Anna's for a celebration braai. Why?'

'Oh okay. It's just that you sound pissed. You're slurring.' Suddenly his tone had changed.

I bristled but wasn't up for a fight. 'I had a glass or two of wine, that's all. I have not been on a big bender, if that's what you think. I have been with your sister. And I'm not pissed either, Ant.'

He could be such a bore on the topic, worse than my mother at times. I sure as hell wasn't going to admit it had been more like a whole bottle of wine.

'Okay. Okay. Okay. Just asking.' Ant backed down, sensing that I was curling my lip and ready to bite back.

I thought it best to end the call before a full-on fight broke out and said a flat good night. Not exactly the nice lovey-dovey call I'd hoped for, I thought, going to sit on my patio and stew.

I pulled a blanket round my shoulders and lit a cigarette. The blue-black sky was slightly faded around the nearly full moon and there was still some far-off thunder rumbling. Frogs, crickets and a nightjar called from the shadows, then the faint hoot of an owl. The songs made me long for the farm and simpler days.

It reminded me that our home and land was about to be torn from our family. I wondered if the farm birds would hang about when the war veterans took up residence and still sound as pretty in the wake of injustice. My eyes glazed over as I drew hard on my cigarette. I watched the flying ants that the rain had brought, mesmerised by their ritualistic suicide dance around the bright lights, flapping their short life away in a frenzy of motion. It seemed oddly familiar.

Perhaps that's what we looked like when we hit the dance floor at the raves, I thought. We too would get caught up in a frenetic trance, with our hands slicing through the air as the drugs took our minds to another world. The speakers would beckon us closer, closer, closer to the music, so loud it was visible. And the lights would hold us there, on the edge, always wanting more. Seductive and addictive. Yes, we are just human flying ants, I thought. Why did we have to complicate our lives so much?

Noticing my rambling thoughts, I admitted to myself that I was drunk. I'd not intended to get plastered that night, it had just kind of happened. Actually, it would just kind of happen fairly frequently these days. Often, I only stopped when the supply ran dry, not because I'd had enough. Up to about my seventh drink I'd feel fine. Eight or more and yes, I'd feel tipsy, but not outrageously drunk or out of control. To my mind, that was in no way excessive. I was not the piss artist Ant made me out to be and I resented the suggestion. My mother was the alcoholic, and my brother had smoked loads of joint but no one ever labelled him a junkie. I just partied from time to time. So what?

Not wanting another heavy head in the morning, I chucked three painkillers down my gob and went to bed.

I dreamt that Sam had given birth to triplets – of the three, only one was Chris's child.

14

It was Ela's big day. The first day of her working life and the day she officially left home. I was going to do everything I could to welcome her to town and keep her company.

I arrived at the welfare centre just as Tim and Linda were unloading the car. Mojo was bouncing around, sniffing every last inch of the flatlet that had been kitted out for the blind. A desk and bookshelf were already filled with text books and teaching manuals, all in Braille. Ela's lounge opened out onto a small garden enclosed by a low fence – Mojo's turf.

While Tim and Linda got things organised, I guided Ela through the space. She only ever needed to be shown a room's layout once. Then, as long as furniture was not moved, Ela moved around as deftly as the rest of us.

There was a knock at the door. 'Hello, anyone home?' we heard someone call.

An extremely attractive man – clearly blind too – introduced himself as James, a fellow counsellor. He ran Ela through some general admin and housekeeping rules, giving her a remote-control alarm device to wear around her neck. In an emergency, someone would come running if it were activated. Promising to check in on her later, he left.

Tim and Linda always stayed at the Umwinsidale house when in town, and that evening we decided to order Chinese and get everyone around. They hadn't met Ben yet or seen Sam in ages.

Ben took an instant shine to Ela, happy lolling in her arms and full of gurgling noises. She ran her hands lightly over his face, visualising his features.

'Ooh, he's going to be a gorgeous child,' she said to Sam.

'Looks just like his gorgeous mom at the moment,' said Chris tenderly, gazing adoringly at his little boy.

Sam totally ignored her husband's compliment and just gave Ela a half-arsed watery smile. After so many years, Sam still never bothered to keep all communication verbal with her. It was arrogant of Sam, but then that was Sam. It embarrassed the hell out of Chris too.

I thought Sam was looking a bit haggard. She was not in a particularly good mood and I definitely sensed tension between her and Chris. Maybe there was a problem in their marriage after all. It disturbed me. She was a great mother and I'd always thought she was a good wife too. Now I wasn't so sure.

Over a bottle of wine, Ela told us more about her windfall from The Clap. She'd inherited far more money than I'd realised.

'Any plans for the money yet?' Chris asked Ela.

'Offshore investments for now. One day, I will find something useful to blow it on, but it's going to be left alone for now. Terribly boring of me, I know,' she said.

When Tim and Linda took the pile of empty Chinese cartons to the kitchen, Ela leant over to me, whispering, 'I'm going to take the folks on an overseas trip. They haven't had a holiday in years. They've spent all their time and money educating me. I'm thinking either Tuscany or South of France.'

'Ela, that's an amazing idea,' I said.

'Not a word, okay?' whispered Ela. 'I want to surprise them.'

'Right, let's get you home Ela, weird as that sounds to your Pa,' said Tim, looking a bit emotional suddenly.

I was glad the evening was over. Sam's sour attitude had made it heavy going.

As everyone headed home, Linda and I were left chatting alone. We had an open and honest relationship. My second mom.

'How are things with Ant?' she asked.

'Umm, okay I guess.'

'You sound lukewarm?'

'Well, he keeps giving me shit about being a party animal and I'm not that hectic, Linds. It's starting to get on my nerves, to be honest.'

'Sweetie, it's probably worse because he's away. Things always feel more dramatic from afar and the mind can play awful tricks. How much are you drinking anyway? And how has your head been lately?'

'Head has been awful. Chris had to take me into Casualty the other night. As for drinking, when I'm out, I have a couple of wines here and there. I haven't got outrageously drunk in ages.'

'KitKat, drinking when your head is temperamental is hardly a bright idea and you know it. How many painkillers are you munching on an average day?'

'Depends. I often take them just in case I might get a headache. I can't function when I'm in pain, and do what I can to avoid an attack.' I paused. It was the first time I'd actually admitted to taking pills on a 'just in case' basis. Maybe I *was* taking too many.

'You haven't answered my question: how many pills?' Linda said. Her tone was caring, with an underlying hint of 'cut the crap, young lady'.

'Ten. Maybe fifteen.' It was an under-exaggeration of note.

'Lord! You know how dangerous they are in large quantities over long periods. Just remember what genes run in the family, my girl.'

'Yup, I'm acutely aware of what Mom is, but that's not me. I'd never get to that level of madness. I just don't need Ant riding my case from five hundred kilometres away. Maybe these nerve-blocker injections will be the golden ticket at last.'

'When do you start that treatment?'

'Friday, so I'll have the weekend to let the black eye subside. I'm gonna look lovely.'

Linda grimaced. 'Ow! Just the mention of needles in the eye gives me the willies. Listen, don't be so hard on Ant. Understand how helpless he must feel and how worried he is. Men like to fix things. He can't fix your head so he probably doesn't know how to cope with it. His rants come from a place of concern, his delivery is just a bit off. He loves you to bits. I'd be more worried if he didn't show any concern.'

Wise words from a wise lady. I hadn't considered it from Ant's side and

Linda had a point. His nagging came from the heart. 'You're right. And I'm too much of a control freak to let myself unravel like Mom, I promise,' I said, feeling better.

'Hang in. Let's hope these injections crack the problem once and for all. Right, I need my bed now and you look a bit buggered too. You've got super black bags under your eyes.'

I hugged Linda goodnight and started closing up. At the door, Linda suddenly turned and said, 'Kat, are Sam and Chris having problems?'

'Why do you ask?' I was surprised she had seen it too.

'They just seemed a little tense tonight. Sam's knickers were in a big knot. I found her very terse.'

'Yes, I noticed too,' I said, deciding not to mention Sam's suspect lunch date. 'I'm not sure if they're fighting. It can't be easy having a baby and toddler and Sam does get a bit pissy, it's her way. Stroppy cow sometimes. Oh, plus they've been renovating their house. They're building another two bedrooms and I know she's been fighting with the builders. And Chris is furious because she has gone over budget.'

'All I can say is, with two kids now, I hope they sort their shit out.' She didn't look too convinced.

I woke up late the next morning. As it was a public holiday, I lazed around in bed reading my book. I even managed a long chat with Ant without any bickering. I decided not to tell him I was going to the cricket with the girls.

Cricket at Harare Sports Club was one of the biggest social gatherings Harare saw. The stands would be packed, there was always lots of bad behaviour, much drinking and after-parties that went on until dawn. It was fabulous. Pulling on a short denim skirt and strappy white top, I then packed a cooler bag with ice, cokes, juice and a lot of vodka.

Vicky collected me and Rolo, and then Andrew who had his cousin, Jake, from the UK in tow. Jake was drop-dead gorgeous and Vicky flicked straight into flirt mode. His frightfully posh accent did it for her, and they soon worked out that they'd grown up a few kilometres from each other in the south of England. Jake was definitely a bit of a bad boy, one of those guys who just had 'Man Whore' written all over him and was right up Vicky's street. Rolo also decided he needed closer inspection so it was game on. Andrew and I soon had bets on who'd win the game of Hot Cousin Jake.

We claimed our spot on the stands, close to the loos and bar; chief concerns at one-day cricket. The grounds were packed and everywhere were the signs of a typical Zimbo social gathering – friends, booze and laughter. We spent the day watching the crowd more than the game and fetching drinks, drinking drinks, then fetching more and munching on gut-lining boerewors rolls in between. A headache niggled so I took a couple of painkillers and felt super chilled, soaking up the festive atmosphere. Our cricket team wasn't doing badly either, or so I overheard. I could have been at a polo match for all the attention I was paying.

Earlier in the day, I'd noticed the TV crews dotted around the grounds, often zooming in on the crowd. Thankfully they'd not swept over our section. Then a Mexican Wave started. Zim was winning and had made a spectacular catch. The crowd went mad. I was jumping up and down on the grandstand, cheering our team on and chanting at the Indian side, 'Go home, Chilli Pips, go home!' when I heard my cellphone ringing. Turning and bending over to find my handbag, I didn't realise my skirt had ridden right up. Even worse, the TV cameras had been on us for several minutes. Blissfully unaware, I answered my phone. It was Ant.

'Hi babe!' I shouted above the noise. There was silence on the other end. I put my finger in my free ear, trying to hear him.

'Helloooo?' I shouted, barely able to hear my own voice.

'Have you any idea what you look like?' I heard Ant say.

'Whadaya mean? I'm at the cricket,' I drunkenly bellowed into my phone.

'I KNOW!' Ant shouted. He didn't sound happy. 'I know you're at the bloody cricket.'

Hang on, I thought. I definitely hadn't told him we were going to cricket so how did he know I was there? I was about to ask when he launched into a tirade.

'My mates and I are watching the cricket on TV. Low and behold, I see my girlfriend acting like a complete fucking hooligan on live TV. The cameraman took a zoom shot right up your skirt just now, by the way. You're wearing those red lacy knickers I bought you.'

Oh. My. God. Fuuuck! And I was wearing the red knickers so he wasn't bullshitting me. Stunned at how I had been bust, but also very drunk, I slurred back, 'Well, they are gorgeous knickers darling. Just think, your knickers may have brightened someone's day, even if not yours.'

As I said it, I realised I shouldn't have. Ant exploded. 'Jesus Christ Kat, I give up. You look like such a complete fucking slag that I am embarrassed to know you, let alone call you my girlfriend. And everyone here is watching. Nice one Kat, class act. And who is that guy you're hanging all over, might I ask?'

Hanging all over a guy? I hadn't even been aware that I was. I looked to my side to see who I was allegedly hanging all over. It was Jake The Beautiful, now shirtless, with his massive biceps and six-pack on display. Even I realised it couldn't have looked good to Ant. I was lost for words, but part of me wanted to roar with laughter too. I mean, I wasn't actually doing anything wrong or scandalous. It was actually quite funny to have been caught on live TV, pissed and rowdy. The crowd erupted into cheers again so I couldn't hear a word for the noise around me, just blah blah blah as Ant droned on about me being a miserable disappointment. The more he moaned, the more pissed off I got. Why the hell couldn't I have some fun? Was I supposed to sit at home every weekend while he was away, being a subservient little woman? And, so what if the world got a millisecond flash of my red knickers. No big secret that everyone wore knickers and they were perfectly respectable knickers too. It wasn't as if I'd flashed my tits on national TV like some of the other girls.

I'd had enough of Ant's lecture. 'Are the cameras still on me?' I asked him.

'Yes!' he replied.

'Okay good, because, you know what, Ant, I am a little tired of your old woman nag act when I'm doing nothing wrong, so here's what I think ...' I paused, looked directly at the camera and gave a quick flash of my middle finger before picking up a vodka bottle and making a 'cheers' gesture at Ant.

'Oh well ain't that just fucking terrific,' he yelled, seeing my televised message, 'and you call yourself a lady—'

I hung up on him. God knows how many times I'd driven him home from cricket, he'd got so plastered. There were more than a few double standards in his rule book. I turned my cellphone off.

'Who were you shouting at? Fiddlypoop?' asked Vicky, handing me another drink.

'Fiddly-fuckwit, more like,' I said.

'Oh dear,' said Rolo. 'Another lecture?'

'Ya, bitching on about me acting like a hooligan on TV. He's been watching us,' I said.

'Cool, are we on TV?' asked Andrew, quickly preening his hair. 'Why's he being such a chop? He's normally the most laid-back dude I know.'

'Fucked if I know,' I said, promptly knocking back the rest of my drink, hoping the camera was still on us.

Seconds later, I was chatting with Andrew and not watching the field when Jake grabbed my arm and sharply yanked me sideways. Suddenly I had my face buried in Jake's crotch and he leant forward into a brace position, shielding my head with his torso. With a loud crack, the cricket ball landed in the grandstand in my now-empty seat. I graciously removed my head and gave him a big kiss as thanks for preventing yet another head injury. Rolo threw her head back and dissolved into laughter. Everyone around us was shouting friendly abuse at me, telling me to keep my eye on the field not the boys. I felt like such a tit and had spilt my drink all over Jake's lap too. We all started laughing uncontrollably. A second later Rolo's cellphone rang. It was my mother! Rolo put her on loudspeaker and my mother opened with the same line as Ant.

'Kat, have you any idea what you look like?' Mom said. I looked at Rolo and pulled an 'eeek' face. We'd been bust on TV again but, in sharp contrast to Ant, Mom was laughing at us.

'That ball came awfully close to landing straight between your eyes, my girl. Who is the gorgeous hunk who saved you?' Mom said.

'Hello, I'm Jake,' he said leaning over to shout into the phone. 'Your daughter's head is fine. Well, fine for now though it's going to feel a bit rough in the morning.'

'Mom,' I shouted, 'are we still on TV?'

'Nope, they've moved on. Have fun girls, chat soon. Just don't drive if you're plastered, that's all I ask. Oh, and Kat, I love the red knickers by the way.'

Hmm, I'd been bust on TV by both Ant and Mom, yet my own mother – the ex-piss artist who went to rehab – had delivered no lecture. To me, it confirmed that Ant was being an old woman.

Zimbabwe won the match and it was perhaps the most festive scene I had ever known at cricket. We partied until midnight, drinking solidly for over twelve hours. God knows how, but Vicky managed to get us all home in one piece and even managed to take Jake home for a bit of 'sexy time', as Andrew called it.

My bed was spinning again. In my drunken stupor, I asked it, out loud, to stand still long enough for me to take a dive at it. Anyone hearing me would have marked me down for the loony bin. I took five painkillers to pre-empt the hangover, waking the following morning with one foot on the floor – the universal position for a bad case of Bed Spins.

Details of the cricket were sketchy and I had a couple of blank spots in my memory. What I did remember was fighting with Ant, something about me being a cricket slag and wearing red knickers.

I turned my cellphone on in the car as I headed to work, not feeling too rough, a Coke at hand, nonetheless. Just as I decided to handle the Ant situation later in the day, I received a text from him, sent the night before. *I'm sorry. Guess I was just jealous you were having such a good time & I couldn't be with you.*

Not wanting to drag the argument out and appreciating him backing down, I replied with a simple X and left it at that.

15

A few days later I got home from work to find Mom, Dad and Grandpa up at the main house, sitting out on the patio. They were in town for a few days. After a catch-up, Mom said she was going to an AA meeting. Although sober for years, she'd still go whenever she was in Harare.

AA had a large local fellowship so there was a meeting every night in some church hall or civic centre. Mom always came home in a great mood, but I had no idea what happened there. What was said in meetings stayed in meetings, according to Mom.

'Grandpa and I are also going to go to a meeting,' said Dad. 'An Al-Anon meeting. Want to come with us?'

Mom had once explained that Al-Anon offered support to the family and friends of alcoholics. Living with an alcoholic could be a tricky, like swimming in shark-infested waters. Alcoholics were not just people who drank themselves stupid. Mom said they had traits and mindsets different to the norm and those close to them had to think differently if the relationship were to survive, no matter how long the drinking boots had been hung up for.

I'd heard Dad talking about his Al-Anon meetings many times. He'd made some close friends in his Harare group. I'd never known Grandpa to attend though.

'It's my first time Kat, tonight I lose my Al-Anon virginity,' said Grandpa, giving one of his wicked laughs.

I looked at Mom sideways. 'Have you been drinking again, Mom? Why's everyone suddenly bolting off to the drunkards' meetings?'

'No,' she smiled. 'I've certainly not been drinking. The meetings are an ongoing thing for all of us. We'll still be going even when I have fifty years of sobriety under my belt. Think of it like servicing a car, an oil and water check.'

'Yeah, your Ma is turning into a rusty old heap. AA keeps her roadworthy,' chuckled Dad.

'Fine pun there, James, old chap,' said Grandpa, the two of them clinking their beer bottles in a 'cheers'.

'Christ Mom, and you want me to go to Al-Anon with these two? They're half plastered themselves,' I said, shaking my head.

'Go on,' said Mom. 'I'd like you to, you'll learn a lot. You can make sure they behave.'

I was unsure where all this was going. I suspected they were getting me into AA because of my piss-up at the cricket. I felt a little sensitive after the way Ant had gone batshit over it, but kept my thoughts to myself.

'Okay, but one day can I come with you to your proper AA meeting? I want to see what that's all about too.'

'Of course, I'd love to take you. It's not the secret clan you think it is. We just don't rehash things outside the meeting,' said Mom.

'Go get ready, we'll leave in ten minutes,' said Dad. 'How's about dinner out somewhere afterwards?'

'Splendid idea,' said Grandpa. 'Let's get Sam, Chris and the kids to join us. How about that new Greek restaurant everyone's talking about?'

'Yup,' said Mom. 'We can give Coimbra a miss for a change.'

I sat there watching my evening disappear as plans were made. Still, it wasn't often we all got together these days.

Dad, Grandpa and I arrived at the church hall where the Al-Anons were gathering that night. I was instantly fascinated, sussing everyone out, wondering who in their family was the nightmare that had them running to a musty hall smelling of old-lady pee and cabbage farts. I counted twenty-five people there, all of us sitting on hard church chairs arranged in a circle.

Everyone fell quiet and the lady in charge asked that the meeting open with the Serenity Prayer. I'd seen this prayer in a pamphlet of Mom's. *God, grant me the serenity to accept the things I cannot change, courage to change the things I can and the wisdom to know the difference.*

Some people were chanting the words and looked a bit like zombies who'd been brainwashed in some kind of satanic ritual. Tonight the words hit home, making me think of Ant. I wondered if he constituted something I could change. Deep down, I knew that if I were to tick a box, Ant would be a 'couldn't change', much like he couldn't change me.

Next, a bunch of A4 cards were randomly handed out around the circle and the rules and traditions of Al-Anon read out, including the 12 Steps that they all followed. The readings touched on accepting having no power over a loved one, in respect of their drinking. They mentioned taking things 'one day at a time', another phrase I'd heard before, then there was talk of a Higher Power and having a faith of sorts in 'a God of your own understanding'. Seemed – though you didn't have to actually call him God or follow any organised faith – you should certainly believe in something bigger and better than yourself, if you planned to get anywhere in your 12 Steps.

Grandpa was absolutely intrigued by it all and soon started his wise-cracks. 'Something bigger and better than me? Surely not,' he said, leaning over to whisper to me.

'Shush Grandpa,' I said softly. We both chuckled under our breath.

Other Steps included removing one's shortcomings with the help of one's Higher Power, as well as taking a 'searching and fearless moral inventory'.

Grandpa started giggling. 'But my morals are all present and accounted for,' he whispered. 'I don'tn't need no inventory or search party, I know exactly where and what they are. As for removing shortcomings, well, where's the bloody fun in that, huh Kat?'

'SHUT UP!' I whispered a bit too loudly.

The lady in charge paused long enough in her reading to give us a vicious stare, making the very clear point that Grandpa and I were to shut up and stop being a disturbance.

'Oh my, she's kinda sexy when she glares like that, all "stern librarian",' whispered Grandpa. I sniggered, he was being a complete devil and I feared we were about to get thrown out.

There were more opening-ceremony formalities as Grandpa later called them, and then the lady in charge cleared her throat to speak.

'My name is Patsy, my husband is an alcoholic. I'm doing okay today and the week has been much better,' she said.

I looked around the circle, bloody sure I'd not heard anyone asking her name or how she was doing. She'd done it spontaneously as far as I could tell. Then everyone replied in unison with a loud and bright, 'Hi Patsy!'

Had there been a rehearsal we'd missed? It all seemed so orchestrated. Next, the person seated beside Patsy also greeted the group and said his name was John, after which the entire circle replied in an equally bright sing-song voice, 'Hi John!'

John also mentioned how things had been at home and poor John, by all accounts, had had rather a shitty week. His brother had been plastered from dawn to dusk, had been caught by the cops driving drunk and in possession of cocaine. The final straw had been him bringing home a prostitute. John told us how he'd got a helluva shock when the scantily clad whore had brazenly sat down to a bowl of cornflakes with his small children at the breakfast table. And, when John had finished his greeting and mood status, the ritual moved on to the next person.

I was starting to understand the pattern, like a reverse Mexican Wave, not driven by happiness. It was coming closer and closer, and I started sweating. What was I supposed to say? Oh my God, Grandpa would embarrass us for sure. Dad would have his turn before us, so at least I could follow his lead. Wish he'd bloody mentioned this part to us before the meeting.

Grandpa, realising he'd soon get his thirty seconds of attention, perked up, sat up straight and rubbed his hands together. Meanwhile, after each person said their name Grandpa was saying, far louder than anyone else, 'Hello old chap!' or 'Hello old girl!' He even said a 'Hello old girl' to someone called Richard. I could have died. And each time he did it, Patsy looked at Grandpa rather fiercely and he was taking great delight in winding her up. If she'd been a dog, she'd have given a low growl.

Four people before Dad was a young man, probably in his thirties, looking a little distraught. Maybe he was new too, also sweating about what to say in his greeting. He wore a smart suit, beautifully polished expensive shoes and looked like some fancy-pants important banker or lawyer type, except he was slouched in a heap looking haggard and deeply pained.

'Hi, my name is Patrick,' he said in a heavy voice. The group gave their sing-song reply and Grandpa's loud, 'Paddy! Hello old chap!' resonated around the hall.

Patrick gave a big pause and the room fell so silent you could have heard the church mouse fart. 'My wife is an alcoholic and—' then Patrick broke down and started sobbing.

'Oh my,' Grandpa muttered to me, 'this is getting a bit heavy now. That chap is in a bad way.'

Patrick couldn't finish his mood status for his sobbing and, once that had been ascertained, the lady next to him gave his hand a friendly squeeze. Without comment they simply moved on to the next person, leaving Patrick to blow his nose loudly on a handkerchief that also looked like it'd had a very long day.

Dad's turn came. 'Hi, my name is James,' he said, also getting the standard sing-song reply. 'My wife is a recovering alcoholic. Life's been good actually, just busy. It's been ages since I came to a meeting and it's great to be here again.'

Great, I thought, that hadn't helped me much with what I was going to say. Grandpa was next.

'Hi, my name is Daniel, friends call me Dan The Man. My daughter, his wife—,' he flicked his head in Dad's direction, 'used to be one helluva piss artist though she's now sober. I came along tonight to see what these meetings are all about. Oh, and I've had a splendid day, thanks. Just a tad worried as we are about to lose our farm but—' He was about to ramble on but Patsy cut him short. The group was laughing openly at him, even the sobbing Patrick managed a small smile. Seemed they did have a sense of humour after all.

'Thank you, Dan,' Patsy said in a clipped voice, her lips pursed tightly in disapproval.

Grandpa quickly leant over to me again, whispering, 'Look at that! She's doing a cat's bum mouth just like The Clap, God rest her soul.'

Well, that was me finished and I got the giggles, plus it was my turn.

'Hi, my name is Kat,' I managed to say.

'Hellooo KITKAT!' came booming from Grandpa's mouth.

'Sorry about Grandpa,' I said to the group, pointing at him. 'Oh, it's also my first time here, my mother is the one who drinks, well, used to.' I simply couldn't go on. I had such a load of giggles on board that all my efforts were on not shrieking with laugher and offending the group. Thankfully the person next to me started their update and I was forgotten about.

The introduction ritual finished and Patsy announced there'd be a ten-minute smoke and coffee break. I went outside to have a cigarette with Grandpa. Dad joined us and introduced us to a friend of his, Cameron, who was very sweet. He'd mentioned in the opening round that his son was the problem, though he'd got his shit together and had sobered up at last.

'So, what happens next in these meetings?' Grandpa asked Cameron. 'When do we get to the good bit, the stories about the mad alcoholics getting rat faced and having bar brawls?'

'Dad, pipe down a bit,' said Dad to Grandpa. 'You're about to get shat on by Patsy, in case you hadn't noticed. And remember that you include your daughter, my wife, when you call them mad alcoholics.'

'Well,' Grandpa answered right back, 'you gotta admit she too was a bit Billy Bonkers once she got to grips with the vodka bottle. Agh, they need to lighten up a bit if you ask me. That chap, Patrick, is in a bad way though. Did you blub like that when Gill was hooching back in the day?' he asked Dad.

Dad just shook his head at Grandpa and told him to show a bit more respect and if he couldn't, then to go wait in the car.

Patsy bellowed out the door that we were starting again. We dragged on the last of our ciggies and went back in, Grandpa very inappropriately muttering something about needing a stiff drink as we sat down.

Patsy introduced Jenna, tonight's speaker, who told us about her seventeen-year-old daughter who was drinking heavily and also doing drugs, marijuana mainly, but she'd also found some cocaine in her school pencil box which, by all accounts, hadn't gone down terribly well. She wasn't tearful like Patrick, she was bloody angry. The rebellious daughter was creating horrendous tension in their household, and Jenna and her husband were heading for the divorce courts. The husband apparently spoilt the daughter rotten. Jenna said he was in as much denial as the daughter and was the enabler, giving her outrageous amounts of pocket money that she just squandered on booze and weed. Jenna said that the pocket money didn't go far when coke was on a teen's shopping list and she'd started to notice things missing in the house. A set of antique silver candlesticks had disappeared and now she was missing a diamond necklace. Jenna reckoned both had passed through a pawn shop before going up the daughter's nostrils.

Then she mentioned something about her daughter being drunk and stoned at the cricket last weekend. Oops, I thought, that's a bit close to home. However, Jenna's daughter had not come home for two days afterwards. Aha, at least I had gone home and slept in my own bed, alone. I wish Ant could hear Jenna's story because her daughter *did* sound quite hectic, a far cry from me.

Jenna wrapped it up, Patsy thanked her, and then it was over to the floor for comment. There was a general rule, I learnt that night. In AA, Al-Anon, or any 12 Step programme, one never lectures or gives sermons. One merely shares one's own experience and others take counsel from that, identifying with the similarities and leaving behind what they couldn't use. That principle fed into the concept that, by being in the fellowship, one never faced these things alone. There was always someone who'd been through it too, come out the other side, and was happy to share how they'd survived. I'd always thought there would be loads of preaching, talk of hellfire and brimstone if one did not stop drinking and repent.

Without lecturing, a couple of people shared their similar experiences with Jenna, who looked vastly relieved to realise she wasn't going insane and others knew how she felt. One man spoke about 'tough love' and another lady said she'd been fortunate enough to be able to send her son to a treatment centre in South Africa, sharing some of the things she'd learnt in the family counselling groups.

There was more talk of rehabs and it became clear to me that still no formal rehabilitation facility for addicts and alcoholics existed in Zimbabwe. To go to rehab in South Africa, you needed foreign currency and a lot of it. I wondered why no one had set up a rehab locally, thinking of Maddie too. There was obviously a real need for one. I also gathered from the discussion that, while the addict or alcoholic could check into hospital or one of the smaller clinics in Harare, no local doctors were trained specifically in treating addictions. The GPs and shrinks just glibly prescribed tranquillisers and piled on antidepressants, masking the issues and never getting to the root of the problem. So, by and large, one simply had to go it alone, using only the 12 Step meetings and literature to get clean and sober. I was shocked that the medical situation was so dire.

The meeting ended and Patsy indicated we were to all join hands and say the Serenity Prayer again. At the end of it, the group loudly chanted a slogan: *It works if you work it, so work it 'cos you're worth it!*

'Huh? Work what?' Grandpa asked me. I just smiled, taking in the incredible vibe, noticing how everyone seemed more upbeat than they had an hour earlier. Even Patrick's face had lightened and he was smiling.

I felt like I had just witnessed something powerful and extremely healing. Perhaps even spiritual.

We arrived at the restaurant just as Mom was parking. Inside, Sam was giving Ben his bottle and the waiters had brought Katie a colouring book. Sam did not look a happy camper, in fact she looked downright angry and had a face like a slapped arse.

After ordering drinks, Mom asked how I'd found Al-Anon.

'It was kind of special, powerful,' I told Mom. 'Grandpa had the devil in him though and was seriously cocking around.'

'Me? Cocking around? Never!' said Grandpa. 'Gill, you should have seen the lady in charge. She was a right stroppy piece of work, though I could tell she was just dying to take me home and ravish me. Bit of a dark horse I think.'

'Was it Patsy?' Mom asked.

'Yeah, that's the one,' said Grandpa.

'Oh dear. She comes to our meetings sometimes, with her husband. She is a bit ferocious, known as the pit bull of Al-Anon. Shame, she's had a torrid time with Ted's drinking,' said Mom.

'You guys went to a meeting? Grandpa, *you* were at a meeting?' asked Chris.

'Yup, would you believe?' Grandpa laughed, now helping Katie with her colouring, except he'd given a cartoon fairy a moustache which had flummoxed the poor child.

Dad took Ben in his arms and gave him the last of his bottle, watching him drift off to sleep. Dad's face was so sweet, just gazing at Ben, transfixed and unable to join in any sensible conversation with us.

'Such a beautiful little boy this. I swear he has a look of you, Dad,' he said to Grandpa.

'Oh, the poor child,' said Grandpa. 'I was such an ugly child, my mother had to tie pork chops to my ears just to get the dog to play with me.'

'Now tell me kids,' said Mom to Sam and Chris, 'how are your house renovations going?'

Well, Sam had a tirade simmering away and she needed no further encouragement to start an all-out bitching session. 'It's a bloody nightmare and I am sick of having odd bods and builders traipsing all over my house. I don't have any privacy at all. Ben can be breastfeeding and they'll march through my house, even into my bathroom. I have to go out to have any peace or privacy.'

'When will they be finished?' asked Grandpa.

'Today the contractor, George, told us it'd be another month,' said Chris. 'I thought Sam was going to kick him in the nuts. There's been some balls-up with materials and he can't find cement for love nor money. Paint is short too.'

'Why don't you all get away for a week or two? Go up to Kariba or do a trip down south. Go to the coast,' suggested Mom.

'We would, if someone—' Chris stopped to glare pointedly at Sam, 'had not gone totally over budget on the building and we weren't in considerable debt.'

Sam looked ready to stick a knife in him. 'Oh, it's my fault that inflation is galloping and prices are going up on a forty-eight-hourly basis, is it Chris?' she said, spitting his name.

'Yeah well, who was the one who, at seven months pregnant, decided she wanted another two bedrooms anyway?' said Chris, an uncharacteristic snipe in his tone. 'And you moan about George and his workmen, but every time I come home I find you sitting having coffee with him and the two of you getting on like a house on fire.'

Chris was seriously angry and my antennae twitched wildly. Yes, there was definitely a problem brewing between them.

'What the bloody hell am I supposed to do when George is in my house sixteen hours a day?' said Sam. 'You just fuck off to work or golf at every chance you get, then come home, pissed, in the small hours.'

Oh boy, I thought, the gloves were off.

'ENOUGH!' said Mom loudly, banging the table with her hand and making people around us stare. 'Settle down you two. And Sam, you do NOT use language like that in front of your children. God help you if I EVER catch you doing it again.'

Mom rarely got seriously angry but hurt her children or grandchildren and she'd come at you flying, claws out. Sam had just tipped Mom's scales, going all guttermouth in front of Katie. Sam went red with indignation at being cut down to size so publicly. Meanwhile, Grandpa was watching her with an interested look on his face.

Dad lifted his gaze from Ben. 'If you're desperate for some peace and quiet then move into the Umwinsidale house until they are finished building,' he said.

Sam smiled at Dad. 'Thanks James, actually that might just be the answer.'

'Excuse me, Sam,' said Chris, tersely. 'We'll discuss it later. But thanks, Dad.'

Sam got up from the table, scraping her chair loudly before flouncing off to the loo.

Chris was irate. 'See what I live with? She's so ungrateful about the things I do for her. Nothing's ever good enough, then she stamps her feet, runs to Daddy darling and paints me as the ogre. Her moaning does my head in. I work my butt off and this is what I get. I don't even get to fly anymore as she gets all militant whenever I go anywhere but the office. I live in a prison.'

Grandpa had deftly distracted Katie and engaged her in her colouring again, but Mom saw Katie trying to eavesdrop, looking a little frightened and close to a meltdown herself.

'Cut it out, Chris, she's old enough to understand there's tension,' Mom muttered, one eye on Katie.

'And,' Chris went on, ignoring Mom, 'there's something up with that builder George. He's a shifty character, too smooth for his own good. Slimy.'

Sam was heading back to the table and again Mom firmly told Chris to cut it out. We managed to get through the evening without any punches thrown but it was heavy going.

Later, Grandpa hopped in my car. After all his chitter-chatter and nonsense a few hours earlier, he'd gone strangely quiet.

'You okay?' I asked him.

'Yes, am fine KitKat. Seeing Chris and Sam bickering like that just disturbs me.' His voice was heavy and he gave a big sigh.

'She's such a princess. Always a diva, once you scratch the surface,' I said.

We drove in silence for a few minutes then Grandpa dropped a bombshell. 'I think Sam is having an affair. My money is on that builder character, George.'

'Shit. You really think so?' I asked.

'Pfft! Is a bullfrog's arse watertight? Of course! It's written all over her. I know the signs.'

'Signs? Like how? How do you know?'

'Well, I don't know first-hand 'cos your gran and I were soulmates but I've seen enough friends having affairs in my time to know what it looks like. Trust me. Sam, the little slut, is playing an away game at the moment and I don't know how I'd tell Chris.' Grandpa sighed. He'd never been fond of Sam though she had no idea what he thought of her. I decided I had to tell him what Rolo had seen.

'There've been similar rumours on the grapevine about Sam. I've said nothing, not even to Mom or Dad, never mind Chris.'

'You're kidding! What rumours?'

'A few days before Ben was born, Rolo saw Sam having lunch with a man and said they looked far too cosy to be just friends. Sam never saw Rolo though, the restaurant was packed.'

'Shit,' said Grandpa. 'Shit shit shitty shit. I was hoping I'd be wrong but this just makes me even more certain. Shit.'

'What do we do, Grandpa?'

'We keep this conversation between us for now. Lemme think about it. I might speak to your mother. If that bloody little tart tears this family apart, I'll throttle her. She's got a nerve huh, messing around when pregnant. Shame on her.'

Again, I felt sick to think of Sam pregnant and in bed with another man.

'That begs the question – how long has she been shagging George and who is Ben's father?' added Grandpa.

'Well, they started the building when she was already preggers – that's not to say she didn't know George before that,' I said. 'I do know George came recommended by her father, so maybe she did know him.'

'I'm glad we had this chat. I thought I was the first to have noticed something was off between those two.'

'Actually, Linda noticed the tension too. Sam and Chris came over for Chinese last week while Linda and Tim were in town. Sam was very uptight and Linda picked up on it right away.'

'Yeah, I'll bet your mother's nose is twitching too, come to think of it. She's no fool.'

Arriving home, I dropped Grandpa up at the main house and made my way to my cottage.

What a heavy evening. My head was pestering me, so I knocked back four painkillers. Seeing the bottle was nearly empty, I rummaged in the bottom of my handbag to see if any had spilt out. I'd filled my prescription earlier in the week, but there were definitely no stray pills in my handbag. I must have cruised through the bottle faster than I'd realised. Still, I had repeats on my prescription so I'd get more from the pharmacy the next day. I'd certainly be needing them as tomorrow I started the nerve-blocker eye injections.

16

'Hop on the bed and lie back, Kat,' said the neurosurgeon, getting various vials out of a cupboard in his examination room.

It wasn't my preferred way to spend a Friday afternoon, but the potential to be free of headaches was so appealing I'd agree to anything, even needles stuck in my eyes.

The doctor explained how he would turn off the nerve endings around my eye. It had to be done with absolute precision so there was to be no squirming. At that point we lost Mom – suddenly the colour of a pistachio, she went to wait outside.

'I'm not going to lie to you. This *will* sting a bit,' said the doctor.

It's fine, I can do this, I thought, suddenly wishing I'd had a shot of vodka before the appointment. At least he didn't tell me to think of happy things. Then I saw the longest, thinnest needle I had ever seen, so fine I wondered how there was even a hollow core in the shaft. I could almost hear *Jaws* music as the doctor drew up the magical numbing potion and came to me, needle poised. Slowly, he plunged it into the area just below my left eye. It stung like hell, and I felt a warm trickle of blood dribbling down the side of my face. I closed my eyes for the next four shots in the same area, I'd been stupid to keep them open in the first place.

'You're doing great,' said the doctor, rubbing my arm gently between shots.

I didn't know what was worse – seeing that needle coming within millimetres of my eyeball or hearing the hard, crunching, gritty sound as it hit the cartilage, with the doctor pushing it down hard. He had to use enough force to wiggle the needle in without snapping the delicate metal.

It was quite the most awful grating sound and sensation, the pain so excruciating I thought I might die. I wanted to scream 'STOP' but moving my mouth was not an option. All I could do was flap my hand like a wounded seal pup.

After the eye shots, I was allowed a break. I was short of breath, my eyes watered profusely, my face felt like a thousand wasps had taken up residence on it, my head throbbed like never before. After a glass of water, I was flipped face down, my head and neck perfectly straight. The needle plunged into the spaces between my first few vertebrae, followed by several shots near my brainstem. Those stung like hell and also felt and sounded like crunchy granola, but were nowhere near as traumatising the eye shots. Maybe because I couldn't see the needle coming, maybe because the tissue was less sensitive than around the eye.

Once it was over, I felt very strange. The base of my head felt numb-ish. My poor eye was another story – a throb, itch, sting, ache and burning fire sensation with a dash of cramp all rolled into one, yet numb at the same time. It was most bizarre, like my brain was not correctly deciphering my pain signals, which I suppose was the whole point.

Ironically, I had the mother of all headaches. Already my eye had started to swell, and in the mirror I could see the bruise kicking in. It was a beautiful shade of dark purple, a stunning colour for anything but an eye area. As time passed, so the agony heightened. The doctor told me to take my painkillers and gave me some sleeping pills too, saying I'd be in some discomfort for a few days. I'd have a repeat session in ten days, then another a fortnight later. Basically, I would have a black eye for the next six to eight weeks. Lovely, I thought, fan-fucking-tastic.

Mom and I stopped by the pharmacy for my painkillers on the way home. As I lifted my sunglasses, the pharmacist took one look at me, and said, 'So, who won?'

Great, I thought, there'll be lame black-eye jokes from everyone.

The pharmacist dispensed my painkillers but not without comment. 'Miss Hay, I gave you fifty tablets four days ago. You should have plenty left. Your dose is four to six tablets *only* per day. I will let it pass this time as I know how you suffer, but you really have to stick to the correct dosage. These are hefty brutes. It's a slippery slope Kat, a road you don't want to go down.'

Shit, I really had hoovered those pills quickly, I thought. Mom too was looking at me with a raised eyebrow, but didn't say anything. I knew I'd get a private lecture later.

'Fifty painkillers in four days flat is a major bloody problem, Kat,' said Mom the second we were in the car. 'Christ Almighty. Do you have any idea how dangerous that is or where it will land you, never mind what it does to your physical health?'

'Mom, I just can't live in pain. It never ever bloody stops. When my headaches strike, I can't do anything – can't work, can't sleep, can't eat. It destroys me and the only thing that helps keep them at bay is the pills. Yes, I've taken too many, but it's for no other reason than to avoid the pain. I don't take them just for fun or a buzz, I take them so I can actually get out of bed each day and function.' My voice was wobbling. I was suddenly overwhelmed. After the neurosurgeon, I was done putting on a brave face. Tears ran down my cheeks and I put my head back on the seat, my eyes closed. I just wanted it, everything, everyone, to stop.

'Relax darling, I'm just trying to understand what's going on here and stop you spiralling out of control. I know you suffer – no one disputes that – but exactly how often do you take them on a 'just in case I get a headache' basis? They're not to be taken as a prophylactic, you know. And they will clobber the lining of your stomach and then you'll end up with ulcers and a whole other set of health problems.'

'I know, Mom. Why do you think I just agreed to have needles stuck in my eye? I'm that desperate for a pain-free life. Come walk in my shoes for a day,' I said, not actually answering her question. I could see Mom had a lot more to say but she let the subject drop, seeing I was on the edge. Actually I got a fright myself, realising how many pills I'd cruised through in just a few days.

At home, I planted my arse firmly on the couch. Grandpa and I found an old movie to watch and I just lay there for the evening, half-heartedly applying ice to my black eye. I had taken painkillers right after the shots, more when I got home, and topped up after dinner, all of which made me both nauseous and zonked. The sleeping pill finished me off for the night. Grandpa walked me down to my cottage, making sure I didn't stumble head first into the hydrangeas and spend the night passed out in the flower bed. I was utterly stoned but finally the pain was bearable. I drifted into a narcotic-flavoured, dreamless semi-coma that lasted pretty much the whole weekend.

'Hey sis, how's the shiner?' asked Chris, phoning a few days later.

'Shining bright and purple.' It was indeed quite a black eye I was sporting. 'What's up? How are things at home?' I asked.

'Crap! Really crap. Sam is driving me round the bend, bitching 24/7, and being a brat. Ben won't settle into a routine so I am severely sleep deprived. Katie is being a handful too. The builders are about to get their arses fired, and if I never see that George slimeball again it will be too soon.'

Shit, I thought, Chris was in quite a state. I didn't know what to say.

'I just need the builders out of the house, a peaceful home and some privacy. Even the bloody dogs have gone nuts and keep fighting.' Chris had two boxers, Tighty's offspring, and it was unheard of for them to fight.

'Sounds like a frigging circus Chris.'

'Yup. Listen Kat, we are going to take up Dad's offer and move into the Umwinsidale house for a week or two, until the builders clear off. Sam is suddenly digging her heels in though. She says we're close enough to finishing to stick it out, but I've had it.'

'Fine by me. Why doesn't Sam want to escape the chaos too?'

'Agh, some bullshit excuse about not wanting to leave her home unattended with builders around. That's fine, she can stay there if she wants, but Katie and I are coming to Umwinsidale. Sam can do her own thing,' he said in a weary voice.

A couple of days later at work, I had to nip home in the middle of the morning. With the Vic Falls congress coming up, I had to put in an order for speaker gifts that day. I'd decided on desk trinket boxes made from old railway sleepers. I couldn't for the life of me remember the supplier's name but knew Dad had one in his study.

I parked outside my cottage, waving at Sam's maid who was taking Ben for a walk in his pram. Sam had decided to move into the main house with Chris for a week or two after all. That morning she would have taken Katie to crèche and then gone to her morning yoga. I went up to the house and straight to Dad's study. Hearing a voice, I wondered if Sam was home after all and on a phone call. I found the box on Dad's desk and quickly jotted down the supplier's details, in a hurry to get back to the office.

Still hearing someone talking, I paused. It was definitely Sam's voice, but I also heard a man so she obviously wasn't on the phone. I walked down the passage, the thick carpet silencing my footsteps. I stuck my nose into the guest room that Sam and Chris were using. It was empty. I went into Mom and Dad's main bedroom. I didn't find anyone there either, but noticed the bed was unmade. Sam must have taken a nap there.

A French window opened from Mom's en suite bathroom onto a walled-in outdoor patio, with a private outdoor shower, a small pond and comfy loungers. Dad had built the hideaway for Mom. It was shaded by jacaranda and msasa trees, and she'd often meditate there. The bathroom was empty and I stuck my nose out, into the patio. Lo and behold, I found the voices. Sam and a man. They had their backs to the doorway where I lingered. On the table was a sheet of building plans and they seemed to be discussing paint colours.

So this had to be the builder George, I thought. I stood there for a minute or so, listening to their conversation. They were talking tenderly and, although not actually touching, they were caressing each other with their eyes and soft tones. It was a scene of raw intimacy, nothing business-like or appropriate about it whatsoever. I knew what I was seeing – sex, plain and simple. My stomach churned in disgust. Still unaware of me watching, the man tenderly ran his hand across Sam's cheek. She leant into him, her back arching and lust oozing from her every pore. I couldn't stomach it any longer.

'SAM!' I said sharply. She got the fright of her life. Quick as a flash she whirled round and George jumped too.

'Kat! Good God, you gave me a fright,' she said, sheer panic and guilt written on her face. 'Why aren't you at work?'

'Sam,' I said, my voice low and threatening, 'who is this man and why are you hiding out here with him?' My jaw was clenched and it took all my willpower not to step forward and slap her.

'Oh, but why aren't you at work Kat?' she asked again.

'What I do in my job and the hours I do it in, Sam, are none of your fucking business. Now answer the question.' My eyes were boring into her. I could see her trying to come up with a way out of the situation.

'Okay, okay, no need to go all Hitler on me, Kat,' said Sam with a sneer, buying time as she thought up an excuse. I was itching to grab her by her hair and march her off the property. The man was just standing there, mouth flapping like a pathetic goldfish.

'Come on, Sam, I take you for many things but not a coward,' I continued. 'So, are you going to keep wriggling and squirming or are you going tell me what the fuck is going on here? Go on, I dare you.'

'It's perfectly easy to explain, Kat,' she said, suddenly all cocksure. 'This is our builder, George—'

'Yes, I realise as much. He fits the descriptions, unless you're infatuated with more than one pig-ugly, fat, middle-aged slimeball,' I said, looking directly at him. Sam ignored my jibe but her face was bright red with anger. George's face also filled with rage at my compliment.

'May I speak without being interrupted?' Sam sneered.

'Oh, please do Princess, because my-fucking-God this is gonna be one helluva story. Go on, I'm all ears, Sam. Thrill me with your lies.'

'As I was saying, this is George. George, meet Kat, Chris's baby sister.'

Baby sister? Now she really was cruising, I thought.

'Hello Kat. Nice to meet you,' George said, stepping forward and offering his hand for shaking. I looked at his outstretched arm, keeping both of mine firmly on my hips. Not a fuck was I shaking his hand. I noticed he had hairy fingers and looked slightly Mediterranean. Overweight, short, balding, with greasy olive skin and dark shifty eyes. His open shirt collar revealed a heavy gold chain nestling in thick, black, curly chest hair. All in all, he looked disgusting.

'George came over to discuss some changes on the plans. See?' said Sam, pointing to the drawings on the table. Then she lost all composure and suddenly started stammering. 'I was, ummm, trying to explain to him what this little private patio of your mom's looks like, then thought

I'd just show him instead. So … well … anyway, I was wondering if we could build something similar off our bathroom. That's all. No need to get overexcited.'

I stood there, glaring, not saying a word, my long silence a tactic to rattle Sam further. George's hand was still extended and it remained unshaken. Clearly, he hadn't got the message, the moron. I noticed he had straightened his shirt a bit. I was willing to bet that five minutes prior, his shirt had been untucked and his trousers around his podgy middle-aged ankles. Obviously they'd been rolling around on Mom's bed. How dare they, in my parents' bed? They'd probably shagged in Chris's bed at home too.

I stepped forward and looked George square in the eye. 'Get. The. Fuck. Out … George. Don't ever let me see your face in this house again, you revolting lowlife piece of shit!' He stared right back but I didn't shift my gaze. We faced off and I stood my ground, almost gagging at the smell of stale garlic mingled with cheap aftershave. Eventually, giving me a derisive snort, he rolled up his plans, told Sam he'd call her later, and swaggered arrogantly past me, deliberately knocking me with his shoulder. I quickly put my foot out, ensuring he tripped.

I was left with Sam who'd gone deathly white. She switched from a stammering wreck to ballsy again, and had the audacity to get defensive and pissy with me.

'Kat, I was actually in the middle of a meeting with him. There's a lot to get through without you sticking your interfering little nose in where it doesn't belong. Why are your knickers in a knot over a simple building meeting? What's your bloody problem?'

'Oh, I see. It's like that then, Sam?' I said through clenched teeth. 'Just a simple meeting. How dare you? You're screwing him. Think we can't all see it? Go on, deny it. Worse still, you were screwing him while you were pregnant. As if that wasn't whorish enough, you bring him here, to your in-laws' house which, might I remind you, they offered you as an escape from the builder – the very toad of a builder who you have just screwed in their bed while the maid amuses your new-born. You really have sunk low and you ask what my problem is.'

Sam spluttered. 'I am NOT having an affair with him. Never heard such bullshit in all my life,' she shrieked, spit flying from her mouth.

'Oh, okay. Then explain to me why your builder, during a simple building meeting as you so righteously insist it was, needs to touch your face? Why did I just find you gagging for it like the filthy whore you are? And the unmade bed? Are you going to tell me you wanted to show him Mom's bed for building purposes, or what?'

She had no answer to that. Then I noticed two round damp patches on her shirt. Her boobs were leaking Ben's next meal. I could have vomited then and there.

'You were caught red-handed,' I continued. 'What do you take me for, the village idiot? You were also seen in public with him. You're still breastfeeding Sam – just how sick are you? For Christ's sake, you haven't even put your bra back on. Has George got a thing for breast milk? Fucking perverts, both of you.'

Sam's face dropped and her hands flew up to cover her milk-stained shirt. She was speechless.

'Stay out of my sight, and don't think for a minute I'm not going to tell Chris about you screwing the builder. Shit, it's a bit of a cliché, even you have to agree,' I said.

'WHO fucking saw me with him?' she suddenly screeched back. 'What ludicrous accusations! Go for it, Kat, you tell Chris how I was meeting with our builder to make sure the house gets finished so we can finally have some privacy and a family home again. Tell him that. Tell him what you bloody want, but I am not – NOT – shagging George.'

'Oh, whatever. There you go again, whining and moaning like a poor, hard-done-by princess. I've met some spoilt brats and divas in my time but you take the cake, Sam. No wonder Chris goes out and gets pissed at every chance he gets. Why would he want to come home to a nagging, whining wife who permanently has a face like a slapped arse? A lying, cheating wife who screws the builder when nine months pregnant?'

'Well, at least I am not permanently fucked on painkillers and walking around with a black eye looking like a victim of domestic violence.' Sam was now all-out shouting, her face inches from mine.

'Screw you, Sam. I'm done with you. I knew from day one that you were trouble, a shallow little brat. We all knew. You were never worthy of our trust, let alone respect. The big question now, of course, is, who is Ben's father? In fact, it has already been discussed in this family.'

Sam's hand came flying up in a blur and, before I could duck, she hit me. Not just a slap, she took a full swing at me with her fist. Her knuckles landed bang centre on my black eye. I stepped backwards, unsure if she'd keep coming at me in her fiery rage. I felt a trickle of blood on my cheek and reeling from the pain, with my hand over my eye, I turned and walked off. Sam stood frozen, her hands over her open mouth.

'Oh my God, I am so sorry Kat,' she shouted after me. 'Please, can we talk about this like adults?'

'You wish you were an adult, Sam, but you're just a common little tart who will never grow up. Get a grip,' I shouted over my shoulder. Much as I wanted to go back and finish the round, I wasn't going to sink to her levels.

'Kat, wait, please. I never meant to hit you.' I kept walking, hearing her dissolve into loud sobs.

I went down to my cottage to put some ice on my eye which was swelling fast. Shit, now my face really was a mess, I thought, assessing the damage in the mirror. With a blinding headache, I knocked back four painkillers as well as a tranquilliser, then sucked hard on a cigarette. I tried to repair my face with make-up, not wanting to go back to work looking like I'd been in a bar brawl. I sat on my bed for a while, replaying the fight. It had been so bizarre that part of me wondered if it had really happened. Wondering what to do about Sam and not sure if I should tell Chris right away, I phoned Grandpa to see what he suggested. He answered right away.

'KitKat! How's my KitKat?' he asked, in high spirits.

'Oh Grandpa, shit, what a mess!' With that, I burst into tears.

'Kat? My God, are you okay? What's happened?'

Between the tears, I described the fight.

'Holy shit balls! She punched you? Wait until I get hold of her, bloody little brat. And still she denies shagging George.' Grandpa was livid.

'What do I do Grandpa? What do I say to Chris? And my face is so bloody sore now I can barely think straight. Why couldn't she have decked me on the other, bruise-free, side?'

'I'm going to chat to your mother. It's time we put her in the picture. Sam is clearly out of control. I don't think the kids should even be around her if she is that unstable. Try to compose yourself, sweetheart, and get back to work. We'll sort it out, don't worry.'

I was still in shock as I drove back to work, but there was no time to stew with so much to do. Nobody seemed to notice the extra layer of make-up hiding the freshly revived black eye, and I managed to place my order for the gifts. Talk about blood money.

17

Mom and Grandpa decided to come to town that weekend, specifically for a heart-to-heart with Chris. Mom asked him to be home on Friday evening but didn't say why. Sam was apparently going to some kitchen tea so at least she wouldn't be around. I hadn't said anything to Chris. Sam had repeatedly tried to talk to me, but I kept blocking her. The mere sight of her disgusted me. To think of her rolling around in the hay with that weasel made me want to puke.

Then things suddenly changed. On Friday afternoon, Chris called me at work to say Sam and the kids were going to live with her parents for a while. It was an informal separation of sorts. I wasn't sure whose idea it had been but agreed it seemed sensible. I still didn't say anything about the fight, knowing we would discuss it later.

That evening, Chris was not shocked in the slightest to hear about George, to our surprise.

'She's definitely shagging that arsehole,' Chris said. 'I picked up on it ages ago. I can't believe she hit you though, Kat. She's unbelievable.'

'Was bloody sore,' I said. 'Still is. I said some pretty nasty things to her, I must admit.'

'Pfft!' said Grandpa. 'Every word deserved, I'm sure.'

'Why didn't you come to me right away?' Chris said.

'Didn't know what to say or how to say it,' I shrugged.

'She's hit me too,' said Chris. 'She's got such a vicious temper. Not just light smacks, also blows. Nothing ladylike about that kind of behaviour. God help her if she ever tries it in front of the kids.'

'She hits you Chris, seriously?' asked Mom, horrified.

'Yup, often.'

'For God's sake! What is wrong with the woman?' said Grandpa.

'She's round the bend. For the record, I've never laid a finger on her in return. I just take it,' said Chris. 'I'm not sure when she started screwing him, but suspect it was just after we started building'

'Ah. That brings me to the next question and there is no delicate way to say this,' said Mom, 'but is Ben your child?'

'I believe so, yes. Sam had never actually met that fuckwit until we signed the building contract, which means she was very definitely pregnant when it started,' said Chris.

'Shame on her,' said Grandpa. Apart from the odd expression of disgust, Grandpa was being unusually quiet. When Grandpa piped down, you knew he was totally distraught.

My heart ached for Chris. He was tired, broken and depressed. All his spark and fire had gone. My brother seemed to have gone from a lively, naughty, adventurous young man to a sad bloke with a failing marriage and two small kids. Sam had killed something in him, his spirit was barely to be seen.

'So, Chris, what now?' asked Mom.

'Well, she can stay at her folks for as long as she wants, but I still need to see my kids. Although Sam denies any affair with George, I'm terminating his contract tomorrow and he can whistle for any further payment. A friend at work has recommended another builder and I'll see if he can finish the job. Then I'll move back home and we'll see how things are between us then.' Chris sighed and ran his fingers through his hair. He looked grey and haggard. It hit me how much he'd aged recently.

We all sat there, mulling things over.

'She's the mother of my children,' added Chris. 'I just don't know what's got into her lately. I've been trying to pinpoint when she became such a miserable cow.'

'She's got father issues,' said Mom, matter-of-factly.

'Oh yes. Big time,' agreed Chris. 'A daddy's girl through and through, but her airs and graces don't wash with me. It's just attention-seeking behaviour. She needs to be adored and put on her little throne. George just happened to be the horny goat who came along and saw his chance. He's married too, you know. I wonder what his poor wife thinks.'

'I'll bet your George is a serial adulterer,' said Grandpa. 'Still though, what goes around comes around and he'll get his due one day.'

'Quite. And it was Sam's father who recommended him. Fine bloody idea that was,' said Chris.

We left the discussion as there wasn't much more to say. For Katie and Ben, I hoped they could get past the affair. I had my doubts.

The next morning, Mom and I decided to ride together, something we'd not done in ages. Our property had such beautiful trails which we hadn't yet explored properly and our neighbours were happy for us to ride up to their dam too. It was a breathtaking late-autumn morning, the crisp air making our breath dance in silvery smoky twirls. Patches of grass were silver with frost and the trees were starting to look bare. A mongoose, busy on his breakfast run, dashed across the dirt track while African doves and guinea fowl announced the start of the day. They were farm sounds and made me slightly melancholy. A squawking crow made me smile, remembering Grandpa's many crow funerals. So much had changed.

We plodded down a track side by side.

Mom asked, 'Sweetheart, are you able to tell yet if those nerve injections are working?'

'Umm, hard to say. The headaches are slightly less hectic than before, if that means anything. I'm still taking the painkillers.'

'Sticking to the correct dose now, I hope?'

'Yup.'

'Not taking them on a "just in case" basis?'

'Nope, I take them only once the headache starts.'

It was not entirely true. From time to time, just the thought of a headache would see a few 'just in case' pills disappearing into my gob. I just didn't want to get into it with Mom and have her roll out another lecture, which she then did anyway.

'I've said it before and will say it again – be bloody careful with those pills, Kat. You don't want to go there.'

'Mom, I know. Actually, talking of all that, I've been meaning to ask you about Maddie. How's she doing?' It was an obvious subject change but was worth a shot.

Maddie had finally gone to rehab last year after they scraped the money together for six months in treatment in South Africa and she was a new woman. She'd put on weight and didn't look like a toast rack anymore, and had a light in her eyes that was wonderful to see, as if curtains in a dingy room had been pulled back. Pete was a new man too, now his mother wasn't a walking talking wildcard.

Maddie and Kevin had been among the first in our district to lose their farm. They'd received their formal eviction notification in the form of a Section Eight and, having little choice in the matter, they'd packed up their worldly possessions and moved to Harare. The last thing they'd wanted was violence so, while it went against the grain, they'd walked away quietly and safely.

Pete had amazed everyone with fantastic A Level results and had gone to the UK after school, cashing in his English birthright to join the Royal Air Force. We all missed him terribly. He'd recently got engaged to a gorgeous South African girl, Meg, also an RAF pilot. We couldn't have been more thrilled. He'd matured into an extremely good-looking man but was so awkward around girls, we'd once wondered if he might actually prefer boys. Deep down, I longed for our little gang to be together again – Chris, Pete, Rolo, Ela and me – without all the drama, spouses, kids and complicated adult stuff.

'Maddie has started working again, would you believe?' said Mom. 'She got a great receptionist job at a veterinary surgery here, in Harare, and loves it.'

'And Kevin?' I asked.

'He's also working for the veggie guys now. Dad used his contacts to get him an interview. Kevin is managing their citrus export division. It's the closest he can get to farming, though strictly speaking it's an office job. But he's very happy.'

'Did they manage to get everything off the farm before it was taken?'

'Pretty much, except some of the heavy machinery. But they themselves got off safely, which is all we can hope for.'

'I'm so glad they're okay. Remember the days when Maddie was a complete liability and always wasted.'

'Well, you go easy on those pills or you'll end up like that too, madam.'

'Yes Mom!'

'And did I tell you Maddie's doing a lot of work with NA?'

'No. Remind me, what's NA?'

'Narcotics Anonymous. Like AA, but for the junkies, the drug addicts.'

'So does Maddie qualify as a junkie?'

'Most certainly. A pharmaceutical junkie. It's not just street drugs that make a good junkie.'

'What's she doing at NA? How does it work?'

'It's much the same as AA really. She still goes to some of the AA meetings – addicts and alcoholics can cross over – but NA is more her thing. She chairs one of the meetings and visits people detoxing in hospital, people who can't go to a real rehab. She gives them counselling based on her experience, plus she sponsors two other girls.'

'Sponsors?'

'A sponsor is the person we turn to on a one-on-one private basis. They're normally further down the line in their Recovery and they hear our nitty-gritty, our hairy-scary issues not fit for public consumption. Sponsors, if they do it properly, kick our arses and take no shit.'

Lordie, I thought to myself, all this jargon.

'It's been amazing to see her transformation,' said Mom. 'There were days Linda and I thought she'd OD.'

'Overdose?'

'Yup. She was suicidal at one point. Even tried slashing her wrists, but she made a crap knife decision. It was way too blunt.'

'Mom! How can you joke like that?'

'I can only joke because she survived it all. We alcoholic addict nutjobs do need a solid sense of humour.'

'I'll never forget that Christmas lunch when Maddie said she was curious about having sex with a woman.'

'Talking of that Christmas lunch, I always meant to ask what you kids did to the gravy?'

I started laughing aloud. 'It was Chris and Pete, they dumped weed in my gravy.'

'Mmm, thought so. Little buggers!' she said, laughing too. 'Anyway, how are things with Ant?'

'Yup, all fine. He also saw me looking worse for wear on TV at the cricket, which caused a major argument. It's blown over now over, but shit, I miss him. I've no idea when I'll see him next.'

'I'm not sure I could handle a long-distance relationship.'

'It sucks Ma but what can I do? He loves his job up in the Valley. *C'est la vie.*'

We walked on, the horses ambling down the farm roads as the climbing sun warmed the nippy air, promising a beautiful clear day. I never grew tired of Africa's vibrant backdrop and could not imagine living anywhere else. A group of farm kids, all giggles and bright toothy smiles, passed us on their way to the dam, strutting along proudly with their rough bamboo fishing rods and rusty cans full of damp soil and worms.

Savouring the long-overdue mother–daughter bonding session, we sat on the banks of the dam for a while, watching the birds and ducks flitting across the shimmering water and thinking of ours back on the farm, soon to be a war veteran's dam.

Grandpa and I spent the morning on the patio with the newspapers, coffee and cricket on TV in the background. Mom had brought more stuff in from the farm. The Umwinsidale house was getting fuller and fuller as the phased evacuation played out.

She plonked a huge box full of old photos in my lap. 'Here. Please organise these according to years and categories, if you can.'

'Hell Mom, there must be over five hundred photos in here,' I said, peering into it.

'No rush,' said Mom, with a grin.

The task became one big trip down memory lane. Grandpa's old photos were in the box too. I came across the photo taken in Malawi that had made me stop and stare before, the one of Mom as a teenager at a Malange Club party looking so haunted. Something about her face in that photo was definitely off. She had a dead expression in her eyes, a sadness that practically jumped off the paper it was so tangible. I decided to ask her about it.

In the study, I found her doing filing, crumpled papers flying over her shoulder onto a growing pile of rubbish.

'Mom, tell me about this photo? What's the story here, why so sad?'

She took the picture from me and sat staring at it for a long time. Her face was difficult to read. 'Wow, this takes me right back. I remember that party well. It wasn't long after that bastard raped me and I was having a hard time coming to terms with it.'

She ran her index finger gently over her own face in the photo. I thought I saw tears in her eyes and got the distinct feeling she wanted to say something more. In an instant she pulled herself back to the present and swiftly changed the subject by asking what we wanted for lunch.

I went back to sorting the photos, intrigued. Granted, I hadn't been raped myself and therefore had no idea of the trauma Mom had experienced, but suspected there was more to it, suspected another story was hidden in that photograph. Obviously, I wasn't going to find out today. I quickly slid the photo into a magazine of mine, to keep for myself.

Grandpa came over to me. 'And why are you sitting there gazing into space?'

'Just looking at all these old photos,' I said.

'Come on then, I'll help you. And, as it's now lunchtime, go find us a nice chilled bottle of wine and let's clobber that and this box together.'

We spent a few hours on the photo exercise, enjoying the memories and a crisp Chardonnay. Mom had gone for an afternoon nap so it was just Grandpa and me, bonding over a box of past lives and different eras. Grandpa told me such wonderful, colourful stories about the various people. I knew many, but there were a few more photos of Mom from the same period in Malawi, looking like a condemned prisoner. I wanted to know more, but my gut told me not to broach it with Grandpa. One day the story will come out, I thought, and I know there is one. Another story.

18

'Fancy a trip to see your other half?' Stephen said, grinning like a kid.

I looked up from my proofreading work, my red pen as exhausted as I was, to see Stephen standing in front of my desk flapping an airline ticket.

'A trip?' I asked, seeing my name on the ticket.

'Yup. I need you to fly up to Vic Falls and start getting all the ground-work in place for Congress. Think you can handle this for me, Kat?'

'Absolutely!' I was thrilled, it was a fantastic assignment and a big responsibility.

'Good stuff. Better start setting up your meetings. I need you to meet with everyone, right down to whoever will clean loos at Congress – the whole shindig has to be flawless. You leave the day after tomorrow and you'll have two nights at the lodge. And, as a thank you, stay on and spend the weekend with Ant.'

I spent the whole day grinning. Just a few days ago, Ant and I were moaning about how long we'd been apart.

I was one happy bunny stepping off the plane in Vic Falls into the warm sun and Ant's arms. It was pure luck that he was at base as he'd had a last-minute cancellation. The next two days disappeared in a whirlwind of meetings but, by Saturday morning, I'd double-checked every detail on my twenty-page checklist. I called Stephen with an update, pleased with what I had achieved, and I then knocked off for the weekend – finally getting to spend time with Ant.

That afternoon, we went for a long walk down to the Falls through the lush rainforest, standing as close to the edge of the deep ravine as possible, drenched by the spray. It's really one of the most wondrous sights and, for me, it rated way up there with a Kariba sunset.

We ambled onto the bridge over the gorge where Ant's friends operated the infamous bungee jump. A group of Germans was queuing to jump, all white socks and Jesus sandals. Ant's friend casually said it wasn't unusual for crocodiles to jump up, with snapping jaws, while the person was dangling just above the rapids. The anxious pacing up and down the bridge that followed gave us the best laugh we'd had in ages.

We slowly made our way back through the rainforest as the sun set. Standing in the spray, tasting the natural, sweet water as it ran down our faces, we could have been the only people in the world, completely lost in each other. Even after so many years, there remained an intense chemistry between Ant and me, a magnetic pull as strong as it had been when we were sixteen. All the silly fights and challenges of our long-distance relationship faded, and I realised just how much I loved him.

Back at Ant's house, I went to soak in the bath, taking a glass of wine. I was exhausted, but deeply happy to have spent a few days with him. The only dampener had been the dry, dusty heat, which had sent my head into a spin and I'd spent the past two days throwing back painkiller after painkiller just to be able to function. I'd had more nerve-blocker injections and even worse black eyes and, while they had helped a bit, I was by no means living a pain-free life. I had noticed a persistent tenderness in my stomach. Even when taken with food, the pills definitely hammered my gut. Realising I was heading into a pity party all of my own, I quickly squashed all 'poor me' thoughts, got out of the bath and pulled on a dress that was probably far too sexy for a night out in Vic Falls. I didn't care.

Ant and I had the perfect evening. He'd arranged a private dining table on the deck of the fanciest lodge in town. It overlooked a waterhole, and had the Zambezi roaring towards the Falls as the backdrop. A herd of elephants came up to drink right below us, while some comical warthogs and baboons ferreted around among them. Pain aside, life felt good. The time with Ant had restored my soul and put my fears to rest. We were okay. I took a long deep breath, suddenly realising I hadn't really been happy in ages. The headaches and injections, the dramas with Sam and Chris, the worry about the farm being taken – it had all been wearing me down more than I realised.

After dinner, Ant and I went into town to meet his mates. Vic Falls had a beer fest on and it was always a legendary party that drew people from far and wide. We got to it with a bottle of wine already under our belts. It was bizarre how Ant never passed comment about my drinking when we were together. It definitely was something that irked him more when I partied on my own. We arrived to find at least four hundred people in two marquees partying up a storm. It was pretty wild and a bit scruffy. I wondered about going home to change out of my slinky dress, then figured if I was going to party up a storm, I may as well do it in style. Secretly, I think Ant loved how I stood out from the crowd.

I'd met most of Ant's friends before but there were a few new faces. Disconcertingly, a particular group of girls seemed awfully familiar with Ant. One girl, Jess, was especially fascinated with him, clearly pissed off that I, the girlfriend, had shown my face in her town. It started a niggle in the back of my mind. Despite all the water under the bridge, I'd never forgotten how Ant had cheated on me at university. Jess, already plastered, was clearly a giggly airhead, her jeans so tight I wondered how she could even walk. Then Ant introduced us, which was when she officially got on my nerves.

'Oh yes, Kat, I recognise you,' said Jess. 'You got rat faced and flashed your red knickers on TV at cricket a few weeks back.'

'Yeah, something like that. Unfortunately, the cameras missed the part where I snorted a line of coke and flashed my tits,' I said, sarcasm dripping. She was flummoxed by my reply and I could see the effort it took for her to process my comment.

One of Ant's friends beside me snorted with laughter. 'Ignore her,' he said quietly to me. 'She's like a really bad smell that follows us around.'

'Are you sure she isn't the smell herself?' I replied, loud enough for her to hear.

Within an hour of arriving, and after three vodkas in quick succession, I started to feel the ground lurching beneath my feet. Our group drifted outside where a joint was going around in the car park. I only took a short puff, not wanting to end the evening early by passing out cold. Jess got high as a kite and was brazenly coming onto Ant right before my eyes, touching him at every chance. Sending a not-so-subtle message, I very seductively leant into Ant, ran my hands up inside his shirt and started a hot and heavy make-out session, straddling him on a car bonnet right next to Jess. Ant certainly wasn't complaining and neither were his friends, but Jess stropped off in such a flounce we all collapsed into giggles.

Back inside, Ant and I were on the dance floor when I suddenly heard someone shrieking at me.

'Kat! Kaaaaat! Over here KitKAAAT.'

In the sea of faces, I saw Vicky sitting on a guy's shoulders, swinging a beer bottle in the air. 'Holy shit, Vicks! What are you doing here?' I laughed.

'Kat, remember Jake?' she said, jumping off his shoulders.

How could I forget Andrew's divine cousin who'd saved my head from an incoming cricket ball.

'We heard about the beer fest and, spur of the moment, decided to drive up. I hoped I'd find you here. How're you Antelope?' said Vicky, drunkenly stumbling into Ant for a hug.

'You drove all the way here for the beer fest?' asked Ant. 'I do love a dedicated party girl.'

'Yeah, why not? Only live once and blah blah!' Vicky laughed.

She and Jake stayed with our group and, after a few more trips to the car park for joint, the night grew steadily more raucous. Vicky and I managed to make the persistent Jess clear off with a few more evil comments, while Jake and Ant got on like a house on fire. Just before dawn, Ant and I weaved our way home.

I woke later that morning and stumbled through to the kitchen for water, my tongue stuck to the roof of my mouth, feeling like I might die. Vicky and Jake were passed out on the couch and I spotted the irritating Jess sleeping in one of the bedrooms, sandwiched between two of Ant's mates. Many more half-naked bodies lay around the house at awkward angles and in odd places. It was the normal beer fest aftermath. Empty bottles and full ashtrays suggested there'd been a notable after-party, yet I had absolutely no recollection of it.

With every step I felt worse and, within minutes, my face was firmly pointed down the loo. I vomited my guts out and my head was about to explode. I tried drinking a flat Coke which merely did a whistle-stop tour of my stomach, making its exit minutes later. Ant came into the bathroom, finding me on the floor hugging the loo.

'If you're finished talking to the Great God of Shanks, can I pee sweetheart?' he grunted.

I crawled out, allowing Ant to pee. I held my bile in long enough for him to flush and then quickly resumed my position, not trusting myself to be more than a few centimetres away.

'Ant,' I said in a feeble voice, 'I'm sick.'

'I know, I can see that darling. You don't look too sparky, but show me one person who went to that beer fest and is not sick this morning.'

'You're not sick though,' I burbled, the words falling out of my mouth in a string of shocking pronunciation. Word gloop.

'I feel fucking awful actually. I'm in two minds about having a vom myself, once you stop hugging the loo.'

Ant joined me on the bathroom floor, the two of us looking like down-and-out scumbags. It must have been quite a funny sight, though laughing was too traumatic a movement to even consider.

'Kat, you had a skinful last night but it will pass. You need to be at the airport in a few hours, so try get yourself together. Can I bring you anything?'

'See if you can find painkillers in my bag, won't you, hun?'

Hauling himself up, Ant found my bag and tossed my bottle of pills over, but not before taking three himself. I swallowed six. Bugger the correct dosage, I thought. I needed relief fast if I was going to catch that plane. Ant just looked at me, shocked. Saying nothing, he got a damp facecloth and placed it on my forehead.

I made it back to bed where Ant gently mopped my brow. With my head on his chest, I prepared for my impending death.

'Babe, you really don't look well. I had far more than you did last night and I'm not feeling half as bad. You're burning up too. I think you're running a temperature.'

'Super,' I mumbled.

'Malaria couldn't hit so fast. Perhaps you have a bug. Or tick fever.'

'Again, super.'

'Do you want me to take you to hospital?'

'No.' It was all I could manage, more word gloop. In my head, I recited the global mantra of the hungover – *Let me live and I'll never drink again.*

'Think you can manage a shower or shall I come with you, my sweet little drama queen?'

'Oh, ha ha! You with the iron-clad guts, come shower with me. I might drown in there,' I replied.

We both got in the shower and I leant on Ant, barely able to pick up the soap. After tenderly shampooing my hair, he wrapped me in a big fluffy towel. I sat on the bed while he rummaged in my bag to find knickers, a bra, and fresh clothes.

I saw Vicky lumbering past our bedroom door, looking dazed and confused.

'Vick!' I shouted, instantly regretting raising my voice as the pain ripped through my head. She turned ever so slowly, one hand on her head, the other on the wall to steady herself and a lit cigarette hanging from her mouth.

'Ah. Kat. That answers my question,' said Vicky.

'What question?'

'Where the fuck am I, would have been the question,' she said, coming in and lying next to me on the bed, letting out a big groan. 'So, KitKat, how do we rate this one?'

We always rated our hangovers on a scale of 1 to 10. Today, Vicky settled for an 8.7 and I opted for a 9.3.

'Good girl! You've not had a nine in ages!' she said. We attempted to high five it but were so broken that our palms were miles apart, and Vicky dropped her cigarette on the duvet.

'You two!' said Ant, laughing as he grabbed the cigarette and flicked it out the window. 'Can't take you anywhere. You're both nutters.'

Vicky and I lay on the bed in silence for a while, watching Ant pack my suitcase, ready for the airport.

'Impressive,' Vicky said to me.

'What is?'

'Your manservant,' she said, pointing at Ant. 'He's bloody hot, your Antelope. I especially like his T-shirt folding.'

I chuckled, both of us lying there flat on our backs like Lady Mucks.

'Oi, Fiddlypoop,' Vicky said to Ant. 'I ain't got no bag to pack 'cos I only brought a change of knickers – do you fancy driving me back to Harare? Shit – an eight-hour drive home with this hangover. KitKat, do you think Jake would mind if I bought a ticket, flew home with you, and let him drive my car back to Harare?'

'Urr, yes, Vicks! He'd mind. You'd never see him again. Didn't think this one through, did you?' I laughed.

'Yeah, yeah. Rub it in, you tart with an airline ticket.'

'Well, Doctor Antelope says I've got tick fever, a tummy bug, and a hangover, so please get your arse back to Harare as there might well be a funeral,' I said.

'Right, in that case I shall leave now and order the wreath. White lilies, okay?'

'Perfect. Just no chrysanthemums. They smell shite,' I replied.

'But you'll be dead in the box,' said Vicky.

'Okay, now you two really are talking complete shit,' interrupted Ant.

With a loud groan, Vicky gingerly hauled herself up and went to find Jake. I heard her bumping into Jess in the corridor.

'Oh lookey here. It's The Jess. Jess The Mess. Jess Who Shags For Less,' said Vicky disdainfully, hamming it up with her posh British accent. 'Shouldn't you be in a kennel or something?'

I was pissing myself laughing before the pain of moving my face forced me to stop. Vicky really was in a league of her own. If I didn't have work the next day, and if I wasn't dying, I'd have driven home with her and Jake just for the laughs.

Starting to feel marginally better, I was tempted to drift into a painkiller coma, but missing my flight was not an option. There was nothing for it but to soldier on and hope it was only a bad hangover.

Ant got me to the airport just as my flight was boarding. I ran onto the runway and up the stairs, every step torturous. Collapsing into my seat, I was asleep before we took off, waking only as we touched down and the pilot had started the Harare weather report. I wouldn't have noticed if we'd flown into a hurricane.

It took me five days to recover from the trip, or rather, the beer fest. It was to go down as one of my best hangovers yet, but it remained a mystery as to why I, the more sober one, had gone down in flames and not Ant. I knew I didn't have tick fever as the headaches seemed normal for me – how sad that my headaches provided a benchmark for normality.

For days I pondered the severity of my hangover and then had an epiphany. It was the first time I'd drunk heavily since starting my nerve-blocker injections. Maybe the medication, booze and smidgen of joint were not a winning combination. It was all I could put it down to but I couldn't exactly phone the neurosurgeon and say, 'Hey Doc, so would it be a train smash to do a spot of drinking and weed on top of your injections?' It passed eventually but was a lesson learnt.

19

'I'm here to see Dr Jackson, please,' I said to the guard at the gate. I'd finished a meeting early and decided to check in on Ela.

At her little flat, I knocked but there was no response and so I let myself in. Ela was sitting with Chris on her patio in the afternoon sun. They hadn't heard me and, just as Mojo woofed to alert Ela, I was sure I noticed a quick flurry of hands. Well, bugger me, I thought, wondering who was making moves on who.

'Hello girls,' I said in a bright voice.

'Kat!' said Ela, smiling.

I gave her a hug and winked at Chris. 'Any danger of some juice? And then I want to hear all the news.'

Chris went to get drinks and, as soon as he was out of earshot, Ela asked me about Sam. 'Can't believe that little bitch. He's distraught. I could kill her.'

'You should see that George character – he's as slippery as snot on a doorknob. Did you hear how she clobbered my eye?'

'Yup, and I don't know how you managed to restrain yourself and not reply with a right hook and a drop kick to the fanny.'

'Little slag,' I muttered, rubbing my eye absentmindedly.

'How's that eye feeling now?' asked Chris, coming back out and handing me a juice.

'Definitely still tender. Now tell me what's happening with Sam.'

'I've fired George's slimy arse. He had the audacity to get aggressive, and made threats about suing me for breach of contract. The cunning part is that I, on purpose, never signed a contract with him so he hasn't got a leg to stand on. I also reminded him that he'd played a part in breaching my matrimonial contract and told him to go shit in his hat. The funny part is that he still denies the affair, yet Sam has now admitted to it. You'd think they'd get their stories straight, huh?'

'And Sam?' Ela asked.

'She says she's in love with him and he's going to leave his wife. He's playing her good and proper. She honestly thinks she has a future with him.'

'Wait – so she actually wants a full-on relationship? She's willing to end her marriage for him?' I was shocked.

'Yup, and she thinks that's gonna happen,' said Chris. 'I know his type. He has absolutely no intention of leaving his wife. He's having his cake and eating it, and right now that cake is my wife.'

'You know what they say: If a man marries his mistress it creates a vacancy,' said Ela.

'Precisely. Oh, and I heard on the grapevine that George had an affair with another pregnant woman years ago. Do you know that having sex with a heavily pregnant woman is a borderline fetish? So, with Sam no longer pregnant, I don't reckon he'll stick around for long.'

'Yuk. It's just so gross,' said Ela.

'He really is a horrible bastard. Cold cold cold. He probably farts hail,' said Chris.

I couldn't help but laugh. 'Sam's the ultimate hail farter. Always been an ice queen, and she clearly has a liking for the bad-boy type,' I said.

'Bad boy? You girls always see things from a different angle,' said Chris.

'She's right,' said Ela. 'You were once the bad-boy type yourself.'

'Me?' said Chris, his eyebrows shooting up.

'Definitely! In your teens you were the biggest and baddest rebel, always up to something,' said Ela. 'But you did the honourable thing in marrying Sam. You stepped up to the plate. However, Sam has slowly sucked you dry of all your spark. Therefore, no more bad boy, by her own doing, and she's had to find herself a new one. Well, that's my take on it anyway.'

Chris looked at me with a questioning expression.

'Go Doctor Jackson. The shrink is in the house,' I said laughing. 'Seriously though, Chris, Ela has hit the nail on the head.'

'Would you ever take her back?' Ela asked.

'Nope. I could probably forgive her in time but I'd never trust her again. Without trust there's nothing,' replied Chris.

'She could have had it all,' Ela said wistfully.

'The builder's no oil painting, but I can see he'd be able to talk the knickers off a nun,' I told Ela.

'Urgh, sounds like such a pig,' said Ela. 'You should report him. Isn't there a builders' council or watchdog group?'

'Nah. But you know how quickly rumours spread. By the time I'm finished, George will never lay another brick in this town, or lay another man's wife for that matter,' said Chris.

'And your divorce process now?' asked Ela.

Chris sighed, looking twenty years older. 'My lawyer is working out shared custody arrangements. My boss is a divorced father himself, and is happy for me to work from home in the afternoons when Katie is back from crèche. It's trickier with Ben as he's still breastfeeding, but we'll work it out. For now, I go to Sam's folks' place to visit, which is horribly awkward. Her father looks like he wants to chop my bollocks off, meanwhile it was Sam who had the affair. She's still got him wrapped around her little finger.'

'And her mother?' Ela asked.

'Well, surprisingly, Jean seems to be on my side,' said Chris. 'She came to me in the garden one day and said she'd tried to talk some sense into Sam, to get her to ditch "that fuckwit George" as she called him. Jean is under no illusions about her daughter's behaviour, in fact she called her a stupid little trollop.'

'That's putting it mildly,' said Ela.

'Agh, it's all just such a mess,' sighed Chris.

Mojo lifted her head and gave a soft bark. James, Ela's colleague, had come in the back door.

'Sorry Ela, I didn't realise you had visitors,' said James.

'Hey! James, come join us. You've met my friend, Kat. This is her brother Chris. Have a seat,' Ela said.

'Hello again Kat, nice to meet you Chris,' he said, shaking hands with Chris.

Chris got up to get more drinks and James sat next to Ela, lighting a cigarette. I was amazed at how effortlessly he did so. If I had to light a ciggie with my eyes closed, I'd lose my eyelashes.

'Right, enough of our family dramas, we shan't bore you, James,' I said. 'I actually came to find out how things have been going for you, Ela.'

'Two words – loving it,' she said. 'James has been amazing, showing me the ropes.'

Having walked in on an intimate moment between Chris and Ela, I watched Ela and James together and noticed some chemistry there too. I could see Chris had noticed it too and was probably a bit jealous.

James had only come to chat to Ela about an art class and didn't stay long.

'He seems lovely, huh?' I said to Ela once he'd gone.

'He's such a sweetie,' said Ela.

'He's really good-looking too. Pity you can't ogle him. Incredible body, I might add,' I said.

'I know,' said Ela.

Aha! There was only one way Ela could tell a guy was in good shape and that was with her hands.

Later, as I was leaving, Ela roped me into doing her a favour. 'I have one or two kids with family members in AA and NA. It occurred to me that I should go to one of those meetings to get some insight. Can you take me sometime?'

'Sure.' My tone was a bit wary though. Suddenly, a tiny paranoid part of me thought I was being ambushed because I was scoffing too many painkillers. I quickly reeled in my mind. It was totally absurd. Ela wouldn't do that to me. I was just being neurotic.

Next, I swung past the pharmacy to replenish my stock of painkillers. The usual pharmacist was on leave but a locum served me, a young guy who looked fresh out of school. He called up my profile and then came to the front of the shop, taking me to one side for a private chat.

'You're not due a repeat yet, Miss Hay, and I see your last refill was early too,' he said. 'If you are using so much more than what's been prescribed, I suggest you chat to your doctor about revising the dosage.'

I batted my eyelashes at him. Suddenly pleased I was wearing a low-cut top, I leant forward slightly to boost my cleavage. 'Yes, I know, sorry. It's just that I suffer terribly from headaches.' A lie then rolled off my tongue with alarming ease. 'I actually have quite a few left but I'm going to be travelling a fair bit so just wanted to stock up in advance.'

'Okay, as a favour I'll dispense fifty tablets but I won't log it in the system. I suffer with migraines and take these same meds, so can sympathise,' he said.

What a nice guy, I thought. 'Ah you're a godsend,' I said in a slightly vampy voice and touched his arm. My heart was racing. I'd had a moment of sheer panic that almost paralysed me, thinking I'd be left high and dry without my painkillers. Fifty pills on the side was hardly an exciting catch, but better than nothing.

Vastly relieved as he handed me the packet, I got out of there fast. Later, when I opened the packet, I saw he'd slipped in a note with his phone number: *If you run short give me a call, Colin.* I didn't quite know what to make of it, but was pretty sure he was breaking every last rule in the pharmacists' book, supplying scheduled drugs without a prescription. Or maybe he was hitting on me? Either way, I was somewhat taken aback but slipped his note into my wallet. Maybe one day I'd take him up on the offer, whatever the offer was.

I swallowed five pills to deal with the bad-head day that I'd had. Four no longer cut it for me, five weren't terribly effective either, but I was trying to cut back, or, rather, trying not increase things any further. I knew I was taking far too many pills. That said, the alternative was living in acute pain. Whether or not I was becoming dependent on the pills, I did not relish the thought of all-out migraines every day.

A few days later, Ela dragged me to an AA meeting as planned. It was much the same layout as the Al-Anon meeting. An assorted bunch – suited businessmen, twenty-something working girls, students, housewives, and pensioners with weathered faces – a story in themselves. Again, I was fascinated by the people and was dying to hear their stories. I tried to describe the crowd to Ela, though it was difficult to do so discreetly, and so she created mental images from the voices. Mojo was a big hit – the first dog to attend AA and the brunt of a few extremely lame one-liners like 'My name is Mojo and I binge-drink water'. I had to admire the alcoholics' ability to poke fun at themselves despite all the shit they'd been through.

The meeting started with the same introductions as Al-Anon – with names stated, the group replying with a sing-song hello, and the one-line mood status: I've been craving like hell; I feel wonderfully serene; my boss is about to drive me back to drink; I'd kill to get pissed tonight; I poured a drink today and just sat holding it for an hour; life is so much better now I am sober; I fucked up today and clobbered the gin.

Any mood, you name it, was in that hall, and they were rawer and a lot more tangible than the Al-Anon moods. It struck me that at least half the people were struggling with cravings to get snot-flying drunk and were generally finding sobriety a challenge.

Meanwhile, Ela was absorbing every sound in that hall and had probably picked up far more than I had. She had an amazing knack of noticing every nuance and lilt in speech and could discern the facial expression that had accompanied the words. Just a frown or smile changed the spoken word and, since becoming a counsellor, she'd become even better at detecting body language delivered through speech.

After the readings of AA Traditions and 12 Steps, the chairman introduced the speaker.

'Hi. My name is Sasha and I'm an alcoholic and addict. Tonight, a grateful recovering one,' she said.

Although Mom and Maddie were in Recovery, I still had the perception of alcoholics being scruffy, dirty buggers. Again, I was wrong. In her thirties, Sasha was an elegant woman wearing designer jeans, a crisp white T-shirt, chunky beads, silver bangles and pretty sandals. With faint lines around her eyes, she had the face of a woman who had many stories to tell. She was strangely familiar and, out of nowhere, I got a weird flash, like a sixth sense, that I was staring at myself in ten years' time. I promptly dismissed the thought as stupid. I wasn't an alcoholic and certainly didn't need any counselling for chemical-dependence issues.

With five years' sobriety under her belt, Sasha's story intrigued me from the start. Her upbringing had been fairly normal, with a good education and a degree in art. University had included the usual drunken shenanigans of student life. In her late twenties, she'd married the man of her dreams but he'd turned into an alcoholic and a beast, regularly hitting her. When he, his brother, and their cousin gang-raped her, she walked out, her young baby in tow. Traumatised by the abuse and wanting to feel numb, she started a long and passionate affair with booze and narcotics. Much as her parents and friends tried to get her help, she preferred her haze of vodka, pills, and denial. It didn't take long for her to lose her daughter. Her parents adopted the child when it became clear that Sasha was just an all-round liability.

Sasha described how she'd go on five-day binges, sleeping where she fell – which was often in a ditch or car park. Her parents tried 'tough love' but still she refused to admit to the problem so they cut the money off. She promptly resorted to petty crime and even prostitution once or twice, utterly desperate for money to support her habit. She'd not been above pawning her mother's jewellery and the family silver, often stealing cash from wallets too. Sasha dabbled in heroin, and then happened upon a 'winner of a cocktail', as she called it – a mix of painkillers, tranquillisers and sleeping pills washed down with vodka and a joint. It put her firmly on another planet and became her way to dodge her demons.

Her rock bottom was waking up in another country with no idea how she'd got there. She'd come round in a Zambian backpackers' lodge, naked, with three men and a woman whose names she didn't know, and bent spoons, tinfoil, dirty syringes and other heroin paraphernalia everywhere. She had only her clothes on the floor and her passport – the stamp in it told her she'd been in Zambia for four days already. It was then that she admitted she needed help, that there was nothing left to lose and a lot to gain, if she sorted her shit out.

It took her many attempts to get and remain clean and sober. A major hurdle was the lack of a proper rehab and substance-abuse counsellors in Harare. Her doctor and shrink glibly prescribed medications to take the edge off her detox. Next thing she knew, they had prescribed so many heavy drugs that she was addicted to those too – a classic cross addiction. Off heroin, but addicted to pharmaceutical narcotics, she'd struggled to equate the pills with being a junkie. She said she'd only ever associated junkies with dirty needles, dodgy dealers and crack houses, not people who bought their fix in broad daylight in a pharmacy and got a receipt for it.

Involuntary tingles shot down my spine and I started fidgeting, finding it all a bit too close to home. Mojo stirred at my feet and looked at me. Christ Almighty, I thought, the bloody dog didn't miss a thing. Worse than my mother! Ela felt it too, but I simply pretended I was uncomfy in the hard chairs. What rattled me even further was that Sasha had looked me square in the eye, like she knew something I didn't. Fuck this, I thought, wishing I could get up and walk out.

Sasha continued, describing her journey in Recovery, the untold emotional and spiritual pain, the physical withdrawals and the permanent damage she'd done to her heart and kidneys. She'd had to make some very tough amends and her biggest hurdle now, even five years down the line, was rebuilding trust. She closed by saying that one day she planned to be a proper mother and a productive member of society, but that it was a hell of a lot harder than it sounded.

I couldn't help it. I had tears in my eyes, moved by Sasha's story. It had poked at my own insecurities and had roused fresh paranoia, but I'd learnt a great deal about the lives of those in Recovery. Many of my assumptions about AA and its members had been blown out of the water. I saw why Mom got so much out of the meetings. Again, I was struck by the fact that there was no preaching, just a safe and honest forum, a place to gain strength from others' experiences – with acceptance and unity in abundance. Guess that's why they call it a fellowship, I thought. Even as an outsider, I could see it was powerful stuff.

As we walked to the car, we bumped into Sasha who stopped to pat Mojo, telling Ela what a magnificent dog she was. Then, Sasha turned to me and suddenly pulled me into her arms in a huge hug.

'Hang in there. It's hard, painful and relentless work, but you can do it,' she said.

Immediately on the defensive, I replied, 'No, no! I'm not the junkie alcoholic. Ela is a counsellor and doing research.'

'Oh hell, I'm so sorry. I saw a familiar look in your eyes and a lot of pain, and thought you were trying to get sober and off the pills,' said Sasha.

Okay, now I was starting to resent this. Who did this woman think she was, making all these outlandish assumptions about me?

'Pills?' I replied, a little coldly.

'Forgive me for being invasive,' said Sasha, 'but people abusing pharmaceuticals tend to get a certain look in their eyes.'

'Nope, I'm all good thanks,' I said in a bristly tone. 'We honestly came here tonight for Ela.'

'My apologies then. I didn't mean to offend you. You take care girls, and good luck, Ela, with your counselling,' she said, walking to her car.

I was extremely quiet on the way home.

'That was a bit awkward,' said Ela.

'What?' I asked.

'Sasha assuming you're an addict.'

'Pissed me off actually, truth be told.' Deep down inside, the reality was that Sasha had touched a nerve but I didn't know how to process what I felt or get past the prickling sensation.

'Clearly this town needs a proper rehab,' Ela said, moving the chat away from me. 'I simply can't get over people suffering, dying even, from alcohol and drug abuse and yet no specialised care is available. It sounds like the doctors are just cowboy prescription writers.'

'Maybe this is your calling, Ela. Maybe Harare needs you to set up a rehab,' I said, half joking.

'That's what I was thinking actually. Maybe, one day.'

As Ela got out of the car, she leant over and squeezed my hand. 'I'm here for you, Kat, always.'

For fuck's sake, I thought, why is everyone acting like I'm terminally ill? I knew exactly what she was alluding to.

At home, I soaked for ages in the bath. I'd been feeling off colour for days, like I was coming down with flu – aching bones and a sore stomach too. I tried to push the noise and clutter of my busy day to the back of my mind, but failed. The thing with Sasha gnawed at me. I eventually plonked myself in front of the TV and tried to zone out with hot chocolate laced with a good dose of brandy. If I didn't fall asleep within the hour, I'd take some more painkillers and knock myself out. Sod it.

20

A week later, I was in a staff meeting when the boardroom door opened a crack and our receptionist stuck her nose in.

'Sorry to interrupt, Kat. There's an urgent call for you,' she said.

Stephen told me to take it. In my office, I noticed nine missed calls on my cellphone. The call was put through. It was Chris.

'Kat. Oh my God, I've been calling and calling. Are you busy?' He spoke so fast that his words were stumbling into each other, barely making any sense.

'Woah! Slow down. What's up?'

'Can you come to the hospital? It's Sam,' he said, almost hysterical. 'Please, I need you here.'

'What the hell has happened? Is she sick?' I was alarmed at the panic in Chris's voice.

'Car crash. Awful, awful, car crash. It's not good.'

'Shit. I'm leaving now,' I said, not even asking for details.

I grabbed my bag and went back into the boardroom. 'Sorry Stephen, my brother's wife has been in a terrible car crash and they need me at the hospital. Can you spare me?'

'Of course, go Kat. Call me with news when you can.'

I ran. I didn't even wait for the lift, bolting down eleven flights of stairs. I tried calling Chris again from the car but it just rang. Beside myself with worry and without any real details, my mind was running away with me. I decided to see if Mom knew what had happened. She answered right away. It was the first she was hearing about any accident. She and Grandpa were actually on their way into Harare to see their accountant, which I'd completely forgotten about. I promised to call as soon as I knew more.

I arrived at the hospital in record time, running straight to Casualty. Chris was in the family waiting room, his head in his hands and deathly pale. Sam's mom Jean came flying in behind me.

'Thank God you're here,' said Chris, hugging me and then Jean.

'Please tell me what's happened?' I was practically shrieking with hysteria myself. 'Where are the kids, Chris?'

'Kids are fine, they're at home. Sam and George were going to view a house to rent,' Chris said. 'A bus in the oncoming lane had a blowout. Witnesses say George was well over the speed limit. The bus driver lost control, but George swerved into it, and there was a head-on collision. The bus rolled and took the car with it, flipping down a small embankment. A third vehicle also got wiped out. So far, eight bus passengers are dead. George died on the scene and Sam just got here. She's in a coma and her injuries are extensive.'

I couldn't believe what I was hearing and had to replay the words in my head. *Bus, blowout, collision, George dead, eight dead, Sam coma.*

'Thank God I was babysitting,' Jean said flatly, shaking her head and dabbing her eyes.

I was still trying to absorb all the information and again recited the facts, muttering the words under my breath as if that would somehow bring clarity to the chaos. *Bus, death, Sam in coma, kids fine, kids at home, George not fine, George dead, passengers dead, lots of death, lots of dead.*

'What have the doctors said?' I asked.

'Both of Sam's legs are broken, one smashed to a pulp. They are trying to assess her internal injuries. There's massive head trauma and they think a rib may have punctured her lung. They are trying to stabilise her, then they'll move her to ICU,' Chris replied.

'Have you seen her?' I asked.

'They allowed me in briefly. There's a huge team working on her, I could barely see a person under all the blood. She has a huge gash across the side of her head. A chunk of her scalp was hanging like a piece of meat. Her left leg is pulverised. They are considering amputation.'

'And George is dead?'

'He probably died on impact. They're trying to inform his wife but she's out of town and her cellphone is off.'

I then asked, 'Is Sam going to make it?'

'Dunno. They can't say. They've asked us not to go far from this waiting room,' Chris said.

Jean, in shock, just sat there like a zombie, gasping, short of breath. I put my arm around her shoulder. It occurred to me to call a nurse, worried she was having an anxiety attack and about to keel over herself.

'Chris, see if you can find Jean some sweet tea. Ask a nurse,' I said, taking charge. Grateful for something to do, Chris stepped out.

Jean smiled weakly when he came back with her tea. 'They left the house in such a happy mood, so excited about setting up home together. They wanted to sign the lease this afternoon and George was going to tell his wife he was leaving her when she got back from her trip. They went to lunch first. I think George was already drunk when he fetched Sam.' Jean's voice was flat, monotone. 'I never liked him,' she added reflectively. 'Pig. I should have put a stop to their bullshit bloody relationship. She'd be fine now if I had. This wouldn't have happened.'

'You can't think like that, Jean. You of all people know how strong-willed and stubborn Sam is,' Chris said, taking her hand in his.

We sat there in the airless waiting room, each in a world of private thoughts and 'what ifs'. My head was pounding and I battled physical nausea as well as emotional nausea, but knew I had to keep it together for Chris. I thought of George, dead and probably already in a morgue somewhere. I wondered if God – if there even was one – had done this to George because he'd destroyed a marriage. I was sad to think that George's wife would soon learn she was a widow. What about her children? They were fatherless and didn't even know it. Then I swung into a wave of anger at Sam. And Jean. Maybe she could have stopped Sam and avoided all this. Then I felt sick to think of the dead and injured bus passengers. Screw you, George, for drunk driving, I thought. Why swerve into the bus and not away from it? Damn you to hell. Then I felt bad for thinking ill of the dead.

I was a mess, overpowering emotions surging through me. I had been at the hospital for just thirty minutes yet it felt like days. Never had I experienced such an intense, varied and rapid range of emotions, the stress making me think of the most bizarre things. As I sat in a plastic chair in that sparse waiting room that reeked of disinfectant and death, I suddenly understood why people paced hospital corridors as they waited to hear about loved ones. Waiting, waiting, waiting.

Somewhere in the distance, I heard church bells and wondered if it was a funeral. Death was at the forefront of my mind. I saw an old man walking down the corridor, sobbing so hard he could barely walk, and I wondered who in his life had just died. Then a pretty lady walked past, smiling from ear to ear, with a tiny baby in her arms and a 'It's A Boy' balloon tied to a pram, the same balloon message Sam had so recently had all over her room two floors up. How unfair that people could be so happy when death was lurking down the corridor – spitting distance – waiting to strike.

Sam's dad Peter arrived and tried to console Jean, though they were as distraught as each other. Peter kept glaring at Chris, throwing daggers with eyes that had untold rage in them. Chris ignored the hostile stares but, after half an hour of it, I couldn't keep quiet.

'Peter,' I said in a firm voice, 'we are all just as worried as you and Jean. It's utter bullshit for you to glare at Chris and act like this is somehow his fault. Sam took it upon herself to have an affair with George, and Chris certainly didn't have any part in the accident. Please dig down and find it in yourself to cut Chris a bit of slack here. I'm sorry, but your hostility is misplaced and totally uncalled for.'

Peter just stared at me, shocked that I'd challenged him. Although I expected a rude answer, he just sat there. 'You're absolutely right, Kat. I'm so sorry. Chris, my boy, I know this has nothing to do with you. I'm so sorry—' Peter broke down, sobbing. 'She's my little girl, my princess.'

Chris got up and crossed the room to sit beside him, giving him a strong hug. Bawling, he clung onto Chris for dear life.

'I'm so sorry, Chris. I'm just so scared,' said Peter.

We suddenly heard a bloodcurdling scream coming from down the corridor and we all knew it was Sam. Chris leapt up, his feet barely touching the ground as he flew out into the long, cold, sanitised corridor. He ran towards the trauma room, but a nurse blocked him at the door.

'What's happening? Why is she screaming like that? Can someone give me some fucking news?' he barked at the nurse.

'Mr Hay, I can't let you go in. Please understand that your wife is in a critical condition,' the nurse said firmly. 'She screamed because she came around as we moved her, but we've knocked her out again. We can't keep her conscious when she's in that much pain. Please, just wait, and the doctor will talk to you as soon as he can.'

We waited and waited, me chain-smoking in the car park. Chris lit up too despite having quit years ago. Mom and Grandpa pulled in at an alarming speed, Grandpa at the wheel. Grandpa took Chris aside and hugged him tightly. Chris dissolved into more sobs and Mom reached for me, crying too as I brought them up to speed.

'Come kids,' said Mom. 'Let's wait inside.'

An hour later, a doctor finally brought some news. 'I won't lie. Sam is not in good shape and, as soon as the surgeon on call gets here, we'll operate. I am not sure we can save her leg. However, my greatest concern is her head and internal injuries. When you take a severe blow to the head there is a danger of the brain swelling from bruising. Once brain tissue hits the skull, it starts to shut down permanently.'

It all suddenly sounded familiar and I was hurtled back in time. I'd heard the same thing in the same hospital all those years ago when I'd nearly drowned.

'Sam is also bleeding internally and has a punctured lung. It won't inflate on its own. A ventilator is breathing for her right now. Basically, it's touch-and-go. Do you have any questions?' the doctor asked softly.

We all had a million questions but they instantly disappeared from our minds and we just sat there, mute. The doctor left, saying he was on night shift and to find him if we needed anything at all. The air in the waiting room had turned stale and fear was tangible, cloying. I felt the walls closing in on me and ran outside, gasping for some fresh air.

Grandpa came to find me and we perched on the edge of a flower bed and smoked.

'I said such awful things about her Grandpa, to her face too. That fight we had – I was such a bitch.' Extreme remorse swirled in me.

'We all said nasty things about her and George, but this is not our fault.

Torturing ourselves by rehashing the angry words will do no good. We have to be strong for Chris and the kids.'

I leant on Grandpa, my head on his shoulder. I was exhausted, sick. His hands were rough, calloused from a lifetime of farming, but his grasp was warm and comforting when he took my hand in his.

Hours crawled by. Daylight faded, the moon rose, and I wondered what the night would bring. Sam had been in surgery for over three hours and we'd had no more news. Jean had gone home to bath and feed Katie and Ben. My headache was acute and I kept taking more painkillers. I'd not eaten since breakfast and my gut felt raw and angry. Too many pills, too many cigarettes, and too much worry had made my stomach a churning cauldron of bile.

We were moved to the ICU family room and at 11 p.m. the surgeon came to find us.

'The surgery was extremely complicated and difficult,' he said. 'We amputated her leg just above the knee. There was too little left of her leg and, with all the dirt, glass and metal debris embedded in her flesh, gangrene was certain. Her other leg had a simple break and has been set in plaster. Her MRI scan shows brain inflammation and cranial trauma. We should be able to control that – the worry is her lung, where a broken rib pierced right through it. We've repaired the puncture, but the lung is still not inflating as it should, so she'll likely require a second surgery tomorrow morning. We just couldn't keep her under anaesthetic any longer tonight. Her heart showed signs of acute stress during the last hour. All we can do tonight is stabilise her and keep her on life support. She's out cold because she wouldn't be able to withstand the pain if we woke her up now.'

'What are her chances?' Chris asked, verbalising all our thoughts.

'She's critical and has lost a lot of blood. Every hour she hangs in is progress and if she gets through the night so much the better,' said the doctor.

'Does she even know her leg has been amputated?' I asked.

'No. As I said, we've not allowed her to come round,' he replied.

I got up and ran, searching for the nearest toilet where I puked and puked and puked, hyperventilating, my body shaking uncontrollably.

Though nothing was inside my gut, bile kept coming. Exhausted and terrified, I sat on the toilet floor sobbing, heaving, retching. Cursing God.

I swallowed six painkillers, poured myself another vodka, lit a cigarette and stared out the window vacantly. I remembered the first time I met Sam at the school dance and her wisecrack about me drinking while wearing high heels, and how I'd laughed at her flat chest and made fun of her donkey laugh. I felt such a shit and wished, more than anything, that I had got to know her better, or just been a better sister-in-law, because now the chance was gone. Sam was dead.

I grappled to absorb that word: dead. I said it aloud to myself. 'Dead.' It sounded heavy and final. Just one short word, two vowels, two consonants. Such simplicity to describe a person whose time on earth had come to an abrupt end.

Sam had died in ICU a few hours after her surgery. Chris had been with her at the end, holding her hand. She'd never woken up, but Chris said he'd seen a reaction on her monitors while he'd been talking to her and he'd found some measure of comfort in that. We were only thankful she'd never known she was an amputee, a terrible affliction for a beautiful and active young woman and mother. They couldn't pinpoint the exact injury that had ultimately caused her death, and Chris said no to an autopsy. It wouldn't bring her back and it seemed invasive and degrading. Chris wanted Sam to keep her dignity, even in death.

Our entire family plunged into shock. Chris seemed to be holding it together, on the surface at least. He'd been very matter of fact about the funeral arrangements, choosing a coffin as if he was choosing a loaf of bread in a supermarket. He even selected the clothes for her to wear in the coffin. I'd sat with him in their bedroom as he sorted through her clothes, painstakingly co-ordinating her last outfit. Veering from tradition, he'd chosen a sexy black cocktail dress and her silver pashmina, his favourite outfit of hers. He then insisted she be buried in her seven-inch black stiletto sandals and even attempted some humour: 'My Sam is gonna knock 'em dead when she arrives upstairs but she's only going to need one stiletto.'

Behind the quip was a broken man. He just wasn't ready to let anyone know how broken he was. The mask would come off in his own time and I knew that when it did, when the brave face faltered, the ensuing breakdown and grief process would be an intensely personal and private affair.

We all helped him with the children, our entire family now at the Umwinsidale house. Jean and Peter were in tatters, unable to cope with the kids, so we'd taken over. Chris, Mom and I had sat down with Katie and explained that her mommy was now an angel and, even though she couldn't see her, she was still right by Katie's side. Whenever she felt the wind blow or heard leaves rustling, that was her mom blowing kisses and the soft breeze was from her angel wings. We weren't sure how much Katie understood. She'd become very introverted, fragile, and prone to sudden tantrums. My heart ached for her. Her entire little world had changed forever and she desperately missed Sam. We all did. For all the drama over the affair, Sam had been a part of our family and her death left a big gap. Ben, of course, wouldn't have a single memory of his mother, another thing I couldn't come to terms with. The biggest hurdle with Ben had been the change from breastfeeding to formula, but Mom was handling it and Ben was coming right.

Feeling guilty, I kept rehashing the bad things we'd all said about Sam and George, as if our negative thoughts had caused them to die. Would we have been nicer to Sam had we known she was going to die so horribly? Round and round I'd go, mentally chasing my tail. In one particularly bizarre and morbid train of thought, I found myself wondering where Sam's leg was, a thought that I simply couldn't drop. I even discussed it with Grandpa. He was about the only one who'd not think I was a total nutter. Together we decided it had been incinerated. I then said it should have gone into the coffin with Sam, but even Grandpa told me that would be 'fucking weird', that medical waste doesn't get filed in case the patient later dies and wants to be buried whole.

Condolences and flowers poured in. Platitudes sprinkled into every conversation. Cards and phone calls all said the same things: *This happened for a reason; it was her time to go; she's in a better place now; only the good die young.* Death really did make people say the most stupid, inane things. None of it would bring Katie and Ben's mother back. Thank God no one had said at least she was with George now. Chris hadn't said much about George at all. He had merely commented that, while he and Sam had been at odds with each other, it was a cruel day when God chose death to formally separate them when a legal document and lawyers would have sufficed.

Privately, I cried a lot. I turned to Ant, my rock. He'd tried to come home for me but hadn't been able to find another guide to stand in for him on a canoe trip. We spent hours on the phone every evening. He'd lost a cousin in a car crash and knew how dark the early days of grief could feel. It was my first real experience of death and, in the days following Sam's, I came to realise that grief has no timeline or order. It takes the soul on a whirlwind rollercoaster ride of intense emotions, a feeling of being stuck in a tumble dryer on the hottest spin cycle. We all felt similar things. Anger, shame, remorse, sadness, fear, denial – you name it, we felt it, and we swung between each emotion. We could only put one foot in front of the other and handle the hurdles as they cropped up, pulling together for Chris. For the first time in ages, our whole family was under one roof again. It was a reunion for all the wrong reasons.

Chris, Peter and Jean had met the priest to plan the funeral mass, at which Ela would play the piano. There'd been discussions about an open casket, but with Sam's extensive facial injuries they'd have battled to make her look as if she was even remotely at peace.

The funeral was, without doubt, the saddest thing I had ever experienced. As a family, we entered the church with Chris and flanked him in the front row, next to Peter, Jean and Sam's brothers. There were at least a hundred and fifty friends packed into the church behind us.

We were surprised when Chris insisted Katie and Ben be there, but we didn't argue. Mom took charge of Ben who lay in her arms gurgling happily; his was the only smile in the church. I had Katie and carried her on my hip. Her little arms clutched me tightly as she buried her face in my neck and hid behind my mass of hair. I could feel her hot, anxious breath coming in short gasps. Her warm tears running down my neck. I whispered to her softly throughout the service, telling her that her mom was with us and was so very proud of her for being such a brave little princess. When we caught the sweet scent of the lilies on the coffin, I told Katie it was her mom's special angel perfume. Her little body was heaving as she kept crying and her grip on me grew tighter and tighter. I slowly rocked her in my arms, my heart breaking. I didn't even try to wipe my own tears away. There was no point.

There we sat, a family united in death. We gazed at the coffin, fighting our consciences, clutching onto the happy memories we had of Sam, giving thanks for her short life and for the two beautiful children she'd given our family.

Later, when the wake was over, the tea cups cleared, the mourners returned to their normal days untouched by death, Chris stunned us by saying, 'I'm going to pay my respects to George's wife.'

Mom did a double take. 'You what?'

'They had George's funeral today as well, and I'd like to pop by and see his wife. I need to do this. Last night I realised I need to forgive Sam and George. If I don't, I'll end up lugging around a load of resentments and never move forward. Paying my respects will help me find some peace and closure. Besides, George's wife never wronged me. Her loss is as big as ours and she also has kids who've lost a parent.'

'Shit Chris, this is a big step,' said Dad.

'Yup, but it's something I must do,' said Chris.

'Have you ever met her?' asked Mom.

'No, but I did speak to her on the phone the other day.'

'Right then,' said Grandpa. 'Come on young man, I'm coming with you for moral support. Let's go.'

Chris smiled, slapped his knees and then stood up. 'Cool Grandpa,' he said, throwing him the car keys. 'You drive, I've had way too many drinks. Oh, and I'm going to make a cash donation to the families of those who died on the bus.'

I looked at Chris, tears in my eyes again as I admired the depth of his emotional resources and strength.

The rest of us spent the day at home. I'd had such revolting headaches over the past few days and, again, had taken way too many painkillers but I couldn't take to my bed. Katie wouldn't let me out of her sight and got terribly distraught if I so much as went to the loo.

When Chris and Grandpa got back, Chris said that showing face at his bête noir's wake had been the right thing to do. Grandpa had taken Chris to the pub afterwards and both arrived home nicely drunk.

We sat down to an early supper as Mom and Dad had called a family meeting.

'Right, kids, we have an announcement,' said Dad. 'Your mother and I have decided to make the final move into town. The land-reform stuff is hotting up and in the last two weeks there've been fresh waves of Section Eights issued, very close to us.'

We knew that receiving your Section Eight meant your farming days were numbered.

'Are you expecting ours soon?' I asked Dad.

'Yup, we reckon within the next month we will be chucked off the farm. Now, what with Sam's death and you, Chris, needing some help with the kids, we've decided to cut our losses and head into town sooner rather than later. It's always been a matter of time and that time has come.'

I knew Dad was struggling to leave the farm loved and nurtured by his family for generations, but Dad was also the king of brave faces and today was no different.

'Wow,' said Chris, he and I both absorbing the magnitude their decision.

'We've all got a lot to adapt to. As much as it's in our bones to fight for our farm and beat the system, we'd never win,' said Dad. 'You all know my stance on this. I've always said that when our time is up we'll leave quietly without digging our heels in. Sam's death has brought it forward but we'll cope. We have to, for Ben and Katie, and for you, Chris.'

And then came Chris's tears, the first tears in the aftermath of the horror. Seeing his chin wobbling, I started too.

'So this is it, Dad. Our farm really is going?' I asked, sniffing rather unattractively.

'Yes, along with thousands of other farms. We are about to become another displaced and uncompensated farming family. I'm sick to the core, but what can we do? All we can hope for now is a good life here in Harare, one where politics leaves us alone. We believe Harare will remain stable for the time being but, should the tides turn here in town too, then we'll look at a Plan C, though that'd mean leaving Zimbabwe for good and I'm not ready yet.'

'It's just so final,' I said. 'And so wrong.'

Sitting next to me, Grandpa gently nudged me under the table with his knee as a gesture of comfort. Shit, I thought, everything sinking in. What a day. Could life get any crueller?

'Obviously we won't hand over the farm until we actually get our Section Eight, but will start in earnest getting our things into Harare,' said Mom. 'We're bloody lucky we weren't one of the first farms to be hit and we've had time to plan this new life.'

Mom looked calm and composed. She was such a strong woman and I knew her hope and optimism about starting over wasn't forced.

'And you Grandpa? GranJilly?' Chris asked.

'Well,' said Grandpa, 'we've been discussing converting the stables into a little cottage for GranJilly and me. In the meantime we'll live here in the main house.'

GranJilly looked somewhat away with the fairies and I wondered how much she was taking in. Poor old duck, she'd taken Sam's death very hard and would cry every time she looked at Ben and Katie, so much so she was starting to freak Katie out. We constantly had to steer them away to avoid the meltdowns on both sides.

'Those stables make the perfect shell for a little two-bedroom cottage and will have a glorious view over the Umwinsidale valley,' said Mom. 'We'll put up three new stables and a tack room at the far end of the bottom paddock.'

We currently had five stables but only three horses so it made sense to downscale.

'Chris, right now no one knows, not even you, how you're going to manage the day-to-day logistics of being a single dad. If we're all in town permanently, things will be more manageable and we can lighten your load,' said Dad.

'Thank you. All of you. I am lost for words,' said Chris, still crying.

Grandpa threw him a hanky that landed bang in the broccoli cheese, breaking the heavy moment and making us chuckle.

'Dad, what's happening with your horticultural contracts?' I asked. 'Are you making progress with the veggie boys?'

'Yup, it's all looking good. I plan to plant the first crop of beans and red peppers within the next six weeks. There's a shitload to be done and I'm bringing in a workforce from the farm. The next month is going to be balls-to-the-wall.'

'And, kiddos,' said Grandpa beaming, 'we're talking my old balls. You're looking at your father's second in command, Dan Hay, Veggie Manager. I'm stepping out of retirement and into gainful employment again.'

Mom laughed. 'Thank God for small mercies. Nepotism Central!'

'Congrats Grandpa, if that's the right word,' I said.

We all knew it would take time for Dad's new venture to gain ground. It would make little return on investment in the short term, but Dad had dabbled in real estate many years back and had made a small fortune on property, providing the financial cushion he needed now. At least his Umwinsidale land would be safe from land reform as it was deemed residential, not agricultural. Dad had had clear method in choosing this property.

'Where will Tim and Linda end up?' Chris asked.

'Well, it's quite exciting,' replied Dad. 'Grandpa heard from the boys at the veggie company that they're opening a new canning factory just outside Harare. Part of the operation is growing pulses – lentils and beans – for the canning factory. Tim had an interview and they've offered him the job of manager.'

'That's great news,' said Chris.

'Yup, a lot of change is coming our way. We have two priorities right now, to help you with the kids Chris, and to get what we can off the farm before the net lands on us,' said Mom.

'Tim and I have a strategy,' said Dad. 'We'll start moving the heavy equipment and machinery, selling what we won't need for the veggies, and, of course, move all the household stuff, three entire households. We've been hearing more awful stories about farmers who didn't move a thing in advance. When the time came, they were run off their land with only a change of clothes. That's not gonna happen to the Hay family.'

'I still can't believe the time has come,' I said, deeply saddened that our farming era was ending.

'End of an era,' said Grandpa, reading my mind.

'It's been quite a day for ending eras,' said Chris.

That night sleep evaded me again. Desperate for physical and mental rest, I took eight painkillers. As I lay in bed, I wondered whether going back to the farm one last time would be a good or bad thing. It may just totally depress me to say good bye to the home I'd loved. Did I really want to see it bare, naked, stripped of us, in the wake of all the other trauma?

Not even sleep brought peace to my cluttered mind and I had awful nightmares. I dreamt I was back on the farm when the men came knocking with our Section Eight. When Dad opened the door to them, it was George who handed over the notice and announced he was the war veteran moving in. Sam marched in too, dragging a plush throne behind her, and told Mom to get out of what was now *her* bedroom.

21

Life went on. Days passed and we all got on with life. Dad had gone back to the farm, taking Grandpa, to start the packing and moving. Mom and GranJilly stayed with us. Chris's house renovation was nearly complete and he reckoned it'd be another two weeks before he moved home. Katie loved it in Umwinsidale. She had the horses to distract her and spent every moment she could in the pool, learning to swim with Mom.

She was still very clingy, and getting her back to crèche and into her little routine again had been traumatic. She'd howled her head off the first day, crying so hard she'd made herself violently ill. Sod's Law it had been me to drop her off that morning, so I got the full force of the tantrum. She'd simply refused to let go of my leg when I tried to get into my car, utterly terrified to let me out of her sight. I caved in, without energy to do the right thing and stand my ground, and I couldn't bear the sheer panic all over her face.

So Katie came to work with me, loving the fuss everyone made of her. All my colleagues, Stephen included, decided she needed a Wimpy lunch with an obscenely large milkshake, and now Katie thought adults went to work and ate burgers all day. That evening we explained to her that crèche wasn't actually optional. Poor thing, the scene she'd made was just her little way of dealing with what she perceived to be abandonment by her mother. We could only love her through it, yet not let her become an overindulged brat. Meanwhile, Ben was growing before our eyes and was an easy baby.

Mom adored her role with Ben. While nobody could ever fill Sam's shoes, Mom came pretty close.

'Kat, good to see you,' said Jenny Merton, my GP, as I sat down.

Permanently tired and stuck in a particularly bad cycle of headaches, I had again cruised through my painkillers. This time the pharmacist did say no when I asked for another premature repeat of my prescription and wouldn't budge, insisting I saw my doctor.

'I've just come to get a new prescription for my painkillers and to chat to you about the dosage.'

She looked up the date of my last script. 'Have you already finished that last script? They should have lasted four months, not eight weeks.'

'I know. What with all the upheaval and stress, I've had a particularly bad bout of headaches and some hectic migraines. I just never have a clear head.'

'How are the neurosurgeon's nerve-blocker shots going? Have they helped? Are you still going to him?' Doc Merton asked, firing questions at me.

'I've had four sessions and therefore four lovely black eyes. They did help a bit but are by no means the miracle cure I'd hoped for. He wants to do another four sessions then let things settle for a while.'

'Mmm. Never mind the bruising, I can see tissue scaring around your eye.'

'Yup. It's bloody sore too.'

'Right, hop on the bed. I want to do a full check-up while you are here.'

My blood pressure was high as well as my pulse. She examined my stomach, gently applying pressure between my ribs and pelvis. I shrieked.

'Sore?' she asked.

'Shit yes! What are you pressing on there?'

'Your stomach. Your gut is raw from taking all those pills. How much are you smoking? And drinking?'

'Smoking twenty-plus a day. Drinking socially, nothing hectic.'

'Thought about quitting the fags?'

'Yeah, I know I should, but now is not the time.'

'There is never a good time to quit smoking but it's always a good time to stop smoking,' she said, getting all cryptic. 'Listen Kat, keep an eye on your stomach and please do not hammer your gut with pills on an empty stomach. You're heading into ulcer territory. In fact, see me in a month for another check-up, okay? And you are to book an endoscopy this week. I want to have a closer look at your gut.' She gave me a referral note for a gastric specialist.

'Mmm, okay,' I mumbled, not keen on the idea of a camera going down my throat.

She wrote me a new prescription, increasing the painkiller dose slightly but saying it was now on the outer limits of reasonable and she'd not increase it any further. Then I got a short lecture about addiction, which fell on deaf ears.

'And please also get yourself back into a physio and acupuncture routine,' she added. 'You absolutely must take a holistic approach to your pain management.'

I thanked her, promising to get back to the normal painkiller dosage, but could see her wondering if it was just lip service.

Feeling the flattest I'd been in a long time, I decided a girls' night with Ela and Rolo might help.

'Right, let's get drinks in and then I want the news,' said Rolo, meeting us at the usual spot, Coimbra. 'Kat, you look awful. That blackish-eye look is really not working for you.'

'Gee thanks, you really know how to make me feel great,' I said. For some reason the neurosurgeon's last round of shots had left a worse bruise than normal. Then again, using the words 'normal' and 'black eye' in the same sentence was a problem in itself.

'Well, you look shite,' said Rolo. 'Ela, you should see the bags under her eyes.'

Ela smiled at me. 'You okay, Kat? What's bugging you? I don't have to see you to sense that you have the weight of the world on your shoulders.'

'I'm tired, girls, so tired. I think everything is catching up with me,' I replied. 'It's been the most awful month hasn't it? Sam dying, us looking after the kids, Mom and Dad moving off the farm. And my head has been outrageously bad. So, yes, I look shite, feel shite, life's been shite.'

'Have you been hoovering too many pills?' asked Ela, shooting from the hip.

'You could say that, but I've seen the doctor and had a check-up.' I downplayed it, not wanting to get into a health discussion.

'Here, get that down your gob,' said Rolo, handing me a double vodka.

Out of nowhere, I started to well up. 'Oh great! Now look what you've done,' I joked, wiping my tears with a serviette.

'You need a good cry, clearly. Go for it, get it all out. Snot is also allowed, in moderation,' said Rolo.

I had my cry. 'I think Ant and I are drifting apart,' I stated matter-of-factly.

'Drifting? You two fighting again?' asked Rolo.

'Nope, no fights, we just seem to be distant with each other. He's got his life in Vic Falls, I've got my life here, we're on different paths. Toss in the long distance and you have a couple who actually have very little in common anymore.' It was the first time I was admitting my fears.

'Except that you love each other madly,' said Ela.

'Quite!' said Rolo. 'And you're just a tad overwhelmed by everything and I'm willing to bet the distance you perceive is in your head. You two are solid. I wouldn't worry, Ant isn't going anywhere.'

'She's right,' said Ela. 'But *you* have to decide if you can cope with the physical distance. It takes a solid bond to ensure love works over long distance but look how you've managed already.'

'I still struggle with being in a relationship while, day-to-day, living the life of a single girl. The weekends really get to me.'

'No one said it was going to be easy. What can you do though?' asked Rolo.

'Dunno, it's depressing me. I don't even know when I'll see him again. It's our Congress in the Falls next week, but he's got a bunch of Americans for a six-day canoe trip,' I said, sighing. I stroked Mojo who'd plonked her head in my lap, reading my mood again.

'Kat, sit tight. They say that just as you're about to chuck in the towel, the answer will present itself, whoever 'they' are,' said Rolo.

'Can we change the subject before I start howling again? My mascara won't withstand a second round of tears.'

'Who gives a shit? Cry if you need to,' said Ela.

I blew my nose, grateful for such wonderful friends. 'Hey, I haven't told you about Sam's Will,' I said.

'Oh jeez, don't tell me she was secretly loaded, like The Clap,' said Ela.

'Yes! Sam, the sneaky girl, had some bucks. Quite a lot of bucks, actually,' I said.

'Never!' said Rolo.

'I shit you not. She had a trust fund. Some wealthy grandmother had a shitload of cash and left it to Sam and her brothers,' I said. 'Sam left most of hers to Ben and Katie, but some to Chris too. He won't need to worry about sending the kids to university as there's plenty in the coffers.'

'Shit, Sam kept that quiet, huh,' said Ela. 'All credit to her that she didn't blab about her wealth.'

'Yup, she was many things but she did have some class. Well, she did before she shagged the builder. But how's this, she also inherited whopping jewels and has left a diamond ring to me. Jean has it and I have to collect it sometime.'

'Good Lord! Diamonds? What's with all these people with loads of money and treasures squirrelled away? I've been making friends with the wrong people. No bloody jewels or cash coming my way,' joked Rolo.

'And Chris didn't know about the money?' Ela asked me.

'He knew there was some but didn't know the extent of it, and certainly didn't know she had a Will.'

'Just goes to show, people aren't always what they seem,' said Ela.

'Talking of inheriting shitloads of cash – Ela, have you started making plans for the Europe trip with your folks?' I asked.

'Yes, I meant to tell you that I've booked. They nearly fell over when I told them we'd be spending two weeks in Tuscany, then on to Rome, then Paris, then we finish the trip with ten days in London and tickets to three West End shows. I brought the trip forward, what with leaving the farm and Dad's new job. I thought it better to go before he starts so we'll catch the end of the European summer – away for six weeks in total.'

'Wow! That's bloody fantastic. What about Mojo? Do you want me to dog sit? Sally would love it,' said Rolo.

'Thanks. I was going to ask one of you, or Chris, to have her. Maybe you can share custody,' said Ela.

'Of course. Ah, it will be an awesome trip, Ela. The folks must have been blown away by the surprise,' I said. 'By the way, Rolo – I've been meaning to ask what's happening with your farm? You've had your Section Eight already?'

'Oh God, it's been a total nightmare and my mother sounds like she's heading for a nervous breakdown and a stint in the loony bin,' replied Rolo.

'So, when do they have to be off and what's their Plan B?' Ela asked Rolo.

'Dad, unbeknown to us, bought property here in Harare a while back so they do have somewhere to live. They're busy getting things off the farm now. They have three weeks. Work-wise, Dad says he has some irons in the fire. He'll be fine. He always lands on his feet,' said Rolo.

'And Ela, how's that dishy colleague of yours?' I asked.

She smiled. 'James? How dishy is he? I have a mental image of what I imagine him to look like.'

'He's super-hot,' I said.

'To answer your question, he's fine. He's a lovely guy,' said Ela, her face suddenly flushed.

'You're blushing,' said Rolo. 'You've shagged him, haven't you?'

'There may have been a few steamy nights . . .' said Ela, getting all coy.

'Good for you! Ain't nothing like a work flirtation to make the days fly by,' said Rolo.

'Shit, now both of you are shagging workmates,' I said, laughing.

'Hey, I haven't shagged mine,' said Rolo.

'Oh sure,' I said.

'Swear to God, but I'd be lying if I said I didn't want to,' said Rolo, smiling.

'I told you before. Don't, Rolo! You'll get your arse fired,' I said.

'So it's okay for Ela to shag at work but not me?' she joked.

'Well Ela, I don't approve either. Now's not the time but I do wish you and Chris would just wake up to what's been under your noses for decades,' I said.

'Me and Chris? Nah, he doesn't see me in that way,' said Ela, blushing again.

Rolo snorted. 'How many times do we have to go over this? You're both as besotted as the other.'

Ela merely grinned. One day, I thought, one day they'll get there.

22

'Shit I'm knackered,' I said to Chris as I got into his car. He'd met me at the airport after my Vic Falls congress.

'You look brown. Did you do any work or just suntan by the pool for five days?'

'Pfft! Worked my sorry arse off. And it was stinking hot too, but it was the best Congress ever. Four days of socials and four corresponding hangovers, the last of which is still in progress. Stephen has given me great kudos, more than I think I deserve – though it's nice to be acknowledged.'

'Well done! I saw a bit of coverage in the newspaper. You made front page and you're also in the photo,' said Chris.

'Yes, I believe so. Fame at last,' I said.

We'd pulled off a sleek event but it'd been a tough week. I was miserable as I hadn't seen Ant, and still had no idea when I would. I lit a cigarette and put my head back on the headrest. 'How're you, Chris? What's been happening over the last week?'

'Same old. They are finally painting my house, so I plan to move back there on the weekend, once the smell has wafted off. Mom is up to her ears unpacking the boxes that Dad sent into town. Grandpa is back in town too. They've finished building the new stables so Jobb's moving the horses in and Grandpa can start converting the old ones into their cottage. Anyway, how's your pip been?'

'Not brilliant,' I replied. My plan to cut back on the painkillers hadn't been a howling success and my supply was low again.

'Oh dear,' said Chris. 'Are we going home or do you need to go to the office?'

'I'm off for the day so home please. I need a hangover nap and have to pop to the shops later.'

I got home to a boisterous boxer-style welcome from Tighty and Gertie, who had also been moved to town along with Grandpa and our other worldly possessions. After just a few days, Mom's new bantams were looking a bit frazzled from boxer chases. Apparently, Tighty had eaten one for lunch on his first day in town.

After a much-needed hour on my bed, I hauled myself down to the pharmacy for more painkillers. The regular pharmacist wasn't in. Behind the counter was the locum who'd slipped me his phone number. Colin. Knowing I wasn't due for a refill, I decided to wing it and see what he'd offer. He called up my history, counted the days and said I was again too early for a repeat, by nine days. Except I sensed it was a charade, that he had to object in some way. He then dispensed twenty painkillers as a stopgap. Instead of letting the shop ladies ring up my bill, he came to the front to handle it himself, saying softly that he could give me more the next day.

'But how are you able to dispense these painkillers without a current script?' I asked quietly, looking around to check no one was listening. I was shocked at the balls of it.

'Ah, well, I have a contact with the supplier and get them wholesale. There are plenty of people like you in this town, people who get blocked by pharmacists when they desperately need refills. Call it a sideline venture of mine,' he said, tapping the side of his nose.

'A case of supply and demand?'

'Yup, you got it in one. Meet me on your way to work in the morning and I'll sort you out.'

I looked at him, one eyebrow raised, not entirely sure how to handle his offer and wondering if it was a trap. I mean, he was a complete stranger. Even so, if he was just a bent pharmacist with a black market, sideline business, what he was doing was illegal too. I was tempted.

'I know you've kept my number from last time so call me later,' he said, winking.

The confidence! I paid and left, a little dubious about the shady deal I'd just been offered, but twenty painkillers wouldn't get me through one day.

I knew it and Colin knew it. I also knew damn well that I'd be blocked by both the regular pharmacist and Doc Merton if I tried for more pills via the legal channels. I carefully weighed up my options. Pain or pills. It was hardly a tough decision.

I called Colin that night.

The next morning, I made the slight detour past the shops at the appointed time. I cruised through the empty car park, finding Colin at the far end. He swiftly hopped out of his car and into mine, handing me a bottle of two hundred painkillers. To say I was surprised would be putting it mildly. Then again, I didn't know what I'd expected – but never in a million years would I get two hundred pills in one shot from the pharmacy. And I wasn't getting another irritating lecture about addiction.

Colin asked for payment and I produced the cash, noting they were cheaper than the pharmacy. He then hopped out of my car, the entire drug deal taking only a minute.

'Give me a shout when you need more. See ya soon and enjoy your day, Katherine Hay,' said Colin in a sing-song voice as he got back into his car.

On the way to work, it hit me that I'd just scored from a dealer in a quiet parking lot, like a dirty little crack junkie. I didn't know what to make of my illicit encounter, but it was done now. I had a decent supply of my drug and didn't have to worry about getting more for a few days so I put it all to the back of my mind. I justified the dealing by, again, insisting to myself that my doctors and pharmacists had left me little choice.

Little did I know then that I'd just stepped onto a very slippery slope. The beginning of the end.

Six weeks later, I was promoted to middle management. With the title of Senior Account Manager came my first-ever set of business cards, which made me feel terribly important. However, I was ready to collapse from exhaustion. Life had been chaotic on all fronts, but the bulk of my stress had been work related. Stephen had signed two new accounts, on top of which a client had us organising a black-tie dinner for three hundred guests to mark their fiftieth anniversary. I was to be the Master of Ceremonies at the dinner. I had balked at it, but Stephen had insisted, saying, 'Any self-respecting PR should be able to stand up and address three hundred people without batting an eyelid.' Talk about a baptism of fire! I was terrified, already planning the neat vodka I'd chuck back before getting behind the podium.

The Friday of the dinner rolled around and I left work early to get my hair done, and to meet Colin on my way home. Scoring pills from Colin was now a regular occurrence and I was pretty much guaranteed a steady and large supply of my prescription painkillers, without the prescription. It was always the same – I'd phone first, we'd meet in a car park, he'd get into my car, give me two hundred pills, sometimes more, and he'd take the cash and go. There was never any chit-chat or personal stuff shared. I knew what I was doing was risky.

The deal with Colin done and my large tub of pills snug in my handbag, I headed home. After a long bath, I put on a slinky, black velvet dress topped with a chunky gold necklace, bangles and Sam's monster diamond ring, which really was rather beautiful. I slipped on some lethally high stilettos and smiled to remember my heels and the rugby incident so many years ago, though I can't say I smiled about the lifetime of headaches it had caused. I vamped up my look with retro scarlet lipstick and smouldering dark eyes, and a good smear of extra foundation to cover the residual black eye I had. I loaded a little black handbag with the essentials – lipstick, cigarettes, cellphone and painkillers. I then took a few pills, mostly to deal with my nerves. After checking my lipstick wasn't smeared all over my teeth, I sauntered up to the main house to see if Mom thought I looked alright.

Grandpa was sitting out on the patio enjoying a G&T as the sun went down. He gave a long wolf whistle when he saw me and bellowed into the house, 'Gill, better get out here. There is some famous celebrity woman straight off the red carpet to see you.'

Mom and Dad came out, gave a full inspection and decided I looked gorgeous. Dad then insisted on taking a photo of me all dolled up like the dog's dinner. As I struck a rather strained pose, Tighty came tearing round the corner, ears flattened, jowls flapping and going like the clappers. He'd been chasing guinea fowl and had the devil in him, a wild and deranged look in his eyes. Unfortunately, deranged boxers have little regard for velvet dresses and, as he tore past me, a long sliver of dog slobber flew off his flapping jowls and landed on the front of my dress.

'Agh, shit, Tighty! Bloody hell!' I shouted.

Tighty screeched to a halt and just looked at me, panting away with his big pink tongue lolling out of the side of his mouth after what had clearly been a very satisfying, high-speed fowl chase. He'd covered me in slobber many times before and couldn't work out why tonight he was suddenly in the shit for doing so. Try explaining the subtle difference between jeans and velvet to a boxer.

'Come inside, it will wipe off easily and the damp mark won't show on velvet,' said Mom.

'Idiot dog,' I muttered at Tighty, who seemed to be laughing at me.

Grandpa was also pissing himself laughing and Dad had taken the photo just as Tighty planted his slobbery signature on my dress, capturing both my look of horror and Tighty's wild-eyed expression.

Inside, Mom took a damp cloth to the slobbery spot. 'Sweetheart, you've lost a fair bit of weight lately. Are you dieting? Look at your shoulders – they're all bony.'

'Me? Diet? Nope, but I have lost some weight, I think. Not sure why. Probably stress.'

'And your tummy looks a bit swollen.'

I peered down at my stomach and then turned to look at my profile in a mirror. It was a little swollen and it had felt increasingly tender of late. I just shrugged it off.

'Have you been clobbering those painkillers?'

'I'm sticking within the normal dosage,' I lied.

'Hmm. No comment,' said Mom, stepping back to check I was slobber free. 'I think you're good to go. You look absolutely stunning, go knock 'em dead.'

'Shit, I'm nervous about this whole public-speaking thing.'

'You'll be brilliant. Just relax, and don't get drunk or you'll make a tit of yourself.'

I arrived at the hotel and worked through my checklist. Happy that everything was ready, I checked my make-up and then ordered a double vodka from my bar staff.

Stephen strolled in. 'Wow Kat! That dress is quite something. Are we all set?'

'Thanks. Yup, everything and everyone is in place,' I said.

After dinner, I got through the bulk of my MC duties and, once I started speaking, all my nerves evaporated and I soon found myself enjoying it. Then it happened. Standing at the podium introducing the last person on the programme, I felt something happen to my stomach. With three hundred people watching, I faltered, suddenly gasping. It was how I imagined taking a bullet would feel. Out of nowhere and with no warning, a sharp and severe pain ripped through my gut, literally taking my breath away. I had no choice but to gulp, grit my teeth, finish my introduction and get off the stage as fast as I could. It was as if a white-hot metal poker had been plunged into my stomach.

As I came off the stage Stephen was waiting for me, having realised there was a problem. 'Kat, are you okay? What on earth happened up there?'

'I suddenly have the most awful pain in my stomach. I have no idea what it is or why,' I said, breathless.

'You're as white as a sheet. Let's get you some water, then come sit at the back of the room and catch your breath,' he said.

Every step made the pain worse. The room was spinning, yet everything was moving in slow motion. Voices and faces merged into one big cacophony of warbled sounds, like it was all happening underwater.

'Let me just go to the ladies, Stephen. I'm coming now,' I said.

In the bathroom, I vomited violently. It was not a familiar pain, making it all the more scary. I eventually composed myself and made my way back. The dinner was wrapping up and guests were starting to leave.

'You okay now, Kat?' Stephen asked.

I didn't want to alarm him or seem pathetic. 'Yes thanks, a bit better. I have absolutely no idea what just happened. Don't worry, it will pass.' I was still very breathless.

'You head home, Kat. You look like shit and I'll handle things here. Can I arrange a lift for you?'

'Ah, thanks a mill, but I'll be fine to drive. Thank you. And sorry.'

I crawled home, my free arm across my stomach as I drove, as if it would make the pain subside. I got home just before midnight, by which time I could only take short, shallow gasps of breath and was unable to stand up straight. I took my heels off and, instead of going to my cottage, decided to wake Mom. I didn't have keys on me so I tapped on their bedroom window. Mom was awake, reading.

'Mom?' I said in a feeble voice.

'KitKat?' she said, flying over to the window. 'What's happened to you?' Dad appeared at the window too.

'Can I come in?' My voice started to wobble and then the tears came, tears of pain. Mom appeared at the front door seconds later.

'What on earth has happened?' she asked again, looking at my stooped posture.

'It's my stomach. I was speaking on stage when suddenly something happened inside my gut. Like a gunshot. The most intense burning pain out of nowhere.'

I hobbled into the lounge and lay on the sofa.

'And you drove home? You should've called me, sweetheart,' said Dad.

Mom gently placed her hand on my tummy, bloated and rock hard. I looked six months pregnant.

Dad dashed to my cottage to get comfortable clothes. I took a couple more painkillers hoping to ease the pain, but they seemed to make things worse. Starting to get scared, I had a sinking feeling it was serious and there wouldn't be a happy ending.

I didn't move from the couch all night and dozed fitfully, trying all positions in a hopeless attempt to ease my discomfort. Mom stayed with me, dozing with one eye open.

Come dawn, the pain was worse – not that I'd thought it possible. Mom announced she was taking me to the hospital. I didn't protest. It took about fifteen minutes just to get me to the car, with me taking small steps and doubled over. Every movement set off fresh waves of pain.

In the last year there'd been an influx of Yugoslav doctors in Zimbabwe, some with questionable degrees but cheap to employ. Our hospitals were brimming with them, most barely able to speak English and, it was widely felt, as medical professionals they sucked. There'd been several horror stories going around Harare. Nevertheless, I needed to see a doctor and with Doc Merton not available on weekends, the Yugoslav was as good as it got. Just my luck, I drew a particularly bad one with an appalling grasp of English, unable to get even 'Hello' right. His weird bushy hair stuck out at odd angles and his breath stank.

After describing what had happened, I saw by the vacant look on his face he'd not understood much. He prodded and poked my tummy, at which point I let out a bloodcurdling scream that probably woke people in the next town.

'Fucking hell, that's sore,' I muttered. Mom squeezed my hand.

The doctor asked what I had eaten the night before.

'Chicken, rice and veggies,' I replied. He had no idea what 'veggies' were.

'Veegers? Vot is Veegers?' he replied in his guttural accent.

I was starting to lose both my temper and sense of humour. 'Veggies. Fuck's sake,' I muttered. 'Vegetables. Vedge. Eee. Tah. Bills,' I said in a slow voice. 'Green healthy things that grow in the ground.' It was like talking to a moron.

'Aha,' he said, looking enlightened. 'Veggertibles. I zee.'

'Yes, those things. I ate some. With chicken. And rice. How is this relevant?' I asked.

'Rize? You had rize?' he asked with wide eyes, as if eating rice was something totally salacious and a banned substance.

I battled to keep a lid on my sarcasm. 'Yes, I ate bloody rice. Those little white grains.'

'Oh yez. Rize. I know rize,' he said.

Halle-fucking-lujah, I thought, he knows what rice is. Even Mom was trying not to snort derisively.

'How is last night's food relevant?' I asked again. 'Surely this is not food poisoning?'

The fool jabbed his finger into my gut again and again I yelped loudly. 'Zat zore?'

'Yes, it's sore. Fucking sore. I told you that the last time you jabbed me. Nothing has changed within the last ninety seconds. I am not screaming because I am bored and have nothing better to do. I am screaming because it is ZORE!' I had now officially lost my sense of humour. With the situation going from bad to worse, I was tempted to walk out and hope the pain went away on its own.

The idiot doctor made a big production of clearing his throat as if to make an important ground-breaking announcement, like life on another planet had been discovered and there was cheap real estate up for grabs.

'I zink you having ze indigyezzion kitt-hiy, zat's all,' he said, pleased with his diagnosis.

'What?' I snapped, not understanding a word.

Exasperated, I looked at Mom for help.

'Are you saying she has indigestion?' Mom asked him.

'Yez, yez.'

'And what is "kitt-hiy"?' Mom asked him.

'Kitt-hiy?' He looked puzzled. 'Zat iz kitt-hiy,' he said, pointing at me then pointing to my name on the patient chart.

'Ah,' said Mom. 'You mean Kat Hay?'

'Yez, Kitt-hiy. She haz indigyezzion, zat's all. I now give her zee renny anz azid,' he said, and then let out the most inappropriate laugh I had ever heard, as if he'd told a filthy joke. Even the nurse looked faintly horrified at his behaviour. Bad English aside, the man was a loon.

'You mean Rennies antacid?' I asked dubiously. I had absolutely no faith in him. I also knew what indigestion felt like and the pain sure didn't resemble any indigestion I'd ever had, not in any way, shape or form.

'Now I give you ze injeczon for ze painkiller in backzide bottom zone and zen I give ze anz azid,' he said proudly, his chest puffed out.

I had a sudden urge to kick him in the nuts. I was exhausted, angry, and his accent was getting on my last nerve.

'Antacid will fix this?' asked Mom.

'Ya ya yez, Missuz, fix for ze indigyezzion. And no greez foods for zum dayz, juz plain mealz. You eat too much ze rize and chicken but I zink you be fine zoon zoon Kitt-hiy.'

The nurse translated for us, feeling our pain. 'No greasy foods for a few days, just plain meals, you ate too much rice and chicken, you'll be fine soon, Kat Hay,' said the nurse, looking a bit pissed off with the doctor herself.

The mad doctor motioned to the nurse to give me a painkiller shot in my arse and about five minutes later, the pethidine brought some relief. I was then offered some Rennies tablets to chew. I took one and snorted, knowing damn well I was not suffering from a bout of acid reflux.

As we left the hospital, Mom asked the doctor if he was quite sure it was just indigestion. She picked her moment to ask the question, making sure one of the local doctors had heard her too.

The other doctor looked up. 'I can assure you madam, Doctor Grabezka is an excellent physician and if he says it's indigestion, then it is. Your daughter needs to watch her language too,' he said in a pissy little voice and went back to his charts without waiting for a response.

I very nearly told him to fuck off too, but Mom shot me a warning look. Meanwhile, Grabezka, the idiot, gave Mom a stupid grin, looking like a lost character from *Sesame Street*.

Back home, I resumed my position on the couch. The pethidine had helped and, despite my doubts, I diligently chewed Rennies throughout the day. The acuteness eased off a bit – the weirdest dose of indigestion I'd ever known. After hearing Mom's account of the moronic doctor, Grandpa called me Kitt-hiy all day, and even got me to see the humour in it, briefly. I dozed off on the couch, exhausted.

Later, half asleep, I felt someone perch on the couch next to me and touch my hair. I opened my eyes slowly, expecting to see Mom, but got the fright of my life when I saw Ant.

'Hey sweetheart,' he smiled at me.

I thought I was hallucinating, perhaps from all the pain and medicine. 'Ant! What on earth? When did …? You didn't tell me …! But how …? You're really here? Or am I tripping?'

He kissed me tenderly. 'Yes, you're tripping but I'm also really here, sweetheart. Surprise.'

'Wow!' I reached up to hug him, wincing in pain as I moved.

'What's wrong babe? You actually look like death. I just saw your Mom in the garden. She said you were in the ER this morning.'

'Yup,' I said drowsily. I told him the story of Kitt-hiy.

'Shit, can we not get hold of your proper doctor?'

'I don't have an after-hours number for her. It will pass, I'll be fine love, don't stress. Sit, tell me your news.'

'Well, as long as you promise to see her on Monday, Kitt-hiy.'

'Yup, I will. But hey, you're here and I refuse to be sick,' I said, trying to sound bright and chirpy but not feeling it in the slightest, although I was thrilled Ant was home.

We talked for hours and hours, lying side by side on my bed. Normally we'd have ripped each other's clothes off in a passionate frenzy but my gut just wasn't up to a romp.

Later, Grandpa ordered pizzas, called Chris and Ela round and everyone came down to my cottage. I lay on my huge patio sofas, too ill and too sore to contemplate food. It was a special evening though and I suddenly got all sentimental, having the people I loved the most around me when I was feeling so ill and a little scared of what my medical diagnosis would be, when we finally got an accurate one. I tried to push the pain to the back of my mind, determined to savour the time with Ant.

For the rest of the weekend, I studiously ignored my body's violent cry for help. Years later, I'd look back and see that it was one of the stupidest things I'd ever do.

On Monday morning, I went to work as usual, still in pain but able to stand up straight, mostly. I had mountains of work to get through but I'd promised Ant I'd see Doc Merton.

I stuck my nose into Stephen's office. 'Just nipping to the doctor quickly to get checked out. I'm nearly done with the proofreading on that annual report. I'll sign off on it when I get back.'

'Good luck,' said Stephen

I stepped into Doc Merton's office. She smiled at me, a smile that faded rapidly once she took a closer look. I explained my disastrous trip to the hospital and the 'idigyezzion' diagnosis.

'Right. On the bed Kat, I don't like the sound or look of this,' she said.

Oh shit, here we go, I thought, lying back gingerly and feeling woozy.

'Did you actually have that endoscopy I asked you to book last time you were here? I didn't see any results come through.

'Urrr, no I didn't. Sorry. Life has been unbelievably hectic and work has been manic.'

'Kat, you really should have gone.' Placing her stethoscope on my stomach, she carefully pressed my tummy, finding the centre of the pain. She applied the gentlest of pressure then very quickly lifted her hand, which was when fresh pain ripped through me and made me shriek loudly. 'Okay, get up. We have a big problem, Kat.'

She helped me off the bed and I sat down again, feeling increasingly faint and struggling to focus my thoughts. It was all a bit of a blur and I battled to absorb the magnitude of her diagnosis, catching only certain words: ulcer, perforated ulcer, perforated gut, internal bleeding, peritonitis, death, hospital, surgery, today, now. It seemed I was sick and it was pretty damn serious too.

Doc Merton whipped out her phone book and said she was calling a gastric surgeon. In my daze and feeling as if I was looking down on us, I listened to her explaining things to some surgeon, telling him about the fool at the hospital too. Many of the words she'd just uttered to me were repeated.

'I know,' I heard her say. 'If it blew on Friday then she should be dead by now yet she's been to work this morning and even drove herself here. But let's see—'

There was a long pause.

'Okay, I'll get her admitted right away. She's probably got a few hours. Less.'

Another long pause as she listened to the surgeon.

'Okay. Call me later, after you've seen her,' she said, and then ended the call by saying, 'That fucking moron at the ER. This is going to be one helluva scandal by the time I'm finished with him. This time I'll have his licence stripped.'

She hung up and turned back to me. 'Sorry about my foul language.'

'No, go right ahead, Doc. I thought he was fucking stupid too.'

Next, she called her receptionist to say she'd be running late for the remainder of the morning as she 'had an emergency on her hands', which I then realised was me. Her next phone call was to St Anne's, one of Harare's better private hospitals. I heard her giving my name, the surgeon's name and saying I'd be a gastro surgical case.

Still listening, I then learnt a hospital bed was reserved and, apparently, I'd be in it within the hour. And still I felt like I was in a dream, struggling to keep up with the speed of things. The more the panic escalated around me, the more confused I got.

Then I vomited. Luckily, Doc Merton saw that one coming and, with one hand, she swiftly lunged forward to shove the dustbin under my nose. Coming round her desk, she gently rubbed my back as I puked and puked. Still talking to the hospital in an urgent voice and still soothing me, she closely examined my vomit colour – a shade of pink.

My God, this woman sure can multitask, I thought, wondering why I could taste blood.

She finished the St Anne's call and turned to me, her hand on my forehead, feeling for a fever. 'Kat, is your Mom in town? We need to get you in fast.'

I assumed that 'in' meant hospital.

'Yes, she is actually,' I said. Even my voice sounded like it belonged to someone else. I gave her Mom's number and she made the next call.

'Gill? Jenny Merton here. I have Kat here with me about her stomach pain. It's not good news. I am ninety-five percent sure she has a perforated ulcer and has had massive internal bleed over the last two days. She needs to get into hospital immediately. St Anne's are waiting for her and the surgeon will meet her there. She'll probably need surgery today. The risk with a perforated ulcer is peritonitis and, if that's what's happened, it's a miracle she's still standing.'

Technically, I wasn't actually standing. In fact, the mere thought of standing right then seemed as impossible as flapping my arms and being able to fly.

'Left untreated, peritonitis usually kills within twelve to twenty-four hours,' Doc Merton continued. 'That said, I'm looking at her now and she is slipping fast. We need to jump around.'

I heard Mom's slightly shrill voice down the phone, 'And they gave her fucking Rennies—'

'Quite! Don't worry, I'll be taking this one to every medical board there is, if it really is a perforation. Although I can't see how she'd have lasted this long.'

With all the phone calls made, Doc Merton smiled at me, shaking her head ever so slightly and now looking a bit pale herself. Apparently, Mom was packing a bag for me and would soon arrive to drive me to hospital.

It was all surreal. I had so many questions but simply couldn't gather my thoughts long enough to ask them.

In another room, I was helped onto a bed where I was to wait for Mom. A double shot of morphine appeared and I was duly jabbed. My mouth was like sandpaper and the blood lingering in my mouth tasted metallic. I was allowed only the tiniest sip of water because I'd be having an anaesthetic for lunch. Lying there as the drug kicked in, I replayed things, bewildered and terrified. Words floated into my head and haphazard thoughts wafted by – morphine-flavoured mental ramblings.

So, I was slipping fast. Yeah, now you mention it, I ain't feeling too hot.

Peritonitis kills in twenty-four hours. But it's been two days since that gunshot feeling – why aren't I dead then? So it can't be peritonitis then. Or am I dead? Is this death, because it's nothing like the brochure.

Hospital and surgery today. Nope, sorry, no can do. I have an annual report that needs to get to the printer today. In fact, I really should get back to the office now. Can't we just wrap this up now? I'm busy. Lots to do. Lots to do.

Ulcer? But I don't have an ulcer. I'm too busy to have an ulcer, never mind a perforated one. I feel fine, apart from this rather sore gut. Wasn't it supposed to be indigestion anyway? Just give her some more anz azid and Kitt-hiy will be fine.

Actually, I'd kill for a cigarette now. Can we smoke here? And this morphine is quite fun too, any chance of another round? Make mine a double, barman.

Obscure thoughts continued as my brain flitted around like a butterfly. Little dots in my vision formed hypnotising patterns. I drifted and dozed as my mind travelled morphine country.

Suddenly, Mom and Doc Merton were standing over me. Mom must have driven like the clappers. She certainly drove like the clappers to the hospital and, as Doc Merton had cunningly predicted, I was in a hospital bed within the hour, not happy about all the fuss, although I was feeling weaker with each passing minute. I'd barely got into the bed when the surgeon strode in very purposefully, a string of nurses on his heels. He was a big burly man, all healthy looking and outdoorsy, with lovely kind eyes.

'Kat, Mrs Hay, I'm Doctor Johnson,' he introduced himself.

Thank God, he's English, I thought.

Much the same as Doc Merton, he pressed my gut with the heel of his hand and then suddenly released the pressure, making the pain flare and me yelp loudly.

'Jenny Merton may well be right about a perforation,' he said. 'Either way, that casualty doctor was certainly way off the mark. This is not indigestion by any stretch of the imagination.'

'Yeah, what a tit he was – OW!' I yelped as he pressed my gut again. 'Can you stop doing that. It's bloody sore.'

'Sorry Kat, here's the thing,' Doc Johnson said, sitting down to deliver the news and looking terribly serious. 'If you had an ulcer and it perforated on Friday night as you describe, the peritonitis from that would have killed you in the same weekend, within twenty-four hours actually. The contents of a stomach are toxic to the body outside the gut, and, when they pour out or leak into your peritoneal cavity, you die pretty damn quickly. When an ulcer perforates, it can tear a hole in the stomach. I will eat my shorts if you have a perforated ulcer and stomach because it would be a total miracle and probably a medical record that you're here today. The internal bleeding is also normally fatal, on top of the toxicity.'

'Well then, just do your thing, tell me what it is, take the pain away and let me get back to my annual report. I really do have a mountain of work to do today,' I said.

'For starters, you can forget about going back to work today. But here's what we'll do. I'll bump my other surgeries down the list and get you into surgery in about an hour. First, I have to have a "look see" in your gut and will attempt that via keyhole surgery. So, you'll just have two little cuts, one in your belly button and one lower down. Let's see what I find and take it from there, okay?' he said, his voice warm and comforting.

'Yup, okay. I don't really have a choice, do I?'

'Nope,' he smiled. 'Don't worry, we'll get you up and running soon.'

'Well, I sure hope you don't eat your shorts Doc. Am sure they're very nice shorts. But still.'

'Put it this way, I too hope I don't have to eat them. Not for my sake, for yours, because that'd mean you've had a very close call.' He squeezed my hand and I got all tearful, terrified.

'See you in theatre just now. The anaesthetist will pop by and give you some happy juice,' he said, standing up and indicating to Mom that he wanted to speak to her outside.

Five minutes later an army of nurses came bustling in to prepare me for surgery. I still had painted fingernails from Friday night, so they took that polish off, saying it was vital for the anaesthetist to see my nail bed. Then they peered at my red toenails and said that polish had to come off too. I freaked! Nobody ever saw me without painted toenails, it was my 'thing' and it was one thing I didn't budge on.

'The anaesthetist has ten perfectly good nail beds on my fingers to look at,' I argued.

The nurse got stroppy. 'If you don't stop messing about, Miss Hay, the matter of unpainted toes will be of little concern because you'll be dead. You don't have much time.'

She won, and the nail varnish remover was hurriedly applied to my toes.

Everything happened in such a rush. The anaesthetist marched in and after his pre-op happy shot, I was soon drifting again, the unpainted toenails forgiven.

While I was being attached to a myriad of machines in theatre, and a platter of sharp, scary-looking instruments was being served, Doc Johnson took my hand.

'Listen Doc, please don't make me make you eat your shorts, okay?' I said with a slur. He just smiled and gently tucked in a strand of hair that had escaped my sexy surgical cap. On my other side, the anaesthetist was good to go and I felt the prick. The thick white anaesthetic slid gracefully and elegantly into my vein, sending a sudden icy chill as well as a burn all the way up my arm.

'Right, gentlemen, let's get a crack on, please. I have work to do and annual reports to get to printers, so make it snappy. Chop-chop, lollipops,' I drawled, wanting to stay in that delicious, seductive twilight zone, not go back, not go forward, just hover. I could never have imagined what was waiting for me on the other side of that nap.

23

I opened my eyes slowly, all groggy, dying to get home and have a long bath and an early night. I reckoned it'd been a short procedure, an hour tops. The wider I opened my eyes, the more aware I became, and was horrified when my eyes landed on a wall sign saying ICU. Then I registered it was pitch-dark outside. A persistent beeping sound was driving me nuts, scratching my brain. I turned my head to see if I could turn the noise off, that was when I saw a collection of monitors and machines around the bed, all attached to me. One machine was hissing oxygen at me and about four drips were up, split between each of my arms. A heart monitor was hard at work drawing spikey lines and various drains appeared to be coming from under a monumental dressing on my stomach. And then I felt the pain and realised this had been far more than keyhole surgery.

The nurse stationed at my bed saw me stir. In a soothing voice, she confirmed I was in ICU, and that I was okay but I'd had an extremely serious op. She then told me to hang five and darted off, quickly coming back with Mom and Dad who'd been waiting outside.

'Sweetheart,' said Mom, finding a spare piece of arm to rub in between all my drip lines. 'How're you feeling?'

'Shit, what happened? That wasn't keyhole. I feel like I've been cut all the way through,' I mumbled.

Dad smiled at me. I was struck by how exhausted he looked as he started to give me the low-down. 'You did perforate an ulcer. And when the ulcer blew, it blew a hole in your stomach lining. The contents of your stomach then spilled into your abdominal cavity. It took them eight hours in theatre to clean up the mess. Right now you have chronic peritonitis and are in critical condition. Most of these drips are antibiotics as they have to get a handle on the toxicity. You're on a morphine drip too.'

'Oh. Lovely.' It was all I could muster.

'They had to take you to pieces and lay your intestines out in order to vacuum up every last speck of food that was free-floating in your abdominal cavity. Everything you ate on Friday leaked out, undigested. And everything you ate and drank since flew straight through the hole in your stomach and into your abdomen too. It took them hours to find every last bit of rice,' explained Dad.

'You're a bit of a mess actually, KitKat,' added Mom, a bit tearful.

'And what does my tummy look like? What's under these bandages?'

'You have a cut twenty-five centimetres long, straight through your middle. You're lucky to have made it. Another hour and we'd have lost you,' said Dad.

'So, it's bad?'

'Yup, very. You've also lost a huge amount of blood and they're about to start transfusions. Your heart nearly gave out during the last hour of the surgery so, yes, you are in critical condition, sweetheart,' said Mom.

'Oh. Mom, I need you to paint my toenails for me tomorrow, okay?' I said. Suddenly, it was the most pressing matter for me. Mom just laughed and the nurse shook her head, Dad too.

'We're considering a lawsuit against that doctor who sent you home with Rennies for a perforated stomach,' said Dad.

'Damn right,' I mumbled.

'How's the pain, Kat?' asked the nurse. At least I wasn't being called Kitt-hiy this time.

'Mmmm,' I replied, remembering I had morphine partying up a storm in my veins.

'I think Doctor will give you an epidural in the morning, to help with pain control,' said the nurse.

'Sweetheart, Ant has been waiting with us outside. He's terribly upset. They won't let him in as he's not family, but he's here and sends his love,' said Mom.

'Tell him I love him and sorry for the worry.' I was dozing off as I spoke. The morphine had a kick like a mule.

The nurse asked Mom and Dad to leave for the night and a while later Doc Johnson marched in. It must have been well past midnight.

'Well young lady, you sure did screw up my Monday night squash plans, plus I have to choose some shorts to eat,' he said softly, taking my hand. 'You are indeed a miracle, my girlie. Did anyone explain what we had to do?'

'Something about hoovering my abdomen.'

'Yup. I've never seen such a mess in my entire medical career. Every time we thought we had all the muck out, we'd find another grain of rice.'

'And what if you'd missed a bit and left rice in there?'

'Well, the toxins would enter your bloodstream and it'd be curtains. The body can't process food outside the intestines. It turns toxic. The peritonitis is what nearly finished you off and, in fact, it still could. You're nowhere near out of the woods yet.'

'Mmm,' I said, battling to keep up.

'I am going to up your dose of morphine for the night and then we need to get some blood into you. I'm just waiting for the match from the blood bank. Your heart is not entirely happy either. You're going to have a long and slow recovery, I'm afraid.'

He looked at my monitors again, something alarmed him and he suddenly moved away to speak to the matron. 'Where's that blood, Sister? She's critical and needs it stat. Look at her vitals, she's slipping again. Give me that phone, let me speak to them.'

There was a bit of a panic and Doc Johnson was suddenly losing his cool. After a terse phone call about missing blood, he left ICU. I was aware of the blood arriving a while later.

By then I had started to drift, not in and out of sleep but in and out of life. The next hour was to remain crystal clear in my memory for the rest of my life. Vivid detail, but I could never quite find the words to truly capture what I felt when I crossed over, when I left my body to gaze down on myself. Drifting, floating, hovering, weightless, comfy, safe – the closest to a description I could get.

And the more I drifted upwards and out of myself, the crazier my machines went. Their frantic beeping became strangely melodic as I floated upwards. I knew I was leaving this part of my life, and there was nothing scary about it. I felt sublimely peaceful and pain free for the first time in years. My world and all its complications suddenly didn't matter. Silly details were of no importance. Stress and angst had no home in that unknown dimension.

While looking down on things, I saw the panic building around my bed and at the nurses station. My blood had finally arrived from the bank, but no one could find the key to the cupboard housing the tubes needed to get it into me. A nurse was saying someone on the day shift must have taken the key home by mistake.

Well, that's fucking helpful, I thought. I floated a bit higher and looked down, almost amused at the matron's panic. Her voice was becoming more urgent.

'You better break that lock NOW! We're losing her,' she said, standing next to me, adjusting my drips and watching me. Beep beep beep. My machines were unstoppable and angry. A new, more serious 'ding-dong' alarm suddenly joined the orchestra.

From my spot somewhere up near the ceiling, I casually watched over my physical self. My body was absolutely still, my chest not moving at all, arms limp, my face an unbecoming pasty grey. I noticed I still had that morning's make-up on, though at some point in all the fun my mascara had smudged, which totally irritated me. I didn't even want to think about the state of my unpainted toenails, grateful they were under a blanket.

I knew my soul had detached, had departed my physical body, but I felt no fear, only comfort. And I felt a warm light on me, on my back perhaps. I couldn't tell where it was coming from, just that it felt lovely, safe. Bizarrely, I thought of Sam, wondering if she'd had a similar experience in the moments before she died. Maybe she had actually known she was minus a leg when she checked out.

Still watching the scene below, I saw a male nurse viciously kick the all-important cupboard open, snapping the door right off its hinges with a helluva noise. As if there was a ticking bomb under him, he grabbed the transfusion tubes and bolted to my bed, hurriedly hooking up the blood and getting yet more lines into me. With the blood transfusion finally running, the nurses began to call my name loudly, staring into my face, firmly tapping my cheek and shaking my shoulder. I wanted to reach down from my aerial position, tap them on the shoulder and say, 'Hey, idiots, I'm up here now.' I mean, why didn't the fools know I wasn't in the bed anymore?

I followed one nurse's eyes, saw that my heart machine displayed an almost flat line, tiny spikes of neon green broke the line here and there, but it was mainly flat. I watched, almost fascinated, as the little blips became more spaced out and less frequent. Still no fear in me at all.

Suddenly things changed, everything slowed down for me, like a sports replay, and I knew the nurses were about to give up and call my time of death. A strange smell saturated the air, sweet, sickly and cloying. It was the smell of sheer human panic, of sweat and adrenaline and 'oh fuck'. It was their smell, the nurses' smell. I was torn between going back down or staying in the safe warmth near the ceiling where there was no pain, only peace and beautiful light.

Then came the pull. It was like an industrial magnet had entered the space and I was just a tiny paper clip. I was being yanked – forced back down to the bed, away from the safe haven above, back to my broken, battered physical self. The force was far too strong to fight. Someone else was definitely driving.

The nurse looked at my now entirely flat green line. 'She's gone. We're too la—' As she was speaking, looking at the clock on the wall and picking up a pen and my chart, I gave in to the pull. Very quickly, I morphed back into my physical self, back into Kat, back to the bed and back to this life. And back to the pain. Small, weak spikes reappeared on my green line and the nurses stood by, shocked.

For the rest of my days, I'd remember the time I'd hovered between this life and the next. The warmth in that light, the delightful peace and sense of relief I had felt up near the ceiling. I would spend years wondering what had pulled me back and why.

Only on the next leg of my life's journey would I discover the true purpose of Kat in this particular life. I didn't know that to find the answers I had to travel a treacherous road, one with no maps.

24

I was told I'd been clinically dead, not that I needed telling. At last, I understood all the stories I'd read about near death, being pulled from this world into another place, another space and dimension. The 'light at the end of the tunnel' stories made perfect sense too, and, from that moment on, I had no fear of death. Death was truly nothing to be afraid of.

That night, after my soul had rejoined my body, what bugged me the most – apart from my unpainted toenails – was not knowing whose blood I had received. I had a certain sense that it was German. Although I had absolutely no basis for that assumption, it didn't sit too well with me. Many strange things happened to my spiritual self in the hours following my surgery. I had so many odd thoughts and realisations about the strangest of things. I couldn't define it, but knew it went beyond just being blasted on morphine. So began my fascination with the spiritual world, the afterlife, other dimensions. It was the start of my being able to live on a higher frequency, more in tune with the energies and symbols around me.

I was horrified, utterly horrified, when I saw my scar. From the top of my rib cage, through my torso to ten centimetres below my belly button, it looked like the handiwork of Hannibal Lecter. No stitches, they'd used a heavy-duty staple gun to close me up. It was the most nauseating thing I'd ever seen in my life. I swore my stomach would never ever see the light of day again.

I didn't remember much of the first few days following surgery. Despite being drugged to the eyeballs and flying very high, reality was a far cry from that ethereal, warm haven I'd visited briefly. I'd be lying if I said I hadn't longed to go back there.

My heart stabilised and the antibiotics got a grip on the peritonitis. I was made to walk on day three, which didn't go particularly well. The pain ripped through me and I collapsed, crumpling like cheap tissue paper.

After a week in ICU, I was moved onto the surgical ward where I had a private room – thanks to Dad sweet talking our medical-aid people. I'd sit on my balcony for hours, aimlessly gazing at the pretty hospital gardens. They started weaning me off the morphine, but I couldn't bear the pain and the hefty doses were reinstated. I never thought it possible to experience such agony and regularly felt like I was losing the plot. I wanted to scream, bite, howl, kick, beg. Anything to make it stop.

Five weeks later I went home, with the drain in my wound. It had to be cleaned daily. The muck still coming out made me feel revolting and dirty. My skin was grey and, no matter how many showers I took, I just couldn't wash 'hospital' out of my skin, hair, everything. It seeped through every pore.

I had good days and bad days. For weeks, I lived from one dose of painkillers to the next, moving between bed, couch and bathroom up at the main house where it was easier for Mom to keep an eye on me. I felt bad, needing so much help from others. The last thing our family needed was another burden after the difficult move off the farm.

Grandpa was the best, ensuring I had a stream of movies to watch, piles of books and the latest magazines. Mom and Dad shared nurse duties, sitting with me whenever they had a lull in the craziness of basically starting over. Even GranJilly chipped in when she could, although she was now about as frail as me. Making tea was about her limit, poor old duck. Ant was at work on the river again, but would be home within a fortnight, announcing he was taking unpaid leave just to be with me, also knowing it would take some pressure off Mom and Dad. He definitely knew how to score points with them. My medical drama had revitalised our love. All the silly niggles and my fears about us drifting apart seemed ludicrous. We had our sparkle back.

Stephen surprised me by popping in one day. I felt awful about leaving him the lurch at work, but he insisted they were coping and told me to take as much time as I needed to recover. Adding to my guilt, Stephen insisted on paying me while I was off. He made a comment about feeling partly responsible for my close call, as he'd worked me to the bone lately.

Rolo came every day after work and Cookie even started setting a place at the dinner table for her. She always made me laugh, telling me what I was missing out on in the big bad world that now seemed so alien to me. On my bad days, Rolo would bring our supper on trays to my bedroom, and, if I wasn't up for chats, she'd just lie next to me on the double bed and read all my magazines, no conversation needed. No matter how crappy I felt, I looked forward to her evening visits. Ela also visited as often as she could. Grandpa would tootle off to collect her and Mojo, donning an old hat on which he'd written Dan's Taxis. Some evenings, everyone piled onto my bed at once – Chris, Ela, Rolo, Ben, Katie, Mojo, Tighty, Gertie and I – not a bit of bed free.

Tighty was never far from my side. I'd hear him come belting down the corridor to my room, taking a run up and leaping onto my bed like a springbok, the sudden bouncing of the bed making me shriek in pain. To his credit, he knew not to land on me. He'd lie sprawled out next to me, panting, farting and chasing rabbits in his sleep. Some days I chased rabbits with him, depending on how close the morphine was.

For the next month, I focused on recovering. Doc Johnson hadn't been lying when he'd said it'd be slow. My biggest issue was pain management. Every time I was weaned off the morphine, I'd soon be yammering in pain. I was switched to a different painkiller, everyone worried about the long-term usage of morphine. After just a few weeks, I was heavily dependent on it and the high doses had seen the side effects kick in, the worst of which was itchy skin. Even after cutting all my nails off, in a fit of Morphine Mads I'd gouge angry welts in my flesh. I was permanently nauseous and dropped ten kilograms. When I could eat, my stomach could handle only toddler-sized amounts and I quickly started to look anorexic on top of everything else. Despite everyone's efforts to keep me comfortable and entertained, a heavy depression set in. I would regularly chastise myself for not taking better care of my health, for not having the ulcer tests as recommended, for ignoring my gut feeling – literally. I knew I had to adopt a healthier lifestyle. The next time I danced with death, I probably wouldn't live to tell the tale.

Three months after my gut went 'bang', I started driving again, finally making it back to work a few weeks later, the annual report long since printed. I felt awkward going back, like the new girl, but soon found my groove – working mornings only for the first fortnight.

Whilst I'd managed to come off painkillers of the morphine variety, I was still suffering from insane headaches and regular migraines. In fact, I think my head was worse. Although I'd basically shredded my gut by hammering it with copious amounts of painkillers, I picked up on my old pill-munching habits and found myself back in that groove. However, I did take them after food or, at least, on a glass of milk in homage to my ulcer. As soon as I could drive, Colin and I also resumed our handy little supply arrangement but, every now and then, as a decoy, I would still fill Doc Merton's prescriptions at the pharmacy. Everyone knew I was taking the painkillers, but no one knew how many.

I hated myself for doing it to my body after what I'd just put everyone through. I couldn't cut back and was terrified of admitting it to anyone. If ever there was a time for me to speak up, to ask for help and admit I was scoring drugs from a dealer, it was then. But I didn't, couldn't. The further down the road I went, the further into my self-built hell I tumbled. I was on that very road Mom had said I didn't want to go down – her road, Maddie's road. Knowing it was one thing, but getting off that road was another. I just didn't know how to turn back, how to ask for help. In many ways it was easier to just keep going.

After all, it was the devil I knew.

Part C: The last six months

25

I was in charge of finishing off the birthday cake but, given the severity of my hangover, it was unlikely to look anything like the one in the picture. Mashing some chocolate icing into a piping bag, I attempted *Happy Birthday Princess Katie.*

I was feeling a little tatty. It had been a particularly raucous and drunken evening the night before and I'd partied hard, crawling into bed just before dawn. We'd smoked a joint before going out, so details of the evening were sketchy and I wasn't even sure who I'd been partying with in the end. Vicky and Andrew had left quite early and I'd opted to stay on the dance floor. On waking an hour ago – before my feet had even hit the floor – I had knocked back a handful of painkillers, just so I could get going.

'Fuck it,' I muttered to myself. A great splodge of brown icing had landed on the cake, looking like something had crapped on it. I scraped it off and decided to practise on a breadboard. I managed a pretty even *Happy Birthday* when, just as I was about to replicate it on the cake, Mom marched into the kitchen looking all purposeful and a bit militant.

'Is that going to take long?' she asked.

'I'm getting there,' I said in a crabby voice. Distracted, I squeezed the bag too hard and another arbitrary splat of icing landed on the cake.

'Oh for God's sake, Kat, look at your hands. You're shaking like a bloody leaf. Here, give it to me. We'll be here till the sodding cows come home at this rate.'

Things had been a bit tense and sparky between Mom and me lately.

Banished from the kitchen, I went outside to watch the birthday games. Grandpa had just dive bombed and emptied half the pool while Dad, Tim, Chris and a bunch of squeaky kids were playing Marco Polo.

Katie had suddenly shot up, the most gorgeous little girl and so like Sam. Chris should probably be nominated for Single Dad of the Year. It hadn't been easy for him, adapting to the life of a widower and single parenting, but he'd stepped up and was doing a fine job. Katie was a polite and well-mannered delight who adored her father, just as he doted on her, and Ben was still the happiest little guy ever, always smiling.

After pouring myself an icy glass of Chardonnay, I joined Ela and Linda in the shade. Ben was bouncing on Ela's lap.

'Wine anyone? Ela, Linda?' I offered. It was late afternoon, sundowner time, though I appeared to be the only one drinking.

'Nah, thanks,' they both said and Ben suddenly gave a happy gurgle.

'Oh hell, Ben,' Ela said. 'That means you've just dropped a load in your nappy, huh?'

In reply, Ben let off a loud fart, just in case there was any doubt, though with the smell wafting from his bum, it was hard to miss.

'KitKat, will you change him?' Ela asked.

'Yuk. No. A shitty nappy won't be good for my hangover.' Already the smell had sent a flood of saliva into my mouth.

'Chris!' I bellowed in the direction of the pool, making Linda wince. 'Your son has a present for you.'

Sam's parents, Jean and Peter, were there too, taking heaps of photos of their grandchildren. Chris was good about including them in our family gatherings, happy they were such hands-on grandparents. A handful of moms were at the party too, mothers of Katie's friends. Chris seemed to be quite the eligible bachelor and it was rather fun watching them being so flirty around him. It all went straight over his head, which only made them try even harder, the dirty slappers. But Chris was off the market.

If one good thing had come of Sam's tragic death, it was that Chris and Ela were finally in a relationship. Their long-awaited romance was only three months old and they were both glowing and looking disgustingly happy. Everyone was thrilled and even Jean and Peter had given their blessing. They'd come to know Ela and adored her as much as we did, happy that Ben and Katie had a mother figure again.

Ela still worked at the welfare centre and loved her job. We all knew she'd had a fling with her colleague, James, but he'd pursued a teaching post in Indonesia and was out of the picture. Ela lived at the centre but spent weekends with Chris. It wouldn't be long before she moved in officially and Chris had started modifying the house for Ela's blindness. Katie still spoke about Sam from time to time, but had wholly embraced Ela's coming into her little world and totally idolised her. Last week Katie had insisted she needed a white stick – making us cry with laughter when she'd squeezed her eyes tightly shut, grabbed Ela's cane, and tapped her way around the lounge, walking slap bang into the coffee table. This week, Katie had requested a golden retriever puppy. 'Just like Mojo, but in pink please,' she'd said.

Katie squealed with delight when Mom came out with her birthday cake, all perfect and pretty as if from a specialist bakery – like she was trying to make a point. Everyone under six was soon covered in sticky icing so Chris and Tim threw them all back into the pool. It was a stinking hot afternoon, everyone lolled around in varying states of relaxation. Finishing my wine, I lay back on the couch and closed my eyes, drifting into a much-needed siesta.

Later, half asleep and half drunk, I was aware of something tickling my nose. I opened my eyes to find Grandpa waving a peacock feather over my face. God, that is so fucking irritating, I thought.

'No Grandpa, stop it man, I'm sleeping,' I said grumpily.

He chuckled. 'You look like you tied one on last night.'

'Yes, apparently I did. Stop with the feather now, it's bloody irritating,' I grizzled. As he stuck it up my nose again, I snatched it from him and lay on it.

It was nine months since my surgery and my life had changed course, not necessarily for the better. My headaches plagued me and some days my stomach hurt like hell. Doc Johnson had given me a clean bill of stomach health but, every six months, under general anaesthetic, a camera was to be shoved down my throat to check all was well and that no ulcers had had babies. He'd also nagged me about quitting smoking and drinking less.

Needless to say, I'd failed on both counts. Meanwhile, I'd developed a high tolerance for any kind of prescription drug and it took much higher doses to get what just one painkiller used to achieve. I now took eight at once without faltering. On any given day, I could hoover eighty, sometimes more.

Thank God for Colin who was still onside, if one's dealer could ever really be considered onside. Doc Merton, however, was onto me. I suspected she'd worked out I was getting something from someone. I'd flatly denied it when she suggested that I was up to something shady. Nevertheless, I'd been on the receiving end of a stern health warning. She'd asked me to consider doing a detox, reminding me what damage I'd already done. I'd argued, saying I could easily stop whenever I wanted to. I also highlighted that I didn't take painkillers recreationally. If I didn't get such bad headaches, I'd never need them. But I did, so I did.

Kat, the queen of justification, I was.

I'd lost a huge amount of weight, too. The 'you're getting too skinny' talks didn't faze me, but the minute anyone mentioned the pills my hackles flew up. Ela, Chris, Mom, Rolo, Grandpa, Dad, Linda – everyone had had a go at me and it seriously pissed me off when the words 'addiction' and 'denial' were sprinkled into every conversation. Their nagging had got so bad that I'd taken to avoiding them, preferring my own company to that of the Pill Police. Mom was leading the crusade over my 'dependence' and the Maddie story had been dragged out countless times, even by Maddie herself.

Deep down – very deep – I knew the line between pain relief and taking pills to quell a craving for narcotics had long since been blurred, but I had no intention of going public with that realisation. Maybe if I didn't talk about it, it would just resolve itself. It was as if the surgery had awoken some kind of beast in me, a monster that made me seek oblivion all day, every day. I hunted numbness and had become petrified of pain, almost to the point of it being a phobia. At the first whiff of discomfort, I'd run to those who never let me down, my pills, my friends.

Colin gave me no lectures, ever. If I couldn't get enough pills via the normal channels of prescriptions and pharmacies, I sourced the balance myself. All I had to do was call in my order, a call that barely took a minute, then Colin and I would meet in some quiet or dark car park and exchange cash and painkillers. He never seemed shocked by the quantities I asked for and I never asked questions or queried the legality of what he was doing, aware that my part in it was as illegal as his. It was a functional arrangement that I kept entirely to myself. I didn't dare think about what would happen if I were caught.

Something had died in me. Some days I wondered if I'd left a part of me on the ICU ceiling that night, that maybe some of my better traits hadn't come back to this world with me. A level of selfishness had moved in and, as long as I had my painkillers, I was happy. They came before most other things in my life.

I pulled myself back to the present, jolted by the kiddies' squeals.

'You okay, KitKat?' asked Ela, sitting next to me on the couch.

'Mmm, yup, just tired. Big night out,' I said. Here we go again, I thought, sensing a lecture.

'Is your tummy hurting?'

'Mmm, kind of,' I muttered.

Grandpa came to sit with us, cracking open a cold beer.

'Ah, don't I get a beer Grandpa?' I asked.

'You hate beer. Besides, by the look of you, you've had more than enough booze. You look like a wreck, by the way,' he said.

'Gee thanks,' I said flatly. I have one night out, one hangover, and everyone comes down heavy on me. Bloody ridiculous.

The Yummy Mummies, whom I'd found increasingly irritating as the afternoon wore on, thankfully started to pack up their little people and cluck about going home.

With all the guests gone, Grandpa decided to get a game of tennis going with Mom, Chris and Linda. They were all being far too energetic for my liking. He led everyone down to the court, swinging a beer as he went. Grandpa was a marvel on the court, fitter than all of us put together. I'd played with him once or twice but got my arse kicked. I also found it tricky to smoke while playing, even after Grandpa taught me how to serve with a lit fag in my mouth.

Dad and Tim took a drive down to the veggies. Dad's venture was doing really well and he'd delivered an excellent crop of runner beans in his first season. He'd been able to expand into other veg quite quickly and next to market was a crop of red peppers and baby potatoes.

Leaving the farm had rocked us all. Our Section Eight had arrived shortly after Sam's death. Dad had managed to get most of his equipment off and what he didn't need in Umwinsidale went to the auctions. Recently he'd had to go back to our farm and returned looking harrowed and traumatised. Our beautiful home had apparently been reduced to a glorified squatter camp, with goats and cows on the front lawn, the house sparse, and the women cooking on an open fire in the middle of the lounge floor. There'd not been a single crop growing. When we asked Dad more, he'd just clammed up, saying, 'No looking back.' It was our new family motto. Mom and Dad's foresight and strategy of not resisting meant there'd been no violence and we'd got out largely unscathed, far better off than some other farming families. The workers had suffered the most with Dad unable to employ them all in Harare.

After the party, I was at last left alone. Tighty clambered onto the couch next to me, not a fan of tennis either as he wasn't allowed on the court to chase the balls, and we lay there snoozing, enjoying the late-afternoon sounds of African doves in the msasa trees and the faint 'clopp' of bouncing tennis balls. My headache had finally receded along with my hangover, my stomach was reasonably pain free and, in that moment, life felt okay again. Given one wish, I'd would ask for Ant to be lying on the couch too. That was another relationship in tatters.

I dialled the number again. For the tenth time in an hour, the number rang and went straight to voice mail. Extremely agitated, I sent another text message and saw it was delivered. Why the hell wasn't Colin answering? He always answered my calls. Bastard.

I had run out of pills. I'd been so flat out at work that I'd forgotten to call Colin in time. It was Friday afternoon and I knew damn well the pharmacy would block me if I asked for more pills. Shit shit shit. I threw my cellphone on my desk and tried to focus on rewriting a client's brochure. I was being ruthless. The grammar was appalling and that alone irritated me but I had to crack on.

A minute later my cellphone rang and I jumped, grabbing it, hoping like hell that it was my stupid dealer finally returning my call. It was Rolo and I didn't do a good job of hiding my disappointment.

'Oh, hi Rolo,' I said, my voice flat.

'Well, I'm so sorry. Were you expecting someone more exciting to call?'

'No, Rolo, shit, sorry man,' I replied, feeling bad but quickly thinking up a white lie. 'I was hoping it might be Ant calling.' That, actually, was true.

'Oh. Has he still not called you?'

'No, he hasn't. Nothing. Not a peep. I'm sick of his nonsense. He's being childish and I've done my best. Anyway, what's up? How're you doing?'

'All cool. Vicky, Andrew and I are going to a movie tonight and then dinner, maybe hit the pub afterwards. You gonna join us?'

'Uhhh, I won't, thanks a mill though. I've got to sign off on some copy tonight and it's so badly written I'm starting from scratch.' I hated lying to my best friend, being more focused on finding my dealer than having a fun evening with mates.

'You sure? Why don't you skip the movie but come for dinner and a toot? You hardly ever come out with us anymore.'

She was right.

'You're turning into a boring old fart. Next you'll get a perm and a Maltese poodle,' Rolo added.

'Ha bloody ha. I am a hard-working woman, not an old lady, you tart,' I laughed. 'Nah, I better leave it, but let's catch up on Sunday.'

'I'll hold you to that, old fart. Let me know if Ant calls,' she said, hanging up.

Ant and I had had a blazing row about three weeks earlier and the argument had ended with us breaking up. With little in common anymore, we'd slowly drifted apart and had perhaps grown out of each other. Sometimes teenage relationships just didn't transition successfully into adulthood. He was still based on the Zambezi so the long distance didn't help. There were so many little things, little issues and little snares that just added up to a relationship going stale and moving backwards, not forwards. I loved Ant – I always had – but I just didn't know *how* to love him anymore. Neither did I have the faintest idea that I had to love myself first for a relationship to work. Even liking myself would have been a good start.

Ant had flown home purely to get 'us' back on track. He wanted it to work, as did I, but the final fight had erupted when I'd been late – very late – for a special dinner he'd booked at one of the best restaurants. I had lied, saying a client meeting had run late. Meanwhile, I'd been waiting for Colin who'd failed to pitch up at the agreed time. There was no way I could even try explaining who Colin was, so it had been easier to lie. He lost it when I eventually rocked up at 10 p.m., livid too that my work had come first when he'd come to town only to see me.

During the fight, Ant had accused me of changing, saying I'd become self-centred and that I didn't vaguely resemble the Kat of a year ago – not on any level. Apparently, I looked like a wreck, was skin and bone, and that I'd become a cold, miserable, sour little bitch, a piss artist and a junkie too. Awful words that felt like shards of glass tearing into my soul. Yet entirely true.

Ant had begged me to take better care of myself, reminding me how I'd nearly died on the operating table after trashing my body. Like everyone else's, his words had had no effect other than to infuriate me and make me slam the proverbial door. All the 'Kat, you'll die' talk didn't work. It meant nothing to me. Ever since the night I'd hovered between this life and the next, I'd had no fear of death. And nobody got it. Death was scary for others, not for the dead.

That night, after the break-up, I hadn't done the girly break-up routine and gone home to sob into my pillow, read old love letters and eat chocolate. Instead, I went to a nightclub on my own and spent the night knocking back double vodkas with some random guy. I didn't even phone Rolo or Vicky to cry on their shoulders, I just wanted to get absolutely plastered and that's precisely what I did.

Despite the bravado, I was gutted over the split and hated myself for what I'd done that night. I'd been desperate to get more pills off Colin. A few days later, full of remorse and the reality of our break-up sinking in, I tried to make comms with Ant to work things out but he hadn't returned any of my calls. Heartfelt emails followed, begging him to speak to me – they too remained unanswered. Now, I was licking my wounds, but also somewhat pissed off that he'd not responded on any level. Hurting and broken, I tried to blame others, telling myself that if Colin hadn't buggered me around then none of it would have happened. However, I kind of knew it wasn't about Colin or about being late for dinner. It was about who and what I'd become.

Now Colin was screwing me around again. If only I could find myself a new Colin, I thought. It would lessen the risk of a supply failure, but I could hardly waltz into pharmacies and announce my desire to appoint a new dealer and score unlimited quantities of the strongest prescription painkillers available, no questions asked. I'd even wondered whether I should turn to more traditional dealers and see if they did pharmaceuticals as well as street drugs.

I kept working until 4 p.m. Colin, the unreliable shit, still hadn't surfaced and there was nothing for it but to make another plan. I would finish my work at home later, being more focused on my priority – scoring pills, knocking myself out and numbing the pain of losing Ant.

I ploughed through the Friday afternoon traffic, considering my plan carefully. I decided on a small pharmacy on the outskirts of an industrial area.

'Hello madam, how may I help?' asked the well-spoken pharmacist.

'Ah, I do hope you can help,' I said, starting my spiel. 'I am from South Africa, passing through Harare on my way to Mozambique. Unfortunately, I've hit some delays on the road and been away longer than planned. I suffer from chronic migraines and I've run short of my painkillers. I was wondering if you might dispense some to tide me over. You'd be a lifesaver if you could, without a prescription.' I rubbed my temples and spoke in a slightly nasal voice, pretending I was in extreme pain and hoping my story sounded plausible.

He just looked at me and, for a millisecond, I thought he'd tell me to press on, seeing straight through my story. Then he smiled warmly and said he'd let me have a hundred pills.

'It's no problem at all. Shame, you look like you're suffering! I just need your name please,' he said.

I thought quickly. 'Mrs Samantha Clapham,' I replied, the names of two dead people first to mind.

Within minutes, I was back in my car. I gave a victory 'Yesss!' and opened the bottle, chucking six pills back. Phew! Colin, you'd better surface soon, I thought. Finally able to think straight, I pulled myself together. I had sweat running down my back. It wasn't a hot day, it was panic.

I headed home. There was actually no excuse for me not to meet the girls other than I wasn't in the mood. More and more, at any social gathering, someone found a way to slip in a comment or express concern about my 'problem'. It was easier to avoid them altogether.

Mom and Dad were at a wedding out of town, only Grandpa and I were home. Dad had recently made the tough decision to put GranJilly in an old-age home. She now needed full-time care, plus she'd recently been diagnosed with dementia. Poor old duck, I don't think she even realised she was in the departure lounge, as Grandpa called it.

Grandpa saw me driving in. He was walking up from the pepper fields, pellet gun slung over his shoulder and Tighty and Gertie in tow.

'Bloody bastard crows,' he muttered. 'They're going for the peppers. Been trying to nab one so I can string it up on the roof.'

I laughed, remembering how he'd waged war with crows on the farm.

'Come on, let's have a little sundowner,' said Grandpa.

'Coming in five minutes. Let me change quickly.' In my cottage, I put my pills away and slipped on a tracksuit.

Up at the main house, Grandpa and I settled down on the outdoor couches. Dad had extended the patio into a far wider deck, adding a fire pit too. It was a perfect place for watching sunsets on lazy evenings. The garden below looked amazing. Colourful rose beds were dotted around msasa and jacaranda trees, and lush lawns met the veggie fields in the middle distance. The sun dipped as we sat looking over the red peppers, bright red splashes amongst the green foliage. I spotted Jobb on Mom's horse, letting off steam on the far side of the pepper field. I took a deep breath. How lucky I was. Such tranquillity surrounded me, yet my own life was turning to shit.

Grandpa sat back with a beer, his pellet gun at the ready in case a crow showed face.

'How's the building at your cottage coming along?' I asked. 'I've not been to look lately.'

'Yup, it's on course and should be ready soon. Now it'll just be me in there. Much as she drove me round the bend on the farm, I kind of miss your GranJilly.'

'Yeah. Remember her fights with the computer?' We both chuckled. 'Shame, I must pop in and visit her over the weekend. Will you come with me?'

'That's a nice idea, we'll take her some goodies. Hope she knows who we are.'

We sat in companionable silence for a while, watching some clouds roll in. A warm wind suddenly whipped through the garden.

'You're not going out with the girls tonight?' Grandpa asked.

'Nah, I need a quiet night in. I'm knackered, work has been manic.'

'Hmm,' said Grandpa, scratching Tighty behind his ears. He looked thoughtful for a while. 'KitKat, what's going on with you, really?'

I took a moment to consider his question. I could see where he was going with it but the way he'd asked the question was gentle. For once, I didn't feel like I was before the firing squad.

'What's happened? Where's the old Kat?' he added.

'Don't know. Everything seems to have changed since the surgery. I've lost most, if not all, of my vim and vigour and I'm not particularly enjoying life. I live in pain. That alone drags me down. So I take painkillers and those put me on another planet. Hey presto, Kat disappears, leaving behind a tired, knackered shell who shuns her friends, her social life and can barely muster a smidgen of enthusiasm for anything.'

Phew, I thought to myself, where did that come from?

Grandpa didn't comment immediately, we both just sat there staring out over the garden, watching the sprinklers that had come on. The miniature rainbows appearing in their wake transfixed me.

'KitKat, my beloved, darling girl, that's the most honest you've been in a long time.'

'Well, it's kind of boring having everyone launch into me and come down on me like a ton of bricks, saying I have a problem. It pisses me off, big time.'

'We're worried about you, that's all. You look awful. How much do you weigh now anyway?'

'No idea. I've never really been one to weigh myself. But yes, I've lost a bit of weight.'

'Do *you* think you have a problem?'

I considered the question for a while. 'I don't think I have a problem on the scale Mom thinks I do. I'm nothing like Maddie was. I take painkillers for pain relief and sometimes I party and get pissed. To me, that's not a problem. To answer your question, no.'

'Kat, remember one thing, I lived through this with your mother. I watched her life unravel, I watched how self-destructive she became, how she allowed her life to become totally bloody unmanageable. I watched as she nearly lost everything – her health, her husband, her kids, her beauty, her soul. And it wasn't pretty. It was the most helpless I've ever felt in my entire life.'

'Yes, but I ain't that bad.'

'Yet, Kat. Not yet. Your mother's right, you're walking the same path. The similarities I see in you two keep me awake at night. We are so worried. She feels helpless, so do I and we're just so scared tha—' Grandpa's voice suddenly broke. He welled up and quickly turned his face to hide his tears.

I kept quiet, shocked at Grandpa's display of raw emotion.

'Kat, your mother wants to help you,' said Grandpa, more composed after taking a deep breath and flattening his beer, 'but she knows how it feels to be backed into a corner.'

'Yes, well, she's doing just that, backing me into a corner.'

'You've become reclusive. A year ago, you wouldn't be caught dead at home on a Friday night. You had an impressive social life, always doing fun things. Now, you just come home from work and isolate in that cottage of yours. You don't even ride anymore. You've shut all of us out too.'

Grandpa's voice was now steady, calm and still gentle. I felt safe and took in what he said, quietly processing his comments. He was right.

'By the way, what's happening with you and Ant? Have you patched things up?'

'Oh Grandpa, I really have been a bitch to him. I have called and called but he won't talk to me.' I burst into tears.

Grandpa let me bawl without a big song and dance or rolling out sickly sweet words of comfort. Then he asked, 'Do you still love him?'

'Of course. Yes. Shit, I've made such a mess of things with him.'

'He loves you too. Maybe he needs some space right now. Don't give up on him just yet. Remember he's also been affected by your change. He has lost his happy-go-lucky, carefree and beautiful Kat, yet he has stood by you. He's terribly worried too. Last time he was here, he said as much to me. He couldn't understand why you have changed so much. In fact, he asked me if I thought you might be cheating on him. Give him space and give him a chance. Ant's a great guy.'

I was surprised to hear he'd had a heart-to-heart with Ant. 'Me cheating on him?' I replied.

'Yes, obviously I told him you'd never do that but I fully understand how he could think it. Tell me, honestly, how many pills do you take on an average day?'

'Dunno, maybe twenty, sometimes thirty. Depends.' I was lying through my teeth.

'Holy shit balls! And how many do you take at a time?'

More lies fell from my mouth. 'Four, five maybe. The normal dose of two has bugger all effect.'

'That's a helluva lot. And on your tattered stomach.'

'Yup, I know.'

Grandpa was no fool and knew I was taking a lot more than that. How could I tell him I was actually taking closer to eighty pills a day, maybe more?

We smoked in silence and finished our drinks.

'Kat, with your ulcer drama and nearly dying, you really need to get a handle on things and be a little kinder to your body. You won't live to tell the tale next time. We love you, we're here for you, you only have to say the word and we'll do whatever is needed to get you back on track, but you've got to want to do it for yourself, not for us.'

'Thanks Grandpa, I know.' My voice was almost a whisper.

'Like I said, I walked this road with your mother. I know bloody well you are taking far more pills than you admit, but I also know bloody well that, until you are ready to accept some help, nothing anyone says is going to make a jot of difference. The hardest part with your mother was getting her to admit to her alcoholism and convincing her that asking for help was not a bad or weak thing. What I *am* saying is that, when you're ready, we're all here waiting. I just pray you don't kill yourself in the meantime. Or get arrested. I know you're getting pills from a dealer. That's all. Enough said and this conversation is over.'

Thank heavens, I thought, but how on earth did he know about Colin? Shit.

'Okay, okay, I hear you. And thank you,' I replied, taking his rough, comfortable old hand and giving it a squeeze.

I put my head back on the chair and closed my eyes, suddenly feeling very sad and very lost. Two seconds later, I leapt clean off the couch. Grandpa had taken a pot shot at a crow, brazenly perched in an avocado tree a metre behind me.

'Fuck!' I shrieked. 'Could you warn me before you fire a gun next to my ear?'

Grandpa chortled, aimed again and let off another shot. There was much squawking from the tree. We didn't see a crow drop to the ground, but did see a flurry of glossy black feathers floating down along with a few avocados.

'Think I got him. Crow guacamole!' said Grandpa excitedly, cantering down to the tree to assess the state of the crow. Tighty was barking madly, Gertie howling, the silence had been shattered.

'Bastard thing!' shrieked Grandpa from under the tree. 'Damn sure I hit it, but the fucker got away, albeit with half his tail feathers.'

Oh Grandpa, I thought, I do love you dearly. As painful as I had found our little chat, I felt better for it.

The next morning, Grandpa and I decided to visit GranJilly and drop off some crunchies I had made that morning. Arriving at Nazareth House, her nursing home, we were cornered by one of the staff. Apparently, GranJilly was not having a particularly good day. She wasn't exaggerating. After an hour of trying to have a flowing conversation, we called it quits and headed to Chris's house in search of sensible conversation.

Katie was going hell for leather down the driveway on her pink bicycle, pink streamers flying and the little basket loaded with Barbie dolls. She insisted Grandpa race her up the driveway. He slowed down to snail's pace, revving his truck and pretending it was no match for the lightning speed of Katie on a bike. She couldn't stop grinning when she won. I was struck by what a happy, grounded child she was.

'Hellooooo?' I bellowed as I went into the kitchen.

Chris was at his laptop in the lounge. Ben was sprawled out on his cushion doughnut with Mojo, perfectly content flinging toys far and wide, chuckling with each throw. It looked like an explosion in a toy shop.

'Hey!' Chris looked up, smiling. 'What are you chaps doing here?'

Grandpa had headed straight to Chris's fridge before coming into the lounge, snapping open a cold beer that he chugged down almost in one sip.

'Aaaah,' Grandpa said in a satisfied voice, 'that's better. We went to see your GranJilly. Need I say more?'

'We really must go see her sometime but she always freaks Katie out,' said Chris.

'No golf this weekend?' I asked him.

'Nah, I'm working. Ela's here too but she's not very well. She's been puking her guts out all morning.'

I found Ela in bed, looking as green as the bucket she was clutching. 'Ela? Oh shit, you look awful.'

'KitKat?' She turned to the direction of my voice. 'Christ, I feel rough.'

'You don't look too sparky, Poppet. Can I get you anything?' I said, plumping up her pillows and straightening her blankets.

'Nope, thanks hun. Must be a gastro bug but it will pass.'

'Pregnant?' I asked.

'That I'm not. Now sit, tell me news. Have you patched things up with Ant?'

'He won't talk to me. Idiot. Shit Ela, what if he's already in another relationship?' I panicked at the mere thought.

'Stop. You'll torture yourself if you start thinking like that.'

'I suppose. I'd have no way of knowing anyway.'

'Well you did screw things up by being so late for your special dinner, especially when he was here purely for you.'

'I know, I know, I know,' I said, tearful.

A minute later, Ela had her head in the bucket again, retching her heart out. I fetched a damp cloth and sat soothing her, remembering what a beautiful soul she was and what a shit friend I had been lately.

Leaving her to rest, I went back to the lounge which looked even more shambolic, Katie and Ben both crawling around like little hamsters on crack. Chris was showing Grandpa a new advertising campaign he was working on, both oblivious to the chaos around them. Next thing I knew,

Ben had my handbag turned upside down and its contents flew onto the floor. I darted across the room in a mad scramble to save my 'handbag' tub of painkillers. The lid had popped open and pills were strewn everywhere like marbles. Grandpa saw my wide-eyed expression and looked at me sideways as I got down on hands and knees. Most people would have worried about Ben swallowing adult medication, but my concern was not losing any pills, what with Colin disappearing on me. Retrieving them, and everything back in my handbag, I stuck it on a high shelf, safe from Ben. I didn't realise I was breathing heavily. The panic was so instinctive.

Katie coerced Grandpa into another bike race, leaving Chris and me alone.

'You okay, Kat?'

'Yup, all good,' I said in a fake bright voice. Sensing a bit of a lecture coming my way, I thought I'd change the subject quickly. 'And you? How's things with Ela? She's not preggers is she?'

'No, but I wouldn't be devastated if she was. Things are great. Never in my wildest dreams did I think I could be this happy. If I had a tail, it'd be wagging. Only now do I realise how miserable I was with Sam. She gave me the two most precious gifts in Katie and Ben but, my God, she wasn't wife material. I don't know why I didn't take the leap with Ela years ago.'

'Well, then you wouldn't have had Katie and Ben. You had to get there in your own time.'

'Yup, you're right. I'm blessed to have beautiful kids and now Ela too. Life, right now, is pretty bloody good.'

'Am so happy for you, really I am. We're waiting for wedding bells now.'

'We'll get there one day.'

A while later, Tim and Linda popped in to see Ela who was still half-dead and vomiting for the World Cup. Chris fired up the braai and it became a typical family lunch. My head wasn't in great shape, so I knocked back some pills when no one was watching, quite tempted to join Ela on the sick bed.

Colin crawled out from under his rock late on Sunday night, giving some wishy-washy story about being out of town on a 'big delivery'. We arranged to meet the next day, which put my mind at ease.

26

I never made it to work on Monday, up all night with my head down the loo, sick as a dog. My gut and throat raw from bile, I wanted to die. I thought perhaps I'd caught Ela's bug, but I knew I'd taken too many pills again and had severely irritated my stomach.

Mom and Dad got back from their weekend away on Monday morning and, realising I was home, Mom came flying in to see me. She jumped around the minute I was ill these days. I didn't admit to why I was vomiting so much, blaming a bug, but I don't think she believed me for a minute. She made me some watery soup, which I managed to keep down, then some anti-vomit pills that finally remained in my stomach long enough to start working. By the afternoon, I felt marginally better and nipped out to meet Colin, as planned.

He handed over two hundred pills, I handed over the cash, and we went our separate ways. Colin really was the most bizarre character and I was dying to ask how he got away with it all. However, I followed gut instinct and kept the transactions brief. Every time I met him, I became jittery, paranoid about being caught and wondering if we were being watched. I wasn't sure, but was willing to bet that I – and certainly Colin – was on the wrong side of the law. Drug dealers generally were. Did the fact that it involved substances available in a pharmacy as opposed to street drugs make it any less of a crime? And did it help that my dealer had a formal qualification – a pharmaceutical degree? Perhaps Colin could be termed a white-collar dealer and thus marginally less of a low life.

I dragged myself through work the following day, managing clients who had decided to all be particularly demanding on the same day. Stressed and tense, I felt like crap.

Mom was waiting for me when I got home from work, having conveniently found a shrub to prune right outside my cottage.

'Kat, what are you doing this evening?' No pleasantries, she just launched straight in.

'Why?'

'Are you free?'

'Why?' I asked again, Mom and I circling each other verbally. She had that look. Come hell or high water, I was going to be 'asked' to do something but I wouldn't actually have any say in the matter.

'I've barely seen you lately, sweetheart. I'm going to an AA meeting. Come with me? We can go to Coimbra afterwards, just you and me.'

Here we go, I thought, she was angling to talk to me about the 'problem' she perceived me to have. Nevertheless, recognising that it was not a request but an order, I chose the path of least resistance.

'Sure, sounds nice.' I smiled outwardly and scowled inwardly. Mom nearly fell over in surprise, clearly expecting more of a challenge. Take that, I thought, two can play this game.

As we arrived at AA, we bumped into Maddie. It was just a tad contrived and I smelt a rat. Someone was going to have a go at me.

'Madds! Didn't think I'd see you here tonight. Will you join us at Coimbra later?' said Mom, obviously not that desperate to have a mother–daughter supper.

'Sounds good, Kevin is away so I'd love some company,' Maddie replied, turning to me. 'How are you doing Kat? How's the tum?'

What a charade! These two couldn't act if their lives depended on it, I thought.

'Am good, thanks Maddie,' I said, giving her a hug.

'Look at you, all skin and bone,' she said.

I ignored her comment but already my hackles were rising. I felt I'd been ambushed, just as I suspected. I decided to ignore Mom and Maddie and play the game.

It was a big meeting, over fifty people, and it started with the usual First Aid round of people announcing their overall mood status. As the ritual went round the group, I noticed a familiar face at the back of the room. Bugger me, it was Colin. I craned my neck to get a better look. He was with a girl, holding her hand. The greeting ritual got to the girl and she gave a fairly non-committal mood status. Colin then greeted the group and merely said he was there to 'support a friend'. Aha! So, my dealer wasn't a recovering alcoholic or addict himself, which would have been a tad hypocritical. I wondered if he was there scouting for new business amongst the weak and vulnerable. Mom was aware of me staring at someone and gave me a questioning look.

Shit, I thought, better put my game face on. I couldn't run the risk of her asking if I knew Colin. I smiled graciously at Mom, shifted my gaze and pretended I was engrossed in the meeting. Mom just looked at me, a serious battle of wits going on and the tension between us twanging like an electric fence on a dry dusty day.

The meeting was fairly ordinary, as AA meetings go, judging from the few I had now been to. The person sharing was a guy who'd once upon a time drunk himself stupid all day and every day. He spoke of shattered relationships, friendships he'd turned his back on in favour of getting plastered, a difficult childhood, and being sexually abused by a male teacher at school. He mentioned the insane things he did to get drunk and the insane things he did while drunk. He talked about fights and debts that were still crippling him, even sober. A tale of unmanageability and despair but, since coming into AA, his life was changing for the better.

Parts of his story resonated with me and got me thinking about the parts of my life that were perhaps slightly unmanageable, though it'd be a cold day in hell before I admitted as much to Mom. How ironic, I thought, to have had a minor epiphany in a room full of drunks, sitting next to my mother with my dealer two metres away. I almost started giggling, it was so bizarre.

After the meeting, when everyone mingled for some chit-chat or a ciggie outside, I tried to avoid Colin. Mom was yakking with another friend so Maddie and I waited on one side. I scanned the crowd and thought Colin had left already. Then I nearly died of fright when he came up behind me.

'Hey Kat,' he said, ambling past.

You cheeky little fucker, I thought. Now what do I say? Thankfully he didn't stop to chat. However, Maddie's had eyebrows shot up.

'Do you know him?' asked Maddie, wearing an interested look.

'Not really, he works for the IT company we use at work. He's a computer tech, or something,' I replied nonchalantly.

'Ah, I see,' said Maddie.

I held my breath, wondering if she knew what Colin really was.

'He's a new face here at AA. Now where's that bloody mother of yours? Am starving,' said Maddie.

Phew! I breathed a slow sigh of relief and lit another cigarette. That had been a little too close for comfort. Little did I know, then, that Maddie knew only too well what Colin was. He'd once been her dealer too. I couldn't have given her clearer confirmation of how far down the slippery slope I was, or known how perfectly I'd shot myself in the foot.

Over dinner I was tense, on my toes and ready to field the blows when comments about the pills started. Oddly, there were no blows. Not one word was said about my health, the pills, my 'problem' – nothing. Mom and Maddie just rabbited away about anything and everything and I was in no way the central topic, in fact, I wasn't a topic at all. I had two glasses of house wine and started to relax, feeling bad for assuming Mom had planned an ambush. Maybe she had just wanted to spend quality time with me after all.

In bed a few hours later, I realised that my varying states of paranoia were only adding to the unmanageability of my life, to the extent that I could no longer enjoy a simple evening with family and friends. Did my being so defensive mean I had a minor problem after all? It was a thought that was entirely private, and would remain so. A thought that made me entirely uncomfortable too.

I wondered about the unmanageability of my life. Hearing that word at AA had triggered something. I was becoming more aware of the chaos and drama following me around. Life just felt shit. Really shit. My reflex reaction was to turn to Ant for comfort. I dialled his number but stopped on the third digit, suddenly remembering that he wasn't there for me anymore. I didn't get to make those poor me solace-seeking boyfriend calls anymore. He'd left me, and for a brief moment I had forgotten that.

27

A few weeks later, Dad called a family meeting over Sunday lunch, including Tim, Linda and Ela. Poor GranJilly had had a bad few weeks and was the only one not there.

'Right kids,' said Dad, calling for order around the table, 'so much has happened to each of us last year and we all need a break. So, Mozambique for fifteen days over Christmas and New Year in a large house on Bazaruto beach. All of us. Any objections?'

'No!' shouted everyone at once. Grandpa did a victory dance around the table with Ben bouncing on his shoulders, both of them giggling loudly until Ben vomited a puree of lamb casserole on Grandpa's head.

'Linda, you and I had better start planning, it's only six weeks off,' said Mom.

'One question,' said Ela. 'What about GranJilly? Will she be alone for Christmas?'

'Shame, yes, I went to see her the other day, to sound her out,' replied Mom. 'She was having a good day and insisted that we all go. She gave us her blessing. Said she didn't give a toss about Christmas anymore, that it's just an ordinary day to her.'

'Bless her,' I said, realising it'd be the first time in my life that GranJilly wouldn't be at Christmas lunch.

And so it was decided that we'd see in the New Year from a beach in Mozambique. The news lightened everyone's mood and, as far as I was concerned, a change of scenery and a beach holiday was perhaps just what I needed to haul my sorry arse out of my deepening rut.

Two weeks later, we didn't have to feel bad about leaving her behind as our dear old grandma died peacefully in her sleep. We all knew it was a blessed relief for her. For over two decades, all she'd ever wanted was to be with her beloved Arthur again. Dad was, of course, terribly upset but also very pragmatic, believing her to be in a far better place. Grandpa was torn up too. They'd had their moments while sharing a house, but the widow and widower had grown fond of each other and been dear friends.

Her funeral was a low-key affair. GranJilly had outlived most of her friends so it was just a handful of old farming friends who came. Dad's sisters flew in too and, while the service marked the end of a life, GranJilly's funeral was very much a celebration of her eighty-seven years. God was thanked – a marked contrast to Sam's funeral where God had been silently cursed and berated by many.

The following weekend, we all went to Raffingora to bury GranJilly's ashes with Arthur's in the little cemetery not far from the farm. It was surreal, being so close to the farm yet like strangers in our own area. As we ended with a short prayer in the shabby, overgrown cemetery, I thought about death again. I wondered if, in the moment just before her death, GranJilly had also had that feeling of being pulled from her physical self. Maybe Arthur had been waiting for her in that warm light and had escorted her in and shown her around. Death. Such a natural process.

Standing in the hot and dusty cemetery, picking blackjacks off my skirt with the sun beating down on me, I mused over how people spent their entire lives dreading and avoiding the one thing that was absolutely guaranteed.

Finally, after an insanely hectic year, Christmas approached and things started to wind down. All I could focus on was our holiday and I was determined to make the most of what was left of the year. As the silly season got sillier, so the various invites to parties came in. Knowing I'd been somewhat of a hermit, I accepted most of them and tried to resuscitate my flailing social life. I even had a few girls' nights out which, surprisingly, proved to be some of our best ever.

I was still gutted about Ant, but realised there were no peace talks on the cards for us. There was nothing for it but to let it go and move on.

Ant was a door I had to close so that other doors might open, though he, my first love, would always be special to me. Wanting to retain some semblance of dignity and graciousness, I sent him a warm email wishing him all the best in love and life, and a happy Christmas. I gritted my teeth and tried not to let the regrets weigh me down. Booze helped. A lot.

Part of seeing the year out on a high note was my fresh resolve to be more aware of the large quantities of painkillers passing my lips each day. I was making a concerted effort not to scramble for the pill bottle when a headache even hinted its arrival. Some days I managed, some days I didn't, but I was trying.

In preparation for Mozambique, I estimated how many pills I'd need to see me through a fortnight, and added ten percent. After all, we were going to a fairly remote place. So, while others placed orders for turkeys and hams, I placed an order with my dealer. Colin obligingly handed over several hundred pills and then gave me, as a Christmas present, a packet of particularly strong and rather scrumptious sleeping pills, beautifully wrapped and with pretty ribbons too. A fine bit of customer relations if ever there was. I wondered if I could discuss some other public relations tips with Colin. A second later I realised how utterly ludicrous my thinking had become.

To avoid raising alarm bells, I also filled a repeat on my prescription at the pharmacy. Nobody realised that what I was allowed from the pharmacy fell way short of what I needed to get by. Nevertheless, with New Year's resolutions nearing, my plan was to cut back enough so as to survive on only the prescribed amount. I had to phase Colin out of my life. He was too much of a risk. In a nutshell, that AA word 'unmanageability' had scared me. Yes, I wanted to regain some control, but I sure as hell wasn't going to make any grand announcements to the family about it. That said, it didn't go unnoticed that I was getting out more and being less of a grump. Mom was delighted to see me socialising again and the lectures about my 'problem' had subsided.

The first day of our holiday dawned and we all congregated in Umwinsidale where Grandpa orchestrated a military-style departure. Making us line up beside our bags, he checked then gathered all our passports while Dad and

Tim loaded up the two trucks and trailers, ready for the twelve-hour drive. And then Dad, Mom, Grandpa, Chris, Katie, Ben, Linda, Tim, Ela, Mojo, Tighty, Gertie and I all piled into the trucks and off we set.

Within the first thirty minutes, Grandpa started the road trip musical torture. First he got a hearty 'Kumbaya' going, then 'The wheels on the bus go round 'n round' for Katie. But when he started the African classic 'Agh please Daddy ...' in the thickest Afrikaans accent ever, I started motioning out the back window to Dad, right behind us, that I needed to swop places with someone in his truck. Dad just grinned and waved, knowing Grandpa was killing us.

Our beach house was heavenly. We spent lazy days snorkelling, swimming with the kids, gorging on fish and prawns, reading, playing board games and taking long walks on the beach. I even braved a bikini for the first time since my surgery and, once I'd tanned up a bit, my scar looked less like something out of a cheap horror movie. Of everyone in the two families, I gravitated towards Grandpa most, the only person I could truly relax with and confide in. In general, I tried to give Mom a wide berth, sensing it wouldn't take much for her to launch into a little lecture if the moment presented itself.

The one drawback of the idyllic setting was the searing summer heat. Combined with being at sea level, I was getting worse headaches than normal but had, so far, managed not to let them spiral out of control. My main stash of pills was hidden in the inner lining of my suitcase with a decoy, the pharmacy tub, by my bed. Thankfully, I'd scored my own bedroom and could get away from my nutjob family when I needed some time out.

Grandpa, ever the family clown, got a bee in his bonnet about spearfishing and had asked a local fisherman to teach him the art. For hours, Grandpa would creep through the shallow waters with the stealth of a ninja, an enormous rusty spear poised above his head. Every now and then he'd roar *'Geronimo!'* before bringing down the spear with lightning speed, the force creating a mini tsunami. Expecting to find a hundred kilograms of blue marlin or tuna impaled on the spear, he'd land a piece of seaweed, at best.

'Why don't you rather shout your *Geronimo* after you go for the money shot?' I suggested. 'I'm pretty sure the fish can hear you. You're kinda giving them a head start.'

Grandpa's profanities would get louder with every piece of seaweed caught. Katie, most interested in this new language, regularly asked us what things like 'fuuuk' and 'blubbybastard' meant. Chris went to great pains to explain that it was special grown-up language, only to get snared in the game of 'But why Dad?' Meanwhile, Ben became like a toddler with Tourette's, shouting 'SHIT!' at every person he saw. Chris wasn't amused. 'Try erasing swear words from the sponge-like mind of a kid just learning to speak,' he muttered after five days of Ben's gutter mouth.

I'd just fielded a question from Katie – 'What's a buggering shithead, Aunty Kat?' – when we heard a particularly loud shriek from Grandpa, and saw him suddenly hopping around like a one-legged man on a pogo stick.

'Help! Help! I've been bitten. The fucker bit me,' he shouted, arms waving like he was in the grips of a seizure. Losing his balance, he then fell face first into the water. We were in hysterics. Tighty belted down the beach, barking wildly as he stood over Grandpa's submerged watery shadow, waiting for a sign of life.

'Are you buggers coming to help me or does only the dog give a shit?' yelled Grandpa, finally dragging himself back up the beach to shore. 'I'm injured, possibly fatally.'

Sure enough, there was blood gushing from his foot, so much so it was hard to see the actual bite.

'Loved the water dance Dad, will you do that again for us?' said Mom, chuckling with Linda. 'What bit you? Shark attack?'

'Oh, ha ha! Laugh all you want, but wait till it bloody bites you,' Grandpa muttered.

'Is a shark really there, Grampy?' asked Katie, her eyes wide with terror.

'No, but they'll smell the blood and be along shortly . . .'

Katie looked like she was about to pass clean out, she was so terrified. Leaning over, Grandpa whispered something in her ear, and she suddenly threw her head back and burst out laughing, rolling in the sand and giggling her little heart out.

'Tell us! Share the secret Katie,' said Mom.

Grandpa was pulling a funny face at Katie, making her giggles worse. 'Grampy didn't get bitten, he speared his toe,' said Katie.

Well, that just finished us. Tears of laughter streamed down our cheeks and we could barely breathe let alone ask Grandpa if he needed a bandage.

'Do you mind?' he asked indignantly, snatching Linda's reading glasses off her head so he could better examine his wound. 'There I was, about to catch your lunch – a beautiful monk fish – and suffer a near-fatal injury while doing so, and all you can do is laugh while I bleed to death. In fact, I think I may have lost the end of my toe, if anyone's interested.'

'So, toes on toast for lunch then,' said Linda, setting Katie off again.

'Oh Dad,' Mom laughed, 'can't take you anywhere. Come on, let's go clean it up and see if we need to alert Intensive Care.'

'SHIT!' Ben suddenly shouted. With that, I was finished, giggling so hard I thought I might wet myself.

Grandpa, making a great show of leaning heavily on Mom as he hobbled up to the house, shouted over his shoulder, 'Oi, KitKat, I'm gonna need some of those magic brain-numbing pills of yours.'

'They're by my bed. Bring some cold wine down when you get back from ICU,' I bellowed back.

A few days later, after too much sun and wine, I woke with a thumping headache and reached for my painkillers. Grandpa had munched all but one of the pills in the bottle by my bed but I wasn't fussed, knowing I had plenty more.

I scrabbled around in my case. I couldn't find my secret stash. I checked they hadn't slipped between my clothes. I even looked in my shoes. I then flung every last thing out of the case and out of my cupboard, shaking everything angrily. Not a pill in sight. I started to panic. I was up shit creek if I couldn't find them. We were about an hour's drive from any pharmacy. Despite knowing they weren't there, I shook my bag out again, heart pounding and head throbbing. I had them just the other day, I thought. Surely Grandpa hadn't found my stash? Even so, he wouldn't have taken a hundred-odd pills for a cut on his foot. I then saw my beach bag in the corner and pounced on it. Only a sarong and a leaky tube of sunscreen in there. Now what? My mind was racing, but Mom started bellowing for help in the kitchen. I went through, a seriously bad mood on board.

'Won't you fry this bacon for me?' Mom said, thrusting a pan at me before marching off.

I absent-mindedly chased the bacon around the pan, trying to work out where my painkillers were. A wave of churning, sickening panic almost paralysed me. Grandpa came strolling into the kitchen, still hobbling with a bandaged toe.

'Ah, Grandpa, have you got any of my pills left?' I asked in a snappy tone, unable to hide my desperation.

'Negative. I took what I needed and left the rest by your bed. And good morning to you too. I slept very well, thank you,' he replied, swiping some bacon and hobbling off again.

The bacon done, Mom then made me set the brunch table in the garden. Soon everyone was at the trough, happily discussing the plans for the day. I was so uptight I couldn't partake in any sensible conversation, grunting only in monosyllables. An intense rage set in and I feared for how it may come out. I was a loose cannon.

Chris and Ela looked as if they had something up their sleeve and were giggling like children, all loved up again. I simply ignored them, focusing only on how I would last another six days without my pills. Mom hadn't missed my twitch and shot me a look to say, 'What's up?' which I ignored too.

Suddenly Chris stood up, clinked a knife on his glass and asked everyone to shush. Grandpa wore a big smile, clearly in the know about something.

'I was going to do this on New Year's Eve but I couldn't wait. So, last night Ela and I ... well, we're engaged!' said Chris, gazing adoringly at her.

There were great cheers from around the table. Everyone hugged Chris and Ela. Dad was beaming and Mom was crying. Katie clapped her hands, loving the excitement and Ben, his face covered in egg, shouted, 'SHIT!'

I was genuinely thrilled and also proud of Chris. 'How fabulous you guys. I'm so SO happy! About bloody time too.'

There was something very special about seeing two people so besotted with each other but, as happy as I was for them, it was a bittersweet moment when my single status, and the massive hole Ant had left in my life and heart, suddenly hit me. I quickly pushed Ant to the back of my mind. It was Chris and Ela's special day and it wasn't right to rain on their parade or start my own pity party.

'Kat, would you do me the honour of being my maid of honour? And Katie, will you be my flower girl?' asked Ela.

'Of course Ela, it would be *my* honour,' I replied.

Katie, beside herself with excitement, clambered onto Ela's lap to discuss flower-girl fairy outfits.

It turned into a long celebration brunch, but I excused myself and went to lie down after an hour. My head was killing me and I was in possibly the worst mood of my life. Much as I wanted to share the happy day, without my pills I couldn't think straight.

I paced around my bedroom, checking my kit bag a third, fourth, fifth time. I was losing the plot and the rage in me swirled. Rage at myself, for becoming so dependent on the pills and for being so utterly useless without them. Rage at my severe craving. I was then angry, furious actually, about being dragged to Mozambique, to holiday in such a remote place. My selfish, irrational thoughts grew darker by the second.

I went to the bar fridge and poured myself a double vodka. I knocked it back in two gulps, immediately pouring another. I then went back to my room and sat on my bed, wondering what to do. I was just going to pour another vodka when Mom came in and sat on the bed next to me.

'You okay? Why are you hiding in here sweetheart?' she asked. 'Isn't the engagement fabulous news?'

'Yup, am thrilled for them,' I said, in no mood for Mom and her chit-chat. 'I've just got a shit awful headache and Grandpa has finished all my painkillers.' I showed Mom the empty pill bottle by my bed, jiggling my foot in a nervous pattern of anxiety and irritation.

'Are you missing something?' Mom asked.

'Huh?' I grunted, rubbing my temples.

'I said, are you missing something, Kat?' Her voice suddenly had a hard edge.

'What on earth are you talking about Mom?'

'Are you looking for these, perhaps?' she said, pulling a packet out of her pocket. It was my stash from Colin.

Shit, this can't be good, I thought. A dozen lies flew through my mind like torpedoes.

'Uh, umm, where did you find those, Mom?' I asked nervously.

'You know exactly where I found them.'

Well, yes okay, I thought, I admit that was a stupid question.

'Kat, I wasn't born yesterday. Remember, I went through all this myself. I watched you this morning. You're like a cat on a hot tin roof. Your nerves are jangling, you're sweating, your eyes are angry, dark and jumpy. You're a complete wreck and now, at eleven o'clock in the morning, I can smell you've been clobbering the vodka too—'

'Well, I feel like shit,' I interrupted.

'Let me finish,' Mom said in a calm yet firm voice. 'Kat, my angel, let's cut the crap once and for all. I know where you're at right now. Apart from me, nobody else in this family understands what you are going through, the dark place you are in and the panic you feel right now.'

I kept quiet for a while, knowing it was game over. At least Mom wasn't shouting. I didn't know if I was more surprised about that or about her sitting there calmly fondling my illegally-sourced pills, the pills I wanted to snatch from her hand and run. I'd have wrestled her to the ground for them.

'I did panic, you're right about that.'

'I know. I've been watching you.'

There was still no anger in Mom's voice. Even though I was well and truly shitting myself, I found comfort in her tone. She really did seem to know exactly how I was feeling. I saw the recognition in her eyes, like she was seeing her own reflection. If I ever had to recall the exact moment I finally realised that drugs had completely taken over my life, it was then, seeing the knowing look of someone who'd been through substance abuse themselves.

'Okay, Kat, here's the deal and I need you to hear me out. Yes, I took your hidden pills. Yes, I knew you had a lot more than was in that tub by your bed. I will not ask how the hell you got so many pills, I don't think I want to know, but I know it wasn't from the pharmacy. I moved your stash because I needed to show you just how dependent you are on them. The only way to make you feel that panic was to let you think they were all gone and that you couldn't get any more while in a strange country. Kat, you freaked out and can't deny that—'

'Yes, but—' I interrupted.

'Zip it and listen. Can you now see that perhaps there is a snag with you and these pills? Can you perhaps start thinking about the word 'addiction' now, because this is certainly not just a 'problem' anymore?'

'But Mom, I have really cut back a lot, since that last AA meeting ...'

'Yes, I've seen you trying but, bottom line, you're still abusing them. Now, this family holiday is one we all need, including you. I will not have any bad moods or your selfish dramas spoiling things, so I am giving these pills back to you. Plus, a sudden withdrawal off these opiates can cause seizures and that's not something to invite without doctors around. I have not counted them, neither will I police you, only because I know what I did when your father did the same thing with my booze.'

I wondered if I'd heard right – that, despite the drug raid, I'd be getting them back?

'But there are conditions,' continued Mom.

And here comes the catch, I thought. I knew there'd be one.

'When we get home, we'll discuss this properly and you will start counselling. I know pain terrifies you, but I think there is much more to your addiction. Maybe there are other issues, better discussed with an unbiased psychiatrist. I've said all along that I am here for you. Take the help being offered. If counselling doesn't work, you're going to rehab.'

'Rehab? Surely not?'

'Yes, rehab. I don't know how to be any clearer. If you carry on taking these quantities, you'll be dead within six months,' she said, waving the bag of pills at me. 'They are opiates, the same class drug as heroin. You're lucky you lived to tell the first perforated ulcer tale, but you sure as hell won't survive a second one. Do you really want to die so young? Want to put us through that? I will no longer stand by and watch my beautiful daughter take daily steps towards her own suicide. End of story.'

I looked at Mom, my tears welling up and then I totally broke down. I sobbed, wracked by pain, shame and guilt.

'I'm so sorry Mom.' She just held me tightly and let me cry, stroking my hair, letting herself cry too.

'I know it's terrifying. Seeing you like this takes me right back and I am reliving all those dark moments of mine as I watch you walk this same road. I swore I'd do everything to keep you off it and feel I've failed you. Do you know how many nights I lie awake thinking about your funeral and what flowers I'll put on your coffin? How I worry what your father will think of me for not taking control of your addiction after I managed to overcome my own? Blaming me forever for his only daughter's death?'

'I'm so sorry.'

Mom put her hands on my shoulders and looked me square in the eyes, her tears glistening on her cheeks. 'No one knows about this and it will remain between us. Wash your face, let's both put a smile on for Chris and Ela, and let's start the day again, okay?' She gently placed my pills in my lap.

Feeling their weight, hearing the soft rustling sound of the plastic, and seeing the chalky dust coating the inside of the bag – the relief was untold. 'Thank you,' I said in snotty voice, tentatively touching the bag to check that this really was happening.

'On condition you start therapy when we get home. End of discussion.'

Mom left me to compose myself and I quickly swallowed the ten pills I'd been so desperate for. After splashing some water on my face and feeling the familiar fuzzy kick of the faithful pills on top of the vodka, I joined everyone outside.

Later that afternoon, Mom came up to me on the beach and merely squeezed my hand, no words needed. I felt like such a shit. My holiday mood had gone and I was very subdued, depressed, and nervous about what lay ahead. Still though, Mom could have made it far worse. She'd given me a helluva scare but some home truths and realisations had at last sunk in.

Yes, I had more than a problem and yes, I was ready to use the 'A' word – addict – a stifling and oppressive word that hung in the air like a stale smell. Yes, I was utterly mad to think I could keep hammering my body and not suffer healthwise. Yes, I'd changed and maybe it was the drugs that had changed me, perhaps they'd even contributed to the break-up with Ant. Yes, I had shed loads of weight in a few short months because the pills killed my appetite and made me vomit. Yes, just about everything in my life that had turned sour could be linked in some way to my addiction.

Then it hit me. My thoughts came to a screeching halt. Not only had I started using the word addiction, I had placed the word 'my' before it. Owning it.

That night I listened to the waves twenty metres from my window and, unable to sleep – even with all the pills in me – a part of me was vastly relieved that things were now out in the open. In being exposed, my true secret had lost most of its power. With a deep sense of release, I saw how living the lie had been weighing me down, as was having Colin in my life. I no longer had to do it alone and knew how lucky I was to have a mother who'd been there herself.

28

It was the beginning of March and our Mozambique Christmas was a distant memory. I'd been going for weekly therapy and, under Doc Merton's guidance, was slowly weaning myself off the high doses of painkillers. It was better than hurtling into it cold turkey, given the seizures and strokes so common with a sudden opiate detox. I had confessed everything to Doc Merton, who was a little shocked to learn that I never took fewer than six pills, often eight, at once. But I was now down to fifteen pills a day and, if I stuck to the regime, within six weeks I'd be down to zero, or in addict-speak, clean. Mom was the control and dished out the day's quota to me every morning, taking a level of temptation from me. I'd not seen Colin since before Christmas, but the bastard had phoned scouting for business several times. He'd completely ignored me when I said I was no longer 'in the market' and to take me off his Christmas card list. Now I just let his calls go unanswered.

While cleaning up my act didn't mean I was in any less pain, I had resigned myself to it. Doc Merton offered me a fresh round of tests to see if they could find a reason and perhaps a cure for my incessant headaches but I couldn't face all that again. I was learning my triggers, just learning to cope, day by day.

I knew the pills had robbed me of many things but, like all good toxic relationships, breaking up with them was neither as simple nor as logical as one might imagine. I had good days – when I'd feel upbeat, focused and put in sixteen-hour work days – but there were bad days too, when the gnawing pain wore me down and I missed them terribly. Those were my 'white-knuckle' days, when I clung desperately to my resolve, when I wanted, more than anything, to loosen my grip and just let go. Should Colin happen to pester me for an order on a white-knuckle day, it took every ounce of willpower to not meet him and succumb to the Beast that lived in me – the Beast that always wanted feeding.

I wasn't entirely convinced about my shrink. In her sixties and of Russian origin, she wore slightly sultry, short skirts and overdone make-up, and looked like she'd just retired from a stripper pole. The most bizarre part was how she flirted with me. I couldn't put my finger on it right away, then she asked to see my stomach scar in my third session. I knew bloody well my scar had no bearing on my mental state, but didn't seem to have a choice. In a creepy way, she ran her finger along the length of it, making my skin crawl. For sure, she was totally hitting on me! After that, I became so uncomfortable that I shut completely down and the sessions were a total waste of time.

She had spent the first month trying to flush out some kind of past trauma, probing extensively for hidden physical or sexual abuse. Other than the fact that Ant had dumped me, that I feared pain, and that self-control and moderation clearly weren't my strong points, there really wasn't much to unearth. She seemed almost disappointed to learn that my penchant for pills was in no way a symptom of something dark, shameful or down to a second cousin twice removed fiddling with me when I was a little girl.

'I buggered up my neck when I was a teenager. I get headaches every day so I take painkillers and I went slightly above the prescribed doses. Boring, but true,' I'd said in the first session and every session afterwards.

Aware that I was detoxing and therefore fragile, she gaily prescribed new pills to help take the edge off my detox. And so Rohypnol and I were introduced. It was love at first sight. I was enraptured from the first hit, loving its warm, silky stroke and how it even helped my headaches. It was only for the Rohypnol prescriptions that I returned each week to Zenka – or whatever her name was – and put up with her flirtations. Despite having had a drug dealer on speed dial for a long time, I remained naïve about the true underworld of narcotics, otherwise I might have known Rohypnol was the drink-spiking date-rape drug.

Mom was amazingly tolerant with me during the weaning process but she wasn't shy about dishing out some good old-fashioned 'tough love', a.k.a. Parental Arsekicking. She'd started attending Al-Anon meetings too, learning how to love an addict. So, in AA meetings, she wore her ex-boozer hat and in Al-Anon meetings, her mother-of-a-junkie one. And poor Dad now attended Al-Anon for both his wife and daughter, 12 Step groups coming out of our family's ears.

Wanting to better understand addiction, I quietly took myself off to a few NA meetings and had been overwhelmed by all the unconditional support from complete strangers. There'd been no judgment and I'd come away feeling accepted and motivated to keep trying to get clean. Maddie's face was a picture when I bumped into her one night. She obviously told Mom who then quizzed me about it, shocked to hear I'd been to NA without telling anyone.

While I tried to get a handle on the pills, another fire started in the opposite corner. I'd never been a big weekday drinker, but had taken to having a glass or two of wine at home each night. My social life had picked up again too and, each weekend, I'd have at least one major bender, either with Rolo, Andrew and Vicky, or sometimes going out on my own if no one was free. The cutback in pills had left a gaping hole and I'd chosen alcohol to fill it. Yet the void never felt smaller the morning after, in fact it felt worse. Yet I kept doing it. Never mind one day at a time, quit one thing at a time, I'd tell myself. I'll look at the drinking once I've overcome the pills, I thought, justifying my binges and adding a heaped spoonful of denial. I did mention my 'slightly elevated social drinking' to the shrink but she pretty much ignored it and the topic was glossed over. She was far more interested in my sex life, the stories about which I hugely exaggerated, just for the hell of it. If anyone challenged me about drinking, I could honestly say my shrink wasn't fussed.

A few weeks later, I was down to one painkiller only if I had an unbearable headache, finding I had even altered my thinking around what constituted 'unbearable'. No more stash, no more Colin, and slowly the good days started to outnumber the bad. Life felt a bit more manageable. Even I could see how things were flowing more smoothly.

And then it all went for a ball of chalk.

29

Rolo, Vicky, Andrew and I were out. It had been a long week and I was anything but sober. There'd been rumours that the nightclub had been pumping drugs through the air conditioning so I was willing to bet I was high too. Both dance floors were a writhing mass of people, our bodies and minds being controlled by the hottest rave DJ of the moment.

I was dancing with Andrew when I noticed a couple on the dance floor. The sexual energy between them was tangible as they ground their hips together, completely lost in each other. I glanced at them a second time, knowing there was something familiar about the guy. As they locked lips in a raunchy snog, I saw it was Ant. Andrew saw my face drop and followed my gaze.

'Come sweetheart, let's get you a drink,' he said, a protective arm around my shoulder as he led me off the dance floor.

As I looked back, Ant saw me. Locking eyes, he seemed as shocked as I was. The girl threw me a look so filthy I practically needed a tetanus injection.

'Are you okay, hun?' Andrew asked me at the bar, handing me a tequila. 'Did you know he was in town?'

'Nope, that was quite a shock. Never mind that he was sucking the face off that chick.' I shrugged, pretending not to care but my heart was pounding. Then the penny dropped and I remembered who the girl was. Jess, the tart from Vic Falls.

Hurting, I had a few drinks in quick succession but I'd lost all interest in partying and called it a night. Thankfully, Ant had melted into the crowd and I didn't see him again.

Fucking great, I thought driving home. There I was thinking I was over Ant but it had upset me far more than I cared to admit.

The Universe obviously had it in for me that week. A few days later I was in the supermarket on the way home from work. Just as I tossed a box of breakfast in my trolley, a voice behind me made me jump. It was Ant.

Shit. At least he was alone today, I thought.

'Hey Kat! I wanted to chat the other night but you gapped it. How are you keeping?' he said.

He looked like he was coming in for a hug, but I quickly moved my trolley to shut it down. Even fleeting contact would be too painful. Be cool Kat, I thought. Be smart, be funny and show him what an awesome girlfriend he threw down the bog. At least I was looking decent today. We'd had a staff photo shoot and I was in a sexy suit, killer heels with my face done by a professional make-up artist.

'Yeah, well you seemed a bit, err, busy the other night. But I'm good, thanks Ant. How long are you in town for?' I asked, all nonchalant.

'Actually, I'm back for good. Vic Falls tourism has taken a nosedive what with Zim going down the tubes, so I've been transferred to the Harare office. I'm in the throes of setting up my new flat. You must drop in one day.'

'Oh,' I said. 'So, are you living with Jess?' I regretted the question the second it passed my lips, knowing how immature it sounded.

'Jess? Urr, no, definitely not.'

Okay, so maybe she wasn't a permanent fixture, I thought.

My cellphone rang. If ever there was a 'saved by the bell' moment, it was then. It was Rolo, but I decided to pretend it was a new boyfriend.

'Sorry, I must take this call. Good seeing you, Ant, and good luck,' I said in the breeziest voice I could muster.

'Cheers Kat, keep well,' said Ant.

Still looking at him, I answered my phone in a low sexy voice. 'Hi darling, I'll be at yours in twenty minutes. Let's stay in tonight ... I've missed you today ...' I gave a coquettish giggle.

On the other end, Rolo was confused. 'What in God's name are you talking about Kat? I love you dearly but if you wanna go lesbian, you're wasting your time barking up my shrubbery.'

Walking off and trying not to giggle at Rolo, I flashed a smile at Ant, aware that he was checking me out. His eyes had very definitely moved to my deep cleavage, the work of a new Wonderbra, then his gaze lingered on my arse in its tight miniskirt. Knowing he was still watching me, I bent right over at the end of the aisle, suddenly needing an item on the bottom shelf. I may have looked calm and collected, but two aisles down my heart was still racing and I had to hang around the frozen peas while I pulled myself together.

Then it happened again a few days later. This time I bumped into Ant in a restaurant while I was at a client lunch. Again, I was tarted up and looking quite sharp for work in a sleek cropped pants suit and stilettos. At least the Universe was engineering the Ant encounters on the days I was suited, booted, and all glammed up.

Ant appeared to be with work colleagues too, all with the scraggy sun-fried River Rat look about them. I deliberately sauntered past their table on my way to the loo, saying a quick 'Hello' to him without stopping. His mouth fell open in surprise as he stuttered a 'Howzit Kat'. I knew damn well that they were all ogling me as I walked past. I came off confident and suave. Again, the complete opposite of what I felt inside.

Each encounter with Ant rocked me for days afterwards and sent my newfound serenity for a total ball of shit. White-knuckle days followed, the addict in me not wanting to feel the emotional pain. I missed him terribly and, more than anything, I wanted us to make up. I wanted to explain what the pills had done to me, to show him that old Kat was back. However, his vibe suggested he'd moved on. And that hurt. I think I preferred him living far away, not having the break-up shoved in my face everywhere I went.

The final straw came a few days later.

I was snarled up in traffic when I saw Ant's truck in the lane next to me. Jess was with him, looking all bubbly and bouncy like a Labrador puppy, practically slobbering on the windows. God, she must be so irritating to be around.

It was all too much. Rage overcame me. Something inside me snapped and I was in the white-knuckle-failure zone. My Fuck-it Switch had just been tripped. I toyed anxiously with my cellphone in my lap.

Should I, shouldn't I? It'll just be once, I assured myself.

Then, at a red light Ant drew level with me again and they saw me. Ant was laughing at something Jess had just said, probably a joke about me. Then the stupid bitch waved at me, and that tipped the scales. With one hand, I gave her the middle finger and with the other hand I hit the number on my phone, turning my face away from Jess and her indignant squawk as they pulled off.

He answered quickly. 'It's been a while, Kat. Hello.'

'Yeah, hi Colin. Listen, can you sort me out?'

'Sure, no problem. The usual?'

'Please. Can we meet now?' I asked. Desperation and hysteria had crept into my voice. Beads of sweat coated my forehead and the back of my neck.

It was as if some unseen force – a lure far bigger than me that reminded me of my time hovering above myself in ICU – was pulling me back into that self-destruct zone and I was powerless to resist. The image of Ant and Jess laughing at me played repeatedly in my mind. I promised myself again that I'd score and use just once, just for one evening, and tomorrow I'd get back on track.

'Once,' I said aloud in my car. 'No one will know because I'll stop again. Just once.' It turned into a chant as I drove, as fast as I could, to meet Colin, speeding back into the arms of the Beast. *Once. Just once. Once. Only once. Once.*

Colin, faithful and as obliging as ever, produced two hundred of my favourite flavour painkillers in a nearby car park. It was a little more than I needed for one night, but it'd be rude to take less, and I could always flush the leftovers down the loo. I belted home, knowing that, within half an hour, the image of Ant with bouncy Jess wouldn't sting quite as much.

Mom wasn't home and Dad and Grandpa were in the veggie fields. I scampered into my cottage, headed straight to the fridge for some wine and took ten pills, hiding the rest behind a sofa cushion. I kicked off my shoes and lay on my couch, taking a long drag on a cigarette, then a longer, very slow exhale.

Hello old friend, I thought, sort this painful shit out for me, please.

Sure enough, within ten minutes I felt the pills reporting for duty, their kick soothing me. Adding to the artillery, I took my evening dose of Rohypnol. At half time, I brought in vodka refreshments and then things began to quieten. Nothing seemed to matter anymore, which was precisely what I'd set out for. Mission successful.

I woke up much later, hearing Mom coming into my cottage, calling my name through the dark.

'Why are you sitting in the dark, Kat?' Mom asked, turning on a lamp.

Shit shit shit. Of all the people to find me passed out.

'Hey Mom,' I said with a bit of a drawl, feeling very groggy.

'What's wrong? Why are you passed out on the couch? We thought you were having supper with us? Where were you?' Mom wasn't asking, she was firing.

I had to pull myself together fast or she'd smell a relapse rat. Saliva flooded my mouth and I realised I was about to vomit everywhere.

'Sorry. I have an awful headache so I lay down earlier. Must have dozed off,' I managed to say.

'Do you want some supper?'

'Urgh. No thanks Ma, not really hungry. I had a huge lunch. I'll bath and get into bed,' I said, gulping as I stood up. I had to get Mom out of there fast.

'Okey dokes. See you in the morning. Feel better. Don't forget our AA meeting tomorrow evening.'

'Yup, got it down.'

Mom shot me one of her special looks but then left me alone. I only just got to the loo in time, vomiting like never before.

Shit. That was close.

So much for 'just once' and flushing the leftovers.

It took just three days to finish Colin's pills and I promptly scored another two hundred from him, plus some tranquillisers – which I'd not got from him before. Encouraged to see me branching out with my narcotic cocktails, Colin had urged me to try some pethidine injections too, showing me where on the leg was the best spot to self-inject. I was terrified the first time, closing my eyes as I plunged the needle into the top outer quadrant of my thigh, thinking I was for sure going to muck it up and be found dead in my bathroom with a vial on the floor. But I didn't, and what a lovely restful night I had.

It was as if the Beast had just been sleeping and, with just that one slip, had woken up and pounced at the chance to destroy me, again. Very quickly I was back to where I'd left off, worse in fact. Soon enough, my life was unravelling faster than ever before. I'd make mental lists of all the reasons why I'd fallen off the wagon and deftly apportion the blame to everyone but myself. Within an hour of taking that first handful of pills, I had justified my relapse and formulated a watertight argument, should anyone ask.

I started to call in sick at work again, seldom working five days in a row. Stephen grew increasingly frosty with me as I made up various illnesses and excuses. Some days it was flu, some gastritis, perhaps car trouble, or even fuel shortages that kept me in bed or forced me to work from home. I then had to field Mom's questions as to why I wasn't at work. The lies became more elaborate, the bullshitting almost a full-time job in itself. Some days I got dressed and left for work, as was my routine, everything appearing normal to Mom. Then I'd find a shady, secluded spot down an unused track on our neighbour's property and just sleep in my car all day. Anything to be alone, and not deal with people either pitying, judging or laughing at me. Unfortunately, one of our workers came across me parked under a msasa tree one day, on his way to see his girlfriend who worked next door. I'd screamed in fright when I woke to him banging on the window trying to rouse me, his oily face pressed against the glass, eyes wide, thinking I was dead. A hefty sum of cash bought his silence. One day, I had to laugh when he brought me a Coke and a packet of chips as he passed by, headed for some lunchtime *jiggy jiggy* with the girlfriend.

In the early days of my relapse, I tried to keep up my social life but it soon became too much effort. I had an inkling that Rolo suspected I'd veered off my much spoken about road to recovery, she'd been fobbed off so many times. Then she rang to invite me on a long weekend to a cousin's swanky five-star game lodge on Lake Kariba.

I sighed down the phone. 'Really, Rolo? I can literally think of nothing worse than driving through dry, dusty bush looking for wild beasties in the middle of nowhere. I'll probably get malaria too. And you know what the heat does to my headaches.'

'I see,' Rolo replied icily. 'I'll be sure to let you know when my social plans are more worthy of your ladyship. Sorry, I'd forgotten that the world revolves around you and only you, and your fucking headaches.' Then she hung up.

Two weeks later I still hadn't heard a peep from Rolo. She was just being a drama queen, in my opinion. We always spoke our minds, so why she'd got the hump this time, I didn't know. I'd not heard from Vicky or Andrew either, which was weird as we always touched sides a few times a week. Feeling bad, I reached out one evening and rang Vicky to ask if she fancied a dinner out. I could hear music and laughing in the background. Apparently, she was at a work cocktail party and couldn't leave. She was definitely a bit off with me. I then rang Andrew about having dinner, only to hear the very same background noise when he answered. He said he was at his grandmother's birthday dinner, also pissy with me.

Screw them all.

Suspecting that Mom was definitely onto me too, I put extra effort into covering my tracks. I also avoided Grandpa, hating lying to him the most. I missed him. He graciously gave me my space, but I could see the hurt and fear in his eyes. Although it tore me to shreds, I was just too terrified of what complete honesty would bring.

Further into the hole I went. Deep down, I was ashamed of my behaviour and grew more disappointed in myself by the day. Still, I didn't stop. In my silence and self-loathing, my Beast took yet more power and control as it got behind the steering wheel of my life again. I'd wake in the mornings to a pillow wet from crying in my sleep, filled with loneliness and dread for the day ahead, exhausted by the lies I had to keep telling. For the first time, I understood how people could consider taking their own lives. I shouted at God, again, for letting me live that night in ICU. Screw you God, I thought, weren't you supposed to be merciful?

And so weeks passed in a haze, with me just going through the motions of life, looking increasingly anorexic by the day. One day I woke up with a face full of spots, something I hadn't had in ten years, and they simply wouldn't heal. And then my hair began to break and fall. Tangled in my own web of deceit and wretchedness, the ground was rushing up to meet me as I tumbled.

About eight weeks after I'd fallen off the wagon, Mom arranged a big Sunday lunch. I had a long and lazy lie-in that morning, processing things, wondering what to do.

There'd been a bit of an incident at work on Friday.

I'd packed up early with the excuse of seeing the printer on the way home, except it was Colin I was seeing. When I said goodbye to Stephen, he asked me to sit down and then closed his office door. He held up a list of dates – fifteen dates. The fifteen times I had called in sick in the last eight weeks. 'Excessive absenteeism' he called it. Apparently, the team was talking about always having to pick up my slack and he'd also had complaints from clients about my erratic and unreliable behaviour.

I agreed that I hadn't exactly performed well lately. Insisting it was just a rough patch, I promised Stephen it had passed.

'Kat, I think we're beyond that now. You were once an incredible asset and you have a passion for language and PR that I've not seen in a long time. But your health problems have turned you into more of a liability than an asset and I just can't risk my agency's reputation. I therefore invite you to tender your resignation with immediate effect. You are welcome to talk to a HR lawyer and argue the fact that you did not get a formal warning first, but you know it will get ugly. You also know the support I've offered and just how many chances I have given you over the years. Your severance pay will be three months' full salary.'

Blinking back tears, deep shame washed over me as I nodded. 'I understand. I'm so sorry Stephen, to have put you in this situation. I'll do as you ask on Monday.'

Not knowing what else to say, I stood up and asked if I could be excused. I wanted to find a middle ground where I kept my job, but was suddenly depleted of all energy and my legs were shaking. I had to focus just to walk out of there.

'Kat, know one thing – if you were operating at full capacity and not completely blotto every day, I'd offer you shares in this agency. You are that talented. I wish you only the best,' added Stephen.

'Thank you,' I said at the door, and left.

Now, having had a day to mull it over, I decided to go to work the next day and see if Stephen and I could work things out. I mean, he evidently wasn't serious about firing me if he thought I could be a shareholder. He wouldn't praise my talents if he really didn't need me. All I had to do was to show him, remind him, of my skills and then make sure I gave it my all and didn't call in sick for a very long time. A frank conversation is all it would take to set things right. This would blow over.

Expected for lunch up at the house, I dragged myself out of bed, into the shower and ambled over a while later.

I poured myself a hefty vodka and settled down for a pleasant Sunday with family and friends. Mom seemed more off with me than usual and Grandpa barely looked at me when I came in, making me wonder what or who had got all their respective knickers in such a knot.

Everyone congregated on the patio deck, soaking up the sun and catching up on news. The men positioned themselves around the braai, as only men in Africa can do, with intense deliberations about the heat and cooking times for steaks. Ela and Chris were talking wedding dates with Linda.

Still though, there was a funny vibe in the air. I gave an internal shrug, knowing that whomever I'd offended would say something eventually. In the meantime, I'll just have another vodka, I thought.

Then Mom's AA sponsor Janet arrived. She'd had meals with us before and it was good to see her again. Not long after that, Rolo walked in. Ela must have invited her. We'd not spoken since the awkward call about Kariba but, nonetheless, she came over to greet me and gave me a tight hug like nothing had happened. I knew our friendship was solid and she'd just been silly about Kariba.

I noticed Mom going over to the men and muttering. All I overhead was 'Come, let's get this over with.'

And the penny dropped. I was before the firing squad. Everyone had moved into position around me, the chatter had stopped, all eyes were boring into me, and the safety catches released as they all took aim. Totally creeped out by how orchestrated it all was, I lit a cigarette, wondering if I could make a run for it.

Janet was apparently the opening gunman. 'Kat, don't look so nervous. We're only here to help you,' she said.

'What exactly is going on?' I asked in a terse tone, looking around the group, seething inside.

'Your parents have asked me here today to act as a mediator of sorts,' said Janet. 'We all know you've been going hammer and tongs at the pills again. It's time to face facts and be honest about your relapse.'

Fuuuuck, I thought. I just stared at Janet and then Mom, my jaw set in a hard line.

'Yes or no?' asked Janet.

'Yes or no what?' I snapped back.

'Are you back on the huge quantities of pills, yes or no?' asked Janet, giving a long pause. 'If you have relapsed, it's okay, we can help and that's what today is about. But throwing daggers and hissing with your eyes like that is not going to make us leave.'

Snotty fucking bitch, I thought. I looked to Rolo for support, but she'd slipped on her sunglasses to avoid my glare. Another traitor.

Nobody else had said a word and there was a huge yawning silence. It struck me that they'd rehearsed who would talk and who wouldn't.

I stood up. I was done.

'SIT. DOWN. KATHERINE,' said Dad slowly. I was shocked by the severity of his tone.

Slowing sinking back into my chair, my mind raced ahead and dozens of excuses came to me.

But I was trapped. While I could have dished out some more bullshit, I was backed into a corner. To come out fists flying wasn't going to get me far. Slowly I began to see all around me the expressions of worry, fear, disappointment, and unbearable sadness. I actually didn't want to fight. I was too tired to keep up the façade. I was furious about the intervention, but I actually wanted the help being offered. I had a flashback to my ulcer drama and suddenly I saw, with absolute clarity, that my pill habit was suicide, plain and simple.

And so I decided to raise a white flag.

I took a deep breath and, just as I was about to answer, the tears came. I let myself sob slowly nodding my answer of 'Yes'. There was an audible sigh of relief around the circle. The army lowered their guns slightly, assessing whether I was being genuine. Mom was also crying, Rolo, Ela, Linda too. In fact, everyone was crying – although the boys were doing a macho job of hiding it, except for Grandpa who didn't give a shit and was trumpeting loudly into his handkerchief.

As my tears flowed, I felt the same profound sense of relief I'd felt in Mozambique when Mom had addressed things. My rage suddenly dissolved too. I really had no right to be angry with them for wanting to prevent my death. 'I'm sorry,' I said, softly. 'So, so sorry.'

'It's okay,' said Janet. 'It's all going to be fine, sweetheart, you'll see.'

'What happens now?' I asked, sniffing loudly.

'Gill, you explain?' Janet said to Mom.

'There are no soft options anymore,' said Mom. 'You now need specialised care and a properly medicated detox, which means a treatment centre in South Africa. There is no help for you here in Zim, not at the level you need.'

'You mean rehab?' I asked.

'Yup. In Cape Town. We fly on Wednesday. You'll be there four to five weeks, minimum.'

Shit.

'Kat, it's the only way,' said Dad, placing his arm around my shoulder. 'Mom did it, and came out of it for the better. You can do it too.'

I didn't say anything. The speed of things and the enormity of how much planning had already been done was sinking in.

'Sweetheart, you are bloody lucky to be getting a shot at treatment in a proper rehab,' said Janet. 'I would have killed to go to rehab back in the day. Accept the help. It will be the best decision of your life.'

'What about work?'

'Kat, come now! Cut the crap,' said Mom. 'When were you going to tell us you got fired?'

I spluttered. 'I have NOT been fired. Stephen and I just need to work a few things out.'

'First of all, this bulletproof denial act of yours needs to stop right here,' said Mom, irritated. 'You *were* fired. Shown the door. Given your marching orders. Arse kicked. Get it? Stephen called me on Friday evening, extremely concerned you may do something stupid having just lost your job.'

Shit, I thought again.

'It's just another consequence of your addiction,' said Janet. 'You're not the first addict to get fired. I got fired too. Shit happens. Get over it, princess.'

They sure were embracing the whole 'tough love' thing.

'Do rehab, Kat,' said Rolo in a wobbly voice. 'Shit, goddamit! You're my best bloody friend and I am terrified you'll kill yourself in an overdose.' Rolo took a huge gulp, tears and snot everywhere. Ela reached for her hand and held it tightly. 'I don't wanna go to your funeral, so will you please sort your shit out once and for all.'

I was silently nodding, giving in and letting go, knowing that I'd definitely reached the end of the road, bankrupted by living the lies.

'Kat,' said Ela, 'everyone has described the state of you to me. Your sunken eyes and the black rings under them, how your shins are just sharp lines of bone.' I ran my hand over my leg and realised it was true. 'They've also told me about your lifeless skin and hair, and your nails all bitten off. When I hug you, all I feel is a carcass, and your skin feels so cold. It'd also be quite nice to have you alive for our wedding. You're my frigging maid of honour, remember? Get your bony arse into rehab. Please.' Ela angrily wiped away her tears.

As I blew my nose, Grandpa jumped in. 'Kat, old girl, you lost Ant because of your drug habit. The poor man came to me and poured his heart out. You pushed him so far away in favour of getting blotto, and he eventually gave up on you. And no one here blames him in the slightest. What guy wants a permanently wasted and depressive girlfriend? No man will put up with that shit long term – just ask your father. And don't be mad, Ant loved you more than anything and still does. He just didn't know *how* to love you. I mean, you're not particularly lovable in this state. You're a wreck and it has been agonising to watch you do it to yourself.'

I honestly thought I'd been doing a good job of covering up my slip – relapse, mistake, whatever it was. They were all right. Ant had left me because I'd always put the drugs before him.

'So, are you going to do this Kat? You're really ready to say cheerio to the drugs?' asked Chris, speaking for the first time and looking deathly pale.

'Yes,' I said quietly. 'Yes, and thank you.'

'With your medical history, we can't delay,' added Mom. 'You're not too far from death right now actually, not that you even know it. You've developed a faint yellowish tinge in the last forty-eight hours, which means kidneys ...'

Suddenly everyone peered at me even more closely. I saw Janet nodding after she'd gawked at me.

'And what happens pill-wise, between now and rehab?' I asked.

'The clinic's doctors say you need to cut back a bit, but not drastically, as we don't want you going into detox here. The potential complications of a sudden withdrawal make it safer for you to keep using until we get to Cape Town. It's what your body knows,' said Mom.

'There's a lot to take in,' I said, lighting yet another cigarette.

'Indeed there is, my girl. Right, everyone. Let's leave it there and have some lunch,' said Mom, thankfully ending my intervention. I felt like a pub dartboard.

Everyone dispersed and the men dashed back to the braai, relieved to escape the touchy-feely emotional stuff. Rolo and I were left alone.

'You're doing the right thing my friend,' Rolo said. 'Be brave, okay?'

'Thanks Rolo. I was such a bitch to you. I can't apologise enough. What have I done to deserve such an amazing friend?'

'Lately, nothing. But it's fine. I saw your bitchiness for what it was – the drugs talking. I just had to distance myself afterwards. It was too hard to be close to you, all "sour bitch" and "me- me- me". Oh, and way to go – you getting fired!'

'One of us was bound to get fired at some point. I took one for the team,' I laughed, starting to cry again at the same time.

'Just don't let your bloody mother hear you joking like that. She's terrifying at the moment,' said Rolo, glancing behind us and checking who might be in earshot.

'You don't have to tell me that.'

Slowly I felt the weight lift off my shoulders, liberated. The Beast had stepped into the ring with some pretty strong opponents. I took a deep breath and visualised it gone for good, allowing me to walk free with no compulsion to engage in such destructive behaviour ever again. The relief was untold. I could breathe again.

And once the storm is over, you won't remember how you made it through, how you managed to survive. You won't even be sure, whether the storm is really over. But one thing is certain. When you come out of the storm, you won't be the same person who walked in. That's what this storm's all about.

HANUKI MURAKAMI

30

Mom rang a buzzer at the door while I admired the view. My home for the next few weeks – rehab – was a hundred metres from the beach in Kommetjie, not that far from the tip of Africa. A fresh sea breeze carried in the smell of kelp, a smell I was never sure I liked or not. Staring out at the ocean as the sun was setting, I felt right at home, as if the wild sea and I were old friends. Something was giving me comfort, though I couldn't quite put my finger on it. Odd, I thought, to find comfort while standing in the entrance of rehab, not knowing what awaits on the other side. Mom smiled at me, the unmistakable glint of tears in her eyes.

Physically, I wasn't doing well. I had a major headache and was fighting waves of nausea. Just the last two days' small cutback in pills, combined with my angst, had made me feel most peculiar. I was definitely a bit shaky.

A security guard opened the door and immediately locked it behind us. Not quite the clanging of a cell door, but close. I began to reconsider that comfort I'd felt outside.

Once an old seaside hotel, the building had been converted into a plush medical facility, furnished in soft earthy colours, gentle art, vases of fresh flowers everywhere, and huge couches scattered around the foyer. Through a doorway I could see a pool. If not for the tight security, I might have thought I was in a fancy spa.

The receptionist took us upstairs to the nurses station where I signed dozens of forms and legal disclaimers. The rehab's director, Carol, welcomed me before whisking Mom off and leaving me with the nurses.

'Right, Kat, welcome,' said a nurse called Pat. 'We have another Zimbo here at the moment.'

I smiled at her, but was completely freaking out inside. I was in rehab. It felt too real, and panic set in. Shit, I thought, is it too late to back out and make a dash for it?

Somewhere down the corridor, a commotion started. 'You haven't got a fucking clue how I feel, so fuck right off,' a guy yelled, followed by the sound of someone putting their fist through a door.

Alrighty then, I thought, looking questioningly at the nurses who acted like they hadn't heard a thing. They kept bustling and seemed to be working hurriedly on my check-in. While Pat pulled out a blood pressure machine and slapped it around my arm, I heard another nurse make a phone call, apparently about me.

'She's here. You'll need to get here pronto, Doc. Stats are not good, all over the show. She's going to start crashing any minute.'

Directly off the nurses station was a small bedroom with a one-way window-come-mirror. Pat explained that I'd sleep there for a few nights, as I needed strict monitoring at the start of my detox. Thereafter, I'd be moved to a regular room. She then asked me to surrender my suitcase and hand luggage, and so began The Search. I stood there, shell-shocked, as she removed every last item and checked, smelt, examined or rattled it.

'Just checking you haven't smuggled anything in,' she said breezily.

It was like having the FBI swoop in. I half expected to see a pack of sniffer dogs trot in next. 'I don't think you'll find much contraband, but anyway ...' I replied.

'Yeah, that's what all you junkies say.'

I got a black mark when she found a couple of painkillers hidden in my suitcase lining. I'd no idea they were there, probably leftovers from Mozambique. Bugger! Then came the body search. She frisked me head to toe, then asked me to remove my bra so she could check its lining. Next, my jeans were ordered off and she had a good hunt around those, checking nothing had been sewn into the waistband. She even checked the reverse side of my belt, which, come to think of it, was quite a nifty hiding place. Then all my shoes got grilled, even one-strap slops, checking that nothing had been slipped into the soles.

'It's your lucky day, I won't give you an actual cavity search,' said Pat, declaring the raid over and helping me fold my clothes again, laughing at how my eyebrows had shot up. 'You'd be surprised how and where people smuggle drugs in here, Kat. Some addicts don't think twice about using their God-given orifices as a hidey-hole.'

I sat on the bed, suddenly feeling as if I might throw up. Pat checked my pulse for the third time in ten minutes, moving a small bucket a bit closer to me.

'Try to relax, Kat. I need you tell me exactly what pills you've taken in the last forty-eight hours. And I need you to be honest as it influences how we medicate your detox. No bullshit, okay?'

'About eighty Stopayne today, maybe more. A few Rohypnol and a bottle of wine last night. I was nervous.'

Pat didn't comment, but noted it all on my chart which was already looking full. My panic was escalating with everything happening so quickly.

Seeing my tears coming, Pat gave me the tightest hug. 'Agh, *pookie*. No man, don't cry,' she said in her broad Afrikaans accent. 'You're in safe hands and it's all gonna be just fine. Now lie down for a bit. The doctor should be here now-now to start your detox medication. The discomfort you are feeling is the start of your withdrawal. I know it's not *lekker*, my *pookie*.'

After settling me on the bed, Pat stuck her head round the door and called out to another nurse. 'Is he coming? She's about to crash.'

'Three minutes,' someone replied.

Despite the nausea, I was dying for a cigarette. Pat directed me to a little balcony off their kitchenette. My brain felt like it might dribble out through my ears and the more I panicked the worse my headache got. After just a drag, I returned to my bed and soon the doctor came flying in.

'Kat, hello. Doctor Steiner. How're you feeling? Pretty grim, huh?'

'Grim? Try deathly,' I said with a thin smile.

'I'm sure. Right, let's check you over. I see that you were using eighty, sometimes more, prescription painkillers a day, Rohypnol, pethidine, and booze too?'

'Yup.'

'And how is your stomach feeling? You have a history of ulcers and perforations.' He pressed my stomach gently.

'It's feeling really tender right now but— OW! Shit!' I said loudly as he hit a particularly sore spot.

'Mmm. With that number of pills in there, it must be like a nuclear reactor about to blow. You're a medical miracle actually.'

'Yeah, heard that before. Sorry.'

'Trust me, I have seen it all and very little shocks me.'

I smiled but, my God, I felt like death. Nervous sweat poured off me, drenching my T-shirt. Every inch of my body ached.

'Your blood pressure is way too high,' he said, scribbling more notes. 'In simple terms, you're nose-diving into detox. So, let's get some meds into you and then—'

I interrupted him by bursting into tears again. I was in so much pain.

'Hey-hey, it's okay. I am going to start you on Valium and methadone. Do you know what methadone is?' He stroked my hand, his bedside manner soothing.

'Is it like purple meths?'

'No! Methadone is a synthetic opioid, part of the opiate family – your painkillers are also opiates. It will replace your pills for now. We'll keep you on it for a few days, high doses to start, given the quantity of pills you've been taking. By switching you to methadone and not making you go cold turkey, we reduce the risk of withdrawal seizures and strokes, which are my major concerns right now. Once stabilised, you'll be weaned off the methadone in stages. It'll make you very drowsy so stay put in this room and don't wander downstairs. The Valium will help too. I hope we can stabilise you on the combination, if not we may transfer you to hospital. You're quite a complicated case, Kat, and your withdrawal is going to be very, very rough.'

Shit, I thought. It can get worse?

Pat came back in and handed me a little cup of dark-red syrup. 'Here, get that down your gob, *pookie*. It's your methadone.'

I chucked back the sticky syrup and then Pat gave me a Valium chaser.

'Right, lie down and rest. The methadone has a kick like a mule. And your mom is waiting outside now,' said Pat.

'I'll be in the nurses station if you need me,' said Doc Steiner as he walked out.

'How're you feeling, Kat?' asked Carol, walking in with Mom.

'Like crap.'

Then I noticed I was already floating. So, this is methadone, I thought, feeling its first kick. It felt kind of cool – a warm glow – but my headache was no better and I still had a deep ache in my core. It was a pain I couldn't touch, itch, scratch, rub or relieve, no matter what position I tried. Like restless leg syndrome, except restless everything.

'Try to relax …' said Carol.

God help me, I thought, if I'm told to relax one more time I shall surely fucking scream.

'Let the drugs work,' she continued. 'You'll be monitored very closely for the next forty-eight hours. I must say, you seem to be quite a hardcore addict. Your detox is going to be hectic, but we'll get you through it. Chin up.'

'Am I worse than the other addicts here?' I suddenly had a morbid interest in just how extreme a junkie I was.

'Well, not everyone comes into this room when they arrive, only those who have a tough detox coming and need specialised nursing. We call it the Fishbowl,' Carol said, tapping on the mirror window.

'So, I'm really hard core? But I was just taking painkillers, not crack or heroin or street drugs,' I drawled.

'Let me put it this way. The particular painkiller you have been abusing is the same class of drug as heroin. Your body metabolises codeine in exactly the same way it would heroin. In other words, it converts it into morphine. You take eight at once, yes? Eight of your pills taken at once is similar to a decent hit of heroin. So, do the math. If you've been scoffing eighty plus pills a day, then you've been doing a fair bit of heroin every day.'

'Oh,' I said, shocked.

'Hell!' Mom said, her eyes nearly popping out of her head.

'Yup. Your pills have a paracetamol base too, which hammers kidneys. It's not surprising that you're looking slightly jaundiced,' said Carol, reading the doctor's notes on my chart. 'I've got a lecture now but I'll check on you later, Kat. Say your goodbyes, Gill. Kat needs to settle in now. Call me anytime, but Kat won't be allowed calls for the first week.'

After Carol left, Mom sat on my bed holding my hand, reluctant to leave me. There wasn't much to say, so we sat in silence, listening to the noises of the clinic. Somewhere a bell rang. Through the open door, I saw a herd of people thunder up the stairs, queuing at the nurses station – for medication, judging by the way they all opened their mouths like goldfish to show the nurse they'd swallowed something.

As one guy stepped forward, we heard a nurse crapping on him. 'I know you sold your last pill to your roommate for cigarettes, Peter. Do it again and you'll find yourself on the wrong side of that front door.'

'Depends what you consider to be the wrong side,' he chirped arrogantly.

'You've been warned,' came the answer.

We saw men, women, young, old, all strolling past, wearing every kind of expression imaginable. Miserable, positively suicidal, sick as a dog, glazed, confused, pasty grey, and the odd person looking vaguely cheerful. They must be the ones leaving soon, I thought, wondering if I would ever smile again.

There was also a group of counsellors milling around. They stood out, in as much as they looked healthy and had an air of authority. On his way to the balcony to smoke, one man saw me in the Fishbowl and stuck his head in.

'Hello,' he said in a bright voice. 'Welcome! You must be the Zim girl. I'm Julian, one of the counsellors.'

I looked at Mom, hoping she would answer for me as I was now high as a kite and barely able to string a few sensible words together.

Mom, however, had gone all odd and was just staring at Julian, her mouth slightly open and her eyebrows almost in her hair.

Great, she can't talk either, I thought, wondering why she'd suddenly gone all 'moron' on me.

'Hi Julian. Yes, I'm Kat from Zim, nice to meet you,' I managed to dribble. He had a lovely face – warm, open and caring. I took an instant liking to him.

'Woah, I see you've started the methadone then,' he said, obviously referring to my slobbery drawl. 'You hang in there, Kat. We'll have you up and about in a few days.'

With that, he wandered off and I looked at Mom, now deathly pale. 'What's wrong, Mom? You look like you've seen a ghost?'

'Sorry. He just seems, I don't know, familiar, but I don't know why. Weird,' said Mom, jerking her head sharply as if to bring herself back to the present.

I looked at her as I floated. Mom continued to sit there dumbstruck and looking gormless, a million miles away. Fine pair we are, I thought. I bet the nurses are watching us through the mirror window and thinking they should check Mom in too.

The crowd outside the nurses station died down and all the inmates went about their business, whatever that was on a Wednesday evening in a rehab by the sea. Pat came bustling in again and chivvied Mom, suggesting she make tracks.

'You're in the best place, my KitKat,' said Mom. 'Stay strong. I'll fly down for Family Day in about three weeks.'

'I love you, Mom. Thank you. And I'm sorry,' I said hugging her tightly, terrified to let her leave me.

'Shush now, it's okay. Having done this myself, I can safely say it gets better.' She gave me one last hug and then she was gone.

Alone, a fresh wave of trepidation and anxiety hit me. Needing another cigarette, I shuffled out to the balcony again, holding onto the walls.

It was a stunning evening in Cape Town and the sea view was breathtakingly tranquil. Well, I thought, at least the setting is awesome. As for the rest of it, time would tell.

Julian was also there, smoking, and gave me a kind smile. 'You're very unsteady on your pins, Kat. You should get back to your bed. That methadone will put you into another dimension.'

'Mmm, I think it already has, but I'm dying for a smoke.'

I took a closer look at Julian, wondering why Mom had been so thrown by him. He did seem vaguely familiar. Maybe he just looked like someone we knew. He was definitely a good-looking guy, with his surfer-style, scraggy, sun-bleached hair, and his body all toned and tanned. I was reminded of Ant.

I suddenly needed to fill the space with silly chatter. 'You ever been to Zim?' I asked.

'Nope, only Mozambique. And Malawi, as a child.'

'Ah,' I said moronically.

'Kat, one of the many rules here is that counsellors can't socialise with patients. So, strictly speaking, we shouldn't be chatting. Sorry. Nothing personal,' he said finishing his ciggie.

'No worries, Julian.'

'Hope you have a good night. Ciao,' he said rubbing my shoulder before going inside.

Back in my room, I dug out some pyjamas and headed to the shower. I stood for ages under the warm water, allowing it to wash over me, and I began to relax, just a bit, trying to ignore the pain.

I felt I was on the wildest emotional rollercoaster ride. The methadone was certainly taking the edge off my headache, but the throbbing in my bones – an ache that seeped through every cell – was driving me to distraction. In bed, I tried every position to find comfort. Pacing up and down the little room didn't work either. I even tried lying on the floor, hoping its hardness and thin, rough carpet would distract me. Nothing helped.

The kitchen staff brought up a tray of spaghetti bolognaise and some fruit salad. It was edible, but after a few mouthfuls my stomach started to cramp violently and I only just made it to the loo.

Pat came to tell me why my body had suddenly turned on me. 'Shame lovey. Acute joint pain is part of detox. You're also going to have the worst shits of your life, so please drink lots of water. Dehydration will only make the muscle pain worse.'

'Super.'

'And stop scratching, Kat. You'll tear your skin to shreds,' she said, walking out.

Scratching? I looked down and saw I was indeed scratching away. Suddenly I realised my skin was on fire, like there was an entire battalion of ants marching to war over my legs.

I was craving something stupid, and not just the pills. I'd have given my right arm for a stiff vodka. I even found myself wishing I had smuggled some hooch in, maybe in a bottle of eye make-up remover. For the next half hour, I imagined the places I could have snuck drugs in. Bored, I then attempted to read my book, but the words were doing gymnastics on the page and so I stared at the ceiling, wishing I could just scream and scream and scream.

I even tried bargaining with God, albeit half-heartedly. He'd hardly been on speed dial throughout my life, and I felt like a bit of a hypocrite, striking up a conversation only because I so desperately needed, somehow, to make it all stop. Hours crawled by in my Fishbowl hell. I had never felt so bleak and lonely. I longed to be in my own bed with my nightjar singing to me sleep. On drugs.

Just before dawn – after a long night of scratching, pacing, fidgeting and diarrhoea like I never knew possible – I was suddenly aware of a presence. A dark menacing shadow, in the corner. It was four-legged, not human, and enormous. A beast. My Beast. Its red eyes pierced the darkness, boring into me.

'How did you find me?' I asked in a whisper, paralysed with terror.

'I will always find you. You can never leave me. Never hide, Kat.' It spat my name from its foul mouth.

Its rank, acrid odour assaulted me, the cloying stench forcing its way into my nostrils. Suddenly I couldn't breathe. The Beast had sucked all the air from the room. As it came closer and the walls of the Fishbowl started closing in on me, I let out a bloodcurdling scream.

A nurse was at my side within milliseconds, two more nurses hot on her heels. I needed to warn them about the Beast in the corner, that it would savage them too, but I couldn't find the air I needed to speak. All I could do was wave my hand and point at the corner, trembling and dripping with sweat.

'Hallucinations,' I heard a nurse say.

I stuttered, gasping, 'No, not halluc— It's there … the Beast … for real.'

As my panic attack escalated and I became catatonic, someone placed an oxygen mask on my face. The hissing from the tank terrified me even more. It became the sound of the Beast breathing over me, right in my face. I tore the mask off, sobbing, gasping and begging the nurses to save me.

They gently tilted my head back, firmly pulled my chin down to open my mouth and poured a cup of the magic red syrup down my throat, making me gag. My eyes rolled back in my head and all I could do was lie there, still fixated on the corner of the room, my eyes as big as dinner plates. I felt a sharp prick in my thigh and a cold rush as a heavy sedative hit my veins.

The nurses knew I was going to throw up before I did and had a bucket ready. The methadone hadn't had five minutes in my gut.

'We'll need this anti-emetic after all,' said a nurse, drawing up another injection and giving me a shot in the bum.

'That will stop the vomiting, Kat,' said another nurse, mopping my face and helping me sip some water.

After waiting a few minutes, they forced down another dose of the magic red potion. This time it stayed put. It was over an hour before I was lucid again and my breathing stable.

With the lights on, I saw that the Beast had gone. For now. I could still smell it though and I knew it'd be back, knew that the Beast wasn't done with me by a long shot.

A few hours later, I woke to find Doc Steiner next to me, writing notes on my chart. I slowly opened my eyes, registering it was daytime, but struggling to get my bearings. My mouth was so dry, I couldn't speak.

'Rough night you had, Kat,' said Doc Steiner, handing me some water.

'Mmmm.'

'Your blood pressure is still too high. If we can't stabilise you then we may transfer you to hospital later.'

'No, please no, let me stay here.' I really didn't want to be moved. The Fishbowl, in daylight, felt safe.

'We'll see. Have a shower, try to eat something, and then we'll give you meds to knock you out for the day. Your body really needs to rest. You're not strong enough yet to go into a full detox, so we will do this very slowly. How is your pain?'

'Everything is sore, top to toe, left and right.'

'Shame, Kat. It's bloody grim, I know. And you have diarrhoea?'

'Yes. Not pleasant.'

'It's normal, although I'm surprised how early that kicked in. I'm afraid it will last several days. Go freshen up now, I'll pop back later.'

Grabbing my cigarettes and pulling on some clothes, I made for the balcony, desperate for nicotine, the only crutch not stripped from me. My smoke was cut short by another dash to the loo.

The rest of the day was a complete blur. They really did knock me out for the day, good and proper. I wasn't complaining. Anything that stopped the rawness that raged forth and the bees in my head, I welcomed. I was mentally exhausted too, tired by a mind that couldn't hold one thought for more than a few seconds.

By early evening, I felt a little stronger. Smoking on the balcony and staring at the sun dipping into the ocean, I inhaled the crisp, salty air. Seagulls' cries mingled with the background rhythmic thump of waves on the beach, not far from where I stood. The sea looked rough tonight. It was all so alien to me, a farm girl from a landlocked country. The shadows deepened and a baboon barked in the hills behind me. I grew uneasy. Night was when my Beast came looking for me. Feeling a sudden shiver – like it was somewhere close, watching me and waiting – I went back to my Fishbowl, hoping like hell there'd be some decent narcotics to stop my night terrors.

Pat was on the nightshift. The later it got, the more like a traumatised child I became, clinging to its mother's skirt. The poor woman had a job to do though, and shook me off gently so she could get everyone else medicated, settled and behaving.

Much later, after lights out and when all the other junkies and piss artists I was yet to meet had shuffled off to bed, Pat brought me a mug of cocoa and a side order of methadone, and then told me to present my butt for a special nightcap – another shot of sedatives. Saying nothing, she marched out, her broad bum jiggling. All I wanted was for her to stay with me but I didn't know how to say it, and my face fell a mile when she walked out. But seconds later she marched back in, dragging a small TV on a trolley and her knitting under one arm. Still silent, she turned the TV on, making sure I had a good view from my bed. Positioning her chair in the doorway so she could still see the nurses station, she sat down with a sigh, kicked off her shoes and started knitting. After two rows, she looked up. I smiled at her, feeling safe, my eyes thanking her for not leaving me alone and vulnerable to the wretched Beast.

'My first grandchild, my own little *pookie*, is due next month. A *pooklet*,' she said, waving her knitting to show me the little bootie in progress. 'God help the bugger if it turns into a crack junkie likes its mother,' she added under her breath.

I didn't comment, realising Pat had just shared something very personal. I didn't want to risk pissing her off by being intrusive in case she left me alone.

A while later I shat myself when a ball of wool hit me square in the face. 'STOP scratching!' said Pat.

Again, I hadn't realised I was merrily giving myself angry welts. The ants were no longer crawling over my skin, they were now under my skin.

'No man! I'm gonna put you in mittens if you don't stop that. I have some in the cupboard 'cos you people on methadone, you all scratch like *fokkin'* flea-bag dogs.'

I laughed as I tossed the wool back at Pat, promising to stop. Whether it was all the drugs or the comfort of Pat there, suddenly the night ahead didn't seem so frightening. God help the Beast if it tried to get through that door with her there, armed with knitting needles and serious sass. I watched TV for hours, not even realising it was in Afrikaans, of which I didn't understand a word. In my methadone mecca, it didn't seem to matter.

31

The next day was a shocker. The methadone kept coming, but the sedative shots lessened as Doc Steiner slowly moved me into position to start my detox. Every symptom was magnified – from the pain in my bones, the awful diarrhoea that pushed me to the brink, more vomiting, the sweating, the incessant headaches, the sudden panic attacks, the ants and now spiders crawling over and under my skin, and the itchy scalp – it all came crashing down around my ears. I also started sneezing uncontrollably. Apparently normal too. My respiratory system was flaring up as the codeine started to leave my system.

Carol organised a full-body Swedish massage with acupuncture to help the crippling aches and to shift the toxins that saturated every cell of my body. I was directed to a room downstairs, catching a brief glimpse of the other patients and normal life in rehab – an oxymoron if ever there was. I found myself in a tranquil meditation room, beautifully scented by vanilla candles.

After a thorough Swedish-style pounding from a lady who, up close, smelt of lentil farts, I was wrapped in a full-body heat pad, skewered with dozens of acupuncture needles, and told to chill for half an hour. It definitely helped my pain, briefly. An hour later, I was back to pacing and vomiting violently. Emotionally, I was hit by a sudden, fresh rage.

Carol brought me some vile ginger tea to help the nausea and I was told, once again, that it was a normal reaction. I snapped.

'You all keep telling me this Carol – this is normal, that is normal, it's to be expected and blah blah fucking blah. Whether or not it is normal, I don't care – it doesn't make it any less excruciating.'

Carol just sat there, smiling ever so slightly, letting me rant. 'And here comes the anger,' she said. 'Don't shoot the messenger, but anger is normal too.'

'Fucking hilarious, Carol!' I yelled, stomping off to the bathroom, slamming the door behind me. I had a damn good cry, wondering if anyone had ever assaulted the staff. I was bloody close to decking Carol.

For the rest of the day, I didn't even try to pretend I was grateful to be where I was, to be getting a second shot at life. My own body was waging a war against me, the soul attached to it was in tatters, and I didn't even recognise the person I saw in the mirror – she looked so alien and had such a dead, cold look in her eyes. What was there to be grateful for? Should I be thanking people that I was in such pain? That I was unable to be more than a metre from a loo or a vom bucket? My mood swung wildly between anger and intense sadness. I even contemplated ending it all, but my razor had been taken off me on arrival, the mugs and glasses in my room were plastic, and the smoking balcony wasn't high enough. At best, I'd get a sprained ankle if I jumped. I barked and snarled at every nurse who tried to comfort me and eventually they left me alone to stew, telling me to sort my sour attitude out.

That evening, Carol arrived with a message that Dad had called and they all sent their love and missed me loads.

'Yeah fucking right. They're glad to be rid of me, the family "problem".'

'Kat, you are one spoilt little madam,' she replied, marching straight out.

'Screw you, Carol. I mean, have you ever been in my shoes and felt this pain?' I yelled after her. She didn't so much as pause, never mind respond, which incensed me further.

A short while later, Carol came back, firmly shutting the Fishbowl door behind her.

'Right, madam, listen up,' said Carol, placing a printed email in front of me.

I gave a loud sigh, barely glancing at it. What she did next, I did not see coming. Reaching into her pocket, Carol pulled out a tub of pills that

I instantly recognised as Stopayne, my lovely drug of choice and dear, dear friend. She plonked them on the table beside me.

'There you go. A hundred Stopayne, especially for you Kat, so you can have a normal, decent day and not be inconvenienced by me or my nursing staff. You clearly don't want to get clean, so go on, all yours. Eat up.' She slid the bottle closer to me.

I just looked at her, gobsmacked. There, within arm's reach, was the very drug that could make me feel like myself again.

'But before you take them, read that email,' added Carol.

Still, I just looked at her.

'Read it.' It was an order.

As I picked up the paper, one eye still on my friends in the bottle, I noticed I was trembling like a leaf. It was an email from Mom to Carol, sent five weeks ago, enquiring about checking me in and explaining the extent of my addiction. I honed in on one particular paragraph:

My daughter has already trashed her body to the extent that she required emergency gastric surgery to save her life, although she did actually die in ICU a few hours after her surgery but was resuscitated. Her frail body simply will not withstand further drug abuse. As a family, we have watched her systematically destroy her life, all her relationships and damage her promising career. I am at the stage where to not get her help feels like I am engaging in assisted suicide. I myself am a recovering alcoholic and thus understand addictions, however I simply don't know or recognise my own daughter any longer, nor do I know what demons are keeping her locked in her addiction. My daughter-in-law Sam was killed in a horrific car crash as a result of drunk driving, leaving my very young grandchildren with no mother, and I know in my heart of hearts that Kat is going to have a similarly tragic death at a very young age. I give it six months, tops, before she is dead.

I looked up at Carol, silent. Then, I just couldn't help it, my eyes darted back to the pills. Not a nervous look, a longing gaze with bedroom eyes.

'Hold out your hand,' said Carol.

I ignored her, meeting her steely gaze. We faced off.

'I said hold out your hand, Kat.'

Slowly I did so and watched in disbelief as she placed the pill bottle in my palm and closed my fingers tightly around it.

'Now feel that. Feel the weight of those pills and feel the relief they will give you. Can you taste them already? I bet you can already feel their familiar kick.'

'What the fuck are you trying to achieve, Carol?'

'Just trying to help – you know, we aim to please, make your stay a pleasant one and all that.' Her voice was cold, cold, cold.

I moved my wrist ever so slightly, making the pills clink in their container. The sound jarred me – such a familiar sound. I used to hear it all the time, that low rattling. Like Pavlov's dogs, I felt my pulse quicken and saliva flood my mouth. I couldn't stop myself.

'Take them Kat, but know that your decision will have consequences. For starters, you'll be thrown out of this clinic within five minutes, for relapsing. I know you don't have any money on you and I don't know if you realise it but your mother took your passport back to Zim with her. And you know no one in Cape Town, which means you'll sleep on the street tonight. But hey, on a hundred opiates, a dry gutter can feel quite cosy.'

I couldn't believe the complete and utter mindfuck Carol had just pulled on me. Common sense screamed at me to hand the pills back, but the Beast was in my head, persuasively telling me that swallowing them was by far the better choice.

'Take your time,' said Carol, nonchalantly picking up one of my magazines. 'I'll just sit here and wait while you decide.'

For long minutes, I sat quietly, thinking. One second I was on the Beast's team, agreeing to take them and agreeing that I could always come back to rehab at a later date, when I was ready. Readier. The next second, Mom's words tore through me. *I give it six months before she is dead.* My conscience replayed Sam's parents' devastated faces at her funeral and made me picture how Mom and Dad would look at mine.

Overcome by guilt, fear and anger, nausea hit me straight between the eyes. I threw the tub of pills at Carol, hitting her on the side of her head and ran to the bathroom, retching violently. Carol didn't move.

A while later, having splashed cold water on my face, I returned to sit with Carol. She casually looked over the magazine at me, questioning me with her eyes. The pills were back on the table.

'Get those pills out of here. Please,' I said.

Saying nothing, Carol picked them up and walked out. At the door she turned, her expression suddenly softer, almost sad.

'You've made the right choice. And don't EVER ask me again if I know how you feel. My own daughter was a Stopayne addict. I buried her on her twenty-third birthday. And she only got up to sixty a day.'

With that, Carol was gone.

That night the Beast came visiting, this time bigger. It was its most sinister and horrific appearance yet. It seemed to know exactly when I was alone and at my lowest of lows.

For two hours, the nurses tried to get me back from my catatonic terror in the Beast's wake, eventually calling Doc Steiner in at 3 a.m., concerned I was having a full-blown seizure, not just hallucinations. Finally, my palpitations and acute hysteria calmed when they whacked me with a different sedative which, I later learnt, was used to treat extreme psychosis. Thankfully, they didn't pack me off to hospital but, for the next twenty-four hours, I had a junior nurse with me at all times, even in the loo.

Looking in the mirror the next day, I was horrified to see that I had pulled huge chunks of my own hair out during my episode. What really unnerved me, though, was noticing that someone had been through my cupboard, probably when I was in the shower. They'd removed the laces from my trainers, and my leather belt was nowhere to be found. It wasn't hard to do the math. I was considered a danger to myself. I was on suicide watch.

The next day, I took a big step forward mentally and started feeling a bit more hopeful about the process, feeling maybe I could do it after all. Perhaps I had needed the last outburst to unblock my emotional drainpipes and release the pent-up rage. The physical symptoms were still grim, but the shift in attitude made them a little less overwhelming. I even found it within myself to apologise to Carol for being such a poisonous brat, which she accepted with grace. She gave me a writing pad and suggested I write a letter to my Beast.

It took me ages to get going, not knowing how to start my letter. Dear Beast, Hello Beast, For The Attention of Beast – they all felt wrong, so I settled on 'So, Beast, you foul piece of evil shit ...' After getting that right, there was no stopping me. An hour of mad, angry scribbling later, I was completely drained, not even noticing my tears had turned the paper into a soggy inky mess. It was a corner turned.

Two days later, I left the Fishbowl for a regular bedroom and was told to join the daily programme. While I was still somewhat unstable, apparently a new gibbering wreck was due and needed the Fishbowl more than me.

Pat took me and my suitcase to a huge room with four beds, an en suite bathroom and a balcony with a stunning sea view. The French windows to the balcony – barred, chained and padlocked – were my reality check, reminding me that I wasn't on a blue-sky holiday, but in an institution.

'Hello love, welcome. I'm Sarah,' said a woman sitting on the bed next to mine. She was a big girl, to put it politely, mid-thirties, jet-black hair in a high pony, incredibly blue eyes, and an Afrikaans accent you could sharpen a knife on. I thought she was lovely. Within seconds I'd forgotten her name, though. My short-term memory had gone to hell. Events of fifteen years ago were crystal clear, but I couldn't say what I'd had for breakfast. Another 'normal' detox symptom apparently.

'Sarah, please "buddy" Kat. Help my special *pookie* settle in and show her around,' Pat asked her.

'Sure thing, come on Kat, I'll help you unpack,' said Sarah, heaving my suitcase onto my new bed. Then she noticed my eyes. 'Woah! You're on the good shit! Methadone?'

'Yup, loaded up to the eyeballs,' I laughed.

Pat just shook her head and left us to it, shouting over her shoulder, 'She sees weird shit late at night, Sarah. Just saying.'

As I sorted out my corner of the room, Sarah began to rattle off the timetable and rules, folding my T-shirts as she spoke. 'We've got to be up, dressed, and at Housekeeping by eight o'clock. It's in the basement which, ironically, was the nightclub when this place was a hotel. We call it the dungeon. Housekeeping is where general rules are hammered into us and issues simmering within the Group are aired. If anyone has broken a rule, they get the high jump. Expect to see fights. Everyone loves ratting on each other. And, if you're in shitty mood or being sarky with anyone, some fucker is guaranteed to bring it up and shit stir in Housekeeping.'

'Sounds like school,' I said.

'Correct,' laughed Sarah, handing me a timetable filled with lectures, group therapy, videos, remedial art classes and one-on-one counselling times.

'Every day at four o'clock, we go walkies with a nurse escort down to the beach, even if you're bleeding from the eyeballs. The boys generally get a cricket game going and we have half an hour to get some fresh air. It's actually nice to just chill. If you try really hard, you can zone out all the snot, tears, and therapy stuff, and pretend you're a normal sane person enjoying a stroll. You need a sense of humour in here, Kat, or you will permanently be in tears.' Sarah gazed out wistfully for a moment. 'Oh, the security is tight and the windows only open twenty five centimetres. People here against their will are usually the ones who try to bolt. Shoulda' seen last week. Some stupid bastard decided he'd try squeezing his arse through the twenty-five centimetre gap. Granted, he was a tiny bugger but he got stuck. Properly stuck. And boy, did he wail like a baby. Not even the nurses could get him out, so the fool sat there, arse wedged in a window frame and was the laughing stock until a handyman arrived to remove the hinges. Great excitement. His wish was granted, except he got to leave through the front door – evicted minutes later.'

'Why was he thrown out?'

'Break a rule in this place and it's cheerio. While the rules don't actually state "don't get your arse stuck in a bathroom window", it's kinda obvious. Another BIG rule is "No Fraternising", meaning no shagging or even thinking about shagging your inmates. They watch us constantly, so don't form any exclusive relationships with the boys – or girls if you're on the other team. Flirting and physical contact will see you on that front step. And don't think anyone will cover for you – everyone is a dirty snitch.'

Sarah described how, like in school, there were rebels, cool cats and nerds. 'Donovan, now – he's the goody two shoes licky-arsey character of the year. Steer clear of him. He's new, but already being all anal and petty. If he doesn't like your T-shirt, he'll somehow get you into shit for it.

Yesterday, he made a formal complaint about his roommate's smelly feet. The roommate told Donovan to get fucked and stuck his filthy foot in Donovan's face. Fists flew and, after they were done thumping their chests like Tarzan, they both got punished. It was the best Housekeeping session in ages. You can't miss Donovan. He wears cardigans, brown ones like a frikkin' pensioner. The dude is twenty-two. Lord have mercy on us.'

I chuckled. Sarah made everything sound hilarious.

My case nearly empty, she held up a pair of my denim hot pants. 'Shit girl, you're skinny, huh? My dog's left bollock wouldn't fit in these. Which brings me to the next rule. No tight, tarty clothes.'

'It gets better and better. Why?' I asked.

'Well, my friend, we have sex addicts amongst us. The sight of flesh can set off dirty urges, so no tits or tushie on display.'

'Fuck me!'

'Not today. I'm good thanks love,' Sarah chuckled with a dirty laugh. She then pointed at the other two beds in our room. 'Cassie and Tina are our room-mates. Cassie snores like a fucking steam train. Coke nose. She's burnt her cartilage to buggery. Tina talks in her sleep, but she's Dutch so it's not even entertaining. And she grinds her teeth – that's from the ecstasy of course. Please don't tell me you have irritating nocturnal habits too. Did I hear Pat say you see weird shit at night?'

'Apparently I had one or two hallucinations in the Fishbowl.' I didn't want to describe the Beast's late-night visits just yet.

'Yeah, I hear the Fishbowl is fertile ground for seeing dragons and shit. Might be all that methadone you're on. Anyway, that's a wrap. Welcome to the nuthouse. If you weren't a nutjob before you came in, then you soon will be.'

'Now *that* I can believe!'

'There's another guy here who also enjoys munching headache pills, though you leave him in the starting posts. Shit, he had a bad detox too. So, how's that methadone? I hear it gives quite a *lekker* buzz? Wish I'd got some.'

I just laughed, the first laugh since arriving. Sarah took me downstairs to join the group smoking on the patio, where I met more colourful characters. Introductions were such as you'd expect in a jail. *What are you in for – uppers, downers, booze, sex, food or gambling?* I forgot everyone's names but the welcome was warm and even a bit comforting. Life outside the Fishbowl certainly was more interesting.

My three room-mates were a mixed bunch. Sarah, widowed in her twenties and single mother of two, told me she had an extreme fondness for gin. She thought nothing of knocking back a full bottle every day, preferably finishing it by sundown, then would top things up with sherry and often a joint too.

Cassie was a girl who seemed to epitomise the darker side of the 'Cape Coloured' underworld, and was part of a pro-murder gang and drug ring in the notorious ganglands on the Cape Flats. Only nineteen, she had a hectic crack cocaine habit, funded by dealing and prostitution – since she was fourteen. She'd already served jail time. She had gruesome cigarette burns on her arms and looked like the walking dead.

My third roommate was Dutch Tina, a 'trance and techno' girl, coming off ecstasy and coke. She was a singer, often in the Euro charts, and also one of the hottest trance DJs. Being a minor celebrity, she'd chosen a foreign rehab to escape the media scandal. In active addiction, Tina would disappear for days, losing herself in the sordid underground of sex, raves, and uppers, forgetting she'd left her eight-year-old son home alone. On one occasion, after four nights alone, the starving child had gone to a neighbour who'd alerted social services and Tina had since lost her son to the welfare system.

With our vastly different backgrounds, we'd never have been friends outside of rehab but, break it down, we were all the same, just substance abusers living unmanageable lives. All crime and dodgy behaviour was overlooked in rehab, and peer judgement was just not on. We'd all been desperate in our own ways. It rocked me to realise that my scoring from Colin was no worse than Cassie's "Two-for-the-price-of-one" blow jobs just before pay day, or her loyalty scheme which made the member's tenth shag free, her marketing tactics she spoke of proudly.

32

It was indeed a full timetable and there was no moping around feeling sorry for yourself. Many of the numerous rules verged on the ridiculous but, with thirty or so very messed-up people living together, I suppose they needed some structure or all hell would break loose. Although it sounded as if it regularly did anyway. Sarah was right about Housekeeping. It was like having a ringside seat and the arguments were mainly petty, yet amusing.

The counsellors were a mixed bunch of different races – young and old – and all recovering addicts and alcoholics themselves. I was assigned to Gina, a stunning woman in an earthy, boho way. She wore flowing gypsy-style dresses, lots of gorgeous chunky jewellery and had a cascade of long dark hair.

Gina scared the crap out of me.

To call her cold would be kind and to call her human would be barely accurate. In my first one-on-one session in her torture chamber, we discussed my childhood and she said some pretty hard-arsed things, including calling me a spoilt brat. Gina evidently had no qualifications in the field of Mincing Words and I came out bawling like a baby. According to Cassie, that was their modus operandi, to break us down and hammer out our denial. Then, when they thought they'd got every last speck of denial out, they'd hammer us further, just to make doubly sure. Apparently that process would take three to four weeks. Only once we got real and honest would they build us back up, glue us together again and prepare us for a clean life in the real world. The rebuild only kicked off in the last week of treatment, which meant I had weeks of intense torture coming my way. After just one round with Gina the evil gypsy, I completely understood how one could be tempted to try to squeeze one's arse through the tiny window gap.

Tina saw me bleeding after Gina's little one-on-one welcoming speech and tried to comfort me. 'Kat, for the next few weeks they will make you feel like scum. They will tear you to shreds with their words and then pour salt on your wounds. You will cry more here than you will anywhere else in life. Everything you thought you knew about yourself will be challenged. In short, buckle up girl.' Said with a Dutch accent only made it more foreboding.

According to the nurses I was on the highest dose of methadone, but my headaches remained relentless. They refused point-blank to give me anything for the pain, saying the monster doses of methadone should take care of it. If it didn't, tough shit. I kept asking for painkillers, hoping they might show mercy, but they soon got shirty with me again. Meanwhile, my fellow junkies were suitably jealous of the quantities of methadone I was getting. They'd have given their right tit or testicle for some too. Only opiate addicts got drugs to take the edge off, and it seemed that a methadone detox earned you hero status within the group.

I soon noticed how we all had a morbid fascination with each other's drinking and drug habits and knew exactly who was on what medication. We'd sit for hours swopping stories. This pastime, known as Euphoric Recall, was theoretically against the rules, though the counsellors had a hard time monitoring our private conversations. That said, in Housekeeping narks like Donovan would rat on any Euphoric Recallers. Our counsellors reckoned we did ourselves no favours in retelling war stories or sharing the mad things we'd done as it just triggered cravings. Still though, we'd sit on the patio late at night, drinking coffee, laughing, smoking and telling wild stories of scoring from dealers and such. Like fishermen exaggerating the size of a catch, so our stories were embellished. There were three other painkiller addicts in the clinic who'd also had tame pharmacists on speed dial and were happy to share their pharmaceutical breakfast smoothy recipe. It all helped pass the time and was a vague distraction from our emotional and physical pain.

The methadone also induced narcolepsy in me. It hadn't been a problem in the Fishbowl, but now I was expected to do more than just lie in bed all day. I kept getting shat on for falling asleep. I could be mid-sentence one minute, fast asleep the next, to the hilarity of all. One morning, during a lecture about what drugs and booze did on a physiological level and hearing about the actual holes many of us had burnt in our brains, I nodded off in my chair, only to be woken by Carol throwing a book at my head from across the room. It hit me on the shoulder and I nearly died of fright, giving a loud girly yelp. There was much sniggering from everyone, but I felt less of a tit when minutes later another poor methadone-marinated bastard woke up to a blackboard duster straight between the eyes. He literally leapt up, screaming in fright, and I swear he'd pissed his pants as he then shot out of the room.

Meal times were a barrel of laughs too. The counsellors ate at a table in the corner of our dining room, creating a foreboding wall of authority that made the food even more indigestible than it already was.

'Don't be fooled,' said Tina one lunchtime, pointing her fork in the direction of the staff table. 'They're watching us like hawks. They're scouting for eating disorders.'

'Eating disorders?' I asked.

'Yup. Many of us here have an eating disorder of sorts, or at least an unhealthy relationship with food. They're watching to see if we're playing games with our food. Oh, and another thing, they watch to see who goes to the toilet straight after eating,' said Tina.

'So our toilet habits are up for discussion too?' I asked.

'Yup. The anorexics and bulimics have this habit of sticking their finger down their throat right after eating and having a good roar into the loo,' said Cassie.

'Yeah, so eat all your scoff 'cos they're watching you,' said Sarah. 'Trust me, you don't want to be put on the eating disorder meal plan. It's awful – they've got me on it and look at this sloppy crap I have to eat.' she waved her hand in disgust over her plate.

Her lunch did indeed look vile and grey.

'So how does *your* eating disorder work?' I asked Sarah, not knowing how else to ask why she was the size of a house.

'As you can see, I am a serious salad dodger. I hoover comfort food at every chance I get. Eating disorders aren't just for skinny people. I am all about the overeating and bingeing, which is why I could kick-start a jumbo jet. Anything with Cadbury on it and there's a stampede. Last year I even painted my kitchen a beautiful deep violet. It's lovely,' she replied, wistfully. She then explained that their meal plan banned white flour and sugar, which caused intense euphoric feelings but equally intense downers after the highs.

'And the entire group knows who is on the eating disorder meal plan. We are supposed make sure they aren't eating sweeties in secret,' said Cassie. 'Anyway, you're skin and bone yourself, you sure you're not a secret tonsil tickler?'

'Nope, never made myself puke on purpose. I'm just skinny because all the painkillers killed my appetite,' I said.

'See those two stick insects over there,' said Tina, pointing at two girls at the next table.

'Yup,' I said.

'They're anorexics and on the meal plan too. Watch how they fiddle with their food. And see how they have no juice. They're not allowed a drink half an hour before eating, and they can't have a drink with a meal,' said Tina.

'Why?' I asked.

'A drink fills you up and then you won't want to eat. It's an anorexic's trick,' said Sarah.

A few days later, out of nowhere, the nurses started making me get on a scale every day – but backwards so I couldn't see my weight. Apparently, it could set off an unhealthy chain of thoughts around food and distorted body images. I managed a sneaky peek one day and got a fright to see I weighed in at forty-one kilograms. Sarah told me to expect an Eating Disorder label to be awarded soon.

Yes, forty-one was a tad low, but it was only a side effect of the drugs. In fact, my appetite had come back tenfold and, for the first time in ages, I didn't view food just as something to prep my stomach for the day's painkillers. Plus, the methadone sparked intense cravings for sugar so, when a clinic runner tootled over the road to a local café to buy all our cigarettes and sweets every day, my order always included a few chocolates. Eating disorder my non-anorexic arse, I thought, they can shove that label. What anorexic scoffs chocolates anyway?

Late one night, after a terrible migraine all day and just as I'd managed to fall asleep, I was woken by a nurse coming into our room with a torch.

'Kat, come with me,' said the nurse.

'Agh, for fuck's sake, why?'

'I need a urine sample.'

'In the middle of the bloody night?'

'Yup.'

Coming out of the loo and handing the sample to her, I scowled. 'Why now? In the middle of the night?'

'We're checking your ketone levels. Your pee tells us if you've skipped meals or induced any vomiting. In other words, if your body is in starvation mode. We test in the night, when the body has been at rest for a while.'

'Fucking unreal,' I muttered, realising this was all about eating disorders. 'Why can't you just ask me?'

I got a filthy look. 'You'd lie.'

'For the record, I don't vomit on purpose and I don't starve myself, and that nice pot of pee you're holding will tell you the same thing. Can I go back to bed now?'

'Yup. Sleep well, Kat.'

'Yeah, whatever.' I was so pissed off it took me hours to get back to sleep.

The next morning, I asked Sarah about the bullshit midnight pee test.

'*Ja*, ketones in your pee tell them what you've been doing food-wise. Better watch out. If they've done the midnight piss test then they're thinking you've got an eating disorder,' said Sarah.

'Bastards,' I said, chewing my pen while doing my daily mood sheet. Every evening we had to fill out a short form, listing how we felt, what had rattled our cage that day, who pissed us off, how angry we were, and so on. A mood inventory, which, if not posted in the designated box on time, got you hauled up in front of Carol to explain yourself. Pissed off about the whole eating disorder thing, I let rip:

Unimpressed about midnight pee test. I don't play games with food. I got

321

skinny from the drugs, not due to an inherent desire to resemble a bean pole. Did I miss something? I thought I was here to get off drugs, not food.

Let's see what they say about that then, I thought. Little did I know I had just put the nail in my eating disorder coffin.

I could not shake the aches and pains, and the throb in my core still gnawed at me. Typically, I had no trouble falling asleep in a Group session, but rest was impossible at night. In the dead of night, I'd often be found pacing the corridors. Sometimes, unable to sleep, I just sat with the nurses and flicked through some Recovery books. Every time I asked for pain relief, the nurses answered with a curt reminder that I was there to quit drugs, not to widen my pharmaceutical research. Carol arranged another Swedish massage to help with the flushing out of toxins – it hurt like hell again and set off a major vomiting session that left me utterly broken, but there was no question of lying around in bed. It all made me permanently angry.

The full group splintered into three smaller batches which gathered twice a day for Group. The counsellors would rotate between the smaller groups so we'd get a taste of them all. Gina was as much of a terrorist in Group as she was in one-on-one sessions. As for Julian – not a whiff of the Mr Nice Guy I'd met on arrival. He was almost as terrifying as Gina. In fact, all the counsellors were hardcore and nobody whosoever escaped their ruthless, biting comments. There was absolutely no point in saying 'No! Not fair!' when annihilated in Group. The counsellors, being addicts and alcoholics themselves, I'd imagined could have been a little more understanding.

The diversity of people incarcerated with me were still a slight distraction, their backgrounds and stories an education in themselves. I had to admit that I'd arrived with a shitload of airs and graces but was soon brought down to size. My so-called snobbery even became the opening topic for a Group session. Group was always a tense hour and, in our splinter groups, we'd sit in a circle and wait nervously, never knowing whose head was on the block or which counsellor would oversee the decapitation.

Today was my turn. As luck would have it, Jackie came in and parked her broomstick. She was a counsellor who terrified me, possibly even more than Gina did.

'Kat,' said Jackie.

'Hello?' I said, dreading what was coming.

'What makes you better than everyone else here?' she asked. 'What's with all the condescending looks? Don't think they go unnoticed. You've been here eight days and already been labelled an all-out snob.'

Fucking bitch, I thought, how could she say that? A wave of anger came over me. 'I'm NOT a snob,' I blurted.

Jackie stared at me with fierce eyes. 'Do you perhaps think because your drugs were available in a proper shop, a pharmacy, that's better than buying crack from a dealer in a dark alley? That you are better than, say, Cassie, because she scored illegal drugs and made a living working in the flesh trade? Because I'll tell you one thing – it's not and you're not. You're the same. Just a self-centred addict with an unmanageable life. Being a precious princess won't get you far in here, Kat.'

Bitch. I was getting tired of being called a princess. Sam, rest her soul, was a princess, not me.

'Does anyone want to say anything to Kat?' Jackie asked the group.

There it was, my head on a plate offered to the group, like a holy sacrifice to the great God of Prescription Drugs. A girl called Linda wasted no time in taking the first bite. She'd been giving me the stink eye for days but I didn't know why.

'Yes Kat, you are totally up your own arse, making out you're something special, like you're better than us because you devoured pills and not crack. You can shove your colonial, stuck-up ways.'

I was seething. Rules stated that you weren't allowed to defend yourself when you were in the ring, but I practically vaporised Linda with my glare.

Then Donovan, never missing a chance to be a complete wanker, said much the same to me. And then the next one got stuck in. Jackie sat back and watched everyone picking away at me. Soon most people had said their bit, even Cassie, which I thought was a bit disloyal seeing as we were mates.

'You're angry Kat,' stated Jackie after everyone had moved off the kill, stepping back from my bleeding carcass.

'No shit,' I replied.

'What's really getting to you?'

I just sat there. Glaring. Thinking. Silent.

'I think you know exactly what's rattled your cage but I'll let you sit with the feelings,' said Jackie.

I looked at her, my face like a slapped arse, tears of sheer anger building. I was hugely relieved when Donovan was hauled up next.

'Donovan, why are you such a teacher's pet?' asked Jackie. 'You're always telling tales. What are you, five years old? Always being a bit of an arsehole. What's that all about, huh?'

Aha, I thought, now that's more like it. About time Donovan got it. I sat up, practically rubbing my hands together. Donovan's face went red as he fidgeted and straightened his brown cardigan.

Jackie went on. 'It all comes back to your relationship with your father, Donovan, doesn't it? You were never good enough for him, as you yourself admit, so is that why you are such a goody two shoes here? Got to be top of the class here because you were such a disappointment out in the real world?'

I almost felt sorry for Donovan, who looked very traumatised. Another guy in the group, James, offered his opinion.

'Yes, Donovan, you shit on Kat for airs and graces yet you're the little arse-wipe who is trying to outshine everyone else. When your father failed to notice you, you snorted coke. Not only did you buy your Colombian Marching Powder with your Dad's bank notes, but you snorted it through them too and even cut your lines with his credit card. All you got was the wrong kind of attention from him. It landed you in here, yet still you want to be noticed, to count for something. You squeal about us for the tiniest thing and wonder why everyone thinks you're such a dick. Leave Kat alone, she has nothing on your act.'

Go James, I thought, starting to like the guy more, suddenly noticing he was quite hot too.

Sarah then went for Donovan's jugular. She'd had an altercation with him at breakfast over a freshly baked jam scone – a banned substance for those on the eating disorder meal plan, but Tina had taken a cigarette bribe to steal it for Sarah. Donovan had caught Sarah in the act and made a citizen's arrest. He'd moved in to snatch her lovely scone and a tussle had followed, bits of scone flying everywhere. Donovan, furious that his cardigan had become smeared with jam, had turned Sarah in and she was one pissed off, sugar-starved lady.

'I'm willing to bet your dad wears cardigans, Donovan – that you copied that fashion statement from him in some attempt to be noticed and loved,' said Sarah. 'You're in your twenties, yet you dress like an old man. It all screams "daddy issues".'

Ouch, now that must have stung.

Jackie was watching Donovan, now a deathly grey and looking like he was considering a vomit.

'They're right Donovan,' Jackie said, but switching to a gentler tone. 'You crave being the centre of attention. Work on your own spoilt brat and goody two shoes image before trying to fix everyone else.'

With that, she left Donovan alone. Shame, he was now blubbing like a baby. Jackie was on a roll and Sarah was the next one up for the chop.

'Sarah, your sister is coming tomorrow for a family chat. Are you aware?' asked Jackie.

'Yes,' said Sarah meekly.

'Has she got custody of your kids now?' asked Jackie.

'Yes.'

'Because you can't look after yourself, never mind them?'

'Yes.' Sarah had tears in her eyes.

'How does that feel?'

We all sat in silence, waiting for Sarah to reply.

'How does that feel, Sarah?' Jackie asked again.

'Awful,' whispered Sarah, starting to cry openly. 'I miss my babies. I've fucked up. Big time.'

'Well, if you'd spent less time getting drunk and more time being a mother, things could have been different. First, they lost their father and now their mother. Tell everyone how you nearly killed them too.'

Sarah had swords flying from her eyes and extreme rage oozing from every pore. Sarah's sorest point was her kids. She'd poured her heart out to me in private.

'Go on, tell the story,' prompted Jackie.

Sarah took a deep breath. 'I had a car accident while doing the school run.'

'And why did you have an accident, Sarah?' asked Jackie.

'Because I was pissed. I guess.'

'And?' said Jackie. 'Pissed and?'

'I was pissed and stoned. I'd smoked a joint.'

'And?'

With that, Sarah started howling. We were all silent, every one of us remembering our similarly insane behaviour and the times we shouldn't have been behind the wheel.

'I'd had a fight with my sister. She was giving me the gears about how I live my life. Bitch. I'd like to see how she'd cope with being a widow. I wanted to blot it all out so I clobbered a bottle of gin, smoked a joint and then picked up the kids.'

'Tell us how it happened,' said Jackie.

'I had one of the kids' friends in the car,' said Sarah, mascara streaked across her face. 'None of us had seatbelts on. I sailed through a red light, hit a pedestrian and then skidded into a lamp post. My son had his head sliced open by flying glass. Twenty stitches. The pedestrian spent a week in hospital and my driving licence was revoked after they breathalysed me. I'd already had one drunk-driving warning.'

'You could have killed someone,' Jackie stated.

'Yes, I could have killed my kids, their friend, and the pedestrian,' replied Sarah.

'Can you see how unmanageable your life had become?' asked Jackie.

'Yes,' whispered Sarah. 'Shit, I just miss my husband so badly. I'd give anything to have him back.'

'Sarah, your husband is dead. You won't find him at the bottom of a gin bottle or in the ashes of a joint. And stop wearing "widow" like it's a label, like a victim. Why define yourself by your husband's death? You're a mother too, remember. Do you think your husband is looking down on you now, in awe of your mothering skills, happy about the life you are giving his kids?' said Jackie.

'No.'

'Tell everyone how you get about without a driver's licence,' said Jackie.

'I hired a driver so the kids could get to school. I had no friends left or favours to call in. My sister has washed her hands of me.'

'And who pays for this driver?' asked Jackie.

'My dad.'

'Lucky you, to have such a loaded father so neatly wrapped around your finger. Pity though, that your children are embarrassed to arrive at school with a driver because all their little friends know their mother is just a common drunk. Do you know that your kids get the driver to drop them around the corner so nobody sees?' asked Jackie.

Sarah had her head in her hands, sobbing uncontrollably.

The lunch bell rang and, thankfully, Group was over. I gave Sarah a fresh tissue, a quick hug and we all headed outside for a much-needed smoke.

I was starting to see what was meant when they said we'd be broken into pieces. Today's session had been just an appetiser and I knew they hadn't even started on me. It wasn't going to be pretty.

Towards the end of my second week, I started to feel a little less like a zombie. I was coming off the methadone and Valium, and the joint pain had lifted ever so slightly, but my head pounded constantly, not helped by the emotional beatings I was getting several times a day. Sleep was still a big issue and the fatigue, on top of everything else, only made me crabbier. When I did sleep, there'd be visits from the Beast, except it wasn't as terrifying or as huge as before. It was the size of a large doll. It still sat in the corner, its menacing red eyes fixed on me, giving a low chuckle. Its smell was unmistakable, a stale stench of death, despair, and destruction, that lingered long after it disappeared. Not wanting to wake the girls by addressing it aloud, I would bravely and assertively tell it to fuck off in my mind, turn over and try to go back to sleep, pretending I couldn't hear its heavy breathing. Pretending I wasn't trembling inside.

In a warped way, the Beast had done me a favour. Its reducing size was a barometer, the only thing showing me I was making progress in this godforsaken clinic. The fact that it had shrunk and lost some power surely meant I was moving away from my old dark, lonely and treacherous life? I was still afraid though. Doll sized or not, its mere presence reminded me that it would pounce the second I grew weak.

With the methadone waning, the next thing to go berserk was my lungs and I came down with awful bronchitis. Wheezing and coughing like a trooper, running a fever, and my confused lungs making gurgling wet sounds, I was still frogmarched through the programme each day.

And, even while I was so sick, Gina was relentless. In our next session, she wanted to know more about the perforated ulcer and the head injuries that had started my cycle of headaches. She also asked how I viewed food and how I perceived my body. They certainly were gunning for me on the eating disorder and I explained, yet again, that I'd always been slim but had lost weight due to the pills killing my appetite, not self-induced puke sessions.

'You've got a healthy dose of denial,' Gina said coldly. 'Your bratty little comment on your mood sheet the other day was really quite telling.'

Agh, fuck, I thought, this woman is *really* starting to get on my tits now.

'There it is again, that raw anger in your eyes. Why are you so angry Kat?'

'I'm angry because I'm sick of all this shit. I'm sick of the accusations about fucked-up eating. I feel like shit 24/7. I feel like I have an angry kangaroo pummelling my brain, day in, day out. I get woken in the night to pee in a jar. I can't sleep. I can't breathe right now. The methadone supply is drying up and a Valium or two wouldn't go amiss. I am here to stop taking painkillers – yet what happens now when I'm in pain? Am I supposed to just live like this, or do you idiots have some magic pain solution up your sleeve that you're not telling me about? I mean, fine, help me quit the pills, but then also address the pain, for fuck's sake. Shall I go on?' I said sarcastically and then promptly burst into angry tears.

Gina ignored my rant and kept quiet for a while, letting me cry. 'I believe your boyfriend left you. Do you want to talk about that?'

'No, I don't actually. What's done is done. Fuck it. Fuck him.' I sniffed loudly and crossed my arms and legs in a huff.

'Kat, I don't think you realise just how severe your addiction is. All you have done since arriving is bitch and moan and, frankly, I am tired of the princess act.'

I let out a big sigh. The princess word again.

'You tore a hole in your gut and nearly DIED Kat, and, if you don't get your shit together, you will still DIE,' Gina continued, being irritatingly emphatic with her mortality forecasts. 'You will continue to lose muscle mass and your heart will get smaller and weaker, and then arrest. Your bones will become as brittle as a stick of uncooked spaghetti, and your liver and kidneys are already showing signs of shutting down. If you don't die by some miracle, you could end up with a colostomy bag – not the most attractive of accessories. Your parents have put you here at great expense and the least you could do is try our suggestions before you discard them. If this doesn't work then fine, go ahead and kill yourself. I won't lose any sleep over your death. Choice is yours.' She looked at me, pausing, shaking her head slowly. 'Kat, you took up to a hundred of some of the strongest painkillers and tranquillisers available, every day. Are you insane?'

'Apparently so,' I said sulkily, a little shaken by 'colostomy bag'.

Gina handed me a piece of paper and a blue book, *Narcotics Anonymous.* 'Read the first five chapters tonight, and complete this worksheet. How are you doing with your Step 1?'

The first of the 12 Steps – admitting to being powerless over drugs and that my life had become unmanageable – was something I was grappling with.

'Getting there, I guess. I can see my life was possibly a bit unmanageable.'

'Possibly a bit?' Gina said with a snort, while doing wiggly air quotes with her fingers. 'Try to finish the work tonight. You've been given the format for your life story and the date you will present it, so I hope you're also working on that. Take a long hard look at yourself. And I know you are in physical pain so I'll arrange some reiki healing for you too. I am also putting you on the eating disorder meal plan as I suspect you are bingeing on chocolates and crap. Sugar won't fill the void, it will send your moods haywire, make you feel worse and—'

'I DON'T have a fucking eating disorder!' I yelled.

'As I was saying,' said Gina, ignoring me, 'the sugar gives you a high and then drops you lower than you were before. The plan will help your headaches. So, starting right now, no sugar, no using the toilet for an hour after meals, no drinks with meals, no white flour. End of story.'

With that, she opened her door and indicated that I was to walk through it. Furious, I left crying. Her words – verbal shrapnel – stung all day.

At supper, a plate of something foul with my name written on the cling wrap, was presented. Sarah related to my disgust and commiserated with me, explaining the meal plan again.

'White flour and sugar have little nutritional value. Food can be used like a drug, to give you a buzz. We EDs – Eating Disorders, or rather Disorderlies in my world – use food to squash feelings. "Eating on emotions" they call it. I call it "eating". You'll get used to the meal plan, hun, but yes, it's a crying shame about the chocolates. I'm totally with you on that. If you crave something sweet, you can eat fruit till it comes out your ears and you can put honey in your coffee, though that tastes crap too.'

'Well, I can't see the logic in this. Surely I need to actively try to gain weight now I am off the drugs? Having no sugar or flour is just dieting as far as I'm concerned, yet I need to gain five kilograms. It's utterly stupid,' I said.

'Yeah well, say that to Gina and she'll just say your body will settle at its normal weight in time,' said Sarah.

I couldn't stomach the unidentifiable grey slop on my plate, or tell whether it had even come from an animal, so it went untouched and I ate only a banana. The next morning in Housekeeping, I was hauled over the coals for not eating my supper. There was no winning.

Mom rang me when I was finally allowed phone calls, but it was hard to have a decent conversation with everyone talking at tops of their voices down the row of phone boxes. It amused me to hear how we all said similar things to those on the other end. *Counsellors are evil, food sucks, petty rules, wanna come home, I hate this place, can't sleep, I'd rather be high, dude.*

Mom passed on messages of love from everyone at home but, too drained to get all deep and meaningful, I kept it short. Little did I know she'd been in touch with Gina regarding my Letter.

I'd witnessed others getting their Letter read out in Group and it wasn't fun. Our friends and families were asked to write to us, saying how they felt and exposing our secrets, lies and appalling behaviour. From where I sat, our Letters were about making sure everyone in the clinic knew what a shit we'd been, in case we hadn't disclosed as much ourselves, which invariably we hadn't. If we were holding back on any sordid behaviour or anecdotes, then our so-called loved ones, via the Letter, would blow it all wide open, putting fresh bait and new material on the table in the verbal slaughterhouse known as Group. If the Letter wasn't harsh enough, the sender was asked to rewrite it and apply themselves more thoroughly to the gory details. For it to work, Letters couldn't be kind. I was dreading mine. It was commonly agreed that Letter Day was one of the worst days in rehab for some, even worse than checking in.

I got the shock of my life on my Letter Day.

Gina handed it to Donovan to read out. 'Before you start, tell Kat who wrote her Letter,' said Gina.

Donovan flipped to the second page.

Shit, I thought, my Letter looked long.

'It's from an Ant,' said Donovan.

My heart farted. I nearly fell off my chair.

'Kat, explain who Ant is?' Gina said.

'He's my ex. Why is he writing anyway? We're over. Done. He's not even a part of my life anymore.'

'Your ex what?' asked Gina.

'Ex-boyfriend,' I replied tersely.

'Letters come from those you hurt, whether they're still in your life or not. Don't scowl at me Kat. Getting Ant to write it was your mother's suggestion. You were a complete horror to him. The mere fact that he has even done this is fairly significant, so get down off your throne, put your big girl pants on, and take it.'

Agh, fuck, I thought, rubbing my temples. I'm toast. The rules of Letter Day stated that the recipient was not allowed to so much as peep during the reading. I quickly snatched a few tissues from the communal box and braced myself.

Donovan made a great show of clearing his throat, puffing out his chest and fiddling with his cardigan.

My dearest Kat,
I don't know how to start so will just write from the heart. You were, and perhaps still are, the love of my life.

For years I have lived with guilt about my part in the night you nearly drowned. If you'd not been trying to impress me that night, not felt pressured into smoking weed and drinking, you wouldn't have had the accident that screwed-up your head and neck for life, and you wouldn't have had to live with chronic pain and headaches. Ironically, it was the night of your accident that I fell in love with you – the night I unknowingly set you on course for your medical hell and your dependency on the very drugs that ultimately broke us up. And I am so, so sorry for my part in that.

I've tried to pinpoint exactly when I lost you to the drugs, but I can't. We all nearly lost you when your stomach perforated, but I'd lost you to the pills and your pain long before then. It would have been easier to have lost you to another guy, something more tangible.

You became so vacant, so empty, and the more drugs you took the less there was of you. You lost all substance and you disappeared before my eyes, both physically and emotionally. The Kat I fell in love with was bright, funny, sporty, clever and very beautiful in body and mind. Hot as hell and very sexy. I was deeply shocked when I ran into you recently and saw how you'd let yourself go. You looked like the walking dead, so rough I barely recognised you. It broke my heart, Kat, to see the immense sadness in your eyes, despite your best efforts to convince me your life was awesome.

The drugs didn't just rob you of your physical beauty, they took your exquisite, kind soul and turned you into a self-centred, arrogant, sour and patronising beast of a woman. You became very difficult for me to like, never mind love. You focused only on your health and we only ever heard about the agony you lived in. I suppose I just got sick of the broken record. It was like dating an old-age pensioner – boring and draining.

Your drinking did my head in too. You seemed possessed once you started and I used to cringe with embarrassment when you got rat faced. It always took over and our nights out were ruined by you going full throttle, drinking until you couldn't remember your own name. Kat, my friends and colleagues used to laugh behind my back. Once I overheard them saying they didn't know why I put up with a stoned drunkard for a girlfriend – imagine how that felt for me? You once told me about your mom's alcoholism. You were angry about the hell she put your dad through. How does it feel to know you created that same hell for me? I had many long talks with your family, with Rolo too. I even attended Al-Anon meetings with your grandfather, I was that desperate to help you and get my old Kat back.

I broke up with you when I realised nothing I did or said would make you quit the pills, the mad drinking, the insane behaviour and the angry, unpredictable moods. You were not going to change for anyone, never mind me. I couldn't stand by and watch you kill yourself. I had to detach to preserve my own sanity. Leaving you was the hardest thing I've ever had to do, but I could no longer breathe in our relationship. I felt trapped. You never thought of my needs, only yours. The final straw was when you left me sitting in a restaurant for over two hours while you chased your dealer around town trying to score, and then lied about why you were so late. As usual, your drugs came first that night. Watching how the lies rolled off your tongue with such ease was, perhaps, my biggest wake-up call. You didn't give a rat's arse that I had taken unpaid leave and come to Harare only to be with you. I had an engagement ring in my pocket that night Kat, which I have since thrown in the Zambezi River.

I've known about Colin for a long time, ever since I happened to spot you meeting him in a car park. I wondered if you were sleeping with him, you'd sunk so low. That said, the nature of your relationship with Colin was even more sinister than any sexual affair could ever have been.

You have no grounds for jealousy about the other women I date. You tossed me aside like a cheap toy, so you only have yourself to blame. I might add that Jess is a breath of fresh air, she doesn't suck the air from the room. She is fun, carefree, happy, considerate and cool. Like you were, once.

Kat, hate me all you like, but I was asked to write this letter for your own good, plus I needed to say these things. Whether you will change your ways or even live to see twenty-five, please know that I loved you deeply and still do. I am just not prepared to hang around, year after year, putting up with your lies and bullshit, and coming second to your drugs, dealers and piss-ups. I couldn't carry on dating an ill-tempered selfish cow in the grips of a love affair with drugs and booze. I have more self-respect than that.

I really do hope things are coming right for you. I speak to your folks every week to find out how you are getting on in rehab. I was so relieved when I heard you'd finally accepted the offer of help.

I don't know what else to say so I guess I will leave it there.

Good luck KitKat, I really mean that. Be strong. The world is a better place with Kat – the real Kat – in it.

Love Ant x

Donovan quietly folded the letter and leant over to put it on my lap. All eyes were on me. I'd started crying after the second line and there was a ring of scruffy wet tissues on the floor around my chair. I felt as if I'd been doused in acid, inside and out, and a burning match flicked onto me. A flame ripped through my chest, my breath came in short sharp stabs. It was a physical burn – brutal, searing, white-hot pain, so intense that I could have just lain on the floor and wept for days.

'How does hearing all that make you feel, Kat?' asked Gina, her tone surprisingly gentle and caring. 'Did you know Ant was going to propose that night you were so late?'

'No, I had absolutely no idea. I just needed to score that night and would have driven to another town if need be,' I whispered, still sobbing.

'Did you know he went to Al-Anon for you?' asked Gina.

'No.'

'And who is Colin?'

'A crooked pharmacist, come dealer.'

'Do you think your life was unmanageable, Kat?'

'Yes. Seems so.'

'Your well-oiled denial system merely served as your shock absorber for life. Denial has kept you entrenched in your disease and your secrets have kept you sick,' stated Gina. Jargon and phrases I'd read in the blue NA book just yesterday. It was all starting to make sense.

Gina then left me alone. I don't even know what was said in the remainder of Group. I was a million miles away, nursing a broken heart – embarrassed, ashamed, and full of remorse. Shattered into a million little pieces. I wasn't angry with Ant, just deeply saddened because it was all so true. I had an overwhelming urge to phone him, but the time for apologies would come later. The list of amends I'd have to make was growing faster than I cared to admit.

And so I joined the ranks in saying that drinking paint stripper would feel better than Letter Day. It took days for the sting to subside. I cried a lot. I started crying in my sleep again, waking to a damp pillow each morning. The Beast came visiting too, never going far away. It appeared bigger than it had a few nights prior and it stayed longer, telling me that if

I left the clinic, right then, it could take all my pain away and I'd feel free again. Free from *all* pain. Suggestions so seductive, sensual almost, that I almost believed the Beast and started looking for my shoes late one night. Everything was raw again, the wound a festering mess, seeping muck. I couldn't stop replaying Ant's words. I had spent years loving the man and being loved by him, yet I had thrown it all in his face.

Soon I was off the methadone and Valium entirely. I still ached all over but, since Ant's remark in my Letter, I stopped mentioning my pain and suffered in silence. It was the first time in years I had no pharmaceuticals racing through my veins like Olympic medallists.

I was clean.

Clean. Such a small, straightforward word for something so mammoth and not straightforward at all. Why didn't we get a fancier-sounding word, more reflective of all the effort? I mean, just twenty-four hours without substances was the biggest achievement in decades for most of us.

Despite the growing number of clean days, my emotional self lay in a heap, still bleeding out like blood through a severed artery. The drugs may have gone but in their place was a gaping void, leaving me with an emptiness and intense craving for my drugs, for booze, and for comfort food. I was desperate for something to fill the cavernous black hole inside me. Had I been out in the real world, I wouldn't have hesitated to fill that dark hole with pills. I longed to feel whole again, not like I was short of a limb. I'd read about amputees who still felt their missing limb and it made perfect sense. I had those same phantom sensations. I still felt the drugs swirling within me, even though they were gone physiologically.

In a lecture, Julian explained that we were grieving for old friends – the drugs, booze, whatever substance we had favoured in order to feel what we wanted to feel, or not feel, as the case may be. The substances had been our partner, lover and best friend, now departed but not replaced. Not a whiff of a rebound relationship.

We were told to 'sit with the feelings'. I didn't want to sit, stand, walk or even hang out with my feelings. Who voluntarily sits with things that feel so shitty? Stripped of our crutches, we were now faced with rediscovering ourselves and understanding the person behind the masks. None of us were fans of our mask-free selves, so we clung desperately to the last vestiges of our screwed-up life of active addiction, just because it was a comfort zone. The alternative, which was to stand butt naked before the world, stripped of the stage make-up, was frankly terrifying. Our masks had served a purpose and now the fuckers were taking those too.

One day Carol gave us each a hand mirror and told us to look ourselves in the eye. It was a literal attempt to face ourselves, but most of us were simply unable to hold our own gaze and quickly looked away. Donovan, of course, proclaimed he could happily stare at himself all day if need be. Carol nearly decapitated me when she overheard me asking Sarah if she had tweezers in the room as my eyebrows needed plucking.

It was a telling exercise, even if it did feel like sitting bare-arsed on a cactus. Doing my mascara every morning, I'd attempt to look myself in the eye. I always failed, cursing when great splodges of black goo got plastered all over my eye socket. Day after day I avoided my own gaze. After I'd got my mascara in kind of the right places, I'd wonder if it would make it to lunchtime without being cried off and dribble down my face. I kept meaning to tell Carol that under "what to pack" in the brochure, they should specify *waterproof* mascara.

When the day was almost done, after buckets of tears and mascara had been shed and our wounds still on fire from the daily doses of counsellor salt, we'd sit outside on the patio, commiserating over cigarettes and hot chocolate. War stories were swopped and, if you'd had a tough day, there was always sympathy to be found out there, and someone to make you laugh. Even if a smile lasted only a few seconds, it helped. There was an unspoken patio rule – if you had whipped someone in Group, all was forgotten outside and grudges were barred on the patio. What was said in Group, stayed in Group, although sometimes easier said than done.

The fascinating characters opened my mind like never before. I heard stories of the underworld, where many of my new friends lived. Alongside criminals, gangsters, sexual deviants and prostitutes, I was the resident hillbilly farm girl. What really shocked me, though, was that, of the fourteen women there, Sarah and I were the only ones who'd not been raped or sexually abused. The girls' accounts of violent sexual crimes were horrific, made worse by the fact that most of their rapists and abusers were relatives. They wanted to get numb and forget – I mean, who could blame them? I thought of Mom's rape a lot and suddenly I saw her alcoholism in a whole new light.

There I was, little old Kat, with no real life-changing trauma to my name – other than a few knocks to the head – sporting an opiate habit worse than most junkies with backgrounds considerably less fortunate than mine.

33

Life suddenly got more interesting with the arrival of Charles from London. A serious plum in his mouth and frightfully upper class – and overlooking his fondness for cocaine and it being his second stint in treatment – he instantly fascinated me. He had gone grey young. It was a crying shame that his thick salt-and-pepper hair and chiselled body were in a rehab where they could not be openly complimented on, let alone stroked.

Tina, Cassie, Sarah and I called an emergency meeting in our room to discuss the new arrival. Until then, the 'No Fraternising' rule had been neither here nor there for me as I hadn't exactly been tempted by any of the guys or their gentleman's log cabins, as Sarah referred to their nether regions. But now that Charlie from the Chelsea Coke Factory had arrived, the rule quickly became my latest irritation.

'How serious are they with this No Fraternising rule anyway?' I asked Sarah. 'You have to agree he is possibly worth testing it for?'

'How serious are they? Kat, break the rule and you'll both get kicked out faster than you can say "Got condoms?" Trust me!' said Sarah.

Charles and I clicked. We started off talking horses, him telling me about his polo days when he played at national level. He could have stepped off the pages of a Jilly Cooper novel. I made out I was a better rider than I was and certainly didn't mention that in the last year I'd been too stoned to do much more than give my horse a carrot. There was definitely a bad boy and rebel in Charles and I was intrigued by the spoilt brat in him. His languid smile and a look from his seductive deep-green eyes would throw me for hours. I even put a bit more thought into what I wore each day, my scruffy cargo pants replaced with the tightest jeans I had packed.

'You dirty slapper you,' chuckled Sarah one morning in the bathroom, knowing exactly what I was up to.

Charles seemed to seek me out for chit-chats. The girls noticed it, and constantly reminded me about the rule. I had to admit I was rather touched by Charles's attention. After Ant's scorching letter, I was in pieces and didn't see what harm could come from a spot of flirty banter.

Charles had managed to cut right back on the Colombian Marching Powder before arriving, so his detox wasn't the worst we'd seen. As luck would have it, he was put in my splinter group so I got to hear his nitty-gritty. It quickly came out that he lived a hectic playboy lifestyle. Daddy was a well-heeled London stockbroker with his own firm that Charles had been earmarked to take over one day. He'd graduated from Oxford with a fluffy degree in art or history or something and then gone to work for Daddy. He was soon entrenched in the glamorous, high-end world of supermodels, designer drugs, and lavish parties, hanging out with English society's upper echelons. Now, thanks to the white powder – never mind that he'd been fired from the family firm – he was about to be disinherited too. Mommy was in love with a daily gin-and-tranquilliser cocktail and Charles remarked how he'd learnt everything he knew about getting plastered and behaving badly from her.

Just another dysfunctional family, I guess. It reminded me again that, no matter the background, the bank balance, or whether the money was old or new, addiction would hang its hat anywhere.

I'd finally completed my Step 1 work and was onto the second Step, which called for a realisation that a power greater than me could restore my sanity.

Oh sure, I thought.

I spent ages looking at the words and tried to sense a greater being. Despite my schooling and being force-fed Catholicism for six years, I was mostly atheist and the smidgen of 'God' I had in my life didn't really have a name. So, I really struggled with Step 2 until Sarah suggested another way to approach it.

'Your God doesn't have to be a formal God from a formal religion. You can have a Higher Power that's different, like something in nature, as long as you believe something actually is bigger than you and that it exists on a higher frequency than you. Don't get hung up on what form he, she or it takes. And don't see this as religious, it's more spiritual.'

She then paged through a Recovery book and shared a saying that made my Step 2 fall into place: Religion is for people who are afraid of going to hell. Spirituality is for those who've already been there.

One afternoon on our beach walk, I was sitting on a bench, half watching the boys play cricket and half staring out to sea. The ocean was grey and angry, and a storm was approaching. The light, colours and textures around me were stunning and surreal. I suddenly felt a deep connection and decided the sea was my Higher Power. It was certainly bigger than me and extremely powerful, plus I'd always had a deep respect for it. Nobody could stop the sea's natural rhythms. Relieved to have cracked the problem, I inhaled the salty air, closed my eyes and relaxed.

Next thing I knew, one of the boys hooked the tennis ball being used for cricket in my direction. The ball whacked me square in the eye socket at high speed. I dropped to the sand, yelping in fright. Our escort nurse was at my side in seconds.

'Drugs! Owwweee! I need drugs!' I howled loudly, my hand over my eye, but also laughing.

'Oh, shut up Kat, and get up,' said the nurse, seeing it wasn't a fatal injury.

It was Charles who'd slammed the ball into my face and he came bounding over to say sorry, looking mortified. He placed his arms around me and plucked a bit of seaweed from my hair, only to catch a firm slap across the back of his head from the nurse.

'Oi! Get your hands off her. No fraternising, you dirty chancer,' she said. 'Time's up anyway. Come everyone, let's go home.'

Home? Yeah right, I thought. Stupid woman had shattered my moment with Charles – a few seconds longer in his to-die-for arms wouldn't have been the worst thing in the world, especially as he'd taken his shirt off for cricket.

As we walked back, I remembered nearly being wiped out by a proper red ball at proper cricket. Now I was in rehab grappling with 12 Step concepts – a far cry from being pissed, stoned, and caught on national TV. I had to kill the thought smartly. The memory of the vodka was making me drool a bit.

With my Higher Power identified at last, I was able to complete my Step 2 worksheet. We came to believe that a power greater than ourselves could restore us to sanity.

Deep down, I knew it would take more than a few written exercises to restore my estranged sanity. I pondered that word for days – sanity – and found it to be completely subjective. I'd listen to other inmates' drug tales, and things that were everyday occurrences for them seemed utterly insane to me. And vice versa. They'd hear about my daily intake of pills and think I was completely round the bend, whereas I saw it as being slightly out of control.

More and more, I realised the disease of addiction was one of the most complex ills of society. Just when I thought I'd got it sussed – thought I understood why I'd done the things I did – some other behaviour of mine would crop up and change my thinking. I thought about Mom a lot and realised that, like her, I would spend the rest of my days battling this disease.

With my brain like scrambled eggs, my emotions all over the show, and Gina still getting on my nerves every time we spoke, I continued to find Charles a charming distraction. He took great interest in my African farm life, saying I was a modern Karen Blixen.

Our conversations became more exclusive and it didn't take long for antennae to start twitching. Housekeeping was where it all kicked off, and Julian was driving it that morning.

'A few things,' Julian announced. 'Sarah, apparently you took three phone calls in a row last night and hogged the call box, so no calls for three days. Group, if people ring for Sarah tell them she's being punished for being selfish. And Kat and Charles, you need to mix with others in the group and stop being so exclusive. We're watching you, you're fraternising. Cut it out. First warning.'

I gulped. Guiltily, I looked at Charles who was opposite me, giving me a lazy, sexy smile. Godammit, you are scrumptious, I thought. I snapped back to reality fast, knowing resident snitch, Donovan, was reading me like a book.

Right after Housekeeping, I went to drop my washing off at the laundry at the back of the building and bumped into Charles, carrying his. The laundry room was in the quietest area of the clinic and there wasn't anyone around. Charles sussed the situation with impressive speed. In a flash, his arm was across my back and he pulled me in, giving me a kiss that rapidly grew in intensity. As our arms tightened, I pushed him into the wall, slamming my body into his and hooking one of my legs up around his waist. His hand slipped under my very short little sundress and he played with the nothingness of my tiny knickers.

'Christ, Kat, if I had just an hour with you alone ...'

I knew exactly how that hour would play out.

Hearing voices around the corner, we quickly pulled apart to a respectable distance, our eyes still locked in lust, extending the intense moment. In an impulsive flash of pure sluttiness, I slipped off my knickers and shoved them into his jeans pocket. I then retrieved my laundry and nonchalantly walked away. I knew he was watching me, still catching his breath.

Later that morning Charles slipped me a folded piece of paper. I bolted to the loo to read it.

Just an hour with you ...

As we walked into Group, I managed to tell Charles without being overheard that I didn't intend to wear knickers that day, then chose a seat directly opposite him in the circle, letting my short dress ride up a bit as I crossed my legs. It was the most fun I'd had in ages.

The following day in Group, Charles was put through his paces and I got a stark reality check. First, we heard more about his fancy family and social life, and then I nearly fell off my chair when Benny, the counsellor, asked Charles about his ex-wife. He'd kept that one bloody quiet! Right after that, we heard about his daughter – the result of a careless one-night-stand with a woman in Italy when he was twenty. Charles soon looked suitably uncomfortable, darting embarrassed glances in my direction and fidgeting like a toddler in church.

'Now tell us about your younger brother, Charles,' said Benny, who was another 'take no shit and no holds barred' counsellor. A brutal man, he could have been a close relative of Gina's, actually.

Charles, a dark angry look in his eyes, gave a slightly arrogant sigh.

'Go on,' said Benny.

'A couple of years ago, I was showing off in a supercar in the South of France. My younger brother Jamie was with me. Jamie was born not quite a full box of chocolates and looks up to me. He worships the ground I walk on, I'm his hero. Going two hundred and forty kilometres an hour, we flipped on a bend. I survived with minor injuries, but Jamie was trapped in the car for two hours. He had to be cut out and his leg was amputated at the scene.'

'And Jamie lived for his polo, didn't he?' said Benny. 'Tricky to play with only one leg, isn't it Charles? You could have killed him. Although, in many ways, that would have been kinder. Now Jamie is not only mentally handicapped but physically too.'

'My mother was both pissed and stoned the entire nine months she was pregnant with Jamie so it's hardly my fucking fault he was born with foetal alcohol syndrome,' snapped Charles.

'That's not the point. Do you ever take responsibility for your actions?' Benny kept prodding. 'Who were you showing off to?'

'A woman. An older woman. I used to visit her in France every summer,' said Charles.

'Visit? Or shag?' asked Benny. 'How old?'

'Shag,' replied Charles, smugly. 'She's in her late fifties.'

'Is she married?'

'Yes. Her husband caught us in bed.'

'Did you end the affair?'

'Yes.'

'And now you shag her daughter instead who, by the way everyone, is fifteen. Is that right Charles?'

'How do you know that?' Charles snapped. His eyes narrowed and he bristled with aggression.

Oh boy, I thought, true colours showing through here. It didn't sit well with me, and I watched with interest.

'It doesn't matter how I know. So, are you, a forty-two-year-old man, seeing your ex-lover's fifteen-year-old daughter, yes or no?' asked Benny.

'Yes. Yes okay, I see her, sleep with her, whatever. Is that a crime?' said Charles.

'Well, in some countries sex with a fifteen-year-old child *is* a crime, though, in France, the age of consent happens to be fifteen. Legal or not, it's still disgusting. Actually, let's call it what it is in this country – paedophilia. It takes a very sick man to sleep with a girl over two decades his junior.' Benny wasn't mincing his words, pausing to let them sink in. 'Whose car were you driving when you maimed your brother?'

'I was driving the woman's husband's car, the girl's father. A Ferrari. He had two and we were racing. The car was a write-off,' said Charles.

'You seem proud of that,' said Benny, reading my mind. 'So, it was all just a macho display of testosterone and chest-thumping between you and the man, meanwhile your brother is minus a leg and the man, whose wife and daughter you screwed, is minus a Ferrari. Tell me, does Jamie still worship you?'

Charles glared at Benny. I thought he was going to get up and throw a punch at him.

'It's all a bit of a cliché, isn't it?' Benny added. 'The rich kid snorting coke, womanising, playing dangerous games with expensive toys. It's always been easy come, easy go with you, hasn't it? I believe you also convinced Jamie that snorting coke is a good idea. Do you think that's going to make him feel he has something left to live for? Will you be happy when he ends up in rehab or commits suicide once he hits rock bottom?'

'Whatever. You'll draw your own conclusions anyway,' said Charles, crossing his arms. The hostility between him and Benny was crackling in the air.

'It's a pity for you that getting clean and actually remaining that way for any decent length of time can't be bought, isn't it? This is one thing you will actually have to work for, it can't be handed to you on a silver platter by Mommy and Daddy,' said Benny.

Charles was fuming. Then he stood up and – horror of horrors – he walked out of Group. The cardinal sin. Walking out of Group would carry a heavy sentence.

'Okay then,' Benny said as Charles reached the door, 'we'll look at your sex addiction next time, if that suits your lordship.'

Charles snorted and gave the door a bloody good slam behind him.

After Group, I found him chain-smoking by the pool. Much of his appeal had evaporated. Charles clearly wasn't as cut and dried as he'd made out to be, but he'd had a rough session and who wouldn't appreciate some friendly support after such a roasting.

'Hey,' I said cautiously. 'Sorry you got so beaten up in there.'

'Fucking arsehole, that Benny. Wanker,' said Charles.

I figured it best to let him process it in his own way and left him to it.

Later that evening he managed to get me on my own.

'Sorry for being so short earlier. I meant to tell you about the ex-wife. She left me for my best friend.'

'I guess we all have our crosses to bear,' I said coolly and walked off, not wanting to get into it. I was far more bothered about him shagging the fifteen-year-old than his divorce.

Donovan saw me talking to Charles and pulled me aside, getting all protective. 'Leave that filthy cot-rocker alone, Kat. What a pervert.'

'Yeah, 'tis quite gross,' I replied, not in the mood for drama.

Later, as I went upstairs to bed, Charles handed me another note.

I'm sorry. And I can't stop thinking about your sensual eyes.
Wish I could have more. C.

Alrighty then, I thought, putting the note away safely and smiling to myself. I attempted a few more chapters of the NA book, but my concentration was non-existent. I was somewhat intrigued by the side of Charles I'd now seen, knowing there was more to be revealed. An issue of *Cosmopolitan* that was doing the rounds in our room seemed far more fitting for bedtime reading than the 12 Steps.

In Housekeeping the next morning, several of us were told we had appointments with a HIV counsellor that day.

'What the hell? HIV?' I asked Cassie, who'd also been summoned.

'Shit, I've been dreading this,' she said. 'Everyone gets tested for HIV.' Poor Cassie was in a helluva state. What ex-prostitute wouldn't shit herself?

I shrugged it off, relatively sure I didn't have cause for concern. Then I started second-guessing myself, wondering if Ant might have cheated on me with a tourist, maybe even Jess who, let's face it, looked like she gave board and lodging to many STDs. Then I totted up my drunken one-night-stands. I had an awful feeling one of them had been unprotected.

Somewhat nervous, I went to the appointed room for my pre-test counselling session. Dorothy, the HIV counsellor, wasn't what I expected – frumpy, grey-haired, three chins, elasticated trousers, sandals with Velcro fastenings and wouldn't see sixty again. I struggled to connect with her in the compulsory discussion about risky sex.

'Should your test come back positive, how would you cope?' she asked.

'Well, that's a stupid fucking question if ever there was. How do you think I'd cope? My life would be over. Not a chance would I stay clean and sober if handed the HIV death sentence.'

'Hardly the right answer,' she said.

'Oh, so there's a right answer? Am I supposed to say I'd skip from the room filled with the joys of spring? This is ridiculous. Do the test and, if I'm positive, let's talk. These "what if" scenarios are bollocks.'

I came out irritated, passing Cassie on her way in. 'Counsellor is a real beaut. Good luck,' I said.

Twenty-four hours later, I was given the all-clear, and Cassie's worst nightmare had come true. She'd tested positive. The counsellors immediately kicked into crisis mode with Cassie, and we didn't see her for the entire day. She was whisked away to discuss her options.

That night in our room, Sarah, Tina and I tried to comfort her.

'What now Cass?' asked Tina.

'Yesterday, I was pretty clear on what I'd do,' she said. 'I'd leave the clinic right away, get wasted, see my family one last time and then end my life.'

None of us was shocked.

'And now?' Sarah asked.

'Not only did my blood test positive for HIV, I'm pregnant too. I'd be killing a baby.'

For two hours, Cassie bared her soul. She was such a good person with the biggest, kindest heart, her prostitution a result of circumstance. She'd thought she missed her periods because she was so messed-up on crack. She and her counsellor had spent the day discussing living with HIV, termination, and adoption. Apparently, she had an option to go into a clean living, privately-funded halfway house for underprivileged women in similar positions. She and her baby would have medical and financial support, and Cassie could work in the home's commercial crafts centre.

Knowing that, Cassie said she had now almost decided to keep the child, even though it could have not only HIV but also foetal drug syndrome. She had hope.

Filled with admiration, we huddled around her, all crying our hearts out. When Pat came in later to check on Cassie, she joined our intimate circle, her motherly nature helping us process this latest consequence of addiction.

The next day, Cassie seemed very quiet, which surprised no one. We gave her the space she needed. On our afternoon beach walk, nobody noticed her drift off further down the beach, until we heard our escort nurse give an almighty yell and start running.

We saw Cassie talking to strange guy in a hoodie, his hand out, giving her something.

'Oh shit, it's a dealer,' said Tina.

'That's a dealer?' I asked.

'Yup. Have you not noticed how there are always one or two weird-looking people around when we come down here?' said Tina. 'Dealers. They know our routine and they know one day one of us will be so miserable we'll want to score. We're easy targets.'

'You're fucking kidding me!'

'Nope, and watch, that nurse is going to go mental.'

Sure enough, the nurse pulled Cassie back from the sinister man, grabbed something out of his hand, and then proceeded to beat him over the head with a piece of driftwood she'd picked up. He fell to the sand, whereupon he took an almighty kick to the nuts and then got an impressive kick in the head from our nurse who'd evidently taken a self-defence class or two. She yanked Cassie by the hand, quickly ran back to us and told us all to get back home. Jogging, we were back at the clinic in a minute.

Cassie was marched off to see Carol and the rest of us just sat around, shaken.

'We can hardly blame Cassie, given her news yesterday,' said Donovan. Beneath the old-man act, he was actually quite a caring, soft soul.

I had to agree, but was distraught that Cassie's resolve had weakened.

Just before dawn, I heard Sarah get up and go to the loo. She flicked the bathroom light on and then let out a bloodcurdling scream that woke the entire building. Tina and I flew out of bed and rushed to Sarah. Cassie, her wrists slit, was lying in the bath. There was blood everywhere. A shard of dirty glass lay on the floor next to a filthy syringe, the needle crusted with old blood. A bent teaspoon and lighter lay next to it.

Hearing the awful scream, two nurses were in our room within seconds and we were asked to step aside. One nurse shouted down the corridor to the nurses station, barking 'Suicide Evacuation!'

In moments of trauma, the mind fixates on curious things and mine thought how interesting it was that a formal procedure existed for handling this. Sarah, Tina and I, standing in the corridor in our pyjamas, watched dumbly as another nurse rushed to each bedroom, flinging doors open and ordering every last inmate to gather downstairs by the pool.

Pat appeared, pulling Tina, Sarah and I aside. 'Girls, did you touch her? Have any of you got blood on you? Sarah, you found her.'

The penny dropped. HIV positive was smeared across our bathroom. We held out our hands and looked at our bare feet – no blood. Everyone was clean.

'Thank God,' said Pat. 'Get downstairs girls, join the others please.'

I didn't even notice Charles placing a blanket over my shoulders and walking me downstairs.

Minutes later an ambulance arrived and went screaming off, sirens blaring. Sirens mean she is still alive, I thought, snatching some hope, but also hoping Cassie might still get her final wish – to find peace in death. No demons, no disease, no unwanted babies.

It was an odd scene by the pool – thirty or so junkies and alcoholics standing around in pyjamas in the nippy dawn air, many still half asleep, not knowing what to do or think. Everyone was quizzing Sarah, Tina and me, wanting details. Carol appeared, wearing a pink tracksuit, her hair a crazy mess – looking more like one of us than the head honcho of a rehab. I heard someone say she lived in a house right on the beach, hence her getting to us in a flash.

'First, thank you all for staying calm and co-operating,' said Carol, addressing us from the garden steps. 'Cassie is still alive, but is critical. She mainlined heroin before slitting her wrists. We'll update you when we know more. Everyone, have some coffee, get dressed, and come back down for an emergency Housekeeping in an hour. Kat, Sarah, Tina, please wait in one of the other female bedrooms while we clean your room. Borrow some clothes until we get things straight.'

An hour later, we gathered again and Carol told us Cassie was dead. Already weak from the years of drug abuse, her body hadn't been able to withstand such extreme blood loss and she'd died in the ambulance. They believed that when her attempt to overdose on heroin had failed, she'd cut her wrists. Having seen her lying there, I knew Cassie's intentions had been clear. She'd known exactly where and how to cut – vertical, not horizontal.

Tina ran from the group, her hand over her mouth. She didn't get far before vomiting in a flower pot. She dropped to her knees, sobbing, shouting at her God. She'd been the closest to Cassie. They'd checked in on the same day.

When allowed back into our room late that morning, Sarah, Tina and I held hands when we opened the door. The bathroom was spotless and smelt of lemons, not a trace of blood. Cassie's bed had been stripped of its linen, the bare duvet and pillows stacked in the corner. Her cupboard was empty and not a single belonging was in sight. It was as if Cassie had never existed. The speed of her removal felt cold and clinical. How could an entire person be erased so quickly?

At sunset, regular activities were cancelled. Every patient and every last staff member gathered on the beach for a simple religion-neutral memorial service. Flanked by the staff and with a large security team scanning the beach throughout the service, we were safe from any dealer trying to approach us. Each of us was given a white rose, we placed our single stems on the wet sand, watching as the waves came up and gently took the flowers – took Cassie – away. We lit candles and left them burning in the sand. Each of us knowing it could have been us.

For days, Sarah, Tina and I blamed ourselves. That week, we were put into trauma counselling where Gina and our respective counsellors tried to assure us that no, we couldn't have stopped her, no, we couldn't have been more supportive, and no, we couldn't have kept Cassie alive. She wanted to die and she'd had a right to die.

All I could think about was Cassie's two-for-the-price-of-one blow jobs just before pay day.

The shock lingered for days. Rehab had just got real.

34

When I thought I couldn't possibly be any more emotionally wrecked, writing my life story damn near finished me off. I'd been working on it all week and was due to present it in Group the following day. My peers would be giving the feedback, so I'd done my best to cover all the angles.

Life-story guidelines:
Part A: describe your childhood
Part B: describe your adulthood
Part C: describe the last six months, i.e., your life and events preceding your arrival here.
In all sections, focus on the unmanageability of your life and factors leading you into active addiction.

I'd heard and marked a few life stories already so I knew the deal. If I glossed over any parts of my life, I'd be grilled. If minimal effort had gone into it, I might be told to do a rewrite. Sometimes counsellors sat in on the life-story sessions, sometimes they didn't, but they did get the feedback sheets. Writing mine had completely drained me. Digging deep – down to my last emotional reserves, dredging up my past and owning my part in the chaos and ruined relationships – had made me want to curl up in a heap and never return to the real world and the people I'd hurt.

Despite the angst, it turned out to be an uneventful session. Everyone already knew a lot of my story, but I did reveal a few more details about the lengths I'd taken to score my pills. It was tactical though, and the overall feedback was mild. I then had to hand in my story and feedback sheets to Gina. No doubt I'd get hammered about the new material I'd just put on the butcher's table but, for now, for today, I'd done it and it was a weight off my shoulders.

That night, lying in bed, I was able to see how cathartic the exercise was. Maybe there was method in their madness after all.

I was now past the halfway mark in rehab. Physically, I felt like a new person – well, nearly new. The headaches were by no means gone, but they weren't as severe and, sooner or later, I came through them, even if only for an hour before the next round of searing pain set in. My stomach certainly felt less inflamed, no longer angered by pills. Emotionally, I was learning new things about myself every day, be they self-made realisations or through seeing the similarities in other patients' crazy behaviour. It still wasn't pretty and, since arriving, I'd cried every day, but now and then I'd catch a glimpse of the old Kat. Gina continued to rattle my cage at every chance, but I'd got used to her biting remarks and was learning not to take her quite so personally.

I watched the newcomers with interest and wondered what I'd looked like when I crawled up the stairs and into the Fishbowl. They all wore expressions of extreme pain and their eyes reflected their inner turmoil. Broken, weary and vacant. As the days passed and their detox subsided, we'd notice their faces lighten and their moods improve. It was as if someone had entered a dark house and turned all the lights on. Watching their awakenings was kind of cool. It made me realise that I was in the throes of one myself. I still had a few light switches to find, though, and they weren't always in the obvious place, by the door.

Charles took some hard knocks in his first week and had not been eased into the programme by any means. The counsellors seemed to dish him a double dose of ruthless, and he'd get it in the neck every day. It had come to light that he was a raging sex addict too. He was still slipping me notes, but we were being watched like hawks so I didn't engage openly. I'd be lying if I said I wasn't fascinated, even knowing his dark side, and

I wondered how much of a death wish I really had. I knew I was playing with fire, but it couldn't go anywhere and, besides, the flirting was fun.

'Kat, I received an interesting piece of info via your mother today,' said Gina, her arse barely in her chair before she opened fire in Group one morning.

Shit, I thought. What new dirt has been dished?

'Do you have any veterinary experience?' she asked me.

'What do you mean? I have dogs.'

'And as such you have a vet?'

'Yes.'

'But you're not a qualified vet?'

'Err, no.'

'What dogs do you have?'

'Two boxers.' I sighed. This was a bizarre conversation for Group. Suddenly it hit me where Gina was going with it.

Shit. Shit. Shit.

'So, you don't have four Great Danes.'

Shit.

I kept quiet for a while, Gina staring at me. I tried everything to avoid her gaze. Sarah was looking at me questioningly, bemused. Charles too.

'Kat please tell everyone about your four Great Danes that are prone to hysteria and howling on Guy Fawkes night when fireworks go off,' Gina continued.

I was so mortified that I wanted to burst into giggles, knowing just how crazy the story about to come out would sound. I could feel my ears redden as I tried my utmost to not laugh.

'When you're ready Kat ...' said Gina.

I let a nervous giggle slip. 'So, Guy Fawkes night—'

'Before you go on Kat, do you think this is funny?'

'No, Gina.' I actually thought it was hilarious, but wiped the smile off my face smartly.

'Good. Continue,' said Gina.

'Guy Fawkes night last year. I'd run out of my pills and I couldn't find my dealer to get more. I happened to drive past a local vet clinic and had an idea. I told them I'd just moved into town, having been thrown off my farm, and that my four dogs were already very uptight and my neighbour had announced he was having a huge party that night, with fireworks. I asked for tranquillisers for my Great Danes.'

'And why were they Great Danes and not your boxers?'

'Because I knew the heavier the dog, the bigger the tranquilliser dose. Great Danes are twice the size of boxers. I figured that four Great Danes would add up to my body weight.'

'Kat, look at you. Two cats would equal your body weight.'

'I factored in a few extra kilograms as a contingency plan.'

Everyone was chuckling softly, and I was having a very hard time not joining them.

'And did you get the tranquillisers you wanted?'

'Yes and no. Normally vets prescribe diazepam for dogs, a version of Valium which, as we know, humans take. But they actually gave me a specific veterinary tranquilliser.'

'And you took them anyway, unknown drugs for dogs used only by vets, not knowing what would happen or how high you'd get?'

'Yes.'

Gina gave me a death stare. 'And what about your horse? Would he not have needed tranquillisers too?'

'I thought that might be taking things a bit far.'

Sarah could hold it in no longer and threw back her head, roaring with laughter and tears streaming down her face. Everyone started laughing. Except Gina.

'I'm glad you all find this so amusing. I have heard some extreme stories in my time, but this is perhaps the best example of complete and utter lunacy and unmanageability I've heard in decades. Kat, I'd be surprised if you ever get to see a vet again in Harare. Your mother's friend, Maddie I think, came across the notes at the vet she now works for.'

Oh my God. So that's how this had come out. Mom must have gone mental. I was extremely grateful two thousand kilometres were between us right now.

Gina shook her head slowly. There wasn't much more to say, the point about me being completely insane having been made. Fairly effectively too, I'd give her that.

After Group, I headed to the dining room for lunch. The story had spread quickly and everyone, led by Donovan, started howling like dogs. More of a tit I could not have felt, and blushed furiously.

'Girl, you have made my week. Hands down, the best story about scoring ever,' said Sarah, high-fiving me.

Thankfully the counsellors appeared for lunch and the howling and woofing died down.

Later, as we assembled at the front door for our beach walk, one of the boys flicked a belt around my neck, saying loudly and all cutesy, 'Walkies Kat. Walky time. Who's a good girl then.'

I kicked him in the shin when he ruffled my hair.

Donovan jumped in. 'Anyone got a bag? There's that No Dog Shit sign on the beach.'

I had to laugh. I really had brought it on myself.

Sarah nudged me, saying, 'Ignore them. They're just jealous that they can't lick their balls.'

35

Family Day rolled around quickly and I caught sight of Mom and Dad by the pool during a tea break. Local patients were kept apart from family for the day but I 'd see them later, since I never got visitors on Sundays. Sundays were shitty days for us foreigners. While the others received their visitors, we got two hours on the beach as our supposed 'treat'. We'd return feeling sorry for ourselves and jealously inspect all the takings from visiting hour.

Mom and Dad would spend the day in lectures and counselling sessions, and then my one-on-one 'family session' – mediated by Gina – was to be tomorrow, before Mom and Dad flew home at lunchtime. I had no idea what to expect. I'd heard accounts of family counselling sessions and, apparently, it could get pretty gruesome. I couldn't foresee a punch-up with Mom and Dad but, then again, I had behaved appallingly.

I watched them and saw Dad draw hard on a cigarette while Mom seemed to be in deep conversation with Julian. I remembered her dumbstruck moment the night I'd arrived, and wondered if she'd figured out their connection yet.

We pointed out our relatives to each other. Charles's father had flown out, but not his mother as she'd finally checked herself into some posh rehab in London. Charles Senior was remarkably suave and dishy, far younger and more hip than I'd expected. From afar, I even noticed Mom having a quick perve when Dad wasn't watching.

There was great hilarity when we, easily, spotted Donovan's father –

his brown cardigan was a dead giveaway. Some of the guys started teasing Donovan, calling him CardiVan which set off a major sulk session. Someone then snuck up behind him and yanked his cardigan up, over, and then down over his face, and held it there. There was a muffled, furious squeal, but a nurse happened to pass by and quickly broke up the tussle. Donovan came out from under his cardi-mask ready to kill, his hair shooting straight up from the polyester static. Unfortunately, he'd had a cigarette in his mouth and now his best cardi had a bloody great burn hole, much to his horror. Everyone was snickering and when Donovan then pulled a small comb from his sock to sort out his hair, we howled even louder, making the family group stop and stare. Donovan really was the most atypical cocaine addict.

Later, I had an extremely awkward half-hour visit with Mom and Dad. Mom was full of eager questions about the whole rehab experience – like I was there on holiday and should be buying souvenirs and sending postcards – while Dad was rather quiet and merely imparted news from back home, delivering love and letters from Rolo, Ela and Grandpa. Nobody mentioned my branching out into veterinary pharmaceuticals or any of the other nitty-gritty that had gone down with Gina, making me even more nervous about what tomorrow's session would bring.

The next morning, I went to the appointed room to meet Gina for my family chat. I had no idea what to expect. Gina gave me a wink of encouragement at the door, so uncharacteristic I wondered how much blood I was about to lose.

I feared the worst, but it never came – no explosive outbursts, just a calm reminder of the hard, cold facts. In the few weeks I'd been there, I'd vented much of my anger, though I did get a bit sparky in parts. Gina sure knew how to poke the bear.

Mom told me how worried they'd been about my health. Dad gave me a stern lecture about Colin, reminding me I was as much a criminal as he was, and then said I'd been a revolting friend to Rolo and Ela, and Mom said I'd become a family embarrassment with my drinking. She also mentioned Ant and his Letter and commented on how I'd screwed-up that relationship, like I needed reminding.

All in all, I was lucky, and what blows came I took on the chin. Every point was, without doubt, valid. Even though guilt made me churn inside, nothing was said that I had not already considered and owned my part in. I admitted to Mom and Dad that I'd wasted my life and that, only now, was I able to see my insane behaviour, the hurt inflicted on those I truly loved, and what a bitch I'd been during my active addiction.

Gina seemed a bit disappointed that no punches were thrown, but she did acknowledge my efforts. For the first time, she said something positive about me and, in that brief moment, I could see she actually did have a beating heart.

'Kat has come a long way in a few short weeks. She gave us a fair bit of grief in the beginning and we're still watching her play games with food. She's in total denial about her eating disorder, but has worked hard, internally, on her drinking and pill habit. It's rewarding to see her thinking shift.'

Hang on, I thought, Gina being nice? I was damn sure I hadn't seen the memo about hell freezing over. Glossing over her eating disorder jibe, I suddenly felt like a child getting her first gold star for neat handwriting. It was short-lived.

'Oh, just one thing, Gill, James,' said Gina. 'Kat has been hurting so badly since Ant's Letter that she has now fallen for the seasoned charms of another patient.'

I spluttered in shock.

'They pass notes as if they are fifteen and still at school. Isn't that right Kat? You're totally distracted by him.'

I snorted derisively, gobsmacked that they knew about Charles's notes. Was there anything they didn't know, I wondered. Unfortunately, the next thing I wondered, I said aloud.

'Gina, next you will tell me how many sheets of loo paper I use to wipe my arse,' I said, instantly regretting my chirp.

'Kat!' said Mom, shocked. 'Don't be so bloody rude.'

'Mom, you wanna hear how rude they are to us?'

'Yup, Kat sure is a bit of a live wire when she gets going. She's got quite a temper,' said Gina. 'Anyway, as I was saying, we've got an eye on her fraternising and sexual distractions. Might I remind you, Kat, that, should you continue to fraternise, you will be thrown out. Consider this your second and last warning. Charles is getting the same warning today. Third strike and you're both out.'

I crossed my arms and sighed, finding it all tedious. Now Mom was glaring at me, and Dad looked like he wanted the ground to open and swallow him. I wondered what Grandpa would have made of Ol' Frosty-Pants Gina.

'Don't look so shocked, Kat. Have you not realised we know everything that goes on in here?' Gina said. 'Fraternising makes you lose focus. Losing focus means you won't do your emotional work at your best level. That, in turn, means you won't do the 12 Steps properly and that, in turn, will see you relapse. From there it's a short trip to your coffin.'

'For Christ's sake, Kat,' muttered Mom, Gina's words hitting her hard.

Gina went on. 'Do you want to throw it all away and set yourself on course for a relapse? Don't kid yourself, you mean nothing to him. He has a severe sex addiction and he won't even remember your name twenty-four hours after you leave here.'

'Kat!' said Mom, now furious. 'Don't you dare! You'd better not, my girl. If you get thrown out for acting like a little slapper, well, I shall wash my hands of you once and for all. Take this as a final warning from me too.'

Dad, hearing that his little girl fancied not just an addict, but a sex addict too, looked pale. I swear I saw Gina smirk, the bitch.

'Okay,' I said finding it within myself to put my ashamed face on. I owed it to them to finish my stint and, while I thought the whole Charles thing was being blown out of proportion, backchat would only make it worse. I decided to not hiss and spit.

We ended the session shortly after that and Gina gave us a few minutes alone to say goodbye. With big warm hugs, I thanked Mom and Dad for all they had done for me.

'Just don't screw this up, Kat. That's all we ask,' said Dad, hugging me tightly.

Mom burst into tears which was my cue to walk them to the door and wave.

With the family stuff done, I felt quite liberated. It would be a nice smooth run to the end of my time in the clinic. I felt like a total shit for what I'd put everyone through, but the load was getting lighter. I found myself enjoying being more like the old Kat. The Beast was still with me, yes, but I'd had my first sip of Recovery and, after the unmanageability of my pre-rehab life, I was definitely contemplating making the change permanent.

Extremely proud of my few weeks' clean time and feeling a strange emotion that I barely recognised – happy – I wrote as much in that day's mood sheet. They could hardly hammer me for being proud of my achievement.

They did.

The next day Gina warned me about the perils of complacency in early Recovery. There was just no winning. Perhaps I didn't qualify for a rebuild, they'd keep picking away at me and just hurl my bloody carcass out the door when my time was up.

That night, I had a bone-chilling nightmare, completely different to an appearance by the Beast. I was naked in bed, in Charles's arms. His alcoholic mother and mine were old friends, sharing a bottle of absinthe in the corner while watching Charles and me in bed. Next, Charles examined the long red scar on my stomach and decided to snort a line of coke along its twenty-centimetre length. He finished the line and dusted off my torso, not missing a speck. I noticed a third person in the corner watching us. Chris. But he had only one leg, and he was using an oversized riding crop as a crutch. Another person appeared. A child. Charles's daughter, and she had the same red eyes as the Beast. Then everyone watched as I prepared my first-ever hit of heroin, Charles showing me how to raise a vein. Thankfully, the nightmare ended there.

It was a sinister and dark sexual dream loaded with symbolism. Two fraught families, brought together by addiction and forbidden sex, against a backdrop that bordered on incest and abuse. I awoke in the morning so nauseous, so disturbed that, within minutes, I was vomiting as acutely and uncontrollably as when I'd started detox.

I didn't know how to start processing the dream. Even drug free, my mind – when allowed to roam free in its subconscious state – was going to some deeply dangerous places. It was a stark reminder that I was – and always would be – just a junkie, with a junkie mind filled with disgusting junkie thoughts. I couldn't even get out of bed. I just lay there, shaken by the darkness of my own mind. I seriously doubted I'd make it in the real world.

Tina called Pat, who quickly came to me in the room.

'What's up *pookie*? What happened that opened up your wounds?' she asked, stroking my hair as I lay in bed, staring blankly at the wall. 'You've been doing so well *pooks*. Did the Beast come last night?'

I shook my head slowly, my tears making my pillow wet. How could I verbalise the nightmare, the people in it and the sick situation? How could I tell them I doubted my ability to stay clean once out when, just yesterday, I had shot my mouth off, so full of optimism?

'I'll give you half an hour and then you must get dressed and join the others. Lying here, isolating, won't help,' said Pat.

I nodded, taking her hand in mine for a moment.

'If you're still puking later, I'll tell Dr Steiner. But I think this is an emotional purge, not a physical illness. Don't keep it inside, it will just get worse, more toxic, and keep you down. Talk to us, or find your own way to release those bees in your head. You're strong *pookie*, one of the strongest here. You can do this.'

A while later, I dragged myself into the shower and tried to wash away the screwed-up nightmare. I was subdued the whole day and everyone noticed it, Gina included. Remarkably, she didn't probe and just let me be.

That night, Pat was working a double shift. Long after lights out, unable to sleep, I crept through to the nurses station where she allowed me to watch TV with her. She made me some tea and showed me her next bit of knitting for her grandchild, the cutest bonnet. We didn't need to talk at all.

My resolve and faith shaken, the coincidence of starting Step 3 the next day was not lost on me. Step 3 was a suggestion to 'turn your will and your life over to the care of a God of your understanding'. I took it to mean that I needed to vacate the driving seat of my life and rather let my Higher Power be the driver and map keeper. Evidently, its way was going to be saner than mine – my reckless driving on life's highways now fully exposed.

While I got the general concept of Step 3, I also thought it was a bit of a cop-out. So, you surrender, you allow an unseen force to take the wheel and then if things go pear-shaped you could blame it on whichever ethereal power you'd allowed to take charge? Handy.

I mentioned my outlook to Gina who promptly told me 'cynicism and pessimism are not our friends in Recovery' and that I should stop paying lip service to my Higher Power and try being 'less of a non-believer'.

While new patients came in every day, one admission really unsettled the whole group. Tim. Cassie aside, he was perhaps the most graphic reminder of just how bad things could get if we didn't cut the crap and stay clean. Tim was so broken and so totally at his rock bottom that it threw us all into shock. The first thing we did when we were rattled was to start bickering with each other. Suddenly everyone was on edge, and just asking for the salt at lunch could quickly escalate into war.

A heroin addict, Tim arrived with only the clothes on his back – a dirty, torn T-shirt and shorts. No shoes, no bag, nothing, just two friends helping him up the stairs. He'd been living rough, clearly. He was covered in tattoos and had the most insane dreadlocks I'd ever seen. The thick rope-like chunks reached his bum and looked like they weighed a ton.

The night he checked in I saw him in the nurses station. Dazed and confused, shaking like a leaf, his tremors uncontrollable, hands and bare feet caked in dirt, his face obscured by grime. He stank too – a rancid, stale odour. He looked up and gave me such a sad smile it almost broke my heart. His teeth were rotten – heroin teeth – but his eyes were the brightest blue I had ever seen. I smiled back, wanting to tell him that things would get better, though I knew first-hand he wouldn't take it in, not on his first night.

Tim was put in the Fishbowl and we didn't see him for two days. When he eventually came down to the patio, he still looked awful. He had showered, but wore his dirty old clothes. They were all he had.

After lunch, I saw Donovan pull the other guys aside and then they all disappeared upstairs, each coming down a few minutes later with some clothes to donate to him. He smiled properly for the first time, but it was a smile as sad and empty as his eyes. When we asked how he was feeling, Tim, battling to speak in full sentences, just said he was sore and struggling.

Even with a whack of methadone, we wondered if he'd make it, he was that ill. My joint pains had been bad enough, but Tim's looked a million times worse. He couldn't sit in a normal chair because his bones ached too much. He'd pace around the garden, then he'd squat in the corner, slowly rocking back and forth on his haunches, his head bowed, skittish, almost cowering.

I was ashamed. I knew if I'd seen Tim lying on the pavement, I would have stepped over him and kept walking. Yet he was an opiate addict, just like me. I hated myself for my double standards. I was shocked to learn that he was on the same dosage of methadone as I'd been on. Because he was a heroin addict and at death's door, I automatically assumed he was in far worse shape than I'd been, yet, apparently, he and I were on a par. I even discussed it with Pat late one night when I couldn't sleep and went for a chat.

'Kat, maybe meeting Tim is what you needed to put the severity of your own addiction into perspective,' said Pat. 'Your condition on arrival was in some ways worse than Tim's. You were far closer to heart failure, *pookie*. We honestly didn't think you'd make it.'

I had a little cry with Pat. On the back of my awful nightmare, everything had started to hit home.

36

I felt like one of the old-timers in the clinic, like a student with graduation day looming except I wouldn't get the celebratory piss-up. Patients continued to come and go, and patients continued to wonder if they were coming or going. There were tears, plenty of tears, some were even mine, though the frequency and severity of my outbursts had reduced. We still shouted and swore at each other, and at the counsellors too. People continued to get verbally slaughtered in Group and family sessions. Rules were still being broken, including one fatal case of fraternising.

There seemed to be a bit more laughing. We old-timers would sit up late on the patio and tell stupid jokes, enjoying the type of belly laughter that gave us stitches. A welcome break from tears. I still felt as if my emotions had been put on a never-ending boil cycle, but it was strangely comforting to welcome new patients and be their assigned 'buddy', assuring them that things got better in time, identifying with the 'yeah right' face they pulled as you said it.

With me taking things a bit more seriously, I had cooled off Charles. Needless to say, he'd quickly moved on to a new girl, a blonde. It took three days for them to get their first fraternising warning in Housekeeping.

Gina and I continued to scrap, though. Eating disorder aside, she was determined to issue a new label or two before I left. Her latest crusade was to get me to admit to being a) co-dependent and b) a love and/or sex addict – whole other addictions in themselves.

She gave me a book on co-dependency. I understood it as a toxic behavioural habit whereby one lives one's life through someone else, can't take a stand on one's own, is excessively needy and is always seeking approval. I read the book, was bored to tears, identified with none of it, and decided I wasn't co-dependent. We all like a bit of approval from time to time, I thought. What's wrong with that?

The love- and sex-addiction topic was, at least, more interesting but – with only one real love and a few casual shags to my name – I hardly qualified as an addict in that arena. Gina, however, brought it up in connection with the Charles dalliance and said I sought affection, affirmation and love in a somewhat addictive and unhealthy sexual way. Memories of my sick nightmare came flooding back, although I didn't say a word to Gina about it.

'Sex addiction is not about how many people you sleep with or if you're having sex day in, day out,' said Gina. 'It is centred more on the behaviours and mind games around sex, the obsessive and compulsive attitudes towards sex, and the objectifying of a person in a sexual and often deviant way.'

'I wouldn't even know where to *start* objectifying someone in a sexually deviant way. It sounds like a porn star's job description,' I replied.

'As I expected, you're making light of it and arguing it. The tell-tale signs of denial.'

I just sighed, crossing my arms. 'Okay, I'm a sex addict. Fix me.'

I got one of Gina's extra-special death stares.

Gina then made me join the sex addiction group sessions, which rounded off my rehab education nicely. I was learning an awful lot about all things weird, freakish, dangerous and of the underworld. I'd already learnt more about drugs and the dark side of society than I would anywhere else in life.

The sex addiction Group was fascinating. One of the guys was, in fact, a virgin – but was a full-blown sex addict nonetheless, and fed his addiction with porn, fantasies and some light stalking of a girl at work with whom he wanted to have his dirty way. His obsessive thoughts had totally taken over and made his life unmanageable.

Charles, of course, was in the sex Group and I was suitably horrified to hear about his fancy-boarding-school dorm sex games, especially Sticky Biscuit. The delightful little boys would stand in a circle, a ginger biscuit placed in the centre. They then all had to masturbate and ejaculate onto the biscuit. The last boy to, well, complete the task, would have to eat it. Super!

That night on the patio everyone assured me it was a common school game. Donovan seemed familiar with Sticky Biscuit too, which was a concern. He got incredibly cross when I asked him why it had to be a ginger biscuit or if shortbread was allowed too. It sparked a huge patio argument and all the sex addicts told those of us with socially acceptable shagging habits to fuck off and show their addiction a bit more respect.

Sarah and I laughed about it for days and, as luck would have it, that weekend Donovan's mom brought him a packet of Custard Creams. Needless to say, he flatly refused to share them.

I thought I'd learnt some weird shit in the clinic but, for a Convent-educated farm girl like me, dare I say it, this took the biscuit. And any lingering desires for Charles had officially been cured. Gina won that round.

Having considered sex addiction and co-dependency with what I believed to be an open mind, I reported back to Gina and told her I wasn't afflicted by either disorder. I also mentioned that I'd been put off ginger biscuits for life. I then told Gina she'd have to try harder for a new label, over and above addict, alcoholic and a possible temporary eating disorder. And to make it snappy as I was going home soon.

A few days after Tim checked in, there was a flurry of activity at the nurses station one morning and I saw Serge, one of his room-mates, having an intense conversation with Julian. Later that morning we heard Tim had relapsed and been chucked out.

Apparently, Serge – a heroin addict himself – had woken up in the night to the unmistakable sound of a fingernail tapping the side of a syringe. Serge, no stranger to mainlining smack, immediately knew what he'd heard. Sure enough, when the nurses tested Tim, they found a fair whack of heroin cantering through his veins.

'But how? He hasn't even had any visitors yet,' was the question flying around the patio.

It turned out that Tim had smuggled the heroin and needle into the clinic inside his chunky dreadlocks. It was the one place the nurses hadn't thought to search, but you could bet your bottom dollar everyone's hair would now be interrogated on arrival.

And so, on his knees and at death's door, Tim was thrown out. We'd seen others kicked out, but just as Tim's arrival had rocked us, his eviction did too, and a sombre mood fell over us. We knew he'd go straight back to the drugs and probably wouldn't survive the relapse. Maybe he hadn't hit his rock bottom after all. Maybe he still had a bit of 'using' left in him, a part of him not sated, still needing more heroin. The dreaded disease of addiction would kill Tim, of that we were sure.

The entire issue was cause for an emergency housekeeping session late that afternoon. When six of the counsellors came in, we knew it was pretty serious. They tried to get us, as a group, to settle and focus again, reassuring us we were safe. Poor Serge called it 'the biggest mindfuck ever'. Having someone shoot up his drug of choice right next to him had really sent him for a loop and he looked terrible. He'd felt so desperately sorry for Tim but, for his own safety, he'd had to turn him in. I couldn't stop thinking about it. Tim had been such a big wake-up call, a reminder that when you get that low, death was far more likely than a successful return from the brink.

Only about one third of us would make it, stay clean, and live to tell the addiction tale, we learnt in Julian's lecture later that day. Pretty appalling odds that didn't cheer anyone up. And, when we relapsed, we would jump back in right where we'd left off. No easing into things, it was straight back to the high quantities we'd used at our previous rock bottom, which is why death by relapse is so common.

A few days later Tim returned, begging to be let back in. He'd been sleeping up on the mountain again and had used once or twice, but nowhere near his norm. He looked marginally better than the last time he'd crawled in, but the look in his startling blue eyes was the same – sad, broken. They let him in, but not before his dreadlocks were practically X-rayed.

I was surprised how happy I was to see him back. Alive. He had unwittingly played a huge role in my journey, making me engage more thoroughly with the programme. I would need to thank him for saving me from myself.

On our beach stroll two days after he returned, Tim did something remarkable. He and our escort nurse moved down the beach where, holding a pair of scissors, he walked into the sea up to his waist. He took the scissors to his dreadlocks, hacking them off and throwing the ropes of hair with all his might into the waves. Almost in a trance, he stood for a long time gazing out to sea before coming back to us, his head full of haphazard tufts of fuzzy hair and looking like a tired Kiwi fruit after a big night out.

'The next surfer is going to SHIT himself when he comes across a dreadlock. There'll be front page reports of a new monster in local waters,' laughed Serge, hugging Tim, as relieved as I was to have him back.

A minute later, a huge dog came belting past us, its owner in hot pursuit and shrieking 'drop it'. Sure enough, the dog had a soggy dreadlock flapping around on either side of its jowls, looking dead pleased with its find.

'Kat, is that one of yours?' asked Donovan, just as we all saw it was a Great Dane.

Everyone roared with laughter and the dog's owner clearly thought we were from the loony bin, which of course we were.

Back in the clinic, the nurse gave Tim some electric hair clippers, and soon he was totally bald. We cheered and clapped for him, knowing his dreadlocks had been his mask and a symbol of the drug culture he was finally ready to leave behind. Whether it was the bald head or just Tim coming back to life, he looked like a different man. Each day his blue eyes got bluer and he seemed to draw strength from our encouragement. Despite facing our own shitty issues, everyone made time for Tim. From the ashes rose a really lovely man.

I was finally being prepared for release back into the wild. As my last week loomed, I was no longer being shredded limb from limb in Group. While I couldn't wait to leave – never to face another dinner of grey slop or see Herr Gina again – I was also shitting myself. I'd come to feel safe in the clinic, to feel beautifully cocooned and protected from the big bad world. Masses of temptation – alcohol, codeine-flavoured pain relief, real sugar, and the deadliest of all, white flour – were waiting for me on the other side.

We were made to do role-playing exercises in preparation for leaving, acting out scenarios to test our resolve. Being offered booze in social situations, hanging out with dodgy friends who did drugs, falling ill and needing drugs – life's regular occurrences were now potential minefields. For me, my greatest fear was still my headaches and how strong I'd be in the face of pain. They may have got me clean, but they sure as hell hadn't fixed my head or neck, which still hurt nearly as much as the day I checked in.

Carol set a scene up for us. 'What to say when your dealer calls.' It hit me between the eyes, realising I'd have to tell Colin to sod off sooner or later.

She put me, raw and unprepared, into the scenario. Donovan asked if he could play the part of the ringing telephone, and Frank, another old-timer, stood before me as Colin.

With a quick straightening of his green cardigan, Donovan started. *'Rrrring ring, rrring ring.'*

With a gormless face, I looked down at my mock telephone – the blackboard duster.

Donovan kept ringing. 'B'ring b'ring. B'rring B'RRRING'.

His ringing got louder and the sniggers from the group made me giggle. I wondered if I could request a better ringtone.

'Cut the crap, Kat!' bellowed Carol. 'This is not stand-up comedy. Start again, try to take this seriously. It's a situation that will occur.'

Donovan cleared his throat, straightened his cardigan again, frowned at me and started a new round of rings.

'Brrr'inga-brrrr'inga. Bringa- bringa, bring bring.'

I answered the phone, holding the blackboard duster to my ear, looking at Frank.

'Hey Kat!'

'Urr ... hi?' My voice was all shaky.

'It's Colin. Been trying to call you for ages. You been out of town?'

'Urh. Ummmm. Yes. Hey. Howzit Colin, you well?'

'Good thanks, all good, how are you Kat?'

'Urrrh. Well. Ummm. Yes, I was meaning to—'

'CUT!' Carol suddenly shrieked, like it was a bloody film set. 'Kat, why are you making chit-chat and being all nicey-nice? He's your bloody dealer, trying to lead you into relapse. Cut the niceties. Tell him you're done with him and he's never to contact you again.'

I stood there, rooted to the floor, staring moronically at my telephone. The mere thought of Colin at the other end of the blackboard duster, and I'd become a mute idiot.

Frank kept the ball rolling. 'You still there Kat? Listen, you must be needing some pills by now. I have a decent supply at the moment and also some new gear. New tranquillisers I thought you might like to try. They're super with a shot of vodka. Let's meet up after work, usual place?'

Jeez, I thought. Super with a shot of vodka? Frank really was taking this to the extreme. I tried to keep going. 'Umm, Colin, sorry, but, you see, the thing is—'

Carol shrieked again and threw her hands in the air. 'Why are you apologising to him? He's your grim reaper, Kat. GRIM REAPER!'

I took a deep breath and picked up the thread again. 'No Colin, here's the thing, I won't be needing stuff from you anymore, if that's okay—'

Another wild shriek from Carol. 'Kat! What do you mean "if that's okay"? Who gives a shit? He's a dealer and you're asking if it's okay not to score? Tell him, NO! And he's never to call again.'

I was getting more and more flustered but, try as I might, even in a fake scenario I didn't have it in me to get straight to the point with Colin. We tried the scenario two more times, but I kept being nice and saying sorry to Colin, and Carol kept exploding.

I crossed my arms and sulked, upset with myself for being so pathetic.

'Kat, my dear child, this Colin is no friend of yours,' said Carol, switching to a gentler tone, seeing I was about to lose it. 'He is a criminal. He *will* screw up your life again if you don't tell him to go to hell.'

Exasperated, she turned to the group for help. 'Hey, peanut gallery, this role play is about as useful as rubber lips on a woodpecker. Any suggestions for Kat?' asked Carol.

Donovan's hand shot up first.

'You in the cardigan, let's hear it,' Carol said.

'Kat must change her phone number,' Donovan said very proudly.

'Not your worst suggestion ever, Donovan. He's right,' said Carol turning to me. 'We could do this role play for days, but I can see you will struggle to be assertive. So, Plan B, changing your number, makes sense. Thank you, Donovan. It's encouraging to see that at least one brain cell is left amongst the thirty of you.'

Donovan looked ready to explode with pride.

'Any other suggestions for Kat,' Carol asked the group.

Tina spoke up. 'Think of Cassie,' she stated flatly.

It hit me between the eyes. It was like a kick to the nuts, if I'd had nuts. I was so disappointed in myself. The Beast was back, bright-eyed and bushy-tailed and doing hopscotch on my shoulder, saying, 'Colin. Say yes to Colin. Meet with Colin. Colin can get you numb. Colin rocks. Colin is our friend. Why endure pain when there's Colin. Colin. Colin. Colin.' My pulse was racing, beads of sweat broke out across my forehead and I felt sick. I just wanted to scream, to drown out the voices.

I sat down again and Donovan leant over to tell me the telephone had left chalk smears all over my ear.

'Oh, just fuck off already,' I muttered, wiping my chalky ear.

It did make sense to change my number. However, I pointed out to Carol that pharmacies weren't going to evaporate from earth for my benefit and there'd come a time when I'd have to go into one. Carol did a role play for me on pharmacies in which I coped marginally better, but it was still a mind-bender and I was only buying vitamin C.

Step 4 was a real bitch of a step. Far harder than all the Higher Power hunting in the Step before it. This one required one to conduct 'a searching and fearless moral inventory' of oneself.

Searching. There's a scary word, I thought.

Moral inventory. Huh? Stocktaking my principles, such as they were?

I had a sudden urge to talk to Grandpa. A sharp pang reminded me how much I missed him. He'd have some good ideas on how to scrum down and start Step 4.

I read it again. We made a searching and fearless moral inventory of ourselves.

Already the word 'fearless' implied that you should be a little scared going into it. Like, guilty as sin, saying to your mother, 'Don't freak out, but ...' You're basically telling her she *will* be freaking out very shortly.

'Fearless' was just a warning, all dressed up. You could expect to be scared shitless in Step 4.

I asked around and, evidently, there was no right or wrong way to do it, as long as we wrote down who we'd hurt or betrayed, and why, and owned our part in each scenario. And, if we'd been hurt by someone, we had to write about that too and dissect any resentments we lugged around. '*Step put-your-big-girl-panties-on 4*', someone on the patio called it.

To list everyone whom I'd ever wronged in my entire life was a tall order. I went hurtling back to childhood to examine the hurts and bruises I'd both received and given. In doing Step 4, I suddenly realised there was a lot more to my drug use than neck pain, headaches and irresponsible doctors with their trigger-happy approach to prescription pads. It brought up events I hadn't thought of in years and I saw how much emotional stuff I'd suppressed around Mom's drinking. Now, with twenty years' interest gained on all the hurt, it was far reaching.

Gina, human sniffer dog extraordinaire, saw my mood change as I cautiously lifted the moss-crusted rocks under which my old resentments lived.

'Kat, you've been particularly scratchy in the last few days,' she said in Group one day.

'Step 4,' I stated in a flat voice.

'Who have you started with?'

'My mother. My childhood.'

'What has it brought up for you?'

I thought for a moment. 'Basically, I'm pretty angry that she chose alcohol over me. She was always too drunk or hungover to play or ride with me. All these years I thought I'd been too young to remember her drinking and the awful fighting with Dad, but actually I remember it all. I was just a little girl! How could she DO that? To a CHILD? HER child?'

Suddenly I was crying, angry tears. Adult Kat had gone and little girl Kat was sitting in Group, blubbing her eyes out. Donovan passed little Kat a tissue from the communal box.

'You're angry that your mother was a drunk?' asked Gina.

'Flippin' furious.'

'Yet you then turned into her. Your relationship with Ant was a mirror image of her relationship with your father. Like your father, Ant begged you to stop using drugs and partying, and he was devastated by all the lies and denial.'

Donovan couldn't pass the tissues fast enough and just handed me the box. Snot and tears streaming, I nodded slowly. I wanted to argue with Gina, but couldn't. It was true.

'While there is never an acceptable reason to become an alcoholic or addict, there is one big difference between you and your mother.'

I nodded, knowing what she meant.

'Your mother drank to forget her rape,' continued Gina. 'You banged your head a few times and have a bad neck and get headaches.'

'I know.'

'Sit with the feelings Kat.' With that, Gina moved on and the whole session became about parents and how, in addiction, we develop the very traits we despised in them. It was comforting to hear it wasn't just me with a messed-up family.

I knew I had to start forgiving Mom. Knowing how hard it was to fight the Beast, one thing I couldn't do was blame her. I wondered how Chris had processed Mom's drinking, as he'd never really talked about it as an adult. I then found myself processing some anger towards Chris, how he'd been the rebel child yet I, the sane one, had landed in rehab.

I plodded on with Step 4, resigned to the fact that it would be shitty but finding a lot of release in writing it all down. Nobody checked it. The value lay in getting the realisations on paper. As healing as it was, it was still hugely draining. Step Sore.

There were goodbyes every week. Inmates who'd done their time took a deep breath and stepped out the front door. All were in much better nick than when they'd come in. I was sad to see Sarah go and cried like a baby. She'd become a dear friend, my rock. Tina had gone into secondary care and would spend another month or two in a halfway house – a stepping stone between the clinic and the real world. It was still rehab, but slightly less hectic than our current lockdown situation. Surprisingly, Donovan's departure left a big gap in the group and we all missed him in his astonishing collection of cardigans in old-man colours, and his licky-arsey, goody two shoes antics. Life was positively dull without the class arsehole always telling tales.

But other weirdos came in and found their niche. Such was life in rehab – a constant rotation of seriously battered, bruised, blood-encrusted and battle-weary soldiers crawling in. Walking out were more confident, healed, clean and sober soldiers, swords raised to their dragons as they started a new life in Recovery, mostly determined to be in the successful thirty percent. Then there were those with a certain look in their eyes. The first thing they were going to do was score, get high and drunk, or both, because rehab hadn't worked for them.

With my epiphany about Mom's drinking unfolding so close to me leaving, Gina called me 'a late bloomer' and recommended I follow Tina and do a month in secondary care to give me extra resolve. I told her to sod off. In a stressful two-session negotiation worthy of a FBI hostage situation, we bargained, finally agreeing on my staying one extra week in the clinic.

At the door, I turned to Gina and said, 'Besides, what with all the crying, I'll be out of mascara in about six days ...'

I sprinted down the corridor before she could catch me.

On my last night while packing, I listened to the chatter of inmates downstairs on the patio, probably swopping war stories and dabbling in a spot of euphoric recall and some fraternising was probably going on somewhere. It was raining softly and the sea breeze floating in was crisp and salty. I considered where'd I'd be in a week's time, fear and anxiety blended with excitement and cautious anticipation. I'd needed the extra week, if I was honest with myself, feeling a lot more grounded now. I did so hate Gina being right.

Later that night, the Beast came. I took notice. I'd been expecting it and, as such, was prepared. It was the size of my hand at most, its smallest size yet. Its presence was more threatening than its size. Time would tell if it would follow me home or if it fed only in Cape Town in a rehab by the sea.

I sat on my suitcase, only just squeezing in all the papers and books I'd gathered. I smiled, remembering it – and me – being lugged up the stairs over five weeks ago.

I'd had my official farewell before lunch. Gina presented me with my badge of honour – a small, but comfortingly heavy, metal disc celebrating my entry into Recovery. Such a simple little medallion for so much blood, sweat, snot and tears. Charles and Tim had said a few words at my little graduation, whereupon I'd promptly burst into tears, suddenly overwhelmed, terrified about what came next.

I said my goodbyes to the nurses.

'One day at a time, *pookie*,' said Pat, giving me the biggest hug ever, with me disappearing into her double-E cleavage for a moment.

'Get a sponsor, do ninety NA meetings in ninety days, and keep it simple, stupid,' said Carol, giving me a beautiful warm smile, genuinely happy for me. 'And pick up the phone if ever you feel a wobble. You know there are people here 24/7 if you need talking down off a ledge. And give my love to your Great Danes.'

I laughed. We all did.

'And remember to change your cellphone number,' said Gina.

Pat, Carol and Gina clucked around me like mother hens. I could have throttled them all in the early days, but these people had saved my life. Now I didn't want to let them out of my sight.

'Oh, come here,' said Gina, pulling me in for a last hug. She held me tightly for a few moments rubbing my back comfortingly, tears in her eyes too. 'Right, KitKat, bugger off now, we have other screwed-up junkies to kick into shape. Your mom is waiting downstairs.' Before she let me go, she whispered one last thing in my ear. 'And – I am sure you already know – when you give your knickers to a man, especially a sex addict, he only does dirty things with them in private.'

I spluttered, and then Gina and I both giggled. 'Just taking one for the team,' I said.

Gina tweaked my nose – her signature mass of bangles jingling – winked and walked off, her pretty skirt swishing. The evil gypsy was human after all.

I found Mom in reception chatting to Julian again. She saw me, quickly ended the conversation and ran to hug me.

'Good luck, squirt. Stay strong.' said Julian.

'Thanks for everything, Julian.'

I officially signed myself out of the clinic and hopped into Mom's hire car. I took a deep breath and looked back. Everyone was gathering at the door for their afternoon beach walk. I waved. Charles blew me a kiss and, still crying, I realised I was happy.

37

Mom and I went on a much-needed mother–daughter weekend shopping spree before we flew home. We checked into our B&B and later drove to a beach restaurant, watching the Cape Town sunset. There was an upbeat vibe in the air and it seemed the world hadn't stopped turning while I'd been in rehab.

'So, how're you feeling now?' asked Mom. 'You're looking gorgeous, much healthier.'

'I'm surprised not to be suffering from malnutrition after that slop they pretended was food. Anyway, I feel all exposed, like everyone can see I've just left rehab.'

'Ah, I remember feeling like a bloody great neon sign was around my neck saying "Drunkard, fresh out of rehab". All conspicuous.'

'Mom, it's been the most insane process,' I said, looking at her and realising she'd now given me life twice. 'I owe you and Dad a huge thank you.'

'Oh shush. We're just glad you did it. You've been given the tools and now it's up to you to stay clean. I can't, and won't, be your Recovery policeman.'

I looked at her properly for the first time since she'd picked me up. She looked so pretty. She'd changed her hair, now a cute short bob with fresh highlights, her face was light and her smile reached her eyes again. I had a rush of guilt about all the angst I'd caused her. I took her hand and just held it for a while.

'So Gina was hardcore, huh? And what did you think of Julian?' Mom asked.

'Umm, he was okay I guess. Also pretty harsh in Group, though he never really annihilated me. Did you work out why he was so familiar to you?'

Mom suddenly glanced up from her menu, but ignored my direct question. 'He seemed really nice,' she said. 'We had a good chat with him on Family Day.'

Mom seemed to want to say more, but obviously decided against it. I felt so disoriented back in the real world that I didn't immediately pick up on the weird vibe coming from her.

The next morning, we hit the shops early. With things deteriorating fast at home and simple items becoming short or unavailable, it was a big shop. We were soon laden with basic groceries, clothes, seven pairs of shoes that I just *had* to have and, finally, new mascara. We then went for an early dinner.

I noticed Mom was like the proverbial cat on a hot tin roof. When I lit a ciggie, she leant over, took one of mine and lit up too.

'Mom! Good God. No ways.' She'd not smoked in years.

'Stress!'

'About me? What's wrong? Now I think about it, you've been all jittery since you collected me.' Never could I have predicted just how big a bombshell she was about to drop.

'Sorry darling. Yes, I'm in a total bloody muddle over something. And no, it's not you. I don't want to overload you, though.'

She'd suddenly gone pale.

'Jeez Ma, what's up? Is someone sick? Dead? Is it Grandpa?' Mom was no drama queen so when something rattled her, it was serious.

'No, nothing like that.' She took a deep breath. Reaching into her handbag, she pulled out an old photograph. 'Remember when we were sorting through family photos, you asked about this one. I found it in your cottage.'

I recognised it immediately. It was the photo taken at Malange Club, when she was a teenager in Malawi. The one in which she had a dark, haunted look.

'Yup, I remember. You said it was taken just after your rape.'

'Yes. But there was more to the story. I didn't tell you everything. I didn't think I'd ever have to, but something unexpected has come up.'

'Huh?'

'Oh shit. I don't know how to say this.' Mom's voice wobbled.

'Mom! You're freaking me out. Just bloody tell me.'

'Okay. As you know, that bastard raped me and he was found dead in Grandpa's dam. What I didn't tell you was that he actually got me pregnant—'

'What?' I interrupted, thinking I had misheard.

'Pregnant. I'd just found out that I was carrying my rapist's child.'

'Holy crap!' I was stunned.

Mom went on with the bizarre story. 'Termination wasn't an option back then, and Gran and Grandpa felt it better to keep my pregnancy quiet. I couldn't face the scandal that would have flown around the community. People were already gossiping about the hushed-up incident on our estate, speculating about that bastard's strange death and his wife suddenly leaving town. So, we hid my pregnancy for about six months. I spent the last three months in a remote convent in the south of Malawi, where nuns took care of me. It was a home for unwed pregnant girls. Basically, a Catholic Church adoption centre. The nuns knew of a married couple desperate to adopt. As soon as my baby was born, he was given to them.'

'A boy?'

'Yes. I saw him briefly.'

'Shit, Ma. And then?'

'Life had to go on. I was seventeen, way too young to be a mother. The fact that he was conceived in such a brutal, violent way was too much for me to handle. I didn't think I could love my child because of what his father was. It wouldn't have been fair for him to grow up like that. It wasn't his fault, so adoption was the best option. After that, I picked up my life again and got on with things. I had to.'

'Does Dad know all this?'

'Of course.'

'So, hang on. I always thought you drank to forget the rape, but you drank to forget the adoption too?'

'Yup. Every day I wonder what happened to my son. It's no longer the raw pain I felt as a young girl, more a sadness and curiosity. I try to imagine where he is, what kind of a man he's become, if he looks like me, if he's successful, and if I have grandchildren. And, every year, I silently celebrate his birthday. It's a day after yours.'

'Shit, how do you even begin to get over something like that and deal with those demons?'

'You put one foot in front of the other and days turn into months, years pass, and life goes on. I met your father, I had you and Chris to raise, I had a home to run and a husband to look after. Yes, I was haunted by it for a very long time and sought solace in booze, which didn't help, but perhaps now you can understand why I drank? And, having been in rehab yourself, you can imagine how much I had to work through. Imagine my Step 4? Took me months to complete!'

Mom sighed and paused for a while, her eyes suddenly moist. 'I'm sorry Kat, I'm so, *so* sorry I was such a bad mother to you.'

'You weren't, Mom. I don't blame you for any of it,' I said, also welling up, not caring about the other diners gawking at us. 'So, that means I have another brother somewhere?'

'Yup.'

'Do you have regrets about the adoption?'

'For a long time, yes I did. As I grew up, I wondered if I should have kept the baby and tried to overlook how he was conceived, but I was young and I made my decision as best I could at the time. Regrets keep you stuck in the past – I finally realised that in rehab while doing my Step 4 actually.'

'Why didn't you tell me this when you told me about the rape?'

'Don't know. I wanted to, but then the moment passed. You were such a mess from your head injury that I left it alone.'

'So, why now?'

'Years ago, after rehab, I decided to find out a bit about my son. I started with the Convent, but they blocked me and kicked up a stink about confidentiality. I persevered. I drove up there and befriended one of the newer nuns. Little did I know that the records had been destroyed in a fire, so my attempts were futile. However, one of the nuns – the midwife – remembered me, but she was gone ninety and a bit loopy. All she could give me was a possible surname, but said that the family had long since left

Malawi. So the trail went cold and I decided to leave it there. I took it as a sign that I wasn't meant to find my son.'

'And then?' Although shocked, I was captivated.

'I knew if, unwittingly, I were ever to cross paths with him, I would recognise him instantly, that I'd feel it in my bones, know my own flesh and blood, so—'

'Oh. My. God,' I interrupted. 'Are you about to tell me you've met him?'

She nodded slowly. My hand flew up, covering my mouth.

'I wasn't looking for him, but he was placed in my path, or I was placed in his – depends which way you look at it. And you were with me. I turned into a bit of a moron,' she said, now laughing.

The penny dropped. Everything suddenly slipped into place.

'Julian?'

'Yup,' said Mom. 'Julian.'

'You've GOT to be fucking kidding me?'

'Nope,' said Mom, smiling.

'If I didn't know better, I'd say you'd been drinking again. No, but Mom, seriously, how the … what the …?'

'I'll never forget that moment. Sitting in that pokey little Fishbowl room with you, about to leave you in rehab, terrified for you, knowing what you were going to go through. Then Julian stuck his head round the door. Well, you saw me. I was completely thrown.'

'You knew straightaway he was your son. How?'

'It's hard to describe. But yes, a hundred and ten percent, no question about it, I knew I had met my son. He was so familiar, like I'd known him all my life. Even you saw a similarity.'

'Well yes. But I thought he looked like someone we knew, not that he was my brother. Hang on, that first evening, he and I were smoking on the balcony and he said he'd been to Malawi as a kid. Shit, this is a lot to take in.'

'I know. You don't have to tell *me* that.'

'But how did you feel about it, Ma?'

'Shocked, Kat. I can't even begin to describe what I went through that night. First putting you in the clinic, then meeting my son. I was scared, but overjoyed I'd finally been led to him. Then I felt like a shit again for giving him up, felt maybe he'd had a crappy life with awful parents and that's why he'd walked the road of addiction himself. He is a counsellor so I quickly worked out that he was in Recovery himself – most addiction counsellors are. I grappled with guilt about that. I didn't sleep a wink, going over it all and wondering what to do, wondering if I should do anything at all. And wondering if I was imagining it.'

'So, what did you do?'

'I got home and spoke to your father. And then we told Grandpa. They both thought I'd gone batty, announcing that my long-lost son was one of your counsellors. I mean, what are the chances? They actually laughed and asked if I'd been back on the hooch. Dad said I was stressed about you and was imagining the whole thing with Julian. Entirely understandable, as I had no hard proof, just that gut reflex to go on.'

'So, you have two addict kids. Julian was a coke addict, for your info.'

'Cocaine, was it? I've been wondering which substance took him down.'

'Have you approached him? Have you actually verified that he's your son?'

'Dad, Grandpa and I talked and talked about it. Dad, of course, met Julian at your Family Day, but making contact with a child after adoption is a delicate process. We didn't know how to go about verifying what I felt. Then, in that Family Day session, one of the parents was talking about her adopted child who was in there with you. It sparked an interesting debate about adopted kids often being prone to addictions. That's when Julian shared his own story. He said he'd been adopted, known it all his life, and explained how he himself had become an addict. He said being put up for adoption, being unwanted, had bred many rejection and trust issues that the drugs had numbed nicely. That, as you can imagine, was just super for me to hear. Little did he know that the woman who'd caused his issues and given him the addict gene was sitting under his nose. I was so upset I went to the loo and had a bloody good cry.'

'Then?'

'Well, then we knew he knew he'd been adopted. That was the first hurdle. By chance, we chatted with him in the tea break and the more I spoke to him and watched his mannerisms, the more certain I became.

Looking into his eyes was like looking into my own. He's left-handed, like you and me. And he mentioned that he'd spent a few years running around on the shores of Lake Malawi as a kid. Dad wasn't convinced, despite seeing a likeness, and said it was all a coincidence. I took a more karmic approach, feeling we'd crossed paths for a reason. Still though, we didn't say anything, we didn't know what to say or how to say it. Oh, and he has the same shaped ear lobes as you and Chris.'

The things mothers notice, I thought.

'This is like a far-fetched C-grade movie,' I said.

'Don't tell me!'

'Okay, and then?'

'Well, we flew home, saying nothing. Then Grandpa suggested we make contact via the Convent. We asked them to write to Julian, saying that his biological mother had come forward and, should he want to connect, they could facilitate a meeting.'

'Did they agree?'

'They were reticent and it was a hard sell. We put a nice little donation forward and eventually they agreed to write one letter only, and, if that didn't bear fruit, then tough titty. They don't like messing with people's lives.'

'Why couldn't you just approach Julian directly?'

'It might have scared him off. Also, we didn't know if he even wanted to find his real parents. It's usually the child who reaches out, not the birth parent. And we couldn't exactly say: Hey Julian, that girl Kat, she's your sister!'

'Yeah, I can see how that would've been a bit of a mind-bender.'

Mom laughed, lit another ciggie and continued. 'Anyway, the Convent sent the letter. We gave them the clinic's address. They gave no names and didn't say how they knew he worked at that address. It really was the most unorthodox way to reach out, but I was determined.'

'Did he reply?'

'Yes, almost immediately. The letter arrived last week. He said yes! He told the nuns that he'd wanted to find me for years and had done a lot of scouting around Malawi, but kept drawing blanks. He confirmed his date of birth and it matched. All he knew was that his mother was the daughter of a tea baron and that her name was Gillian.'

'Bugger me,' I said softly.

Mom stared into the middle distance for a while, lost in thought. I was reeling.

'Oh, he did ask the nuns how they knew where he worked, but obviously that will be revealed when he and I talk. Now the ball is in my court. It's time to make myself known. It's somewhat complicated with him being one of your counsellors, and I couldn't do anything until you'd left the clinic.'

'Sorry,' I said meekly.

'Hardly your fault. I have such mixed feelings, but I think it's something I have to do. Too many coincidences that can't be ignored, don't you think? I need to ask if you're okay with it? You're fresh out of the clinic, and vulnerable, and I would never do anything to jeopardise your Recovery, darling. If you want me to wait, I will.'

'Don't be daft, Mom. Of course you must do it, and do it now, face to face, while you're here. You have my blessing. What's Dad's stance?'

'Dad's such a rock, says he supports whatever I do. He's actually quite excited to welcome his stepson into our family, bless him. I have been putting a lot of faith in the Universe and asking to be shown how to do this. I'm decided on my approach.'

'And what's that?'

'I've drafted a letter saying I received his reply via the nuns and am thus initiating the contact. I've said nothing about his father, just that I'd been very young and adoption was the better route for me.'

'And have you mentioned the connection with me?'

'That was a tricky part. I've said we met unknowingly and by unbelievable chance. That Gillian, the Malawian tea baron's daughter, is now Mrs Gill Hay, Kat from Zimbabwe's mom.'

'Boy oh boy! That's going to be one letter he won't forget. You sure you shouldn't tell him in person?' I wondered how I'd feel to get such a bombshell in the post.

'Doing it via letter allows him to take his time and absorb the information and not be put on the spot.'

'Shit Mom, this is massive. I can't quite get my head around it all. It really is like a movie plot – bizarre coincidences you'd never expect in real life. I thought I'd leave rehab, spend some time with you, a spot of shopping, and then we'd fly home. Now I get a new brother thrown in too.'

'I know! Why it's all happening, I don't know. I guess the reasons will be revealed in the fullness of time,' said Mom, all pragmatic.

'Well, the addictive gene sure runs strong in our bloodline – two addicts and one alcoholic – two if you count GranJilly,' I laughed. 'You couldn't have just found him in a more clean-cut, traditional way, could you Mom? No, you gotta walk bang into your lost kid while checking your other kid into rehab in a foreign country. Shit, all I can say is thank God I didn't get wind of this whilst I was in there being counselled by him.'

'Isn't life bizarre?' Mom mused. 'If you're really okay with it, I'll drop off the letter tomorrow. I can't sit on this any longer. I'll mention that we are in Cape Town for another day or two if he wants to talk in person. We could even stay on a few extra days – but let's see what he says first. Thank God I have you for moral support, except I'm supposed to be giving that to you.'

'Nothing dull or predictable about us, huh? It's going to be interesting to hear his addiction story.'

'I have a feeling that he had a pretty rough time. I'm dying to know what made him become a counsellor.'

'I can't understand why any of them are counsellors, actually – the abuse they take,' I said, remembering the hatred and bad language we'd hurled at them.

'It takes a very special person to dedicate their life to helping those who've walked the same road.'

We headed back to the B&B, both of us emotionally shattered. That was one chat I wouldn't forget in a hurry, but I'd noticed my relationship with Mom seemed to have mellowed. We'd become friends again. Being included in one of her toughest decisions ever was something I'd treasure forever. It struck me, again, that she was a woman of incredible depth and strength. For her to smile, embrace life and remain sober after experiencing such trauma and loss – and at such a young age – was beyond inspiring. I hadn't faced a fraction of the things she had, but the Julian news had sideswiped me far more than I let on.

It would definitely take me a while to digest that I had this older brother, who was both a stranger and already a friend of sorts, who knew many of my secrets. It truly was the most unbelievable situation, bordering on fantasy. I understood that, in life, there are no coincidences, and wondered whether everything was part of a plan far bigger than any of us.

'Kat,' said Mom, thoughtfully, coming into the bathroom holding an envelope as I was brushing my teeth. 'It's a lot to ask, but will you read my letter to Julian?'

I suggested only a few minor changes. She sat down to write the final letter while I watched TV, giving her some space. As she sealed the envelope, she smiled. A shadow had lifted from her face.

The next morning, we set off for the clinic. It was a stunning warm day and the view of Cape Town was magnificent as we drove over the mountain and back to the clinic almost to the tip of Africa. Mom seemed upbeat and happy, confident she was doing the right thing. Dad had called to wish her luck too.

When we parked outside the clinic. I felt a twitch running down my spine to be back there so soon.

'Come on then,' I said. 'Let's do this.'

Mom gripped the steering wheel, her knuckles white. 'I can't move KitKat. Will you run in and leave it at reception?'

She was pale, her hands shaking as she lit another of my cigarettes. Then she burst into hysterical laughter and we both sat there giggling. The guard at the door looked warily at us, probably thinking we'd been on a bender and I was about to check in again.

'Will you, Kat? Please run in for me,' Mom asked again.

'Okay, here goes,' I said, grabbing the letter, jumping out of the car and darting to the front door.

I gave the receptionist the letter. As I turned to leave, I felt a warm, firm hand on my bum, snatching a forbidden feel. Knowing it was Charles, I turned around, smiling to see he was carrying his laundry.

'Such a nice arse,' he said languidly.

Chuckling, I gave him a kiss on the cheek before walking to the door. 'Try behaving, Charles. Don't miss me too much.'

I saw Julian coming down the corridor. I didn't think I'd be able to handle an interaction with him, knowing what I knew, so I darted out.

'Done!' I said to Mom, jumping in and slamming the car door.

'You see him?'

'Just in the distance. The receptionist said he'd get the letter right away.'

'Well, nothing for it now but to wait. I think some more retail therapy is in order.'

We spent the morning in the mall again, Mom with her cellphone at the ready, having given Julian her number. The day crawled and, by dinner, Mom hadn't heard a peep. We imagined all the reasons he hadn't called. Maybe he hadn't had a chance to read the letter, maybe he was upset or angry, maybe he was too shocked to call having realised he'd already met his mother. Round and round we went, until we were both exhausted and I insisted we stop. I could see Mom second-guessing herself. She looked knackered and was smoking so much she'd now bought her own.

The next morning, we were woken by Mom's phone ringing. She leapt up from a dead sleep and lunged across the room to answer it. It was Dad. I rolled over and continued to doze while they discussed an issue with the veggies. Mid-sentence, Mom suddenly shrieked and said she had a call waiting, cutting Dad off. It was Julian.

They didn't talk for long.

'He seems okay about it all and wants to meet me,' said Mom, after the call.

'Serious?' I asked, yawning. 'What did he say?'

'He thanked me for the letter, said he's doubly stunned to know we've already met, but suggested a proper chat over lunch.'

'When?'

'Today.'

'Yay! You nervous?'

'Yes! No! Yes! I don't know! Oh shit!'

'Well, better get a crack on, Mumsy. At least you don't have to wear red carnations to identify each other.'

'What will you do while I'm out?'

'Babysit your credit card.'

Mom raised an eyebrow.

'Ha, ha! Jokes,' I said. 'Am all shopped out. I'll stay here, do some reading. Do Step work maybe. Don't worry about me, this is your big day.'

By 4 p.m., I started to wonder if Mom was okay. She marched in an hour later, exhausted yet elated. I made coffee and, for the next hour, she unwrapped her son, my brother.

Julian's adopted parents, Sandra and Vincent, chose to adopt when they'd been unable to conceive, but, after Julian's arrival, they did get preggers and Julian had a younger sister, Amanda. Vincent was from 'old money' in the UK. In his twenties, he'd fallen in love with Africa and started a successful career in tourism. Julian and his sister were toddlers when they'd built a small resort on Lake Malawi. They'd moved to South Africa when Julian was ten and built a luxurious lodge near Kruger National Park. It seemed Julian and Amanda wanted for nothing and were educated at the best schools in South Africa.

Julian was a rebel at school, but highly intelligent and got the second-highest matric marks in South Africa that year. At Rhodes University in Grahamstown, he did a business science degree, graduating cum laude and had then started his career as a broker with one of the top financial institutions on the Johannesburg Stock Exchange.

His drug use started at school, first experimenting with weed. At nineteen, Julian was drafted into the South African army, and saw a lot of apartheid-related violence. Drugs were rife in the army – used to blot out the racial savagery the conscripts were forced to partake in. When Julian cruised into the high-flying financial markets, cocaine was the perfect complement to the 'go, go, go' lifestyle. It was also the era of LSD and magic mushrooms and so, in his early twenties, he was doing some serious drugs.

He did exceptionally well for himself, falling in love with the glamorous world of big money. By his thirties he had all the accessories – luxury properties, fast cars, lavish overseas trips, wining and dining with the crème de la crème of South African society, a string of model girlfriends – and access to every drug imaginable. The bubble was always going to burst.

When his friends started to grow up and settle down, Julian couldn't get off drugs. Sandra and Vincent tried to intervene, but failed.

Julian then married his best friend's sister, thinking domesticity was the magic antidote to addiction. They had a child within a year – a daughter – but couldn't make their marriage work and got divorced. Julian, permanently high and thinking he was invincible, started to take bigger and bigger risks on the stock exchange. He also got sucked into the underworld of illicit gambling and high-stakes private poker games.

From there, he went down in flames as his life spiralled out of control. He was still doing coke and was addicted to gambling. He quickly lost everything. His marriage, his daughter, wealth, status – all snorted, swallowed, smoked, or gambled away. Then he was convicted of fraud and insider trading. Julian maintained he was framed, but, at the time, he was just too messed-up to realise that he'd been set up as the fall guy. He served two years, and then got out of jail early after an appeal. He still used drugs in jail, always freely available, but it was light use compared to previously. Finally, during the appeal process, he had an epiphany and decided to straighten out. He got out of prison and used what was left of his money to get clean, spending nine months in rehab and halfway houses.

After rehab, he knew the world of high finance would take him back down the same path. Somewhere along the line, a Catholic priest got through to him and he decided to start helping others and give back to society. He got a bog-standard admin-clerk job in a bank to pay the bills and stayed away from the high life. He put himself through night school and got his diploma in addictions counselling. Then, with a few years of Recovery under his belt, he got his first job as an addictions counsellor and has worked in rehabs ever since.

'And the family?' I asked Mom.

'Sandra and Vincent own and live at a resort on one of Mozambique's Benguerra Islands, close to where we were for Christmas actually. Amanda is a shrink and lives here, in Cape Town, with her husband. Julian himself recently got engaged to Victoire, a French–Mauritian girl whom he met in Mozambique. His ex-wife married a wealthy fruit farmer here too. Julian has his daughter to stay during school holidays. My granddaughter – your niece – is called Hayley.'

'Hayley? And we are Hay? Don't tell me – another weird coincidence?'

'Good Lord, you're right. I didn't even see that one,' Mom said.

'So how long has he been clean?'

'Nearly twelve years, I think he said.'

'And what did he say about you making contact?'

'He was absolutely dumbfounded to learn that he'd already met me. He thought it was a really bad joke at first and went screaming off to find Carol, needing a friend to talk to. Apparently, Carol was floored too.'

'And did he ask about his father?'

'Yup. That was the hectic part. He thought your father was his father too.'

'Oh shit!'

'I told him about the rape. I needed to be totally honest with him. It was quite a blow, but then he said something weird.'

'What?'

'Many years ago, in Paris, some girlfriend dragged him to one of those hocus-pocus, fortune-teller psychic women. The psychic told him a load of bollocks, but then said he was adopted, which made him sit up and take notice. Then the psychic told him there'd been some kind of violence associated with his birth or early childhood. He asked her to elaborate, but she clammed up. Ever since, he's had a sixth sense that his father had been a good-for-nothing bastard, perhaps a wife beater. He just never imagined he'd been a rapist.'

'Hell, that man's head must be spinning.'

'KitKat, he took it all so well. He's a fascinating man, gentle, very spiritual, and in tune with the Universe and into karma. I've not seen serenity like that in a long time, if ever. What a remarkable man,' said Mom reflectively. 'It says a lot about Sandra and Vincent too.'

'What did he say about there being three of us, so closely related, with addiction issues?'

'Nothing much. Remember that addiction is his profession now, so he's seen it all. He just said he fully understood why I drank to forget. He also understands your story. We're not that remarkable. We are all just bog-standard drunks and junkies.'

'And, the million-dollar question, how are *you* feeling about it all?'

'A little bewildered, darling, to put it mildly. I've lived with so many questions that are finally being answered. It's going to take a long while for it all to sink in. I owe you a huge thank you, actually.'

'Why on earth are you thanking me?'

'Well, if you hadn't been a real nutcase of a pill junkie, I'd probably never have found him.'

'I suppose that's one way of looking at it. My pleasure, then. At least some good came of my wayward behaviour.'

'Plenty of good has come from it. Look at you, back to your old self again, looking stunning and healthy. And alive. We thought you were going to die, Kat, we really did. As for your games with that English chap, I really thought you'd get tossed out. Your father was mortified.'

'Charles was bloody hot, Mom. I seriously considered it.'

'I know, I saw him. His father made my knees a little weak too.'

We both giggled. Then her tears came. Mom quickly turned into a gurgling mess of snot, tears, and laughter, and started me crying.

'So, what happens now, with Julian?' I asked, sniffing.

'We're going to do a DNA test. I know in my heart that I am his mother and I think he does too, but we both want proof. He told me where to go. You and I then fly home tomorrow, as planned, and Julian and I will obviously keep in touch. And I guess life will go on. Our family has suddenly changed shape and it's just a new dynamic for us all to adapt to.'

'I always thought Chris would be the addict. The amount of weed he smoked with Pete as a kid was nobody's business,' I said.

'Oh, I know. I always knew one of you would fall foul of mind-altering substances and for a long time I also thought it would be Chris. At least I didn't have wishy-washy boring kids.'

'Wishy-washy we are not. Poor Dad, living with us lot.'

'Poor Grandpa, too. Those two have seen it all.'

'Can we maybe just have like a stretch of dull and boring normal life now, for a change?' I asked.

'Nope! We are in full swing with wedding plans and Ela needs you to pick up your maid-of-honour duties. Oh, and we're all invited to Julian's wedding in Mozambique. The date is to be confirmed.'

'Awesome,' I said. It could only be better than my last Mozambique trip.

38

'The leather is still new, very stiff, Miss Kat,' said Jobb, helping me saddle up and adjust my stirrups. '*Eish*, Miss Kat, but it's nice you are home.'

'Thanks Jobb,' I said, mounting and settling into Mom's beautiful new saddle. 'Yes, it's good to be home. How is your family?'

'My daughter will have her first baby soon-soon,' he said, grinning proudly. I'd missed his big smile.

'Congratulations Jobb! *Sekuru!*.'

I'd been longing to ride again and today, my second day home, I was on Mom's latest addition to the stable, a palomino mare, rescued from displaced farmers in our old district and the most magnificent horse I'd seen in years.

I'd had dozens of phone calls to welcome me home and was feeling a little overwhelmed, still quite vulnerable and exposed. Needing some space, I set off for Dad's red-pepper fields, loving the hot and dry African air and the sounds coming from the dusty bush around me. The African doves in the msasa trees, the crickets and cicadas, the squawks from the odd crow that Grandpa hadn't killed, and a hawk playing high up on the currents – it was good to be back.

Coming home had been harder than I'd anticipated. I'd underestimated the power of the clinic in terms of the protection it offered and, while I'd not yet had any real temptations placed before me, I knew they were out there. A simple supermarket would be temptation, given the alcohol aisle. I already knew from Carol's role play that a pharmacy would challenge me and poke the Beast. It had come to me last night, the Beast, but in a dream rather than a physical presence. It was still small, but it was a clear message that the bastard had a passport and had not stayed in Cape Town.

Dad and Grandpa had had a beer with supper the night before and I'd felt a slight twitch when I heard the unmistakable glugging sound of beer being poured. I couldn't expect everyone around me to curtail their habits for my benefit. I was the one who had to change.

Last night I'd gone to an NA meeting with Maddie and tonight I'd go to AA with Mom and her sponsor Janet. Until I found my groove, I'd do a mix of NA and AA. They followed the same 12 Steps, merely interchanging the words 'drugs' and 'alcohol'. The NA group had once again been warm and welcoming and I'd left with five phone numbers – new friends I could call on day or night should I get a speed wobble. No one judged and there was genuine unconditional acceptance in 'the rooms'. Last night, I was told that getting clean was the easy part, but actually staying clean was a far bigger challenge – something I understood immediately.

The meeting formats never changed, which was grounding in itself. Even little Harare had a strong fellowship. There were only three NA meetings a week, but AA had gatherings every day. Drinking was, after all, practically our national sport. The ninety meetings in ninety days recommendation sounded like overkill to me, but nobody had promised this would be easy. Apparently, it could also be enjoyable.

I was sponsor-shopping at the meetings, scouting for a woman I could relate to. I'd thought about asking Maddie, but having to filter myself for fear of Mom hearing it all simply wouldn't work.

'Sponsors aren't necessarily friends,' Maddie had said last night. 'They're there to keep you real. One day when you're one yourself, you'll see how it helps the sponsor too.'

Mom and Maddie had given me Recovery books and were already like mother hens around me. Much as I loved knowing they were there for me, I needed to set some boundaries and not allow my Recovery to be their Recovery.

As I'd realised on my first night as a free woman, the world had not stopped turning while I was in rehab. I just wished it wasn't turning quite so fast now, while I was rejoining it. I wanted to hit the slow-motion button, gingerly put my foot back onto the carousel, and gently move forward. Instead, it felt like I was taking a flying leap at a fast-moving object, being hurtled back into the mainstream. And it all made me a little queasy.

As I rode alongside Dad's gorgeous crop of peppers, trying to ignore a thumping headache on top of all the anxiety, I savoured the earthy scent of clean and uncomplicated life and suddenly longed to be a red pepper. Far simpler than life and all its landmines.

I saw Grandpa's truck approaching, dust flying as he bombed down the track, shattering the silence with an old Rod Stewart cassette playing at full volume. It was a tape he'd been playing since 1991 when the eject button had snapped off and Rod took up permanent residence. Grandpa refused to get it fixed, so Rod was well stretched and it wasn't pleasant. Tighty was in the truck, his wild barking adding to the cacophony that made my horse skittish. Grandpa pulled up alongside me and cut the engine, Rod giving a strangled burp, mid-Maggie May.

'KitKat! What you doing out here on your own? Everything okay?' he asked cautiously, jumping out of the truck.

I smiled, realising this was going to happen a lot. We'd been warned in the clinic that the minute we were quiet and introspective, people would twitch and worry. Or suspect relapse.

'All fine, all good. I was just wishing I was a red pepper actually.'

I dismounted and we sat on the end of an old storm drain. Tighty, a panting heap, went to lie in the shade of the tree I had tethered my horse to.

'Ah, I see. Peppers you say?' said Grandpa. 'And why red, not yellow? There's a lot to be said for being a yellow pepper you know?'

I laughed. We were, and probably always would be, on the same wavelength.

'So KitKat, what's got you all dreamy and having pepper fantasies?'

'Just easing myself back into life, I guess. It's like I am about to step back out there, but as who or what, I don't know. I feel like I've been stripped naked and nobody's given me any new clothes to go out in.'

'Ah, a mini identity crisis?'

'Yes, I guess, but not so mini. I don't feel whole yet, Grandpa. Less broken, yes. But whole? Not entirely.'

'Sweetheart, don't underestimate yourself. Kat is back, I can see her. I think you got so lost in the wilderness that you wouldn't recognise Kat if she bit you on your own arse, but she's back, trust me.'

'In rehab, they taught us a load of stuff about wearing masks. Thing is I quite liked wearing them. They served a purpose.'

'No, correction – they served a purpose in your active addiction, not in your Recovery,' Grandpa said, picking his teeth with a piece of dry grass. 'You've got everything to live for, Kat. You can do great things with your life. Try not to complicate things and don't analyse the crap out of everything and anything. You'll have no fun if you live like that. Simple things, my dear child. It's the simple things that will sustain you from here on.'

'That's why I thought I'd rather be a red pepper. Much simpler.'

'Yeah, but then you'd just end up in a salad or a stir-fry and then into the sewerage. Where's the fun in that?'

I giggled. I'd missed Grandpa's nonsense.

'Don't waste your youth, Kat. I'd give anything to be a youngster again.'

'Would you do anything differently?'

'Probably not. I've had a good and happy life. It's not been without hurdles or heartache though. I miss your Gran like hell, but we'll meet again one day. That I do believe. Until then, I shall just enjoy what's left of the ride,' said Grandpa, gazing into the distance.

I leant over and took a cigarette from his pocket. We both lit up, enjoying the moment.

'I lie,' said Grandpa reflectively, 'I would do one thing differently.'

'Mmm?' I said, inhaling.

'I'd never have let that bastard rapist in Malawi anywhere near my family. Or I would have killed him with my bare hands. At least the Bush Court saw justice was achieved. My men didn't let me down.' There was an uncharacteristic flash of anger in his eyes.

I took Grandpa's lovely, big, rough hand and held it. We sat in companionable silence.

'Must say, I'm looking forward to meeting my new grandson though,' said Grandpa a while later.

'Julian? Ah, he's great. Bloody scary counsellor but a lovely man under that.'

'I still think it's the coincidence of the fucking century, but anyway. So Kat, what about Ant now?'

'What about him? He's moved on, I must too,' I said, shrugging, feeling a sudden sting.

'He still loves you.'

'Says who? I've not even heard from him.'

'Says me. He phoned me yesterday. He phoned me every week you were away.'

'Really?' I was very surprised.

'Yup.'

'And what does he say?'

'Well, he asks how you are – but it's not about what he's saying, it's about what he's saying by calling me. He adores you. His fling with Jess, the Vic Falls trollop, is over by the way. He says he's had more intelligent conversations with a fence post.'

I snorted a laugh.

'You should call him,' said Grandpa.

'I didn't think he gave a shit about me.'

'Pfft! Is a bullfrog's bum watertight? Course he gives a shit. The boy is crazy mad in love with you and was beside himself with worry. I half expected him to fly down and visit you in rehab.'

'Fuck no! Serious?'

'I shit you not.'

'In the clinic we were told to avoid relationships for the first year. We must get a plant and if the plant lives for a year, then we can get a pet. If we don't kill the pet after a year, only then can we go relationship shopping,' I said. 'Knowing me and my fantastic relationship skills, never mind plants and pets, I'd probably kill the boyfriend too.'

'Pah! You gotta take some of what they say with a pinch of salt. That's two years' celibacy! What about people who leave rehab and resume existing relationships? Like your mother who came home to her husband? And even she hasn't killed him yet.'

'Yes, I asked that too and was accused of backchat.'

'Listen Kat, rehab has saved your life, no question. But you have a good head on you, now that you're not shit-faced from dawn till dusk. Just go slowly and carefully. Ant is a good man who will support your Recovery.

I am not saying rush in, I'm saying give him a call and just have a meal together. Keep things simple. Make your amends and, if there is anything left after your damage control, take it as it comes. You do know he came to Al-Anon with me, huh?'

'Yes, he said so in the letter he wrote. Shit that was a harsh letter, Grandpa,' I said, remembering the intense pain, like metal claws, that had gripped my heart and ripped it out.

'The level of harshness reflected his level of love. It hurt him to write that letter, more than you know.'

'You two really do get along like a house on fire. How come he's been calling you and not Mom?'

'Because your mother scares the shit out of him and he's convinced your father still oils his shotgun purely for his benefit. Dunno Kat, we get along, that's all. Nothing sinister.'

I was stunned to realise Ant was still in the loop, on the fringes of my life.

'Right, my little red pepper, it's getting hot as hell and your horse and dog need water so let's trot on. I'll see you later. Good chat,' he said, hauling himself up with a dramatic moan.

Grandpa gave me a leg-up, then he and Tighty clambered back into the truck, disappearing in a haze of dust with a very ill Rod Stewart.

That afternoon, life wasn't feeling quite as scary. There was a glimmer of hope regarding Ant. I had to admit it had cheered me up more than anything. Still, I didn't dare get my hopes up, fearing the crushing pain of rejection.

My next hurdle was my cellphone. I had yet to turn it on, delaying for one reason alone – Colin. After my role-play fiasco, I was terrified. One call, and the Beast would sit up and say 'Hey ho, Kat! Check what the cat dragged in – it's our old friend Colin. Meet him. Score drugs. Yum! Get wasted. Yum!'

Over dinner, I asked Dad about changing my number.

'That's going to be tricky,' he said. 'The cellular networks are over-subscribed and they're not issuing new numbers. Chris is battling to get a line for Ela too.'

It was Grandpa's idea to swop my cell number with his. He was quite eager to tell Colin where to go anyway. It seemed the best option and so we switched our SIM cards, Grandpa checking he'd saved Colin's number so he'd be identified. I then started the laborious process of sending texts, advising everybody of the switch. Grandpa only had us, Jobb, and his muckers at the pub to notify, so he was done in minutes. He said he'd leave it to me to tell Ant, pointing out it was the perfect reason for me to make contact. My gut lurched. I'd wait a few days and just hope Ant didn't call Grandpa in the interim.

An hour later, Dad, Grandpa and I were on the couch, sharing a pile of biltong and watching Australia whip South Africa at cricket, when Grandpa's phone rang. He looked at the screen and snorted.

'Aha. That didn't take long,' he said.

Colin. My pulse started racing.

'Hello,' said Grandpa, answering the call and switching to speaker phone.

'Urh, is Kat there?' said Colin.

Just hearing his voice made my gut turn. I hugged a cushion to my chest.

'Who's asking?' replied Grandpa.

'Why?' said Colin.

'I said, who is asking?' Grandpa spoke slowly, his tone hostile.

'Umm, a friend of hers. Colin. Is she around?'

'Ah, Colin old chap, I've heard all about you. Kat raves about you. I'm a friend of hers too. How're you doing?'

'Err, I'm fine. Is Kat there?'

Grandpa ignored the question. 'How's business been? Kat says you only supply the good shit?'

'Yup, only the best for my people, you know,' said Colin.

'No seriously, Colin, how's business? Must have been a bit slow what with Kat being away,' Grandpa goaded.

'Actually it's been flat-out busy as always. Supply and demand, you know. There are plenty of Kats in this town. Plenty of fucked-up junkies to feed.'

I was disgusted and wanted to grab the phone, reach in and gouge Colin's eyes out.

'Yeah, can't beat 'em join 'em, huh?' said Grandpa.

'Umm, so do you need some gear? Who are you though, first? You sound ancient,' Colin said.

Oh fuck, I thought, here we go.

'Do I need some gear you ask, Colin?' said Grandpa, lighting a cigarette and sighing. 'What I need, you little scumbag drug-dealing piece of shit, is for you to get fucked. Kat has changed her number – but if you so much as think about finding her you will regret it. First, a few associates of mine, specialists in the ancient art of kneecap remodelling by baseball bat, will find you, beat seven shades of shit out of you and make walking a thing of the past. Then I will expose your dealing to the Medicines Control Council, which means you will be struck off and will never work as a pharmacist again. Finally, I will let the police finish up with some nice criminal charges. And Colin, I am sure you know, a little boy like you in a Zimbabwean prison is just fresh meat for all those big strapping boys. And boy do they love a nice, fresh, tight, virgin arse. You may well pick up a pesky little virus too. You may have heard of it? HIV? Or does the idea of violent gang rape within minutes appeal to you? You piece of scum.'

Grandpa let the question hang, taking a casual drag on his cigarette. Dad's eyebrows were resting somewhere behind his ears. There was dead silence from Colin.

'Any questions Colin? Shall I fax you a picture?' asked Grandpa.

The line went dead. Colin had hung up.

Grandpa leant back in the couch, took a deep breath and looked at the TV. 'So, what's the score now? Little wanker made me miss that last over.'

Mom, standing in the doorway, wore a look of total shock. Meanwhile I was practically hyperventilating. Go Grandpa! Done, dusted, message delivered and there was no further discussion needed. Colin had been dealt with and Grandpa was my hero. I simply looked at him, thanking him with my eyes.

'Biltong, Grandpa?' I said, handing him the bowl.

'Lovely, Kat, ta. Would ya' look at that,' he said, pointing at the TV. 'Bloody useless butterfingers, how could he drop that catch? Disgrace!'

Our family evening resumed as if nothing had happened.

Late that night, alone in my cottage – thrilled to have the first Colin phone call out the way – I had an overwhelming urge to tell a friend about it. She answered the phone right away. I knew she'd be on night shift.

'*POOKIE!*' she shouted. 'How's my *pookie?*'

Pat and I had a long chat, like we we'd been friends since childhood. She loved hearing how Grandpa had sent Colin packing, her big laugh from a million miles away making me so happy but oh-so homesick for my family in a rehab by the sea. I asked Pat to tell Gina and Carol the story. I went to sleep happy, but also wishing I could tell the story on the patio, with Sarah, Tina and Donovan cheering me on.

Early the next morning, I had a short email from Carol.

Is Grandpa available to do freelance role-play coaching in a rehab by the sea? Love Carol.

It made my day.

That week, I settled into a comfortable routine of NA meetings, family time and a very tame social life, trying to keep life simple. My feelings of exposure were subsiding and life was feeling okay again. I lived with a degree of pain and daily headaches, but was no longer caught in a vicious cycle of rebound headaches caused by the painkillers. I was learning to manage my pain and pretty much kept it to myself.

I hung out with Ela and Chris, loving being around Ben and Katie again. I also met Andrew and Vicky for lunch and they couldn't get enough of my funny stories about rehab and all its weirdos. Rolo was away on some work training course, although I suspected it was a dirty long weekend.

With every catch-up, I made suitable amends to those I'd hurt. And everyone accepted my apologies with good grace. Slowly, the slates were being wiped clean. I still had to speak to Stephen though. I grappled with it for ages and finally sought guidance from my new NA mates who urged me to arrange a lunch and just do it. Amends to bosses who'd fired your arse were evidently common in NA.

Stephen sounded genuinely pleased to hear from me when I rang. Our lunch was long and draining, but I managed to start setting things right. At no point did I ask for, or expect to be given, my old job back. In fact, Stephen gave me some good advice on finding a new job and how to get my CV into shape, even saying he'd write me a reference, now he could see with his own eyes that I might just live after all.

I got home all fired up, and rewrote my CV. I started to flick 'please can I have a job' emails out to other PR agencies, selling myself like never before. I'd have a job by the weekend, for sure.

There was a deathly silence in my inbox. Only the odd joke and one or two notifications about winning a million dollars in an international lotto, urging me to reply immediately with my bank details. Bored out of my bracket, I replied to one of them, saying they were welcome to defraud me but my bank account was empty. I was broke and jobless.

39

'She's a pill muncher, like us,' said Maddie, kissing me hello.

Maddie had asked me to go with her on a 12th Step call, which was all about 'carrying the message to the still-suffering addict'. Maddie had volunteered to do these calls for NA and they'd had a request from the patient's doctor for a visit. A 12th Step call in a hospital meant the person was in bad shape and she figured it'd be a good reality check for me.

The girl sure was screwed-up and in a deep hole, her tale so like those I'd heard in the clinic. I had a vivid flashback to Cassie, how suicide had been her best option. The girl's doctor had hospitalised her to detox from prescription drugs, and yet, when we asked what medication she'd been put on, she rattled off a list as long as her arm. She was now on more drugs than when she'd crawled in. Maddie and I left feeling drained, acutely aware of how fortunate we'd been to do proper rehab.

'There is just no one in this town who specialises in addictions,' said Maddie over coffee afterwards. 'You ask for help detoxing so they throw you in hospital and load you up to the eyeballs with tranquillisers, antidepressants and sleeping pills. Basically, kicking off a whole new set of drug dependencies while you're supposed to be getting clean.'

'That chick is nowhere near clean,' I said.

'Indeed. No doctor in this hick bloody town has the first clue how to treat a detox. We need a proper rehab, with correctly managed detoxes and an active four-week programme. It's a sad case of haves and have-nots. That poor girl will never have the money, but she's hardcore and will be dead in a matter of months, just like you would have been.'

Maddie sure was getting worked up but I could see her point.

'Look, some people can manage cold turkey detox on their own, and stay clean by working the programme and doing meetings. But others need specialised care, yet will never get it as long as it has a hefty price tag and is in another country,' Maddie continued.

'But then, why has no one opened a rehab here?' I asked.

'Exactly,' Maddie sighed.

'And there is no shrink here who understands addiction?'

'As far as I am concerned, no. Look at that winner of a shrink you went to. She just gave you Rohypnol, a HECTIC drug that you never even knew about until she meddled. I couldn't believe it when I heard.'

'Yes, my mates in the clinic were quite impressed that I was good friends with Rohypnol.'

'You were on methadone in the clinic, weren't you?'

'Yup. It came with free day trips to Mars. And Pluto. It dried up before I could do Saturn.'

Maddie shook her head at me, chuckling. 'Well, methadone has not been used here in years. Don't think it is even available now.'

'I didn't realise how dire the situation is.'

'In the few years since I saw the light, I have been to many funerals. Deaths that could have been avoided. And it's child's play to get drugs to the addicts in these hospitals. No search on admission and visitors aren't controlled. Your mate Colin does a lot of dealing in the hospitals.'

'Really?' My heart fluttered, hearing his name.

'Yes. The little arse-wipe. He was my dealer too, for your info. Remember when we saw him at that AA meeting. "He's our IT guy," you said, like butter wouldn't melt in your bloody mouth.'

Ooops, I thought, also suddenly remembering my four Great Danes and wondering if Maddie would bring that up too.

'For years, NA and AA have tried to get more doctors on board and have highlighted the need for a local rehab.'

'Are there really enough addicts and alcoholics in this town to warrant one?' I asked.

'Plenty of us. A small twenty-bed clinic would be full all year.'

'So, what are we waiting for?'

'A lot of money and counsellors. That's all Kat. No biggie.'

40

'You're glowing,' I said to Rolo as I hugged her tightly. 'Actually, you look like the bloody cat that licked the cream.'

All she could do was grin at me. So pleased to finally see her, I got all tearful, setting her off too. In the middle of Coimbra, we hugged, cried, and then giggled.

'So, what has got you all glowing and twinkling in the eyes?' I asked.

Rolo gave a guilty smile.

'You're in love,' I said.

Rolo blushed ever so slightly and nodded, still beaming.

'Who?' I asked.

'Mr Financial Director—'

'No! Rolo! He's married.'

'Not anymore. It's been such a whirlwind . . .'

I braced myself for tales of adultery.

'They – Shane and his wife – split up. So we're officially together.'

'Oh Rolo, that poor woman. Don't you feel even a little bad for breaking them up?'

'No, no, no – *she* left *him*! She was having an affair and came clean.'

'Oh. So you don't qualify as a home wrecker?'

'No! Thanks very much, but that's not a badge I wear.'

'Then I'm very happy for you.'

'A couple of people at work aren't too happy but I don't give a shit.

Anyway, enough about my man, what's the status quo with you and Ant?'

'Status schmatus. The status is that there isn't one.' I still hadn't had the courage to contact him. 'Grandpa insists he still has feelings and that I must make comms. Ant wrote me a letter in the clinic that nearly killed me.'

'Yes, I heard about the letter. It nearly killed him too. I saw him a few weeks ago at a family lunch. He and I spoke for hours. It turned into a bit of a mini Al-Anon meeting and we both ended up in floods of tears. But basically, all he could talk about was you.'

A sharp stab of fresh guilt hit my heart, a physical pain.

'I want to reach out and apologise, but I don't think I'm strong enough yet. It's too sore still. I'm too terrified to take my eye off the ball. I don't want to relapse, Rolo. It was a living hell.'

'None of us wants to see you go down that road again. Do you still love Ant?'

'Yes. But I shouldn't. I've had the fear of God put into me about how relationships in Recovery are Russian Roulette.'

'Take a leap of faith with Ant.'

'But how?'

She sat back and looked thoughtful. 'Pass me your phone.'

I plonked it on the table and within seconds Rolo was typing a message.

'Show me before you send it.'

'Yes, yes, keep your slippers on.'

Ant, hope you're well. Am back from boot camp & living on this planet again. Would love to meet for a coffee & chat, if you're keen? Love K

'See? Short, simple, light,' said Rolo. 'Shall I send it?'

I curled my lip. 'But what if he rejects me?' It truly was my biggest fear.

'Well, then *c'est la vie* and your life won't actually be any different to what it is now. You will live. But if he gives you a second chance you have everything to gain. Stay focused, and remember that text is about making amends, not about dating again. Make your peace, and see where things go.'

My tears welled up and Rolo started passing tissues. 'I feel terrible about what I did, not just to Ant, to you all. I'm so sorry, my friend.'

'Yes, you were a mess and none of it was pretty. We were all traumatised by your behaviour, some of us still are. I, personally, could have throttled you, but we still love and stand by you. Now love yourself too, and be proud of yourself. I'm proud of you. And start thinking about peeling off that first layer of cotton wool you've now wrapped yourself in. Don't take risks, but don't hide behind your Recovery either.'

Nodding, I gave a snotty, wet, gurgle of a laugh. While Rolo toyed with my phone, her own phone beeped and we both jumped. It was a message from Shane that made her all smiley. She gave it to me to read.

Sweet Caroline, my angel, the minute you're out of my sight I want you back. Enjoy your dinner darling. x

I raised an eyebrow. 'Sweet Caroline? You're dating Neil bloody Diamond. Can't remember when I last heard you called Caroline.'

'See now, wouldn't you like to be getting messages like that, lovely words that make your knees wobbly?'

'I suppose.'

'So, shall we send Ant the message?'

'Umm, okay. Yes. Shit – no! Alright, do it,' I spat the last two words out before I changed my mind.

Quick as a flash, Rolo hit send. My phone beeped, confirming delivery and we sat back, staring at the phone on the table, willing it to beep again with a reply. Then we started giggling like schoolgirls.

'Right, now let's forget about it. Tell me more about this new brother of yours? I still can't quite get my head around it. Are you sure our Gill hasn't been drinking again?'

With many weeks of news to unpack, we were the last ones to leave Coimbra that night. As we got up, I waved my phone under Rolo's nose.

'See – two hours and no reply. He's probably with some chick, laughing at me.'

'Be patient. And stop being such an addict and drama queen.'

In a huff, I threw my phone into my handbag. As I rummaged in its depths looking for my car keys, there was a beep and my handbag lit up. I got such a fright that I dropped everything. I fell to my knees and lunged for my phone, ignoring the lipstick, chewing gum, and tampons that had flown out, landing next to the manager's foot as he waited to lock up behind us.

'Is it Ant?' asked Rolo excitedly.

I gulped, nodding. I hadn't even stood up to read it.

Hi babe, so good to hear from you, glad you're doing ok. Yes, would love to catch up. Up at Kariba at the mo but back in town next weekend. I'll call you then. x

'Babe?' said Rolo, joining me kneeling on the floor, peering at my phone. 'And he's put a kiss there. Happy now?'

I grinned like a fool. I came back to the present, hearing someone standing over Rolo and me pointedly clear their throat.

'Is this perhaps yours?' said Coimbra's manager, holding a tampon.

'Oh, keep the change,' Rolo said chuckling as we both stood up.

I smacked Rolo on the shoulder and relieved the poor man of my tampon. We headed out, chuckling.

'And you girls haven't even been drinking tonight, for a change,' said the manager, laughing too.

'Yeah, she just spent five weeks in rehab and is off the sauce,' replied Rolo, getting another smack from me.

That night in bed, I read Ant's message another twenty times. A feeling of nervous anticipation set in. Some clever person at NA had recently told me that Higher Powers only ever give us what we can handle. Humpf, I thought, we shall have to see about my handling abilities.

My Higher Power obviously decided that I couldn't handle seeing Ant, not that weekend anyway. On Friday, he called me to say one of their guides had malaria and he had to fill in. He'd be away for at least three to four weeks. Oh well, more time to get my head straight, I thought, both disappointed and a little relieved.

I began to wonder if I'd ever find another job. I'd not had a single nibble in response to my emails, the tone of which now bordered on begging. Chris pointed out that, with the economy so tumultuous, I couldn't be job hunting at a worse time.

Knowing that the Beast loved boredom, I did everything I could to keep busy. I even worked for Dad – up early and overseeing the pepper pickers in the sorting shed. Then I'd go for long rides in the afternoons or do some Step work before shooting off to NA or AA in the evenings. I felt horribly unfulfilled though. Having to ask Dad for cigarette and petrol money was somewhat soul-destroying too.

Suddenly, the Universe started playing nice.

One day, as I was about to send my CV in for a menial secretarial job, my phone rang. It was Jenny Merton, asking me to pop in. Why my doctor had called me in, out of the blue, was beyond me. I headed off albeit a little nervously, convinced some shady behaviour from my past was about to resurface and bite me on the arse.

After a lovely hug, some chit-chat about rehab and the parts they didn't put in the brochure, and a minute or two on how I was handling my headaches, Doc Merton placed an envelope in front of me. I found a cheque inside. A rather large cheque, made out to me. Seeing my jaw hit the floor, she began to explain.

'Remember that ER doctor who misdiagnosed you as having indigestion? Well, both I and your gastric surgeon were so outraged that we couldn't *not* take formal action. On your behalf, we appointed lawyers to sue the doctor and the hospital itself. Actually, we appointed my father's legal firm as he specialises in medical malpractice – part of the reason I became a doctor. Anyway, we expected a lengthy court case, but they came to us early, wanting to settle out of court. They put some money on the table, we bargained a bit, got them to raise the offer and, well, it's all yours, Kitt-hiy.'

'Bloody hell!' She was going to tell me it was a joke, for sure.

Doc Merton laughed. 'I have been DYING to see your reaction.'

'So, this is for real? You're not playing?' I asked incredulously, flapping the cheque. I was holding at least twelve years' worth of salaries.

'For real. Doctors always have hefty insurance policies. Turns out this one had a similar malpractice case last year and wanted to buy our silence quickly. He was under big pressure from the hospital to settle too.'

I went around her desk and threw my arms around her. 'Thank you *so* much.'

'Ah Kat, my pleasure. You have a special place in my heart. I was so terrified we'd lose you and wanted to help you, in some small way, to get your life back on track.'

'This is hardly small. And the timing couldn't be better, what with me being an unemployed lout.'

'Enjoy it – treat yourself.'

That night over supper, everyone thought I was talking shit, even when I passed the cheque around. Although I had a feeling Mom knew all along as she'd winked at me. The sneak!

The next day I deposited the money and immediately transferred the cost of rehab into Dad's bank account. Then I phoned Rolo, Vicky, Andrew, Chris and Ela and told them to take leave as I was booking a Kariba houseboat.

I felt liberated and independent again, although still bored to sobs every day. I had to find a job.

Mom announced that Julian was coming to visit, en route to Sandra and Vincent in Mozambique for three weeks' holiday. Aside from meeting the family, he'd be wearing his addictions counsellor hat. Mom had told him about the dire rehab situation and he was going to meet some of Harare's so-called medical professionals and enlighten them, especially around medicated detoxes. Who knows, maybe he could make a difference.

All flappy about Julian's visit, Mom kicked into manic domestic mode and the guest bedroom suddenly got a major face lift.

'I don't want him thinking we are backward hillbilly farmer types,' said Mom as I helped her with pillow cases in the guest room.

'Sorry Gill, I didn't get that memo. Are we no longer hillbillies then?' said Grandpa, coming in to inspect Julian's room. He chuckled at Mom's faffing, tenderly stroking her new scatter cushions and wearing a wicked look.

'What does one have to do around here to get fancy cushions on their bed? Oh wait, do you have to be adopted?' he said.

'Give that here Dad. Tsk! You'll make it all grubby, look at your bloody hands, they're filthy,' snapped Mom, snatching a cream cushion from Grandpa. 'Out, both of you, scat. And I don't want Tighty coming in here and buggering up the bed, Kat.'

'Come on Kat, let's leave Martha Stewart to her soft furnishings,' said Grandpa. 'Let's go shoot some crows. Bastards have been in my red peppers again.'

The following weekend Mom went to meet Julian at the airport while everyone gathered at the house for what Grandpa had coined The

Unveiling of Julian. Mom had invited her sponsor Janet, and also Linda and Tim, Maddie and Kevin. Rolo brought Shane, also being unveiled. In the kitchen making salads, Rolo pointed out that only in our family could we gather five recovering addicts and alcoholics around one table and consider it perfectly normal.

'Maddie, Janet, you, Julian, and your mother,' said Rolo. 'I should ask for the magic password to access the inner circle.'

'Careful what you wish for,' I laughed. She was right – junkies and piss artists everywhere. Meanwhile, Grandpa and Chris were sinking beers as fast as possible, nervous about meeting Julian.

Mom came striding into the kitchen a few minutes later, with him in tow.

'Julian! Welcome. I don't think you'll miss the clinic too much with all the nutters here,' I said, giving him a hug before introducing Rolo.

'Good to see you Kat. You're looking fantastic,' said Julian.

Rolo swooned as he left. 'Jaaayzus, Kat, why didn't you tell me your new brother was so hot?' she said, flapping a tea towel to cool herself.

Outside, Julian was passed around like a bowl of peanuts but he didn't falter; he was full of warmth as he met the gang. Dad, usually the most cool and calm of us all, suddenly came over all shy. Chris seemed a bit awkward too, meeting his big brother. Grandpa shook Julian's hand and then changed his mind mid-greeting and went for the full bear hug, both thumping each other on the back like dear old friends.

'Right, who needs drinks?' said Grandpa, 'Julian, beer?'

'Urh, well I don't—' said Julian.

'HA! Gotcha,' said Grandpa, laughing. 'Don't stress, I know you're a teetotaller. Bloody overrun by them these days.'

'Dad, go easy on him,' said Mom. 'Julian, you'll get used to it. Meet the family clown.'

We had a long, happy lunch. Julian, the poor man, didn't draw breath. Despite it all going well, Mom looked tense and was smoking again. She wanted everyone to accept Julian and for him to feel comfy and part of our quirky, odd-shaped family. Much later, when I was clearing up, I overheard Linda and Mom chatting.

'You did good today Gill, what a lovely day. You must be shattered though. It's a big step, having him here. Big for both of you.'

'I hope I don't screw it up,' I heard Mom say. 'I'm a bundle of nerves, terrified he might reject us and rather stick with the family he knows. We are, after all, a bunch of lunatics and he works with them all day.'

'Relax Gill, just enjoy his company and stay in the moment. Ground yourself – you'll both find your groove.'

The next few days flew by and Julian slotted into our family effortlessly. It helped that he shared our sense of humour – a bit warped and always dry. Grandpa and Dad spent some time alone with him, proudly showing off their veggie empire. Chris took him off for eighteen holes and every night Julian came to either AA with Mom or NA meetings with me. Mom couldn't help proudly introducing Julian as her son – a 'highly respected addictions counsellor'– to all her AA muckers. The three of us made quite a splash in the meetings that week. Talk about a family disease.

Julian had also managed to meet our so-called addictions specialists and shrinks, and was appalled by the lack of treatment available.

'Look, I'm not a doctor, but I do know the drugs they are prescribing are from the Ark,' said Julian over dinner on his last night. 'I mean, drugs for bipolar disorders, Rohypnol cocktails and even epilepsy drugs, all being prescribed for addictions. It's outrageous. Okay, so you don't feel the detox on them – you don't feel anything at all – but you quickly form a dependence. It's pure substitution, one addiction for another. Detox my arse!'

'I told you it's dire here,' said Mom.

'Your doctors don't see addiction holistically, they see a medical problem and treat the symptoms, not the cause. No thought is given to the behavioural aspect behind addictions, or what made the patient seek oblivion in the first place. But, if you go to a shrink about it, hey presto, you come out with another prescription.'

'Yup, go figure,' I said.

'I honestly can't get over it. I mean, look at you, Kat. A neck injury created a chronic pain condition and cavalier doctors just ushered you into a very dark place, knowing how addictive those pharmaceuticals are. And look where you landed up – one of the most extreme addictions Carol and I have seen in all our years as counsellors. Granted, in the end you scored from a dealer not a doctor, but your neurologist could have been more responsible and your GP could have intervened much earlier, before your gut blew. Shit, the first few nights you were in the clinic, we seriously doubted you'd make it, you were that sick. Your blood tests that first night showed opiate levels that would take a horse down, and you weighed thirty-eight kilograms. As for your hallucinations, even Pat was scared and you know she's one tough cookie.'

Julian's recap hit me like a ton of bricks. I was shocked. Mom looked at me sadly, shaking her head to remember me at my worst.

Julian went on. 'And one of your Chinese doctors I spoke to laughed when I said that painkillers and sedatives are as addictive as heroin. I don't think he even knows codeine is the same class of drug as heroin. Where do these fools get their medical degrees? Methadone seems to be a contentious issue too. It's not available here, even under monitored controls. Any rehab, African or otherwise, uses methadone, or a variety thereof, for an opiate detox. I've not made myself very popular with your doctors, I'm afraid.'

'Good, they need a shake up,' I replied. 'The pharmacists need educating too.'

'Pah! Addicts are their gravy train,' said Mom.

'Remember though, these old-school doctors are men of science and don't subscribe to the fact that addiction is a disease and, largely, a behavioural and compulsive disorder. It's almost too "touchy-feely" and new age for them,' said Julian. 'I find younger doctors far more holistic. You just don't seem to have any of them in Harare. Look, there isn't a magic pill that will cure addiction. The only way is by abstinence, be it in a 12 Step programme or a similar, controlled way of life. Doctors can hardly write a prescription saying "Don't get high, don't get pissed, repeat every twenty-four hours". But rehabs exist the world over because they work.'

Then, that night, something big was born, but we weren't really aware of it at the time. Julian took Mom's dream, rewrapped it and gave it back to her.

'So, Gill, how serious are you about setting up a private rehab?'

'It'd be a massive undertaking, just the medical side alone,' replied Mom.

'Yes, but not impossible,' said Julian.

'Nah? You really think it'd be viable? I mean the country is fast going down the bog – how can we set up a rehab in these conditions? It'd take masses of money too. It's a pipe dream, Julian. The ramblings of a sober middle-aged woman.'

'Don't look at it so negatively. See the opportunity under your nose,' said Julian.

Mom looked extremely sceptical.

'Gill, I've been thinking long and hard about setting up the first real rehab in Zim. I want to help. Why don't you write a business proposal and let's see exactly what we'd need. Medical and nursing staff, premises, legal issues, medical licences, housekeeping, and so on. Think of every detail.'

'Wow,' I said slowly, looking at it from a business angle for the first time.

'Hey, perhaps this is the bigger reason for us reconnecting at last, because together we can actually help some very sick people,' said Julian. 'I know many people in the rehab world who'd be happy to advise us. I might even have an ace up my sleeve for funding.'

I could almost see Mom's dream come to life right there. She was looking a tad shell-shocked.

'Start small. Fifteen beds,' said Julian.

'And your funding ace?' Mom asked.

'Ah. Money. The fun part,' said Julian. 'It's an interesting story about a private Trust in the UK. In the sixties, there was this Englishman who was an alcoholic—'

'Sounds like the start of a bad bar joke,' I interrupted.

'Yeah, it sure does,' replied Julian.

He went on to tell the story of an Englishman with buckets of old family money, who'd moved to South Africa where he spent many years as a practising alcoholic. Eventually his wife threw him into a rehab where he finally got his act together, but he died when he was in his sixties, the years of drinking having left his liver in tatters. But, for the last few years of his life, his marriage had been happy again and his wife was eternally grateful for all things Recovery. She promised to use their considerable wealth to help the less fortunate with drug and alcohol problems and to fund treatment centres. The grieving widow set up a Trust which, every year, donates twelve months of operational funding to one rehab. With a clinic's overheads covered, patient fees get slashed and the facility can offer treatment to those who'd never be able to afford it normally. The Trust specifically favours rehabs in Africa that are struggling to start up or stay in business.

'What a fascinating charity model,' Mom said.

'It's slick and smart, and a well-kept secret, this Trust. You only get to hear about it in the rehab world. They frown on any publicity and it's highly discreet. The widow has since died, but the Trust has a Board of Administrators in London. You also get free business mentorship from the head of the biggest rehab in the UK,' said Julian.

'So how does one take a shot at it?' I asked.

'It needs a business proposal, hence my suggestion. Then you submit and the Board appraises all the bids.'

'Sounds like a tender process of sorts,' I said.

'Similar. The first rehab I worked at submitted an application and I did most of the paperwork. Let's apply for start-up costs and then overheads for the first year,' said Julian.

'That, Julian, is a shitload of money,' said Mom.

'I happen to know that the kind of money we'd need would just be skimming off interest. Oh, and it helps to give the presentation in person. Let's both go, Momsy,' he said smiling.

'What? To the UK? You really think we should take a shot at it?' Mom asked both Julian and me.

'Julian, would you really consider moving to Harare?' I asked.

'Why not? I'll help you set this up Gill, spend a year, maybe two, in Zim. As you said the other day, despite the political nonsense the lifestyle here is still bloody good. This town needs proper addictions counsellors. If I can help people, especially the less fortunate, overcome their demons, that's what matters, not my home address.'

'What would Carol say?' Mom asked.

'I've been there nearly five years and am getting itchy feet. You get rehab stale in this business, and counsellors move around to stay fresh and focused. I've always dreamt of a project like this, I've just never met anyone as mad as myself who'd want to open a rehab. But my mother is definitely mad enough. I'd considered doing something similar in Mozambique, but now see that Zim is probably more viable. And I need a business partner otherwise I wouldn't have the time to counsel. I'd just be a business owner, which I'd hate.'

'And what about your fiancé?' I asked.

'Victoire has always known I might do something like this and has actually encouraged it. We'll work it out. Don't stress about that part because, girls, we've got a goddam rehab to open!' said Julian, all fired up. 'The key to a successful Zim rehab will be the medical side of things. You'd need to import the best specialists. For that, you'll have to dangle decent foreign currency salaries,' he continued.

Mom nodded. 'So, in year one, patients pay a subsidised rate. In year two, we step up the rates and make money?'

'Yup, but we'd always keep a few free beds for the less fortunate,' said Julian. 'Word of advice – the Trust doesn't like to get involved in real estate. We should try to secure premises, provisionally.'

'That's tricky – to lease or even buy a house provisionally. Plus, it'd have to be a huge place,' I said.

'A large house can be converted fairly easily. Four beds in each room is normal, so look at a five- or six-bedroomed house,' said Julian.

Mom sat there, still shell-shocked.

'Come on Mom, for years you've been thinking about this. At least give it a shot or you'll never know,' I said.

'Yes, writing a business plan won't cost you anything. What's to lose?' said Julian.

'Okay, okay. I'll start put some thoughts on paper. I must be bloody crazy,' said Mom.

And there it was. A dream of Mom's now growing into far more than just a good idea.

41

It was just gone dawn and the new sun had made pretty patterns in the sky. I was plodding down to the sorting shed to deal with the pepper picking, a fag hanging from my mouth as I threw sticks for Tighty. I was just wondering what my life had come to when my cellphone rang. It was Stephen.

'I hope I haven't woken you,' he said.

'Believe it or not, I'm up at dawn sorting red peppers these days.'

'Ah. I wanted to ask a favour, but if you're busy, don't worry.'

'No problem. What's up?'

'We're running a two-day conference and the new admin girl just called in sick. I wondered if you might fancy two days' temp work, running the registration desk for me? Four hundred delegates are arriving in ninety minutes, if the peppers can spare you?'

I nearly fell face first into a bush in surprise. 'Err, yes, of course. Gosh. That'd be awesome, Stephen.'

Within milliseconds I'd turned on my heel, sprinting back to my cottage to get ready, my purple gumboots making a deep, rhythmical *flump flump* sound as I woke the garden. Tighty, a big fan of any running gumboot, was trying to maul my left ankle as I belted along.

In my excitement, I didn't realise I hadn't ended the call. A voice wafted up from my hand. 'What's that noise, Kat?' I suddenly heard Stephen ask.

'That, Stephen, is the sound of my purple gumboots rushing in your direction,' I said, panting loudly, holding my side as a stitch took hold. Shit, I was unfit.

'Well, if you could bring a change of shoes, that'd be great,' he said.

I flew into the shower and within an hour I was looking every bit the career girl, face painted, suited and stilettoed as I sped into town, grinning.

They were the best two days of my year and there wasn't a single glitch at the Registration and Help desk. Shame on you, new admin girl, for calling in sick. Oh, the irony.

I had to laugh when I got an email from Dad that night, a written warning for my 'absenteeism without suitable notification'. I worked a double sorting shift on Sunday as penance.

I didn't dare get my hopes up about Stephen giving me a second chance. But maybe he would.

Ant was already at the coffee shop. My gut flipped when I saw him, looking all fit and tanned, and way more gorgeous than I remembered him ever being. I'd put much thought into my look, settling on jeans with a bit of bling on the bum pocket and a classic white shirt, a few undone buttons announcing a new lacy Wonderbra, lots of bangles and a chunky red-and-bronze roped necklace. I'd had my hair done yesterday, lovely bold highlights, all casually piled up high on my head, and I felt tall in strappy red polka-dot wedges.

He saw me and stood up, taking me in. Suddenly, I didn't think I could do this, wondering if I could just leg it out of there.

'So good to see you,' said Ant, giving me a long, tight hug and a kiss on the cheek.

His arms just felt right.

'Hey!' I replied, wondering if I sounded as strung out as I felt.

'Wow, look at you. Gorgeous Kat is back.'

He hugged me again, this time tighter and longer.

Ant and I spoke for ages. I apologised for the shit I'd given him and the worry I'd caused. And I tried to explain that my addiction had made me a walking nightmare, had created a monster. I gave him the space to speak openly.

'Kat, I said as much in the Letter – I would despair over that dead look in your eyes. There was no depth or substance to you then. As for Colin, well, I won't even go there.'

'I didn't shag him, for the record.'

'I know that now, but back then nothing about you would have surprised me.'

Ant told me many other home truths. He was trying to hide his anger, but I kept getting flashes of it, simmering just below the surface. I guess he had a right to be angry. Still, I felt an argumentative wave come over me, almost instinctive. Suddenly the Beast was awake and, as Ant vented, it was urging me to object and fight back.

'You don't have to listen to this shit, Kat.'

'Who the fuck does he think he is, calling you selfish?'

Thankfully, I found the strength to not engage with the Beast's internal dialogue.

We eventually moved off my being a handful and onto lighter topics. The awkwardness subsided and then I knew that, more than anything, I wanted a second chance. It was difficult to gauge Ant's feelings.

Three hours later, he walked me to my car.

'Kat, believe it or not, I miss you terribly. I've been worried sick, but I'm very proud of you, that you're on track. You really look amazing too.'

Proud of you. Three small words which, to someone in early Recovery, meant everything. I glowed, but feared a blow was coming. There'd be a 'but'.

'And thanks for your honesty and your apologies too,' said Ant.

'No, thank *you* for the support. And for seeing me today.'

Mentally, I put myself in the brace position, waiting for the crash, the sound of breaking glass and crunching metal.

'I will always support you KitKat ...' Ant took a deep breath.

Here we go.

'Much as I would love to take you in my arms and whisk you off, common sense tells me not to. Kat, I've never stopped loving you, but ...'

And there it was.

Shit.

'... it's early days for us to go down that road again. I say let's give it another month then meet again. You're still so vulnerable, babe.'

I was blinking back tears, feeling utterly rejected, wanting to slap him yet beg him too.

'Kat, I don't want to mess with your Recovery. I know about the risks of early relationships. If I have to wait another year for you I will, but, first and foremost, I want you to stay clean and sober. This is not about me, it's about your life. Your body won't survive a relapse, and I'd rather take a shotgun to my own head than bury you. Why risk it all by rushing this?'

'Umm, I guess you're right. I don't really know what to say. I wasn't expecting this,' I said, feeling shaky.

'Well, what were you expecting?'

Looking away, I tried my damnedest not to cry, but still the tears came – tears of disappointment, fear, regret and hope at the same time. Ant was right, though. I was so very raw. His one-month rain check actually made a lot of sense.

'Were you expecting me to whisk you off to bed and for us start over like nothing happened?'

'Yes. Kind of. No. Fuck, I don't know,' I said, blubbing.

'Babe! Why the tears?' he said, pulling me in and holding me tight. 'Think I'd be here if I didn't give a shit, you big silly?'

I laughed, giving an unladylike sniff. 'Sorry, I'm being stupid.'

'Don't be so hard on yourself,' he said, his hands cupping my face as he wiped my tears with his thumbs. 'One month from now we'll have this conversation again. In the meantime, if you need a shoulder, you call me, okay? Call me a hundred times a day if you want. And hey, I also need a friend, so I'll call you too. Cuts both ways. Let's get to know each other again. I'm not going anywhere and before you ask, no, there is no one else in my life.'

'Jess?'

'Done. I'm not proud of that liaison, but I was hurting and thought some freelance shagging was the answer. I know that makes me a big pig, but let it go. Nothing for you to worry about.'

'Oh,' I said flatly.

'You'll love this – I kept calling her Kat by mistake. Seriously pissed her off.'

'Well don't call me Jess 'cos you'll only do it once.'

There wasn't anything more to say so I got into my car. 'Thanks Ant. For everything.'

'Call me, okay? Any time, you gorgeous thing. Now I'm going home for a cold shower. You and your Wonderbra tactic, you cruel woman.'

I drove home crying and laughing.

As I was getting out of my car, Grandpa, Tighty and Rod Stewart came belting past on their way to the veggies. I waved and Grandpa did a sharp U-turn, narrowly missing a flower bed as he pulled up alongside me.

'KitKat, you look nice. Where've you been?' With one look, Grandpa noticed I had more mascara on my cheeks than on my eyes. 'Hang about, what's wrong? You've been crying.'

'Just seen Ant.'

'Right, hop in and tell me while I do my evening rounds.'

All I wanted was to mope but, knowing that Grandpa would persist, I climbed in. Tighty scooted over on the seat, first giving me a slobbery hello lick, right across the chops. Grandpa dropped Rod Stewart a few hundred decibels and we tore off down the driveway.

'So then, why so upset?'

'I'm perhaps being oversensitive. We had a lovely chat, but he's still very angry. I didn't expect that.'

'He's allowed to be angry. You really fucked him around, pardon my French, Tighty,' said Grandpa, nudging my dog in the ribs like he was a person. Tighty just nodded.

'I fully accept that my behaviour has had consequences, Ant's anger is just one of them,' I went on.

'Now you're sounding like a sodding NA textbook again. Anyway, are you crying because he is angry?'

'No, what happened was that he said he loves me and wants to be with me, but not yet. He wants us to wait a month as I'm still vulnerable. He doesn't want to jeopardise my progress, but did say he'd wait for as long as it takes. In the meantime, I can call him anytime I need to chat. Basically.'

'Sorry, let's back up a bit here. So, you gave him untold shit. He spent *days* writing your rehab Letter. He spent hours talking to you today. He loves you, but is willing to put his own feelings aside purely for your benefit. He doesn't want to put you in any danger of going off the rails. You can call him anytime you want if you need a friend. He's done all his homework on dating an addict. A mere four weeks from now, you two will more than likely be a couple again. And you're crying. Why?'

'Well yes, now you put it like that, it does seem stupid.'

Grandpa smacked his hands hard against the steering wheel. Even Tighty gulped in fright, the whites of his eyes showing as he shot me an 'Oh shit' look.

'Katherine Hay, will you stop being so melodramatic. What did you expect?'

'What I didn't expect was to be put on the back-burner.'

'It's for your own good. Actually, I think it's fucking amazing – sorry, bad French again Tights. I am blown away by his maturity.'

'I know. It just made me feel like a shit.'

'You were a shit. To him, to us, to everyone. Face facts! You're not in any position to call the shots, I'm afraid.'

'I'm just not used to feeling feelings.'

'Yeah, you're gonna have to get used to that, my girl. You don't feel when you're living in other galaxies. You'll have to earn Ant's trust again too. Don't think for a minute it's a given. Took me, and your father too, a bloody long time to trust your mother again.'

'Yup, I know.'

Grandpa pulled over next to a field and turned to me. 'KitKat, please don't think I'm being unreasonably harsh. I support you and want to see you happy again. But there really is no need to be upset. So, send him a nice text message tonight, thank him for his support and just chill, okay?'

'Thanks Grandpa. Me and my super-sized insecurities, huh?' I said, already feeling way better.

After checking on Dad's new bean field, Grandpa decided to take a different road home – a barely used dirt track than ran along our neighbour's fence. We noticed a 'For Sale' sign on his gate.

'Well, well, well,' said Grandpa. 'The Brigadier must have built a new palace. I wonder why he's selling.'

Our neighbour was one of the army's big shots. We rarely saw him and it was rumoured that he spent his time on his several newly acquired farms.

'I've been inside that house, it's absolutely enormous. I think there's a cottage too. Must be asking an absolute fortune,' mused Grandpa.

Dad was on the couch watching golf, half listening to Mom and Maddie talking about the rehab business proposal. Mom was going all out and had roped Maddie into it too, the Trust deadline just six weeks away.

'Hello you two. Been shooting crows again?' asked Dad as Grandpa and I came in.

'No crows bled today. Did you know next door is up for sale?' said Grandpa.

'Gosh. Really?' Mom looked thoughtful and then looked at Maddie. 'Are you thinking what I'm thinking Madds?'

'Premises for the clinic?' asked Maddie.

'Yup. It's enormous. It'd be perfect,' said Mom.

'Yeah, but how?' said Dad. 'It's for sale, not for rent, unless you rent from the new owner but chances of that are slim.'

'Very slim. We'd need an investor to buy it for us. Also unlikely! I'm going to find out the asking price though, just out of interest,' said Mom.

Grandpa looked at Mom and shook his head. 'Gill, you're nuts. You do know this, don't you?' he said, passing Dad a beer and opening one himself.

'I actually think she's getting nuttier with age,' said Dad.

Recovery's next big challenge was thrown at me by NA itself. We'd received a request for someone to talk to schoolkids about drug abuse. The guy who normally did the teen 'just say no' talks was away and no one else could do it.

'You tell them your story, the scariest version of it with no watering down. Then explain where drugs will land them and take along all the NA pamphlets,' said my new sponsor Nicky, noticing I was contemplating putting my hand up.

'Bugger it. I'll give it a shot,' I said nervously. 'Which school and when?'

'Tomorrow. Convent.'

'Oh shit! No can do. That's my old school,' I said, horrified at the thought of going back to the nun house even for an hour.

After some hard bargaining, Nicky promised to buy me lunch and go with me for moral support, saying it'd be a healing experience. Next thing I knew, I'd agreed to march into my old school and tell God's women I was a drug addict. Clearly, I had rocks in my head.

The next morning, I put extra care into my outfit. I didn't want the girls to think I was a prissy old maid and I didn't want the nuns thinking I was a junkie slag. I decided on some trendy white cargo pants with a floaty navy-blue sleeveless top, adding some heavy silver jewellery and flat white sandals.

I pulled up at the Convent, seriously regretting having had my arm twisted. My chest felt tight and, soon enough, I walked slap bang into old Mother Superior, Sister Maria.

'Goodness gracious,' she said. 'Katherine Hay, what are you doing here? We are expecting an addict to talk to the girls about drugs and drinking.'

I pulled my shoulders back, took a deep breath and faced my old bête noir.

'Yes Sister, that would be me, the addict. The recovering addict,' I replied.

She paused for a moment, looking me in the eye. I was suddenly twelve again, wondering how severe her lecture would be. I braced myself, waiting for her judgement of me, head of the Old Girls Junkie Society. But then she simply stepped forward and gave me a tight hug, her starchy habit making my nose itch.

'Then well done, Katherine. Good for you,' she said, paying tribute to my personal war.

And in that moment, it all came to pass. Everything was laid to rest and Sister Maria and I were, at last, two adults on an equal footing.

As luck would have it, Nicky then messaged me to say she'd been held up, but wished me luck. The slag. I knew I'd been stitched up.

Sister Maria led me to my old classroom where the musty wood smell hurtled me back in time. It was overwhelming to the point of suffocating. All I could think was, 'If I'd known then what I know now ...'

I took a deep breath, reminding myself that I wasn't twelve and yes, I'd made some notable screw-ups since I'd last stood in that classroom, but this was my new life, my better life.

Composed again, I was ready to start. Then Sister Maria sat down at the back of the classroom.

'Sister, I am afraid I have to ask you to leave,' I said. 'The girls need to speak openly if this is to be of any benefit.'

Sister Maria merely stood up, nodded in a gesture of respect and quietly left the classroom.

I spent two hours talking to the Form 6 girls, and I came out shocked to have heard the extent of the drug experimentation going on. Marijuana use was rife, seventy percent of the girls drank heavily and most had already experienced a complete blackout. They had no idea that prescription drugs were as lethal as street drugs, and a good number of them regularly scoffed their parents' painkillers and sleeping pills. Some had already discovered the delights of washing painkillers down with vodka.

Sadly, the girls thought it was kind of cool and glamorous that I'd gone to rehab. I explained just how unglamorous my first night in the Fishbowl had been – what it really meant when a nurse was with you twenty-four hours a day and they removed the laces from your tackies, and how uncool it was to spend five weeks being torn limb from limb by counsellors and producing more snot and tears than you ever thought humanly possible. Finally, I told them about Cassie's unglamorous end. By the time I'd finished, a lot of the girls were crying. But there'd definitely be some causalities in that class.

Afterwards I thanked Sister Maria, who said again how proud she was of me, 'still the most honest girl in the school'.

I left feeling somewhat cleansed. My first school talk had been a massive step. Doing it at Convent had made it cathartic too.

The Universe, on a roll, finally started to address my 'unemployed lout' status. Stephen had now called me in twice for temp function work and then the miracle happened – he offered me a job. It was a demotion, though. I was back at the lowest rung on the PR ladder. For six months, I'd be on probation and I'd be out if I took more than four days' sick leave in that period. I told him I wanted no pay for the first three months and to treat me as a volunteer. He sure looked surprised, but I wasn't going to tell him why the money didn't matter. He just needed to know that I was serious about kick-starting my career.

I had to share an office with Jonathon, a new guy and theoretically my senior. He was my age and somewhat dishy, but I kept my head down and my nose clean and just got on with things. It felt a little weird, returning as the new girl and way down the food chain. The last thing I wanted was people gossiping and speculating about my history, so I was open, addressing it head on by telling everyone about my time in Summer Camp coming off drugs. I quickly noticed that Stephen never gave me late-afternoon meetings, knowing my NA and AA meetings kicked off at 5.30 p.m.

I duly handed in my resignation to Dad and asked when I was having my leaving party and if I could expect a gold watch. The next morning, I found a red pepper, spray-painted gold, on my front step.

'God I'm knackered. There's a lot more to this clinic business proposal than you'd think,' said Mom, finding me in my cottage on a Saturday afternoon. She lay on my bed next to me. 'Remind me why I am doing this?'

'Because you're tired of seeing addicts die because they couldn't go to rehab,' I said.

'Oh yes, that rings a bell.'

'Second thoughts?' I asked.

'Nah, not really. Maddie did a 12th Step call in the hospital the other day. Eighteen-year-old, full-blown addict, but no money. He'd give his right nut to go to rehab. Those stories are what's keeping me going.'

'Any luck with finding premises?'

'Nope. El Brigadier wants stupid money for his castle. So frustrating! Our dream premises right next door yet priced out of reach. Madds and I must have viewed fifty rental properties in the last week. It's a bit of a turn-off for any property owner, to have their place turned into a rehab. Looks like we'll go to the Trust with zero ideas for premises.'

'And have you decided if you're going to London to present in person?'

'Unlikely. Dad and I don't have the spare cash. The veggies are yet to start making a profit,' said Mom yawning. 'Anyway. How are you?'

'Good, Ma,' I replied.

'How's work?'

'Great.'

'How are your headaches?'

'Not great. But I manage.'

'Ant?'

'We speak every day. All good.'

'Fantastic! Right, back to work now. Good talk,' said Mom, hauling herself off my bed.

'Hang in, Ma. Keep the faith!'

I'd just had a brilliant idea.

The next weekend, our usual Sunday family gathering was at Chris and Ela's. Mom had brought the paper and was scouring the property classifieds. Ten minutes later, she tossed the paper aside in a huff.

'Fuck it,' said Mom.

'Mom!' said Chris.

'Oh, sorry,' she said, realising Katie was in earshot. 'But there's not one possible property in this paper.'

'How's the rest of the proposal looking Gill?' asked Linda.

'Great. It's just the premises giving me a headache,' said Mom. She then rattled off the various other elements she'd costed and the hurdles she'd identified.

'Gill, we have a proposal for you,' announced Ela a while later.

'Oh?' said Mom.

'I've spent the last week doing the sums with Chris and Kat,' Ela said.

Suddenly our parents were all paying attention. I was dead excited to see how Mom would take our idea.

'Chris and I are going to buy the Brigadier's house as an investment and offer it to you as a rental,' said Ela, a big grin on her face.

'Err ... what?' said Mom, spluttering loudly.

Ela laughed.

'How on earth can you get hold of that kind of money?' asked Mom.

'My inheritance from The Clap,' said Ela.

Mom gasped. 'Oh my God! I can't ask you to do that.'

'You haven't asked, I'm offering. It's a business deal. We buy the property as an investment, you pay rent. Simple. It doesn't make too much of a dent in the capital either, bless The Clap. I'm as passionate about this clinic as you and Julian are. I may well ask you for a job, though. I'd love to counsel in a rehab.'

'You're hired!' said Mom. 'Could knock me down with a feather.'

'Isn't it exciting?' said Ela. 'We couldn't wait to tell you. I've always said I'd put that money to good use. This just feels right. Remember, too, that The Clap's husband was fond of the bottle.'

'I'm completely blown away,' said Mom.

'So, is that a yes?' asked Ela.

'Hell yes – it's a yes!'

'Okay Mom, here's what we thought,' said Chris. 'Obviously the house would only be used for a rehab. Ela wouldn't buy it for any other reason. It's all in the timing now. List the place as potential premises in your Trust proposal. Only if you get the funds will Ela buy it.'

'I see where you're coming from,' said Mom.

'Well, the agent said it's been on the market for months and hasn't exactly flown off the shelf, so maybe time is on our side,' said Ela.

'We'll be totally upfront,' said Chris. 'Let's all meet the agent again and explain why Ela will only make an offer in a few weeks. We can ask them to hold out on any other offers until they hear back from us.'

'Sounds sensible,' said Mom and promptly burst into tears.

'And the other part of this comes from Kat,' said Ela.

The folks all rubbernecked and looked at me. 'Oh, Ela's way more loaded than me. I'm just throwing in three air tickets to London,' I said. 'Mom, you and Julian can present the rehab bid in person, and afterwards you and Dad are going on a proper holiday.'

'Lordy!' said Mom.

'Gotta love medical malpractice settlements!' I chuckled.

Grandpa was beaming, tears in his eyes too. 'I think it's safe to say that you chaps have raised three remarkable children,' he said, looking at Mom, Dad, Tim and Linda. 'Even with all the grey hair they've each given you.'

'Speechless,' said Linda, a soggy mess too.

'I'll never be able to thank you kids enough,' said Mom.

'Open a clinic and save lives. That's all the thanks needed,' said Ela.

'I'm going to phone Julian,' said Mom, galloping off with half a

Yorkshire pudding in her paw and dribbling gravy down her shirt.

'Well then,' said Dad turning to Grandpa, 'think you can hold the fort for a week or two? It seems I'm going on holiday.'

'Lucky bastard,' said Grandpa. 'I'm still waiting for new scatter cushions on my bed.'

42

Stephen had given me the tedious task of capturing the results of a client's research exercise. While I was stacking five hundred questionnaires in piles around my desk, Jonathon was gnashing his teeth over updating our media list. Despite sharing an office, I didn't know much about him but, late that afternoon, I couldn't help overhearing a phone call he received. There seemed to be a family drama in swing and, when he ended the call, he just sat there, his head in his hands.

'What's up?' I asked.

'That was my brother. The police raided his office premises last night. They have trashed the place.'

'Police? Why? What does he do?'

'He has a wholesale medical supply business.'

'Why the police, then?'

'He thinks they were looking for evidence of foreign currency deals. The moron left a fat wad of US dollars in his desk, which they took.'

'Oh hell! But doesn't everyone have forex from the black markets?' Ever since banks had frozen the exchange rates, the black market for hard currencies had boomed, while the economic meltdown worsened by the day.

'Yup, he won't see that cash again. But that's my brother, always cocking things up and in the shit over something. Proverbial black sheep. Anyway, he's coming here now to borrow some money, but I need to nip to the ATM and draw the cash. If he arrives before I'm back, won't you ask him to wait?'

'Sure, no probs.'

Ten minutes later, the receptionist sent Jonathon's brother through to our office. I looked up and thought I was hallucinating. There, standing in front of my desk, was Colin, drug dealer Colin. My mouth dropped open.

'You've got to be fucking kidding me,' I said. '*You're* Jonathon's brother?'

'Well, well, well,' he said, arrogantly. 'Fancy meeting you like this.'

'For fuck's sake. Actually, why don't you wait in reception rather,' I said, my hands suddenly clammy.

'Oh no. I'd far rather catch up with my favourite junkie,' he said, perching on the corner of my desk. 'So, you work here? You're one of them PR dolly birds who does cute things like organise company Christmas parties and golf days?'

'Grow up,' I snapped.

He gave a slimy smirk, which I'd have loved to slap. 'Oh my, you're a frosty little bitch aren't you, now that you don't want any gear from me. Must say, you're looking good Kat, got some meat on you now. Nice,' he said, his eyes running over me, lingering on my chest. 'Very nice, actually,' he added, licking his lips in an obscene way before adjusting his crotch.

My stomach churned. Saying nothing, I stared at my computer, refusing eye contact.

'So, you're off the pills then? I'm guessing Mommy and Daddy sent their precious little darling to rehab,' he said, picking up a bundle of my research papers and reading them.

I leant over and snatched the papers away.

'How's Grandpa? Still fighting your battles for you?'

'How's your girlfriend? Still a drunk whore?'

He laughed derisively. My skin was crawling and sweat trickled down my spine. He even smelt foul – dirty, unwashed, and with stale whisky breath. I refused to let him see how unnerved I was.

'Colin, I won't ask again. Go and wait for Jonathon in reception or do you want to chat to Security about it? Much as I'd love to chit-chat with a lowlife scumbag of a drug dealer, who's just had his balls busted in a well-deserved police raid, I'm busy. Get the fuck out of my office. Now.'

'Ooh, crotchety. You were far nicer when you were a permanently stoned prescription whore. You sure you don't need a few happy pills? Got some in the car if you're keen 'cos, my God, you need to chill out. I reckon you need to get laid too – all frigid and uptight, you are. Happy to oblige with that too. For a fee.'

'Get. The. Fuck. Out,' I said, teeth clenched.

Colin stood up and sauntered out, sneering. In the doorway he turned and winked at me. 'I can give you a hundred pills right now if you want to change your mind, my hot, sexy Kat.'

Overcome with rage, I didn't realise I'd picked up my stapler until I saw it hurtling through the air. It was a perfect throw and hit the side of his head, sending staples flying.

He gave me a filthy look and left, not letting on just how much that stapler had hurt him. I sat there frozen, breathing in short gasps. The Beast was awake, urging me to go after Colin and score. The pull was so strong, so sudden, I nearly did run down the corridor. In that split second, a million thoughts sandblasted my brain, thoughts of the wrong kind. A flashback to the night Carol had offered me drugs brought me to my senses.

I grabbed my cigarettes and dashed to the balcony, my hands shaking as I tried to light up. I was horrified by how much power Colin still had over me, and upset that he now knew where I worked. I mean, what were the chances of working with my dealer's brother? This shit only happens in my family, I thought, wondering if Jonathon was part of his dealing operation or if he even knew what his brother was. God knows how we'd work together if they were in cahoots.

Once I'd got my breath back, I went in. Jonathon was at his desk – there was no sign of Colin.

'Hey. Did you sort things out?' I asked cautiously, unsure how to play things.

'Yup. Stupid wanker, my brother.'

Well yes, amongst other things, I thought.

'He's always getting into shit and I shouldn't bail him out. He's really screwed-up his life. My parents refuse to cushion his falls anymore, but he's so good at emotional blackmail that I always get suckered in.'

'How has he screwed-up his life?' I asked, tentatively.

'He's a pharmacist but got himself struck off recently when he got caught dispensing scheduled drugs without a prescription.'

Thank God Jonathon was not part of his brother's racket. And Colin obviously hadn't mentioned that he knew me.

'So, let me get this straight, he was dealing drugs?' I asked.

'Yup. All over town it seems. You should see his girlfriend – a raging alcoholic and on every drug out there. Total whore. Twenty-one with three kids from three different fathers.'

I took a deep breath, knowing I needed to address the elephant in the room that Jonathon didn't even know was there. I had to take steps to safeguard myself right away.

'Jonathon, you know how I told you all that I was recently in rehab?'

He looked surprised by my sudden question. 'Yes?'

'Well, I just found out that my dealer is none other than your revolting brother. He sauntered in here earlier, recognised me, and then did his level best to get me to relapse.'

'Shit, I'm so sorry Kat,' said Jonathon, absolutely mortified and suddenly pale.

'Please understand that for me to stay clean, certain people have to stay out of my life. If Colin sets foot in this building again, I'll take the issue to Stephen and that could affect your job. Stephen fully supports my Recovery and he won't want me to be at risk at work. Please don't let Colin come here again.'

'Of course. I'm really so very sorry.'

'It's not your fault at all, and thanks for understanding. Take my advice and listen to your folks – cut Colin off and walk away before he takes you down too. Because he will. Anyway, I'm going home now. Your delightful brother has completely fucked with my serenity.'

I was still rattled when I got home. I went for a swim and did fifty laps, fast, venting my rage on the water. Before I got out, I sank to the bottom of the deep end and let out a monumental scream, stopping only when every drop of air had left my lungs and I felt dizzy. I screamed at Colin. And at the Beast.

Most of all, I screamed at myself for being an addict.

Grandpa was having a beer on the patio, chatting to Mom about their London trip. Drying off, I joined them, lit a ciggie and sighed.

'You were beating the crap out of the water there, Kat. Bad day at work?' asked Mom.

'Colin strolled into my office today,' I said.

'WHAT!' said Mom.

I told them what I'd learnt about Colin. Grandpa was delighted about the police raid. Mom congratulated me for throwing him out.

'Shit Mom, does it get easier? He woke my Beast up. Bam, an ordinary work day and it starts jumping up and down and demanding a feed. When does that stop? Does it stop?'

'In time it gets easier. You did good today, darling. Be proud,' said Mom.

'I'm not proud of being such a wimp and letting him get to me like that,' I replied.

'Scoring from him would have been wimpish,' said Grandpa, suddenly busy typing a message on his cellphone.

'It's a small town and it's getting smaller, so you're probably going to bump into him again. Just stay on top of your game. We're all around you, darling,' said Mom.

That night I sat up late on my patio. It was a hot, still night and I couldn't sleep. I was churning inside and had a massive headache. I had a gut feeling that Grandpa may have had a hand in Colin's police raid. He never used his cellphone but, tonight, he'd had it out a few times. Over his shoulder, I happened to catch a glimpse of one text he'd received, simply saying *Done*. Oh well, shit happens when you're a dealer.

After some paracetamol, about the only painkiller I could take these days, sleep finally came to me. It was restless, filled with dreams of being chased by a wild creature. I was running, feeling something closing in on me from behind. It wasn't the Beast though, it was a completely new kind of monster, almost feral, with sharp claws and lime-green feline eyes, and I felt its hot, humid, rancid breath on my neck. I kept running, searching for safety, but never quite reaching it. Unable to put any distance between myself and the creature with luminous eyes.

The night before the folks left for London, I sat with Mom watching her pack.

'I'm having such a flashback,' I said. 'I can clearly remember sitting on your bed watching you pack for rehab. Now, twenty years later you're going to open one.'

'We've sure come a long way,' said Mom.

I flicked through her thirty-page business plan, impressed. Every last aspect of a rehab had been accounted for, right down to garden tools and toilet brushes.

'Nervous?' I asked her.

'No. I'm shitting myself.'

'At least Dad will be there. Julian too.'

'I'm so excited to see Julian again. This whole venture has really helped bring us together in a weird way. If, six months ago, you'd said I'd find my son and go into the rehab trade with him, I'd have laughed in your face.'

'Everything for a reason Ma,' I said. Julian and I had become close too, often chatting for hours on the phone. I loved hearing his funny patient stories. He'd given me some solid advice about Ant and our getting back together. Our waiting period was up and after another long and brutally honest chat, Ant and I had declared ourselves a couple again and had promptly fallen into bed. We were still all honeymoonish, but I had a lot of trust to earn back.

The house seemed strangely quiet when Grandpa and I got home from dropping them at the airport the next day. Grandpa suddenly came tearing through, waving a new scatter cushion in my face and dragging me to his bedroom. Mom had bought him so many scatter cushions we literally couldn't see the bed. Tighty, impressed too, opted to spend his day on the mound they made.

A few days later, with both sides on speaker phone, we huddled round to hear about the presentation to the Trust.

'Well, we think it went very well,' said Mom. 'They were mainly asking about Zim, and whether we could sustain a rehab in such a volatile environment. They were fascinated to hear how I found my son when checking my daughter into rehab. Clearly thought our bizarre African story was all very exotic. Then we explained the dire rehab situation. Having Julian onside as a counsellor really gave weight to our bid.'

'Sounds like it went great,' I said.

'Yup! And the story of your misdiagnosed perforated ulcer all served to illustrate the calibre of doctors in Harare. They were horrified,' said Julian.

'When will they announce the winning bid?' Grandpa asked.

'Within three weeks. So now it's off to Spain and France on holiday.'

'Not bloody fair, Gill,' said Grandpa. 'By the way, I love the new overkill of cushions on my scratcher. Tighty does too.'

We heard Dad give a loud chuckle in the background.

'Please update Ela, Madds and Linda. And is everything okay at home?' said Mom.

'Yup, all fine here,' said Grandpa. 'Bar the fact that my new cottage nearly blew sky high as a result of dodgy wiring done by that bloody idiot cheapo electrician we used.'

There had indeed been one mother of an explosion when Grandpa first turned on the mains in his new cottage. I thought a bomb had gone off. Seconds after the monumental bang – that had shorted my cottage too – Jobb had streaked across the garden towards the new cottage, screaming his lungs out, arms waving madly, yelling, 'Baas! Baba! Boss Grandpa dead!' I think Jobb had come close to setting a new land-speed record as he belted off to Grandpa's aid. Grandpa, even after nine beers in rapid succession, had worn a pained look. Jobb had disappeared into the nearest shebeen to recover.

'WHAT? Dad, you blew up your cottage?' asked Mom.

'Yeah Mom, mine too. Don't even ask,' I said. 'Tighty howled for a good two hours after the explosion. I even considered a trip to the vet for a tranquilliser – for Tighty, mostly. The horses nearly left home too and, four days later, there are still no birds in the garden.'

'One way of dealing with your crows, I guess,' Dad shouted down the line, and we heard him and Julian cackling.

We all shouted 'bye' at the phone and Tighty, strolling past, added a bark, frowning because he could hear Mom but couldn't see her.

43

The weeks had flown by and nothing exciting had happened, apart from the wedding planning. Mom and Dad were home from their holiday and they'd never looked happier. Dad had announced he was going into fresh herbs – chives, basil and parsley. He was all fired up by the veggie markets he'd seen in Paris. He was equally chatty about Julian, and it seemed he and his stepson of sorts had formed a special bond in the UK. Meanwhile, Mom was sure their presentation had gone well but was taking anxiety to a whole new level while they waited to hear whether or not they'd be given a lovely fat cheque. Suddenly, the whole idea of a real rehab next door seemed awfully close to becoming a reality.

A week later, Mom was still jangling, jumping whenever the phone rang and checking her email every half hour. They were due to hear from the Trust any day. I even tried to get her to ride with me, but she'd found any excuse to stay within arm's reach of a phone or computer. Days dragged by and when Friday rolled around there was still no word, which meant Mom had another whole weekend to stew. She was getting crabbier by the minute. Grandpa and I quickly worked out it was safer to stay out of her firing line, after witnessing Ant get the biggest bollocking of his life for flicking a cigarette butt in her flower bed, something she did herself all the time.

Early on Sunday morning, I was woken by raised voices wafting down from the main house. I looked at my clock and saw it was six o'clock. Suddenly Mom was banging on the front door of my cottage, like war had broken out.

'Oi! Are you decent in there, Ant? Can I come in, Kat? Hurry!' she bellowed, then she cantered round to bang on my bedroom window, flattening a flower bed in the process.

'For God's sake, Mom, what is it? What's happened?' I asked, wondering who had died as I unlocked the door, half asleep.

Mom, in her pyjamas and with crazy hair, started doing some kind of wild maniac dance on my patio, flapping a piece of paper in the air and making funny squeaks. I snatched the paper from her and scanned through it. It was an email from the Trust sent an hour earlier.

'We've only gone and got ourselves one shitload of money for a rehab,' she shrieked. 'It's way more money than we asked for.'

She started her victory dance again and this time I joined in, hugging her, hopping and shrieking in delight. She'd done it!

Dad and Grandpa came strolling down wearing broad smiles. Ant had crawled out of bed to see what the commotion was about, while Tighty and Gertie barked like dogs possessed. Even Jobb had heard the noise and came running up to see who was shrieking, fearing another explosion had occurred. His face was a picture when he saw us all being hysterically stupid in our pyjamas, prancing around on the front lawn at dawn on a Sunday morning.

'Phone calls,' said Mom, panting from the exertion. 'Phone calls to make. Julian. Ela and Chris. Madds, Linda. Estate agent.' And with that Mom bolted off back up to the house.

'Pity it's six o'clock on Sunday morning,' said Grandpa lighting a cigarette. 'I quite fancy a beer after all the excitement.'

'Better watch out, boozing so early in the day,' said Dad. 'She'll have you as her first patient.'

'Pah! Like to see her try,' said Grandpa, casually diving into the pool in his pyjamas, having decided on a swim in the absence of beer.

I looked at Ant, who was laughing. 'You lot truly are an utterly weird but totally amazing family,' he said.

'Stick with us, you'll be a nutter in no time at all,' I said.

Ant grabbed my hand, dragging me inside and back to bed. 'Come. I'll show you nutty …'

A few hours later, Ant and I joined everyone up at the house. A celebratory brunch had evolved after Mom had phoned the troops with the news, and a steady stream of bacon and eggs was flowing from the kitchen. Mom and Ela were discussing the Brigadier's house, sure they could close the deal within a fortnight, while Linda and Maddie flicked through the original proposal again.

'Well, here's the sticky, tricky, challenging part. The Trust wants us up and running within five months. In the sixth month they will do a trip out and assess everything,' said Mom.

'Jeez Gill, you've got your work cut out then,' said Maddie.

'Don't tell me! And they gave me an extra month because they know we have a family wedding. I need to start interviewing and hiring people right away,' said Mom.

It was a long, happy day, with Mom glowing, but also looking increasingly nervous. The train had left the station and there was no calling it back now.

That evening Dad, Grandpa and Ant went to the pub and left Mom and me at home talking about clinic stuff. After all the excitement had died down, the reality of just how much she had to do was sinking in. While we bounced ideas around, she handed me a list of staff she needed to hire.

'I am going to invite Maddie to apply for the bookkeeper job,' said Mom. 'I promised her I'd find her a role.'

'I see you also need people for Catering and Housekeeping?'

'Yes, someone to manage a team of cooks and maids and to plan menus, possibly consult a dietician on it too. I'm thinking Linda.'

'Are you sure you can handle working with your best friends and being their boss?' I asked.

'I think so. I trust them implicitly and we're all old enough and ugly enough to handle a working relationship in a mature fashion. This little clinic is as close to their hearts as it is to mine. Don't forget Julian will be their boss too,' said Mom, rubbing her eyes, looking exhausted.

'Gotta love nepotism!' I said, laughing.

'Speaking of, I need your help on PR and marketing strategies. We have to target the medical fraternity, such as it is, and tell them about Harare's first rehab. It's one thing to be up and running in four months, but we need a few patients too. I also need a name, a logo, and a website, which I'll leave to you and Chris.'

'I can easily create a campaign for you. Off the top of my head, you need a launch function. Invite all the doctors, shrinks and pharmacists, also school heads seeing as most high schools in this town now have more drugs than text books. I'll invite media too.'

'Brilliant idea,' said Mom, writing in a notebook, which was already full after just a day's planning.

'So what happens now with Julian and his current job?' I asked. 'And how are you going to interview counsellors if they're based in South Africa?'

'Julian will hand in his notice next week, pack up his home and make his way here to Harare. He's bringing his puppy, by the way. He's going to take the little cottage by the dam on the property. Victoire may or may not follow in a few months' time, but Julian is very laid-back about that side of things and says it will work itself out. And, as for hiring counsellors, he has a shortlist of people he has already spoken to who are, amazingly, very keen on a stint here in Harare. Julian will do the counsellor interviews before he leaves South Africa.'

'And how are you going to structure the patient fees?'

'Julian and I discussed that in detail with the Trust. This clinic's overall objective has always been to give the less fortunate a shot at rehab and we can't lose sight of that. While there's capital to subsidise the fees, we can't offer a poor person a place for free and then make a wealthier person pay. And we can't charge absolutely nothing at all. There's some psychology behind that – people will work at it harder and take it more seriously if they've actually parted with some money. So, rich or poor, it will be one nominal fee for the first year and the grant will absorb the difference. However, we will also welcome donations over and above the basic fee, should someone feel so inclined.'

'But will anyone actually donate? Sounds complicated.'

'It was the Trust's idea. They've seen similar rehab models work with great success. It's like an Honesty Box and, apparently, people do make donations, especially if rehab works for them and they get their lives back. This is why it's so important to get the crème de la crème of counsellors and a high success rate from the start. In year two, when the fees go up, we'll have a strong reputation to trade on.'

'Sounds highly involved, Mom.'

'Yup, but we've taken a lot of advice and tried to find the balance between helping people while, ultimately, building a sustainable business. Charity models are always complex. The second year is when we'll feel the pressure, once the Trust cuts financial ties.'

'Shit, you're brave,' I said, truly in awe of her determination.

'Either brave or stupid.'

It was the night of Ela's kitchen tea, and I was definitely on edge at my first real party in Recovery. We'd started the evening at our house and then moved on to the pub, to where Chris's bachelor party had also migrated and, with the stag and hen parties merged, plus the general public, it turned into one major pre-wedding jump-up of about a hundred people. As usual, Grandpa was the life and soul of the party. He kept dragging Ela off to dance. She, as drunk as he, was in safe hands and their dancing so slick it cleared the floor and made the entire pub stop. *Scent of a Woman* had nothing on Grandpa and Ela as they took to the floor in a tango that looked like it had been rehearsed for months, everyone standing in a ring around them cheering. Ela was beaming. There wasn't a happier girl in the world.

Mom and I, taking a breather from dancing, watched everyone let loose.

'Gosh, KitKat, if the Trust boys could see us now,' said Mom. 'Here we are, opening a rehab and our entire family is completely wrecked.'

'I can't believe Chris and Ela are finally tying the knot,' I said.

'Yup. And I'm hoping you'll be next,' said Mom.

I choked on a mouthful of juice, spraying Mom.

'What?' laughed Mom, dabbing herself. 'You and Ant are going great guns, aren't you?'

'Well, yes, but let's not get ahead of ourselves, Momsy.'

'Pah! Wait, you'll see. Pity he threw that first engagement ring in the Zambezi – now he'll have to save up for another,' joked Mom, except I knew she wasn't joking at all.

I chuckled. Watching Ant on the other side of the pub, I felt my gut lurch. After all this time, I still got butterflies around him. I'd scoffed at

Mom's comment because I didn't dare hope, but, if he were to propose then and there in the middle of the pub, I'd not skip a beat in whipping out my hand and presenting my ring finger. Overcome by a wave of deep love, I went over and hugged him.

'Oh, hello babe. What's up pussykat?' he said grinning like an idiot.

'Nothing. Just wanted to tell you I love you,' I shouted over the noise.

'Aaah, I love you toooo my schweet KittyKittyKitKat,' slurred Ant. 'Your brother isn't going to know what hit him in the morning.'

'None of you will know what hit you in the morning,' I laughed. 'Listen hun, I'm heading off with Mom just now. Is someone sober enough to drive you buggers home?'

'Yup. I hired our office driver for the night,' said Ant, hiccupping on every second word.

Grandpa walloped Ant on the back to cure his hiccups.

'Enjoy yourselves,' I said, laughing. 'And look after my brother.'

I waved as I left, and Mom and I finally made it outside. I spotted our friendly slapper, Jess, about to go in. I was torn. I could go back and glue myself to Ant, or I could be horribly mature, trust Ant not to go there, and go on home. I took a deep breath and pulled out my phone to message Rolo, Vicky, and Andrew, all still inside.

Just seen Jess at the door. Give it horns …

They'd know exactly what to do with that.

Just as I'd shaken off the moment, I saw Colin across the car park.

'Oh shit, Mom, it's him again,' I whispered. The Beast had been twitchy all night and these little things were really starting to get to me.

'Who? What?' Mom asked, looking around.

'Colin, coming towards us,' I said.

'Ignore him, let's cross over the car park, quick,' said Mom.

Colin didn't see me. He was engrossed in conversation with a woman dressed like a hooker and draped all over him like a cheap shower curtain. They were barely able to walk they were so high and were openly passing a joint between them, its acrid, sweet smell wafting across the car park.

'Horrible little shit,' said Mom, starting the car.

Between Jess and Colin, I just wanted to get as far away as possible.

It was 3 a.m. when I collapsed into my bed, feeling grateful for two things. I wouldn't have a hangover in the morning and I didn't have Colin in my life anymore.

But the Beast took a long time to settle that night.

44

The following weekend a string quartet played the Wedding March under the shade of our big msasa trees on the front lawn. Katie, the prettiest little thing, walked the garden aisle in front of Ela. We hadn't told Ela we were laying a thick carpet of fresh lavender blossoms down the aisle and among the seats. As the masses of purple flowers were crushed underfoot, the sweet smell of lavender hung in the air as a surprise for her. Ela paused at the top of the aisle with her arm linked in Tim's. She lifted her nose and inhaled deeply, smiling, looking beautiful in every way.

Following her down the aisle, I glanced ahead at Chris who was openly crying as he watched his serene bride approaching. Her long auburn hair, sprinkled with tiny rosebuds, fell softly down her back. Her grace and inner beauty were breathtaking. She wasn't just smiling with her lips, with her whole body too. I noticed Mom and Linda fiddling discreetly with tissues.

We were halfway down the aisle when I saw a flurry of movement at the outer edge of the chairs. It was one of Mom's bantams and I braced myself, knowing a boxer was in hot pursuit and chaos was about to enter. The bantam chick was confused by the rows of chairs in its normally wide-open garden, and squawked in panic, darting between people's legs and the chairs as it frantically tried to escape the jaws of death, sending up sprays of lavender as it flapped around looking for an exit. Sure enough, a second later Tighty came flying into the gathering, jowls flapping, ears flattened, a wild look in his eyes and long strings of slobber landing on guests' smart wedding gear. The bantam did a sharp turn to outwit Tighty and made a break for it, dashing out through the eight legs of the string quartet. Tighty, however, veered straight into one violinist who went flying off her chair. The Wedding March turned into a strangled warble, but it was barely audible over the shrieks of laughter from all present.

Poor Ela, her big moment was trashed. She quickly realised that Tighty had just outdone himself when she heard Mom shouting, 'That bloody lunatic nutter dog!' Ela threw her head back and laughed loudly with us, everyone in hysterics except the violinist who picked herself up and busily pulled sprigs of lavender out of her hair.

Still chuckling, we made it to the end of the aisle. Tighty had more important things to do than witness a wedding and was long gone. Sitting on the pastor's feet, Mojo watched Ela coming towards the altar, but she didn't get up to guide her, knowing Tim had it covered. She merely nuzzled Ela's hand when she got to the end then went off to sit on Linda's feet. In many ways, Mojo was giving Ela away as much as Tim was.

As I followed my dear friend down the aisle, I glanced at Ant, hoping one day I would be the one in a pretty white dress. He winked at me, as if he'd read my mind. I was hit by a surge of butterflies and suddenly felt terribly sentimental. I kept it together until Chris and Ela read the vows they'd written. When Chris took Ela's hands and gave her his pledge, staring intently into her non-seeing eyes, out came everyone's tissues.

Later, during the reception, Grandpa, the Master of Ceremonies, called Chris up for his speech. I was blown away when Chris reached out to Ela, who stood up beside him. Katie was on his other side, holding his hand and Ela took Ben from me, bouncing him on her hip. The new family of four faced their guests.

'Before I start,' said Chris, 'Ela and I would like a moment's silence to remember Sam. She gave us the most precious gifts in Ben and Katie and, for that, Ela and I want to give thanks and honour her memory today.'

The crowd fell quiet, some were surprised that Chris had toasted his first wife with his new bride at his side, but it was a powerful moment. Then Ela raised her glass.

'To Sam. Thank you, Sam. I will always love, honour and guide your children as if they were my own,' said Ela.

Ben gurgled with laughter in Ela's arms and tugged on her veil just as everyone raised their glasses. Ela sat down, leaving Chris to clear the lump in his throat and start his speech. Mom was tickets and had buried her face in Dad's shoulder, overcome by emotion. Sam's parents, Peter and Jean, were there and I noticed Jean discretely head to the loo to compose herself.

The rest of the speeches were, thankfully, lighter. Everyone loved Grandpa's funny anecdotes about how Ela and Chris had been making eyes at each other since they were toddlers.

'And Chris, as a boy, used to make talking books for Ela,' said Grandpa. 'The boy would spend days reading books into a dodgy old tape recorder. And, much to his mother's horror, recording these books always took priority over any schoolwork. Then his balls dropped and his voice started to break. Poor Ela had to put up with a somewhat squeaky storyteller but, luckily for her, puberty arrived around about the time she could finally get proper talking books in Zimbabwe.'

Grandpa gave a signal to the DJ and suddenly we heard Chris's childhood voice booming through the speakers. Ela had kept every tape and given Grandpa one of his very first ones. It was hilarious to hear a young Chris narrating *James and The Giant Peach*. I'd never seen Chris blush quite to that extent while Ela laughed her head off, her blind friends giving a loud cheer of approval.

Later, as the sun dipped and washed the sky with a blend of oranges and pinks, Chris took Ela's hand, saying he had a surprise for her, and led her out of the marquee. I had no idea what he had up his sleeve until I caught sight of Grandpa, Dad, Tim and Jobb wheeling out the old farm microlight at the very top of the driveway.

'You've got to be kidding me?' I said to Mom, who'd also been kept in the dark.

'Oh, good Lord, no! Surely they aren't going up in that old heap,' said Mom.

'Looks like it. And looks like they're going the use the drive as the runway. Is Chris's pilot's licence even valid?'

'Oh shit, don't ask me,' said Mom. 'This is against every aviation rule in the book, but there's no point in trying to stop them, they'll do it anyway. Your grandfather is involved, need I say more?'

The entire wedding party followed Chris and watched in delight as he got Ela strapped into the microlight, her wedding dress scrunched up around her like clouds of candy floss, holding her bouquet and a look of absolute excitement on her face as she waited for Chris to complete all the checks. A few minutes later, the engine spluttered to life and they were belting down our, thankfully very long and straight, driveway. That's when we all saw the Just Married sign on the back of the microlight.

They lifted off with a metre of driveway to spare and soared up into the sky, doing an immediate turn and coming back over us, hardly clearing the trees. We waved and cheered, just able to make out Ela's huge grin. She chose that moment to toss her bouquet. I had Ben in my arms and was saying something to Ant when I suddenly looked up and saw the sizeable bunch of flowers hurtling down towards me. Ant stretched his arm in reflex and was the one to catch it. Much debate followed about whether or not it still counted if a man caught the bouquet.

'Ant's next up at the altar. Play your cards right and you'll be the culprit,' said Mom on the side, elbowing me in the ribs.

'Oh funny, ha ha!' I said to Mom. 'For God's sake don't let him hear you talking like that. He'll run a mile.'

Chris and Ela did a few laps over the veggie fields and then over the Brigadier's house which, of course, was now Ela's house. Twenty minutes later, he landed the microlight safely on a longer stretch of dirt road running alongside the veggies and Dad set off in his truck to get them. They came back beaming and laughing, Ela barefoot and her hair all loose and wild, looking more exhilarated than I thought humanly possible.

'Who got the bouquet?' she asked excitedly.

'Ant!' Mom said, laughing while I cringed.

Ant took me in his arms and held me tight. Everything around us stopped and we lost ourselves for a moment. It was as if we were sixteen again, at Jack and Anna's wedding on the farm, me in a little sundress, us kissing in the shadows of the rose garden and just realising how completely infatuated we were with each other.

It was the most perfect day our family had had in a very long time.

'Am I in the right place to open a rehab?' said Julian, getting out of his car and stretching.

He'd left Cape Town four days ago, with his entire life in boxes and his old Land Rover packed to the hilt, and had trekked north and over the border. I saw a little black nose peering out from between some crates on the back seat and, next thing, the cutest bull mastiff puppy with enormous paws flew out of the car like a tornado, cocking her leg on the nearest bush before taking in her surrounds.

'Meet Pringle. The only bitch to cock her leg,' Julian said to us, everyone having come out to welcome him.

'Ah well, the dog's a bit odd so you'll fit right in here. Welcome home, son,' said Dad, hugging him.

'Not sure about the surfboard old chap, but we can give it a shot in the dam,' said Grandpa, peering at all Julian's clobber in the car.

Tighty and Gertie were deeply fascinated by the new arrival and, after the bottom-sniffing can-we-be-friends ritual was out of the way, they were galloping around the garden with Pringle, all puppy fat and wrinkled skin that she had yet to grow into.

After a Saturday lunch filled with the usual family nonsense, I went next door with Mom while she gave Julian the guided tour of his new home, the little thatched cottage by the dam on Ela's new property.

'Gill, this is gorgeous. So quiet and peaceful. I love it,' he said, hugging Mom.

'I thought you'd like it. I've furnished your cottage with the basics. We can get some more stuff for you out of storage, but you should be okay for now.'

'Basics?' said Julian. 'Gill, the place is fully furnished and looks like home.'

'It's the addict gene. No half measures,' I said.

Mom blushed before wittering on. 'I've put some goodies in the fridge, though you have a standing invitation to join us for meals at the house anytime you want. Make yourself at home and don't ever wait to be asked. Tomorrow I'll show you where the DVD shop and Chinese takeaway are – the important things in life.'

We then headed up to the main house, which would soon be a fully fledged rehab. In just a few weeks, Mom had done an unbelievable amount of work and it was looking more like a luxury African resort than a rehab.

The décor throughout was warm and gentle, nothing clinical or cold about it at all. Linda's kitchen was fully equipped. Bookshelves everywhere were laden with Recovery books as well as some lighter reading material. The bedrooms were all ready, waiting for the first check-ins. In the smaller rooms, designated for group sessions and one-on-one counselling, I chuckled to see Mom had put in some industrial-sized boxes of tissues.

The nurses station was also finished, shiny nursing paraphernalia neatly stacked on the counters. A small two-bed medical ward was off the nursing centre – Mom's version of the Fishbowl. I felt a definite shiver down my spine, knowing exactly what would go down in that room and knowing, here too, Beasts would probably walk the corridors late at night. Suddenly unable to breathe, I left.

The Brigadier's old eight-car garage block had been converted into the clinic's offices. French windows opened onto a private courtyard where staff could relax between their target practice on patients. Andrew had done wonders with landscaping, putting in lush lawns and massive flower beds everywhere. Around one side of the pool was a huge thatched patio with comfy sofas and loungers where patients could laze during free time, but it was also a space for art therapy or poolside group sessions in summer. The view of the valley below was incredible, far nicer than our own view, and I could just picture patients sitting there reflecting, looking down on the dam and across onto bush and farmlands, pondering life and all their shit decisions that had landed them in treatment.

The all-important security was nearly complete, ensuring the patients' protection from the outside world, and vice versa. There could be only one way in and one way out, achieved with electric fencing, twenty-four-hour guards on the gate, CCTV and a security team patrolling the perimeter. To keep nearly eleven hectares, a lot of it bush, secure at all times was no small task.

Whereas we'd had beach walks in rehab, Mom's patients would be trotted down to the picturesque dam for fresh air and exercise every afternoon. Next to the dam, Dad and Grandpa had built a notable combat-style obstacle course, worthy of any army barracks. Mom and I had even started talking about equine therapy on weekends – a programme I would develop and oversee, when I was ready. We'd need more horses and stables, and Jobb and I had already had a long discussion about 'Junkie Jockeys', as I'd titled it, and he was dead excited to be my right-hand man.

Julian and I were blown away by what Mom had achieved. She was flushed from the excitement of showing him the fruits of her labour, anxious for his approval.

'Jeepers Gill!' he said. 'I'm super impressed. We could practically open tomorrow.'

'Hardly! Your job, now, is to start writing the house rules and creating a few systems and procedures,' Mom said. 'I am about to finalise all the medical licences and we should be legal by the end of the week, not that we're even close to opening the doors.'

I left Mom and Julian to their clinic stuff and strolled home. It was a beautiful afternoon for a walk through the veggie fields, but I had a filthy headache setting in and my mood was fast going downhill. Ant, Dad and Grandpa had gone off to golf and it was wonderfully quiet as I climbed into my bed, willing my headache to pass and feeling inexplicably irritable.

Ant rocked home at midnight, completely plastered. Flinging himself on my bed, reeking of beer, he announced that the nineteenth hole had been particularly challenging.

'Ant, how many times must I ask you NOT to lurch all over me reeking of booze?' I snapped. I'd not been in such a vile mood for a long time and my headache had worsened.

'Jeez, alright. Keep your hat on, madam. I was only at golf with your Dad,' he said.

'I don't care if you golfed with King-fucking-Tut. You don't pour your beer-soaked self into my bed, ever. Show a bit of respect, please,' I said curtly, turning over and ignoring him.

I knew I was being a bitch, but just couldn't pull myself together. I didn't exactly protest when Ant grabbed a pillow and stomped off to sleep on the couch. I'd not had a headache so bad since rehab and waves of nausea kept washing over me. I wondered if I was coming down with flu, confused by the suddenness of it all.

The next morning, my headache had subsided a bit, but I still felt flat and angry. Ant was definitely pissed off with me and I knew I owed him an apology, but I couldn't bring myself to do it. Instead, we walked on eggshells around each other. To make matters worse, Ant and I had to go to a lunch at his boss's house, which I could have done without. Their company had just signed into an exciting business venture which, apparently, needed celebrating.

We arrived at the lunch and, lo and behold, there was Jess, still a groupie and shagging her way through the team of guides, be they in Harare or Vic Falls.

It was going to be a lunch from hell.

Whether it was to punish me for being a cow, or because he didn't give a shit about my feelings, Ant instantly gravitated towards her and spent the better part of the day engrossed in funny stories about their past, blatantly excluding me. Jess may have been a skank, but she was no fool and picked up on the tension right away, loving the drama. I sat on the fringes, simmering, as Ant threw me dark, angry looks and Jess threw me sour little one-liners. Then, someone brought out a bottle of tequila whereupon Ant loudly called for everyone to do shots. Jess gathered shot glasses and went around handing them out. Then she got to me.

'Oh, sorry Kat,' she said, way too loudly. 'You're fresh out of rehab aren't you? No tequila for you then?'

'No, thanks,' I said, curtly.

'But you're just a junkie though, or does that make you a raging alcoholic too? Are your binge drinking and blackouts over too?' she smirked.

Bitch.

'Jess, don't,' warned Ant in a low voice, watching me nervously.

I took a deep breath, savouring the chance to take Jess down in front of everyone. Half the guys were cheering me on with their eyes, equally irritated by her. Just as the biting words formed on my tongue, something made me stop. I held all the power in the situation. Walking away from the cat fight would count for so much more. As sick as it made me feel, I just smiled sweetly. 'You can have my shot, Jess.'

She looked positively disappointed and I still wanted to scratch her eyes out. The rest of the afternoon was like drinking paint stripper, with Ant getting drunker and Jess getting more whorish by the minute, always touching Ant in some way, and both of them loving winding me up. It didn't go unnoticed by the others and I overheard Ant's boss, taking him aside for a chat.

'Listen Ant, you need to cool it with Jess. Your Kat is about to blow sky high and you, my friend, are being a total dick. No matter what you two are arguing about, you don't treat your girlfriend like that, especially in public. Kat is worth a hundred of Jess.'

I could have kissed him! Pleased to know others were on my side, I managed to get through the lunch without committing assault, even though Ant remained on a mission to take pissing me off to a whole new level.

'What is your fucking problem, Katherine?' Ant said when we got home.

The gloves were off. He'd called me Katherine.

'My problem?' I hissed back. 'Excuse me, but who just spent the day making his girlfriend feel like a total idiot and a pathetic loser of an addict?'

'Nobody can make you feel that way, that's all your shit. Own it.'

'Don't you fucking DARE rattle off clichés from my own addiction books. Give me a break, Ant.'

'You've done nothing but snap and snarl at me since last night and I haven't the faintest idea why. What I do know is that I will not put up with this. What I see standing before me is the addict Kat, the selfish, sour bitch of a year ago, the one I couldn't stand to be in the same room as. And, right now, I'm asking myself why I even bother.'

'And so the first thing you do is throw yourself at Jess. Nice, Ant, fucking nice. And I am wondering why I have to put up with that from you. You've still got a thing for the slag, I can see it.'

'Christ almighty! Do you know how insecure and pathetic you sound? Jess is nothing to me. And despite all your childish shit today, I was proud of how you walked away from that dust-up with her. It was the only thing you've done in the last twenty-four hours to show you're still a decent human being.'

'Screw you, Ant.'

He sighed, running his fingers through his hair, just looking at me with immense sadness in his eyes. 'I can't do this, Kat. I really am trying to understand you, but you've suddenly turned into a monster again. I won't go down that road a second time. I see what your mother meant when she said dating an addict is a minefield. I won't do this. I'm doing all the giving, you're just taking. Again.'

There it was, my relationship unravelling before my eyes and all my own doing. The old Kat was back – Ant was right, but I was powerless to smooth things over and put it right. The Beast was swirling in every part of me, holding me down in the riptide that was getting stronger by the second. It had completely overpowered me and Ant wasn't the only one who didn't know why.

'What is it, Kat? Talk to me. What the *hell* happened yesterday when I was at golf? You were fine when I left,' he said in a softer tone, though still unbelievably angry.

I shrugged, but kept quiet, not trusting myself to open my mouth as I kept making things worse. I truly didn't know what had caused my sudden turn and it scared me. I sat on the couch hugging my knees and buried my face. My head was pounding and when bile started to rise in my throat, I only just made it to the bathroom. I sat on the bathroom floor sobbing, hating myself. Minutes later, I heard Ant packing his gear and heard the jangle of his car keys. I didn't even try to stop him leaving, part of me thinking maybe I should be single for a while. Another part of me wondered if I needed Colin in my life more than Ant.

I sat outside on my patio smoking, unable to make sense of the self-inflicted mess and unable to stop my mind going to some dangerous places. Just when I thought I was understanding myself again, it had all blown up in my face.

As it grew dark, I saw Julian walking past on his way up to the house. He waved, and then changed course and came over to chat.

'Hey, how was your lunch?' he asked, joining me on the couch and lighting a ciggie.

'Fucking horrible,' I said, and promptly burst into tears.

'Oh no, what happened?'

I poured my heart out to Julian, begging him to help me make sense of this sudden toxic funk that had come over me. I spoke to him as a brother, a friend, a counsellor, and an addict who'd been in the same dark places as me.

'Shit Kat, sounds like you really have screwed-up. I thought you were a bit flat yesterday when we walked around the clinic and wondered if you were struggling with things.'

'Two days ago, I was fine. Loving life.'

'Are you freaked out about having me here as a part of your family?'

'I don't think so, Julian. Why would it bother me?'

'Well, it's a huge adjustment for you, having a new sibling. I know everyone has supported me and our mother through this totally bizarre situation, but I often wonder how you and Chris have processed it, gaining a brother overnight.'

'Honestly, on no conscious level am I unsettled by you, but maybe you're right. It's change – and change can be uncomfy. I'll tell you one thing – while walking around the clinic yesterday, I was completely freaked out when I went into that Fishbowl room. Took me right back to my own detox, to the worst few days of my life.'

'Aha! Now we're getting somewhere. That's what pushed your buttons.'

'Huh?'

'Well, you're relatively fresh out of rehab and it must be a bit of a mindfuck, having a rehab next door and ingrained in the family.'

'Surely a clinic next door would be a good thing for an addict? I mean, it's a pretty stark daily reminder of where addiction takes you.'

'Still not easy though. Don't beat yourself up, Kat. You've come so far in a short space of time and you're bound to have some demons lurking. Just being in a clinic environment will have stirred it all up for you. It's very common. In Cape Town, we regularly saw old patients coming back to say hi and tell us their news. Even years down the line, just popping in as a visitor would bring up huge issues and old emotions for some of them.'

'Well, I can't walk around permanently pissed off because you guys have a rehab next door.'

'No, but you can reboot your thinking and get out of this addict mindset that has crept back in. And stop being a cow. Don't be threatened by these changes in your life. They're good changes. See them as part of your healing.'

'What do I do about Ant? Am I even fit to be in a relationship if I'm still so raw?'

'What you *don't* do with Ant is make this his problem. He's a fantastic guy, Kat. Take out your fears and insecurities on him and it will be the biggest mistake you'll make. And yes, you can handle a relationship. Don't doubt yourself.'

Julian and I sat chatting for hours. I was surprised at how alike we were. He shared some of his biggest relationship mistakes, which gave me a better perspective regarding Ant. He also spoke openly about how finding Mom had thrown him for a loop and stirred up a heap of issues from his active addiction. He even shed a tear or two, which I found touching – that he was comfortable enough with me to do so. Then we had a good laugh at ourselves, two junkies both facing monumental changes.

When Julian left, I climbed into bed, noticing my headache had cleared and I was feeling a lot saner as the Beast slunk back into its dark den. Still, I felt awful about Ant. I contemplated phoning him, but then decided to go and make my peace in person, not caring it was past midnight.

At his flat in town, Ant answered the door half asleep, stunned to find me standing there in my pyjamas. I threw my arms around him and just held him for a very, very long time. At first his body was tense and angry, but I clung on, refusing to let go. Slowly I felt him relax, soften, and finally his arms tightened as he returned the hug and pulled me closer, his face buried in my neck. We held each other, rocking gently, as one, not saying a single word the entire time I was there. I slowly drew back, kissed him softly on the cheek, turned and drove myself home, knowing Ant and I would be okay.

Ten days later it was all go next door. Mom and Julian had appointed their full complement of staff. Seven people were coming from South Africa, five of them counsellors handpicked by Julian and a psychiatrist and a nurse from Carol's clinic. The rest of the staff were local. On the first of the month, the entire team would report for a fortnight of intensive internal training and to finalise all the rules and timetables. The kitchen – Linda's domain – would also be functioning, trying out recipes and producing a full lunch for the staff every day. Mom had announced that we, the family, were also kitchen guinea pigs and all family meals would be at the clinic for a fortnight.

They'd written announcing the new rehab to doctors around the country, with invitations to the official launch of Two Hays House – the name of the clinic having been debated for weeks by all, but now finally decided on. I loved the quirk of humour coming through in the name. Besides doctors, heads of all the senior schools were invited too, as well as over fifty pharmacists and hospital administrators. The Minister of Health was even sending a representative.

'Everyone in NA and AA is buzzing with excitement,' said Mom over dinner one night. 'For your info Kat, it's strict policy that we never use NA or AA as a means to promote Two Hays House. Ant, Dad, James, same goes for you lot and Al-Anon. No self-promotion please.'

'But it will be brought up in conversation at meetings,' I said.

'Yes, but it can never be brought up by us,' said Julian. 'We're already the talk of the town. Gill, even your sponsor Janet found me at AA and greeted me like I was some kind of saint, saviour and local hero. Then I was approached by a kid, barely twenty – a heroin addict – who asked me to sponsor him. He seemed to know all about me and the clinic, said he wished it'd been open three months ago when he'd decided to clean up his act, which he did through sheer willpower.'

'I just hope we get some patients and get them straight, and hope they bloody stay that way,' said Mom.

'We will, Gill,' said Julian. 'We have some of the best counsellors in Africa. If they can't get the buggers straight then no one can. But some people will fall off the wagon – you know the statistics.'

'Yup. Anyway, let's discuss veggies rather. I'm tired of clinic talk. How's the herb empire?' Mom asked Dad and Grandpa.

The clinic property was so big, with so much empty land, that Ela had given Dad several hectares for his new herb venture, which meant he didn't have to forsake his existing veggie fields. She also gave Dad the dam for irrigation so it wasn't only Mom benefitting from her property investment.

'My herbs are going great guns,' he said. 'Linda already has her beady eyes on my parsley and chives for your rehab scoff. I've promised to plant a herb courtyard off the kitchen for her.'

'Personally, I think we should be planting a few happy herbs,' said Grandpa, 'but I don't think I'll get management on side with my weed beds.'

Mom and Julian just laughed. I sat looking around the table, loving how our family and friends had come together and how everyone was still so positive about the clinic. I'd got over my recent wobble and was back on track after the fight with Ant, able to see that, yes, the clinic was changing our lives but it was also going to save lives.

Suddenly sentimental, I raised my glass and called for a toast to Mom and Julian. Mom, Ant and Grandpa raised their eyebrows, but Julian, my knight in shining armour, knew exactly where I was coming from and gave me a supportive nudge under the table.

I collected the first batch of Mom's stationary from the printers on my way home from work and headed to the clinic. I found Pringle amusing herself with the sprinklers, barking wildly and covered in mud.

She'd been crowned the official leader of the clinic's menagerie, which was growing by the day – animals being powerful tools in therapy. Ela had rescued five kittens from the SPCA. A tortoise had wandered in from the bush and decided to stay in rehab permanently. Mom had installed four geese and a new flock of bantam chicks, which Tighty promptly taught Pringle how to nail. A flock of guinea fowl already lived down by the dam, as well as a couple of ducks. Julian bought an African Grey parrot that lived in the patients' lounge area. No doubt it'd soon be squawking Recovery slogans and profanities.

To top it off, after Mom and Linda had been banging on about how they missed our farm cream, Grandpa had rocked in from the pub one night with two young Jersey cows in tow. Except he'd been too pissed to tell Mom about them and there'd been much shouting when she'd gone to ride her horse the next morning, only to find two cows in its stable. I'd got a fright too. I'd opened my front door to go to work, only to find Mom's horse tethered to a chair on my patio. For days, there'd been much banging and crashing as Grandpa and Jobb obeyed Mom's orders to build a milking shed and move 'the bloody *mombes*' to the bottom of the property.

Dull moments definitely still gave our family a wide berth.

Ela was in the offices, deep in conversation with Mom and Julian about what roles she could take on at the clinic.

'Your printing,' I announced, dumping the box on the floor.

'How exciting! Thanks sweetheart,' said Mom, admiring her first-ever business cards. 'Ooh, while you're here, can you count up RSVPs for the launch?' A piece of paper was thrust into my hands.

'One hundred and six invites and seventy-eight people confirmed,' I announced ten minutes later. 'Are the guys from the Trust coming for the launch?'

'Nope. It's all part of their stance on discretion. They don't publicly associate themselves with their projects,' said Julian.

'I can't believe this is all finally happening,' said Ela.

The moment was shattered by a loud puppy shriek from outside. Pringle had just been nipped by an angry goose.

'Oh, I do love this nuthouse,' chuckled Julian as Pringle belted into the office and leapt into his arms, terrified of the raging goose who'd run inside after her, looking to finish the fight.

Two days later on a hot, stormy Friday afternoon, the launch kicked off with every detail perfect at Two Hays House, now looking even more like a fancy spa. I did a walk through on my own, processing what it all meant for me. In the Fishbowl, I allowed my memories to flood back and, rather than fighting to forget the horror I'd known in a similar setting, I made peace with what came up for me. Memories of Cassie and her slashed wrists popped into my mind. All I could do was hope that Two Hays House never had to implement their patient suicide protocol.

Chris, Ant, Rolo, Ela and I sank into the couches outside and watched the event kick off. Mom and Julian, supported by their staff, dashed around playing host. The kitchen was buzzing, huge trays of snacks being carried out, while Grandpa was overseeing the bar under a jacaranda tree.

'I guess it's the last time there'll be booze at Two Hay House,' said Rolo, swinging her wine glass.

'Yup. Cheers to Too High House,' said Ela, also with a wine in hand.

'Damn, your wife's funny,' Ant said to Chris, all of us giggling like schoolkids.

It was, indeed, slightly incongruous to serve beer and wine in a rehab, but, then again, it hadn't officially opened for business.

A while later, I got the fright of my life when, behind me, I heard Julian calling my name, followed by a big voice I'd know anywhere.

'POOKIE!'

I swung round to find Pat and Carol standing there. They threw their arms around me in an embrace that knocked the breath out of me. I nearly wet my pants with excitement. Mom came over too, amazed.

'Surprise!' said Julian, explaining that he'd flown them up and they were staying at his cottage. For the next week, they were going to mentor Mom and Julian, with Pat working with the nurses and Carol with the counselling team. Apparently, they'd offered their services the day they'd heard the Trust money had been granted, and Julian had been plotting the trip ever since.

Carol, Pat and I spent ages chatting alone and I suddenly realised they'd come to see me too. No words could capture the significance of the moment and, when I personally gave them the clinic tour, we stood together holding hands in the Fishbowl while Carol said the Serenity Prayer. The memory of my own Fishbowl fight with Carol hit me straight between the eyes and I apologised again for being such a bitch. She accepted graciously. Any lingering doubts about whether or not I could handle the changes coming at me were laid to rest then and there.

I took them back downstairs to introduce them to Ant, who, of course, they knew all about. Next thing I knew, Carol and Grandpa were engrossed in conversation.

'Check it out,' said Ant. 'Your grandfather is hitting on Carol.'

'Oh God. Looks like she is lapping it up too,' I laughed. That was all I needed, Carol shacking up with Grandpa. I wouldn't put it past him.

A while later, Julian stood at the top of the patio steps and gave a short speech explaining the medical facilities' scope, the fee structure, and the principles of the programme. Choosing his words carefully, so as not to alienate the medical fraternity, he managed to get the point across that addicts and alcoholics in Zim had had a pretty raw deal, until now. There was an audible 'hear! hear!' from all the NA and AA members there.

Mom was up next, snatching a hug from Dad before she stepped forward.

'This journey – my journey – started a long time ago when I was a teenager. I was a victim of violent abuse and I turned to substances to take away the pain. In turn, those substances – alcohol in particular – took my life away. I nearly lost everything near and dear to me, and my disease of alcoholism didn't torture only me, but my family too. In the absence of any specialised care in this country, I was fortunate enough to go to a rehab treatment facility in South Africa, and that gave me a second chance at life. I wouldn't have made it on my own. Not without rehab.

'My entire family has walked the road of addiction and alcoholism too – some suffering the disease first-hand, others suffering the disease through us. An alcoholic or addict, it is said, directly affects an average of fifteen people around him or her. With three of us in Recovery – mother, daughter, son – that's forty-five people who got some nasty bruises from us. It's surprising we have any friends left at all.'

The crowd chuckled and Mom took a sip of water before continuing.

'Many times over the years, similar people have reached out to me for help, all of them desperate for specialised treatment that was out of their reach, financially. Many of them found release in death, not in Recovery, and all I could do was watch. For years I have bored my friends and family with my dreams of offering affordable treatment to Zimbabweans who are trapped in the spiral, but Julian – my son, business partner and an addictions counsellor – was the one who urged me to take the dream further, and he showed me how.

'Harare has a massive drug problem and alcohol abuse is rife here. The average age is getting younger. Two Hays House is about saving lives, it's not intended to ruffle feathers or alienate our medical fraternity. Julian and I, with our team of experts, are here to work with you, the doctors. We will never eradicate drugs, or dealers, and we can't get alcohol taken off shelves. What we can do is to help those who fall into the pit. We will follow a 12 Step programme here, not whimsical or religious approaches. The 12 Step programmes are not just band aids on the wound, they are a proven way that works for millions of people worldwide. Rich or poor, everyone who comes to us will be offered life without mind-altering substances, in a secure and confidential environment. Patients will leave this clinic clean, sober, and with tools and resources for a better, more manageable way of life. They will leave with choices too.

'So, ladies and gentlemen, it gives me great pleasure to announce that, from tomorrow, there will be affordable and specialised in-patient treatment in Harare for addicts and alcoholics. Today marks the start of a new era in Recovery in Zimbabwe. And lastly, I thank our benefactors and those who helped me follow my dream. You know who you are and I love you all.'

I held my breath, not knowing if Mom would be booed or applauded. A second later the loud clapping started and people chatted excitedly, roused by the speech. Mom, meanwhile, had shot off to have a cigarette. She got to take a few puffs before her guests caught up with her, congratulating her and full of questions. Julian was swamped too. The media people I'd managed to get there were hounding Mom and Julian for interviews and one had already invited them to be regular guests on a weekly health show on radio. She and Julian couldn't have wished for a better response. Even Carol came to tell me that she thought Two Hays House would give the established rehabs in Southern Africa a run for their money, hers included.

Ten minutes later, Chris, Ant and I were chatting when Jobb came running over, looking anxious, but not wanting to raise alarm or draw attention. He quietly told us that there was a problem at the gate and Dad and Grandpa needed the boys for support.

Chris and Ant quickly went down to the main gate while I stood on the lawn watching from a distance. There was a helluva scuffle going on and a man was trying to barge his way in. Either stoned or absolutely drunk, he was swinging his arms wildly, trying to land a punch on the security guards. I wondered who the hell would want to gatecrash the launch. Intrigued, I moved closer to get a better look.

It was Colin. My gut lurched.

Shouting the odds, he was insisting he was an invited pharmacist, but was obviously unable to produce his invitation. Hearing his name, Dad and Grandpa had quickly put two and two together.

I caught snippets of the row. Grandpa was, in no uncertain terms, telling Colin to fuck off. Giving up the fight and realising he was against several men, Colin stopped struggling and looked like he would turn and leave. Then he saw me.

'You! You little bitch,' Colin bellowed loudly, pointing at me. 'I will get you. I will fucking destroy you for ruining my life. I know it was you and your gutless family who tipped off the cops. Watch your back, all of you, especially you, you uptight bitch – you're no better than a crack whore who'd fuck anyone to get high.'

Colin started struggling again, trying to make a break for it in my direction. Well, with that Grandpa saw red, and grabbed him by the neck so tightly he could barely breathe.

'Gutless?' shouted Grandpa right in his face. '*You* are calling *us* gutless. You miserable little piece of shit.'

Then, still holding him round the neck, Grandpa stepped back and gave Colin an almighty kick in the shin and then a knee to the groin. Next, Chris came from behind Grandpa and landed his fist straight between Colin's eyes. Colin dropped to the ground screaming, his hand over his bleeding face. Then Ant stepped forward and kicked Colin several times in the kidneys.

Colin lay curled up in a ball on the ground, crying like a toddler, blood gushing onto the gravel as the men stood over him. One of the security guards dragged him to his feet and threw him past the gate.

Grandpa shouted after Colin. 'Don't you ever, *EVER*, speak to a woman like that again, you little troll. And if you ever come near this clinic or this family again, trust me, you will beg us to let you die. Now fuck off. For good.'

There they stood – Dad, Chris, Grandpa, Ant, Jobb and two security guards – forming a human wall at the gate. A foreboding signal that no one, absolutely no one, messes with our family.

As Colin stumbled to his car outside, a guard picked up a large stone and hurled it at him, just clipping the side of his head. Yelping again, Colin got into his car, still throwing evil looks at me, and tore off. Only then did I realise that Pat and Carol had come down to see what the fuss was about and were flanking me. Carol knew, of course, all about Colin's effect on me from my disastrous role play.

'It's alright, Kat, he can't get to you. Piece of shit. I wish I'd noticed the tussle sooner. I'd have given anything to contribute to that conversation,' said Carol.

I gave her a watery smile but my chin was wobbly – I was far more shaken by the incident than I cared to admit. After all, the attack had been directly targeted at me.

'Jeez *pookie*, your grandpa don't take no shit. *Sjoe!*' said Pat.

Carol looked at me, fluffing her steely grey hair, all coquettish, a twinkle in her eye. 'He's single, yes? Your grandpa.'

'Very!' I had to giggle. It was just such a bizarre situation. Standing at my mother and brother's rehab, my old counsellor making moves on my grandfather while my dealer drove himself to hospital.

The men came over to us and, once we'd all regained our composure, we headed back to join the gathering.

I pulled Grandpa to one side as we walked up. 'Grandpa, Colin's police raid. Was it you?'

All he did was tap the side of his nose discretely, taking my hand in his and walking me back to the party, whereupon he and Carol disappeared into a quiet part of the clinic for what I suspected was the clinic's first incidence of fraternising.

Thankfully, the Colin incident had gone unnoticed by the guests. Julian had known, though. Confident that the guards had Colin under control, he'd distracted Mom rather than join the fight, more worried about how she'd cope with an ugly drama on her big night.

Ant and I didn't stay late. Yet again, Colin had seriously rattled me. That night, I had the same dream, of being chased by something evil, bloodthirsty and a lot bigger than me. I wondered if I would ever be free, truly free, of the Beast.

The next morning, Ant said I'd screamed in my sleep.

Six months later

45

A few days after the launch, Two Hays House had admitted its first two patients, both direct referrals from doctors. The next day, another five were admitted and within a fortnight the clinic was full. A lot of foreign patients – South Africans, Zambians and even some Dutch addicts – had also stumbled in. The imported counsellors had settled well in Harare, despite the worsening economy. Some had moved their families up to Harare, preferring the slightly slower pace of life to the rat race in South Africa.

The NA and AA Fellowships had been delighted to welcome professionals to the meetings and on any given day a few staff from the clinic were at NA and AA meetings. After all, the counsellors still had their own Recovery to work on. They were also hot property for newcomers needing sponsors.

Two of the UK Trustees had been out for the standard inspection, after which Julian and Ant had taken them on a no-expense-spared trip to Kariba and Victoria Falls and they'd fallen in love with Zimbabwe. Clinic-wise, they'd been impressed. In their feedback, they'd recommended appointing another counsellor and, given that there was such a demand and a permanent waiting list, they'd produced further funds to build a new bedroom wing, adding ten beds.

Judging from how many patients we saw sticking with NA and AA after treatment, there seemed to be a generally good 'pass' rate – testament to the level of care and expertise at Two Hays House. Some did relapse, which was always expected, but a good number of the relapsed and remorseful came crawling back to do another twenty-eight days of treatment. Mom called it the Relapse Refresher Course.

Meanwhile, I found my Recovery groove and was starting to enjoy it. I religiously attended NA meetings and did a lot of the school talks – and I'd been asked by a new girl, fresh out of Two Hays House, to be her sponsor. My headaches made regular appearances, but I'd learnt to live with them. Doc Merton had offered me more tests to find out why. However, just seeing a stethoscope terrified me these days. I was haunted by my torrid medical experiences in Harare. The Beast still stirred within me from time to time, especially when I was in pain, but, so far, I had won each round. It was finally accepting who was running the show, not that it ever rolled over purring and wanting its tummy scratched.

At work, a series of promotions saw me step into senior management, with a team of three reporting only to me. Stephen really had been good to me and remained one of my biggest supporters. It had come to light that his girlfriend in London had been a heroin addict, found dead in a crack house. With Two Hays House in the spotlight, and me being so public about my battle, Stephen had finally found the strength to talk about his girlfriend and thus start his own healing, realising that addiction didn't have to be shrouded in shame. Jonathon, Colin's brother, hadn't stayed at our agency long. I suspected he was involved in Colin's dealing, and I was certain he did a bit of the old white powder himself. Nobody got 'head colds' that often and the constant sniffing drove me round the bend. Despite being warned, he'd still allowed Colin to visit him at work, creating a major altercation with me each time. After the fourth time, Stephen fired Jonathon, not prepared to have his agency associated with known drug lords who put his staff at risk. It was all well and good, but we knew Colin was still out there and still gunning for me. Even more so now that his brother had been fired because of me.

'Smile! Say cheese,' said Dad, positioning the camera. He pressed the auto-timer button and rushed over to join us. It was Mom's birthday and, because she was always so busy at the clinic and never did anything for herself anymore, Chris, Ela, Julian, Ant and I had thrown her a surprise party.

Later that evening after the party, I sat on my little patio. My faithful nightjar was singing from the shadows and the familiar sound of crickets, frogs and sprinklers on the lawn reminded me of the farm. I had a sudden pang for my childhood, when life was simpler. Before addiction had kicked down my front door.

I plugged the camera into my laptop to print the photo taken earlier. Ant came to find me, giving my neck a massage as he looked at the photo over my shoulder.

'Look at Ela, she's glowing. Chris too,' said Ant.

'Yup, I've never seen them happier,' I said, looking at their expressions.

Ela was six months pregnant. She still worked at the welfare centre but had restructured her life to fit in family and welfare work, and one or two group sessions a week at the clinic, often filling in when someone was sick or on leave. No doctor could say whether their baby would be born with the same sight disability, but it didn't matter to her or Chris. Katie and Ben were shooting up too. Katie was gorgeous, looking more like her mother every day and Ben, ridiculously cute, was always laughing, and the happiest child I knew.

Dad, Tim and Grandpa had been caught on camera with wild-eyed expressions and laughter on their faces, obviously sharing a filthy joke. Grandpa still caused much hilarity wherever he went. He also remained one of my biggest anchors in life, always able to ground me in five seconds flat, especially when it came to Ant.

'Did you hear that he's going to Cape Town on 'holiday' again?' Ant asked me, fingers wiggling as he did an air quote.

Grandpa kept denying it, but we all knew he and Carol had a bit of a steamy romance going on. They'd gone out together the week Carol had been staying at Julian's place. An early riser, Julian had caught Carol slinking in, doing the walk of shame a few times, much to all our amusement. Suddenly, Cape Town had become a place Grandpa 'always wanted to explore' and he'd flown down twice in the last four months. Winding him up about his new girlfriend had produced some of the best laughs we'd had in years.

Dad's veggies and herbs were thriving and making decent profits. Of all of us, Dad missed his farm the most, but it was a life gone by and he knew we'd been very lucky to start over. So many of our old farming friends were on the bones of their arses, desperate for work, often coming to Dad to ask for jobs.

Even Tighty, Gertie, Mojo and Pringle were in the photo. Pringle was still a chubby bundle of puppy but with gangly legs now. Despite her size, she loved nothing more than to snuggle in the arms of Julian's wife Victoire, who was pulling a face in the photo as Pringle had just licked her nose. We'd all gone to Julian and Victoire's wedding in Mozambique, which had been a fabulous trip. Sandra and Vincent were lovely, a little wacky, but so down-to-earth. Victoire and Julian had struck a balance with their jobs and she came to Harare fairly regularly. She worked as a freelance legal consultant in Johannesburg and would often hop on a flight for a long weekend in Harare, working via email. As a family, we loved her as much as Julian did. Warm, full of fun, and absolutely gorgeous, her chic French style and accent made her an alluring woman. I often caught Chris and Ant having a quiet perve when they thought no one was watching.

Rolo had also been at the party, with Shane, although things were a bit rocky between them. Rolo, young and independent, struggled with his kids, with being a stepmother of sorts on weekends. It cramped her impulsive style and she was starting to question if it was the right situation for her. Added to which, Shane wasn't keen on a second marriage and more kids.

'I hate to say it, but I saw some unrest in Rolo tonight. Not sure if those two will go the distance,' Ant said, reading my mind.

'Yup, they're fizzling.'

'Ah, but Rolo will be snapped up, if she wants to be,' said Ant. 'All my mates adore her.'

'She does love Shane though and he's been really good for her. Hats off to her. I don't think I could handle a man with kids in the package, not even one as hot as Shane.'

'Have you been eyeing out your best mate's man?' joked Ant.

'Damn straight! And far more than you eye out Victoire.'

Ant shook his head, laughing at me. Feeling the nip in the night air, he pulled a blanket over me before joining me on the couch. I swung my feet onto his lap, and sighed happily. With so much chaos in our high-octane family, I had come to cherish these simple, quiet moments. Feeling very blessed to have so much love in my life – having managed to restore my broken relationships and mop up most of my addiction-related mess – I looked at Ant and me in the photo. The camera's flash had caught my diamond ring, causing a pretty flare of light. I put the photo down and stretched out my left hand to admire my engagement ring. I was still getting used to wearing a ring on that finger, still in shock too.

Ant had completely surprised me six weeks ago when he'd proposed up at Kariba. We'd gone with his friends for five glorious days on a houseboat. One evening, Ant had taken me out fishing on the tender boat. I could never stomach putting worms on my hook so he always did it for me. This time, he turned his back to me, and quickly tied an exquisite diamond and platinum engagement ring onto my hook instead.

Thankfully, I noticed it glinting in the sun before casting my line, otherwise that would have been a second engagement ring gone into Zambezi waters. I nearly fell out of the boat in surprise and, after I'd said yes and thrown my arms around Ant, nearly capsizing us, we heard cheers coming from the main houseboat. Everyone had been in on the proposal and was watching with bated breath through binoculars. I smiled every time I thought about it. A more romantic setting for a proposal I couldn't imagine – Kariba-orange sky, shimmering water, a lone fish eagle's call and an elephant twenty metres from us – as I finally got asked to produce my left hand for some bling.

Ant was watching me gaze at my ring and smiled at me. 'You okay, sweetheart? You seem a bit quiet. Tired?'

'There are so many stories in just this one photograph,' I said.

'KitKat, my darling, wherever you or your family go there's a story. Life is simply never dull around you.'

'Wanna hear another not-dull story?' I asked Ant, smiling, unable to contain myself any longer. I'd waited all day for the right moment.

He looked at me questioningly, one eyebrow raised.

'I'm pregnant,' I said. It came out as a whisper.

With an incredulous look of happiness, love and excitement coming over his face, and a grin so stupid and so big it could only be genuine, Ant took me in his arms, holding me tightly. I felt his tears on my neck.

Gently holding my face, he stared into my eyes. 'You truly are the love of my life, Kitt-hiy. Marry me now.'

I laughed as we clung to each other, both crying happy tears. Wiping my eyes, I pulled back and looked at him, thoughtfully.

'What?' asked Ant. 'What's wrong?'

'I'd kill for a cigarette right now.'

* * *

ACKNOWLEDGEMENTS

This manuscript was first written years ago and spent many happy years under my desk serving as a footrest. Life and work got in the way but, in 2021, the time was finally right to haul it out, share the message and for it to start its journey - and hopefully save lives by shining the spotlight on addiction once again.

Over the years, I have bored people to sobs with promises of this book. So many people have had a part to play, both in publishing it and on the personal journey that got me here.

To my mother, thank you, for *everything*. I wouldn't be telling any stories, with happy endings or otherwise, if it weren't for you.

To my editor Alexia Lawson, thank you. I am humbled by your mastery of the written word and relentless attention to detail. You took such care with my story, all the while keeping me motivated.

To Vanessa Wilson and the team at Quickfox Publishing – what a pleasure to publish with you. Thank you for seeing a story that needed to be told and not just another book.

To Bron Kausch, for believing in the very first edition and pushing me to see it through, much barging and many leftward trajectories later, thank you.

To Lisa Daubermann, thank you for putting so much thought and effort into my photography.

For the evocative cover image, thank you Ambra. What a privilege to use a prominent work of art on my cover.

And lastly, to my people, my inner circle, in Cape Town, Harare and around the world, your faith and endless support over the years is so appreciated. You all know who you are.

It has been quite a ride so far. And yes, in parts, it did sting a bit.

Printed in Great Britain
by Amazon

67602008R00281